THE GENIUS WARS

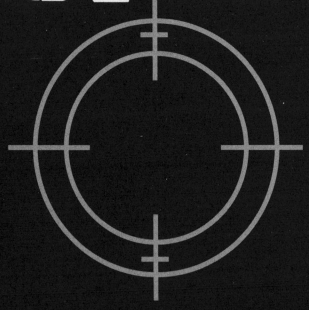

CATHERINE JINKS

GENIUS WARS

*G*RAPHIA

HOUGHTON MIFFLIN HARCOURT

BOSTON   NEW YORK

With thanks to Ken Wilson, Margaret Connolly,
and Peter Dockrill for their assistance.

www.hmhbooks.com

Published in 2009 by Allen & Unwin, Australia
First U.S. edition 2010

The text of this book is set in Ehrhardt MT.

The Library of Congress has cataloged the hardcover edition as follows:
Jinks, Catherine
The genius wars / Catherine Jinks—1st U.S. ed.
p. cm.
Summary: Fifteen-year-old genius Cadel Piggott Greeniaus sets aside his new,
crime-free life when his best friend Sonja is attacked, and he crosses oceans and continents trying to
track down his nemesis Prosper English, breaking whatever rules he must.
[1. Genius—Fiction. 2. Identity—Fiction. 3. Crime—Fiction. 4. Good and evil—Fiction.
5. Australia—Fiction. 6. Science fiction—Fiction.]
I. Title.
PZ7.J5754Geq   2010
[Fic]—dc22
2009049979

ISBN: 978-0-15-206619-2 hardcover
ISBN: 978-0-547-57727-2 paperback

Printed in the United States of America.
DOC 10 9 8 7 6 5 4 3 2 1
4500315711

To Richard Buckland, Andrew Hellen, and Erica Jacobson

ONE

Two dented lift doors were embedded in a wall of pebblecrete. Between them, the up button looked slightly traumatized, like a punching bag. It was hard to believe that the University of New South Wales had just installed a state-of-the-art, web-based management system to run its elevators.

Cadel was convinced that they had to be at least thirty years old.

"Right," he said, eyeing an indicator panel. "We'll wait till they're empty before we give it a go."

Ping! The words had barely left his mouth when one set of double doors slid open, revealing a lank-haired student in a Metallica T-shirt who blinked in sheer astonishment as he surveyed the line of people confronting him. Then he ducked his head, adjusted his backpack, and shuffled off toward the nearest lecture theater.

He must be in my course, Cadel decided, cursing himself for being so slow off the mark. Even after three weeks of seminars, he still didn't recognize many of his fellow students.

"Do you know who that was?" he asked, in the faint hope that Hamish, at least, might be able to help. But Hamish simply shrugged. He regarded Introductory Programming as an insult to someone who could boast a genuine police record, and had roundly dismissed many of the other teenage hackers with whom he was forced to associate as "a pathetic bunch of script-kiddies."

Cadel couldn't help thinking that Hamish had an attitude problem. Though the two of them were in exactly the same boat, Cadel wasn't perpetually bitching about its shape or its color. Like Hamish, he had been *forced* to attend university; the demanding nature of his computer engineering course work was supposed to keep him so busy that he wouldn't be tempted to engage in any illegal hacking operations. Unlike Hamish, however, Cadel had been quite happy to enroll. He had always wanted to attend a proper university, with legitimate teachers. And if that meant relearning all his painfully acquired programming skills . . . well, he was prepared to make the sacrifice.

Hamish wasn't. He had left high school a year before, at the age of sixteen, to pursue his own, very specialized interests. Only the combined urgings of his parents, his lawyer, his psychiatrist, and the juvenile justice system could have pushed him back into a highly structured academic environment. "It's not like there's anything they can actually teach us in a place like this," he'd said to Cadel on one occasion. "We're in a totally different league. We've been out in the real world. We've fought real b-battles, and you can't do that without breaking a few rules. We're *cyberwarriors,* not schoolboys."

It had been hard to keep a straight face, because Cadel couldn't imagine a more unlikely pair of warriors. Hamish looked like an archetypal computer geek, with his glasses and his braces and his bleached, knobbly frame, while Cadel had no illusions about his own appearance— which was unthreatening, to say the least. Angelic blue eyes and a halo of chestnut curls had rescued Cadel from more sticky situations than he cared to admit. And despite the rapid approach of his sixteenth birthday, he was still unusually small for his age.

Mind you, he thought, glancing at the three people lined up next to him, *none of us are exactly unobtrusive.* It wasn't surprising that the lank-haired fellow in the elevator had blinked at the sight of them. Though Hamish belonged to a physical type that was quite common in most computer engineering classes, he wore a wholly unconvincing "tough-guy" outfit: biker's boots, ripped jeans, studded belt. Beside him, Cadel looked like a cherub from a church ceiling. Then there was Judith, massive and middle-aged, with long, frizzy gray hair, fluorescent pink glasses, a shoulder bag made of recycled tea towels, and layers of tie-dyed hemp flapping around her ankles. As for Sonja, she was the most conspicuous of them all. Her cerebral palsy meant that she was racked by continual, eye-catching muscular spasms. What's more, her wheelchair was an imposing piece of technology that tended to dominate whatever space it occupied, thanks to the huge amount of equipment attached to it.

Not that any of this equipment was as big or as clumsy as her old Dyna Vox machine. Once upon a time, Sonja had been forced to spell out her remarks on a keyboard, which had then transmitted them as spoken language. For someone with unreliable motor skills, it had been a slow, laborious, tiring process.

Now, thanks to Judith Bashford, Sonja was hooked up to a revolutionary speech synthesizer. From one of her mysterious offshore bank accounts, Judith had extracted enough money to pay for the very latest kind of system. "If Sonja's going to be studying at university," Judith had declared, "then she'll need all the help she can get." This help included a cutting-edge neurological interface device that interpreted signals sent by Sonja's brain to her vocal cords. A tiny wireless transmitter resting on her voice box then relayed the signals to a portable computer that decoded them, matching them against a set of prerecorded words in its databank. As a result, Sonja was not only able to utter her thoughts aloud—via the speech synthesizer—but also direct her wheelchair to stop, go, slow down, speed up, turn, retreat . . . whatever she wanted it to do.

At first, Cadel had assumed that this new system would give her complete independence. He had expected to see his best friend making her own way around town, or at least around the university. Most public buildings now contained ramps and lifts and automatic doors; as far as Cadel knew, it was illegal *not* to provide access for people in wheelchairs. He'd been convinced that Sonja would soon find the trip to her Advanced Mathematics class just as easy as the course itself.

He hadn't reckoned, however, on the large amount of push-button technology standing in her way. Sonja couldn't manage wall-mounted buttons. She would hurt herself trying vainly to hit them as she wrestled with her own wayward limbs. Pole-mounted buttons were almost as bad as the wall-mounted variety. So when it came to crossing roads or operating elevators, she was at a serious disadvantage. Without help, Sonja couldn't be sure of reaching her classes on time.

To Cadel, this was unacceptable. He found it hard to believe that all the money, effort, and sophisticated research lavished upon Sonja's new wheelchair could be undermined by something as basic as a little plastic button. It was ludicrous. It was *unfair*. Cadel knew how hard her life had been. He knew that, after being abandoned at an early age, she had been shunted from one group home to the next. Her only real friends (before her first meeting with Cadel) had been nurses and nurses' aides. She had fought to speak, fought to move, fought to learn. Every day had been a battle. And despite the fact that she now had Judith to take care of her, Sonja's life was still far from easy. She couldn't even tie her own shoes or wash her own hair.

The last thing she needed was yet another obstacle blocking her path to freedom.

So Cadel had decided to tackle the problem himself. After doing a little research, he'd realized that every up and down button on campus could be circumvented, given the right tools. And it just so happened that he had the right tools. He had Sonja's wireless transmitter, which could be reprogrammed. He had the university's own wireless Internet connection, which could pick up her signals and pass them on to a special server. Most important, he had the new elevator management system (or EMS), which was connected to the World Wide Web.

Cadel had quickly worked out that, with elements like these in place, there was no need for Sonja to push any buttons. All she had to do was think of a command and it could be routed through to the EMS via her wireless transmitter. Of course, that meant hacking into several secure networks, but he had no qualms about doing so. Not for a good cause. And if the arrangement actually worked, it could be used to help other people with similar disabilities.

He told himself this, though he still felt bad. Having promised not to do any more unofficial hacking, he couldn't help struggling with a faint sense of guilt as he stared up at the indicator panel. It wasn't that he had straight-out *lied*. He had simply chosen not to keep everyone properly informed. Sonja knew what he was doing, naturally. So did Judith. Hamish was in on the secret because he and Cadel were classmates; it was inevitable that they would have bumped into each other, purely by accident, just before the first test run of Sonja's modified transmitter. But nobody else was aware of Cadel's latest project. Not even his foster parents, Saul and Fiona Greeniaus.

He was hoping that if he presented them with a completely successful, exhaustively tested, thoroughly worthwhile service to humanity, they would overlook the fact that he hadn't been entirely honest with them. Surely they would understand? It wasn't as if he had *liked* keeping them in the dark. It was just that Saul happened to be a police detective. And police detectives are notoriously unsympathetic when it comes to illicit network infiltration.

Once Cadel's system was up and running, however, even Saul was bound to see how beneficial it was.

"Right," Cadel said again. Then he turned to Sonja. "Are you ready?"

"*I'm-ready,*" was her synthesized response, which had a slightly less robotic tone to it than anything produced by her old Dyna Vox. "*Shall-we-go-up?*"

"Remember, you have to be specific." Cadel felt that this point was worth repeating. "Just to be on the safe side. Code, location, level, destination."

"*I-know.*" Sonja sounded calm. She always did, because she talked through a machine. Only by studying her appearance was it possible to tell if she was agitated; for one thing, her muscular spasms became more violent when she was stressed.

But as her brown eyes strained toward him, Cadel could see that she was excited, rather than anxious. Her flushed cheeks gave her away.

"*Audeo, EEB, level-G-up-level-two,*" she intoned, her synthesizer responding to directions that were also being channeled toward the EMS.

Cadel immediately lifted his gaze. Above him, the indicator panels showed that elevator one was stuck on level three. But elevator two was still on the ground floor; its doors parted just as he glanced at them.

Sonja's wheelchair began to move. She guided it carefully into the mirrored box, which shuddered beneath the weight of all her equipment. Judith followed her. Cadel was next in line, and made room for Hamish by pressing against one wall.

When the doors banged together again, they nearly squashed Hamish's enormous, overloaded backpack.

"*Going up,*" said a disembodied female voice.

"Did someone press that?" Hamish asked, gesturing at the button labeled "2." It was glowing softly, unlike the buttons surrounding it.

"Nope," Judith replied. "It was all lit up when I got in."

"Then it's worked!" Hamish crowed. But Cadel raised a cautionary hand.

"Just wait," he said. "Let's see. We can't be sure, yet."

With a lurch, the elevator began its ponderous climb. Cadel checked his watch. While Sonja's next class wasn't for another half hour, he and Hamish were due at the Rex Vowels lecture theater in less than ten minutes. It would have been nice to run a whole series of different tests, at a variety of different locations. Unfortunately, however, that wouldn't be possible. Not yet, anyway.

"*Second floor,*" the elevator announced, grinding to a halt. And Hamish punched the air in a victory salute.

"Yes!" he exclaimed.

Cadel wasn't convinced, though. When the doors opened to reveal another startled-looking student, he realized that he had mistimed the whole procedure. *I should have done this at night,* he fretted. *There are too many people around. Too many variables. I wasn't thinking.*

He said as much after he'd hustled everyone out of the lift.

"We can't get a clean set of results," he observed. "Not right now. We're up against the scheduling algorithms. That girl who just got in, she might have affected the outcome."

"*I–don't–think–so,*" said Sonja. "*The–button–lit–up, remember?*"

"It's still inconclusive. Someone else might have pushed it by accident." Though Cadel could sympathize with her desperate optimism, he didn't approve of unscientific methods. "We should do this at night. Or on a Sunday, when no one's around. It'll be the same with the traffic lights, when I tackle those. We'll have to trial them *really* early, like at three o'clock in the morning."

"Traffic lights?" Hamish echoed. "What about the traffic lights?"

"I'll tell you later." Cadel had just spotted a woman marching toward them down a nearby corridor. He didn't want anyone else listening in. He didn't want the whole world to know that he was about to target the Sydney Coordinated Adaptive Traffic System. "I've got to go," he informed Sonja. "I'll be late otherwise. Do you want to meet for lunch?"

"She can't," said Judith. "She has a physio appointment."

"Oh." Cadel accepted this, but wouldn't let Judith hijack the conversation. She was always doing it, nowadays, and it annoyed him. In his opinion, she was being overprotective; Sonja would be eighteen in less than a month, at which time she would become an adult, with an adult's right to choose. In other words, she would be taking charge of her own destiny.

And if she decided to miss a few appointments, that would be her privilege—no matter what her new foster mother might think.

"Well, what about this afternoon?" Cadel continued, addressing Sonja. "You could come over to my house, and we could talk about a weekend test run."

"She'd be better off at home," was Judith's opinion. "It's set up properly."

By this she meant that Cadel's house didn't have ramps, sensor lights, or automatic doors, whereas Judith's seaside mansion was fitted out with all these features, and more besides. It was a fully wired Smart House—an "intelligent environment."

Cadel's house, in contrast, was as dumb as a doorknob. Or so Judith seemed to imply whenever she compared it unfavorably with her own.

"I'll-come-over-to-your-place-if-I'm-not-too-tired," Sonja interjected. *"Physiotherapy-can-wipe-me-out-sometimes."*

"Sure." Cadel gave a nod. He was aware of how tired she could get doing the simplest things. "What if I call you?"

"Okay."

"I'll be working at home, so you can reach her there," said Judith, causing Hamish to frown. He was jealous of the work Judith did. As a condition of her parole, she had recently set up some kind of forensic accounting consultancy; Hamish envied the amount of time she spent helping the police to track down dirty money while he himself was stuck in school. "*I* could help the police," he'd often said. "Why don't they ask me to help? Why does Judith get all the b-b-breaks?" He didn't seem to realize that he had been very, very lucky—that he could easily have ended up in a juvenile detention center, or a community service program. For some reason, he remained unconvinced that he had done anything wrong by joining the illegal operation known as Genius Squad. The fact that at least one of its former members was now in prison didn't appear to faze him in the least. Nor did the attitude of his fellow squad members Cadel and Sonja, who wanted to put the past well and truly behind them.

As far as Hamish was concerned, trying to bring down a corrupt organization could only be a good thing, no matter what questionable means you might employ to do it.

"Okay—well, I'll call you," Cadel assured Sonja before Hamish could make one of his sour remarks about Judith's busy schedule. "Some time after lunch, say? Around two? And we can work out who should go where."

"All-right," Sonja agreed, her calm, metallic delivery undermined by her eager expression. *"See-you-later, then."*

"Bye." Cadel began to edge away. "Bye, Judith."

"Bye, boys. Have fun."

Hamish snorted. He didn't respond to Judith's cheerful wave. And on his way downstairs, he accused her of "taking the piss."

"Like we could possibly have any fun in Pediatric Programming," he complained. "Do you know what she told me last week? She told me she was chasing after money that *Prosper English* has tucked away in some tax haven somewhere. Can you b-believe that? The police are going after Prosper English, and they haven't come to you for help!"

"Because I don't want to help." Cadel slammed through a fire door. "I wouldn't help even if they asked me."

"Yeah, but they *d-didn't* ask you. That's what I'm saying. It's like they think you're useless, when you probably know more about Prosper English than anyone." Hamish then launched into his usual rant about the criminal stupidity of disbanding Genius Squad: how it wouldn't have cost too much to run, no matter what the accountants said; how its teenage members had not been the least bit "unreliable," no matter what the police commissioner claimed; and how, if Genius Squad had been permitted to survive, Prosper English would have been caught within weeks of his escape from prison. "Instead of which, we're all given a slap on the wrist and told to go home! And nine months later Prosper's still at large, free as a bird and breathing down our necks!"

"He's not breathing down our necks," Cadel said shortly. "He's gone to ground."

"Yeah, b-but he's still out there, isn't he? And you know him better than anyone. The police should be *begging* you to help."

"No they shouldn't, Hamish! Because it wouldn't do any good!" Cadel suddenly became aware of how loud his voice was as it echoed around the concrete walls of the stairwell. So he continued more quietly. "I don't want Prosper English in my life anymore. If I leave him alone, he'll leave me alone. It's a tradeoff."

"You can't be sure of that."

"Yes I can." Cadel *was* sure of it. He had calculated the probabilities. There could be no other explanation for the nine months of perfect peace that he'd enjoyed—unless, of course, Prosper English was dead and buried. "If he saw me as a threat, he would have got to me by now," Cadel went on. "He could have killed me the minute I left the safe house. But he didn't. So I'm going to be fine, as long as I keep my nose out of his business."

"Do you think he'll go after Judith, then?" Hamish queried, following Cadel down another flight of stairs. "Since she's sticking *her* nose into his b-business?"

"I don't know." It was a good question. It had certainly crossed Cadel's mind. Saul Greeniaus, however, had assured him that Judith was just a very small part of a large long-term, ongoing pursuit of Prosper English, whose criminal empire was slowly being taken apart, piece by piece, all over the world.

According to Saul, police from half a dozen different countries had so far failed to uncover any evidence that Prosper was trying to undermine their investigations. There had been no attempts to bribe or kill or intimidate any members of the task force. And this meant that Judith would probably be safe as well.

Because they're nowhere near Prosper, Cadel had decided upon hearing this news. *If they were getting close to where he is, they'd find out soon enough.* But he had said nothing. Not even to Saul.

He wasn't going to make himself a target by offering up any unsolicited advice.

"Anyway, I'm happy as I am," he said. "I don't want to get involved in stuff like that. I like things the way they are."

"You must be joking." Hamish sounded genuinely shocked. "Aren't you b-bored to death?"

"No." Cadel pushed through another fire door, emerging into a wide, sloping hallway near the Rex Vowels lecture theater. "I'm happy."

"How *can* you be? In this place? It's so *dull.*"

"It's not dull. It's normal. It's a normal life." It was, in fact, Cadel's first taste of a normal life, and he'd been savoring every moment. Things were so easy. So free. He could go anywhere he wanted without having a surveillance team tagging along. He could say anything he wanted without wondering if the people who were listening to him had some kind of hidden agenda. He could stroll around campus secure in the knowledge that none of his fellow students was going to explode.

For fifteen years, he had lived under constant scrutiny. He'd grown accustomed to being closely monitored, first by Prosper English, then by the police—who had been afraid of what Prosper might do to him. As heir to a criminal empire, Cadel had been brought up in an atmosphere of invasive scrutiny, subtle manipulation, and unending lies. Even his education had been an exercise in duplicity. At the age of thirteen, he'd been enrolled in a college known as the Axis Institute, which had been established for the express purpose of turning him into the world's greatest thief, liar, and con artist. What's more, he had escaped that particular trap only to fall into another one—which, like the Institute, had been the work of Prosper English.

As far as Cadel was concerned, Genius Squad hadn't been a fearless team of brilliant crusaders secretly working to bring down the world's most evil corporation. It had been a naïve group of opinionated suckers who had become more and more entangled in one of Prosper's cunning schemes. Cadel didn't mourn the loss of Genius Squad. Not one little bit. He didn't need Genius Squad to give his life meaning.

Now that he had a real home, and real parents, and real friends—now that he had enough room to move, and talk, and make his own decisions about his own future—why would he want anything else?

"Hey, Cadel." Hamish wouldn't let up. "Can I ask you something?"

"I suppose so." Cadel wasn't keen to continue their discussion. A crowd was gathering outside the lecture theater, drifting in from every point on the compass, and he didn't want to be overheard. "As long as it's not about Prosper English."

"But what if he doesn't *know*?" Hamish demanded, blithely ignoring Cadel's request. "What if that's why he hasn't tried to kill you: b-because he still thinks you're his son? What do you think will happen when he finds out you're not?"

"Oh, shut up, Hamish," Cadel said crossly. Then he darted forward, swerved past a press of rumpled students, and plunged through the open door beyond them.

TWO

Introductory Programming was divided into two classes: basic and advanced. "Advanced" students didn't have to fight for a place in the Rex Vowels lecture theater, which was big enough to accommodate every one of them. Scattered thinly across three hundred or so brightly upholstered seats, the advanced class could afford to spread out a little.

At times, however, Cadel almost wished that he belonged to the larger group. There were so many "basic" students that they were never asked to "move down to the front, please." Cadel would have felt less conspicuous in a crowd like that. He would have found it easier to keep a low profile. And he could have chosen a seat up at the back without attracting any kind of attention.

Not that he was intimidated, or scared of being caught out. He didn't find the course work especially hard. But he preferred to keep a low profile because he wasn't sure how much his teacher actually knew about him. Although the campus admissions office knew everything there was to know, Saul Greeniaus had insisted that certain aspects of his foster son's background remain completely confidential. Cadel had even enrolled under Saul's name—Greeniaus—despite the fact that the adoption process was taking a long, long time.

"You're *my* son, now," Saul had declared. "Mine and Fiona's. You don't have to worry about Chester Cramp anymore. Chester Cramp is irrelevant."

Chester Cramp was, in fact, Cadel's biological father. But since Chester was sitting in an American jail, charged with all kinds of offenses (including conspiracy to commit murder), Cadel could only conclude that he *was* irrelevant—in the legal sense, at any rate. And since Cadel had never even met Chester Cramp, there wasn't much of an emotional connection between them. In fact, of all the various "fathers" who had cluttered up Cadel's life over the years, Chester was probably the least important.

Phineas Darkkon had been important; he had tried to mold Cadel into a criminal mastermind. Prosper English, Darkkon's right-hand man, had also been very important; he had engineered the death of Cadel's mother, before proceeding to mess with her infant son's head. Saul Greeniaus had been the most important of the lot, kindly rescuing a lonely, mixed-up, homeless kid from a life full of social workers and group homes. All three men had viewed themselves as father figures and had behaved accordingly.

Only Chester Cramp had displayed a complete lack of interest in his own flesh and blood. Though a brilliant scientist, he was also (in Saul's opinion) "a totally deficient human being."

"He's done you a favor," Saul had once remarked. "You can ignore Chester Cramp, because he's ignored you. Unlike Prosper English." Prosper, unfortunately, had always treated Cadel as his personal possession—until a few months ago. Perhaps news of Cadel's true paternity had filtered down to him at long last. Perhaps *that* was why Prosper had gone to ground.

Perhaps he wasn't interested in Cadel now that he knew they weren't blood relations.

Whatever the reason, he had suddenly withdrawn from Cadel's life. So had Phineas Darkkon—who was long dead—and Chester Cramp, who had never been a big part of it to begin with. Therefore, for all intents and purposes, Cadel was now just a policeman's son. An ordinary kid. And although he might have been a little younger than his classmates, with more memorable features, he was careful not to dress or behave in a manner that was going to get him singled out. If anything, he was one of the quieter students.

Nevertheless, he had a funny feeling that his teacher knew something about him—something more than just his name and student number. Richard Buckland was in charge of Introductory Programming; he had been given the tricky job of coaxing several hundred budding computer engineers through the first year of their degrees. Despite the size of his class, however, he always seemed to remember who Cadel was. And occasionally, when Cadel asked a question, Richard's benign regard would become rather more intent than usual.

Had Richard been told the full story? Or was he simply impressed by the insightful nature of Cadel's questions?

It was hard to decide.

"What was all that stuff about traffic lights?" Hamish queried as he sat down beside Cadel in one of the middle rows. "Why d-didn't you mention it to *me*?"

Cadel sighed. Hamish saw himself as an expert on all things traffic-related because he had once hacked into the Digital Image Department of the Roads and Traffic Authority. His aim had been to tamper with various speed camera photographs.

"It's just an idea I had," Cadel muttered, glancing uneasily over his shoulder. But no one was listening. "If Sonja's wheelchair could get a signal through to the regional computer that runs all the controller boxes around here—"

"Then she wouldn't have to press a 'walk' button," Hamish concluded. "Yeah, I get it. Hack the loop detector input, somehow."

"It depends what's in there." Cadel cast his mind back to his former infiltration of the Sydney Coordinated Adaptive Traffic System. He'd been in elementary school at the time, and his approach had been a little heavy-handed. "It's a while since I poked around in SCATS," he confessed, almost sheepishly. "I don't really know what's been happening. I don't know if they've got any kind of new strobe preemption program for emergency vehicles. Or how many microwave detectors have been installed."

"Oh, I can tell you that," said Hamish in a condescending tone. But all at once Richard Buckland appeared, laden with technology, and Hamish couldn't risk uttering another word.

Even a whisper would have been audible in the sudden hush.

Richard dumped his laptop on the podium, where various plugs and cables allowed him to connect his computer to the theater's audio-visual system. He was tall and bespectacled, with neatly trimmed brown hair and an open, genial, squared-off face; he wore a baggy old T-shirt over jeans and sneakers. For a minute or so he flicked switches and pushed buttons, peering back at the big white screen on the wall behind him. Then he addressed his audience, delivering information in explosively rapid, breathlessly excited bursts like machine-gun fire.

Words and ideas seemed to erupt out of Richard, as effervescent as a carbonated soft drink.

"Today we'll be looking at stack frames and buffer overflows," he observed, getting straight to the point. "I used to save this one for my third-year course, but buffer overflows arise from poor programming practice, and by the time you're in third year, it's too late to fix *that* up." With a fleeting smile, he added, "The problem is that if your data is stored next to your program, and your users are allowed to put in as much information as they like, then the data can become *part* of your program."

None of this was news to Cadel. He'd launched quite a number of buffer overflow attacks in the past. But he was interested to hear Richard's thoughts on programming solutions. As a matter of fact, he was interested in *everything* that Richard had to say about programming—because it completely contradicted what the Axis Institute had taught.

There, the emphasis had been on infiltration. Cadel's Infiltration teacher, Dr. Ulysses Vee (a.k.a. The Virus), had delighted in loopholes, weaknesses, vulnerabilities. And Prosper English had been the same. "You can only tell whether you've mastered a system if you isolate and identify its weakest point," he had once advised Cadel. "If you knock that out and the whole system collapses, then you know you've got a handle on it." This opinion had been endorsed by Dr. Vee, who had created only to destroy. He'd created computer viruses and malware. He'd constructed labyrinthine security programs with built-in flaws, which had given him free access to many a company's databanks. He'd been a consummate hacker, with a hacker's mind-set.

In other words, he had been deficient in what Richard liked to call "style."

Cadel was still coming to terms with this concept. It had something to do with simplicity, and something to do with practicality. It was a measure of how you approached a problem—of how well you understood the fundamentals of programming. But it was also an attitude: a kind of inherent appreciation of all things clean, clear, and beautiful. Cadel couldn't help thinking that Sonja would have grasped what Richard was talking about. Her love of numbers was almost aesthetic; she would go into raptures over an exquisitely balanced algorithm. For Sonja, it wasn't just getting there that mattered. It was the *way* you got there.

Apparently, Richard felt the same. He wouldn't have liked Genius Squad's scrambling, headlong, piecemeal approach to solving problems. And he would have deplored the Axis Institute's choice of problems to solve. "When you're really young," he had pointed out during his very first lecture, "it's all about puzzles, about unlocking secrets and cracking codes. But as you mature, you come to realize that none of this *means* anything unless it helps people and makes the world a better place." Trashing networks or sabotaging software clearly weren't stylish goals, in Richard's view.

Cadel sometimes wondered if he himself was making the world a better place by helping Sonja to push buttons. He certainly hoped so.

"Psst." Suddenly Hamish jabbed him in the ribs. "Look who's here."

Cadel hadn't been watching the door. He'd been staring at a stack-frame diagram projected onto the screen behind Richard—who abruptly broke off in the middle of his lecture. "Can I help you?" asked Richard. "Are you lost?"

He was addressing the new arrival: a neat, wiry, dark-haired man wearing a suit and tie that looked bizarrely out of place among so many hoodies and cargo pants. It was painfully obvious that this man didn't belong in Richard's class.

Cadel's stomach did a backflip.

"I'm here for Cadel," said the newcomer, so quietly that his Canadian accent was barely perceptible. Cadel stared at him, paralyzed.

Only something very, very urgent would have prompted Saul Greeniaus to interrupt an Introductory Programming class.

"Oh . . . well. Okay." Richard seemed hesitant. He glanced at Cadel, who was slowly shutting his laptop. "Are you all right with that, or . . . ? I take it you know each other?"

Cadel nodded, flushing. He pushed his computer into its bag, uncomfortably aware that almost every single person in the auditorium was studying him with intense curiosity.

Only Hamish appeared to be more interested in Saul.

"Do you want me as well?" asked Hamish. But the detective shook his head.

"No," he rejoined. "You can stay." Then he turned to Richard. "Sorry about this. If it wasn't important . . ."

"Oh, look." With a wave of his hand, Richard signified complete understanding. "These things happen."

"Yes. They do. Unfortunately." Saul's tone was grim. He watched Cadel sidle past eight pairs of denim-clad knees while Richard adjusted his glasses. The strained silence was broken only by the pad of Cadel's rubber soles and a muffled cough from the back of the hall. Cadel tried not to look at anyone. On his way to the exit, he kept his head down and his pace rapid.

He was *mortified*.

As a schoolkid, he had always been a detached little weirdo, isolated from the rest of the herd. Since then he'd adopted a kind of camouflage, having learned how to dress and talk and conduct himself like other people. But at this precise moment, he felt as if he were twelve all over again.

"Okay," said Richard, addressing his other students as Saul followed Cadel out of the room. "So those integers, they take up how many bytes?"

Then the door creaked shut, muffling Richard's voice.

"Wait." Saul grabbed at Cadel's shoulder, lengthening his stride in an effort to catch up. "I'm sorry. I tried to call, but you weren't answering."

"I always put my phone on mute before a lecture." Struck by an awful possibility, Cadel stopped in his tracks. "Is it Fiona?" he asked hoarsely. "Is she—is she all right?"

It was a measure of Saul's preoccupation that for a moment he stood blank-eyed, as if he didn't recognize his own wife's name. Then he blinked, tightening his grip on Cadel.

"What? Oh yeah. She's fine. At the moment, she's . . ." Saul checked his watch. "She's on her way home from work."

"Why?" Cadel demanded, searching the pallid, fine-drawn face that hung over him. He knew that his foster mother wouldn't have canceled her appointments for any minor reason. She was a social worker, with an overwhelming caseload and very little support. Only a real emergency would have prompted her to drop everything.

Saul didn't answer immediately. Instead he surveyed the wide, empty hallway in which they stood. At last he said, "It's Prosper English. He's been seen."

Cadel swallowed.

"We can't talk about it here," Saul went on. "We should get in the car first."

He guided Cadel out of the building, which opened onto a terraced plaza decorated with a giant ball of matted, rusty wire. Cadel had always wondered if this sculpture was somehow connected with the nearby electrical engineering department. He couldn't see the point of it, otherwise.

Saul headed straight across the plaza.

"I'm parked on the road," he explained, scanning his immediate vicinity for signs of trouble. All at once Cadel realized how exposed they were out on the brick-paved pedestrian concourse.

They must have been visible from at least half a dozen multistoried structures, each sporting hundreds of windows.

But he can't be here now, Cadel decided. *Prosper can't be here now, or the place would be crawling with police.*

He wondered if Saul had a gun. It was hard to tell; no bulge was discernible beneath the detective's neatly buttoned jacket.

"Where are we going?" Cadel mumbled as they passed the computer labs.

"We're going home," Saul replied. "You have to pack your things."

"I have to *what?*"

"Fiona will help you."

"But—"

"Just wait. Not yet. Wait till we're in my car."

So Cadel waited. He numbly allowed himself to be removed from the campus, shuffling through a side gate and into the tree-lined street beyond. Saul's gray sedan was sitting just across the road in front of a picket fence. The car was empty. Like an eager pet, it chirped when Saul waved his keys to unlock it. Cadel, however, wasn't allowed to open the front passenger door.

"Back seat," Saul instructed.

"Oh, but—"

"In the back, please."

Cadel complied mutely. He remained silent as Saul slipped behind the wheel, started the engine, and pulled away from the curb. Only when they were heading down Barker Street did Cadel finally remark, "You're not sending me to a safe house, are you?"

"I'm sorry." Saul's voice was tight. "I have to. Prosper's in Sydney."

"In *Sydney?*"

This news was like a punch. It was hard to absorb.

"He turned up yesterday, in a multistoried car park," Saul revealed. "And again last night, at a railway station. But I didn't hear about it till this morning, when he was spotted in the foyer of a downtown office block." Glancing up into the rearview mirror, Saul added, "It's all closed-circuit TV footage. That's how he was identified, through a security company. They reported today's sighting, and we sent out an alert. There might be other footage that we don't know about, yet."

Cadel cleared his throat.

"Have—have you seen the pictures?" he squawked. And Saul heaved a sigh.

"Yeah," he said flatly.

"Are you *sure* it's Prosper?" Cadel was stunned. The whole thing didn't make sense. "Closed-circuit footage can be really rough . . ."

"I know. You're right," Saul agreed. "But we can't afford to take chances. And if it isn't Prosper English, it's his identical twin. With Prosper's taste in clothes."

"You mean he wasn't disguised?" Cadel didn't wait for an answer. "This is crazy! Why would Prosper come back now? I haven't *done* anything! Why isn't he laying low?"

Saul shrugged. "Maybe he didn't come back from anywhere. Maybe he never left the country." Before Cadel could protest, Saul plowed on. "He could have been in Sydney for the last nine months. We've got guys going through old CCTV footage, looking for him. Maybe he's surfaced before, and no one recognized his face."

"He wouldn't be that stupid."

"Cadel—"

"He's been leaving me alone on purpose! I know it! Because he doesn't want me trying to track him down!" Cadel leaned forward, gripping the headrest in front of him. "This is a stupid thing to do. It's *stupid*. And Prosper's smart."

"Not that smart," the detective retorted. "Smart people don't end up as fugitives. They don't break the law." He changed lanes smoothly, weaving his way through the traffic with quiet confidence. "Smart people don't slap their wanted faces all over CCTV networks," he finished.

"Exactly! Which is why he must have a *reason* for doing it!"

"Other than the fact that he's on his own, with no one else to buy his groceries for him?" An undercurrent of savage scorn marred the detective's otherwise measured delivery; he hated Prosper English with a vengeance and couldn't conceal it no matter how hard he tried. "There could be a million reasons, Cadel. He could be getting careless. He could be trying to freak you out. He could be going senile. What matters right now is that we find him before he finds you."

"If he was looking for me, he'd have found me already. It's not like I've been keeping my head down."

"No. You haven't." Saul sounded regretful. "But that's gonna change. It *has* to change. I'm sorry, Cadel," he murmured, once more lifting his solemn gaze to the rearview mirror. "You'll have to go back into hiding until we work out what the hell is going on."

THREE

It was the same old room in the usual safe house. Cadel couldn't believe that he was back.

Nothing had changed. The room was still a bleak white box full of plain white furnishings: white desk, white chair, white cupboard and bedspread. There was even a white plastic litter bin tucked away in one corner. The only touch of color was the beige of the carpet.

Of course, this carpet was also strewn with Cadel's belongings—but they weren't very colorful, either. Even the book jackets were bleached and grubby. Whatever wasn't black or gray seemed to be either brown or olive; now that he really looked at his wardrobe, spread out across the floor in tangled heaps, Cadel could see why Fiona was constantly complaining about the way he dressed.

"Anyone would think you were in some kind of guerrilla army," she'd grumbled on one occasion. "These aren't clothes; they're camouflage." And she was right, to some extent. Cadel knew he wasn't the only teenager in the world who chose outfits that were designed to repel interest. Nevertheless, as he contemplated the lack of variety in his pants and T-shirts, he wished that he'd had the sense to bring his quilt with him. A bright red quilt might have done something to alleviate the sheer dullness of his surroundings.

I should have given it more thought, he glumly reflected. But then again, there hadn't been much time. Saul had been anxious to get him into a secure environment, and the little weatherboard cottage that they shared wasn't particularly secure. "You could find our place in the phone book," had been Saul's reasoning when his wife had objected to the whole notion of a safe house. "There isn't enough protection; not against someone like Prosper English. He wouldn't *need* to trip any motion sensors. He could throw a Molotov cocktail through the kitchen window without setting foot in the yard. It's just not an option, Fi—I'm sorry. Cadel can't stay here."

So Cadel had been moved. After packing a rather haphazard selection of clothes, books, and computer equipment, he'd been whisked off to Roseville, where he'd been installed in a two-story house behind a screen of rhododendrons. This house stood in a large, flat, featureless garden; there was a sweeping view of every approach from its top floor, and full CCTV coverage of every single entry point. The bedrooms were numerous enough to sleep four bodyguards working twelve-hour shifts. The security system included automatic gates and isometric locks.

But the décor inside was abysmal: all blank walls and featureless space. Cadel had never liked it in the past, and now—having lived in a proper home for six months—he loathed every single white door, white tile, and white cornice that currently imprisoned him. After his brief taste of freedom, the blandness of the safe house was even harder to take.

And his name was *still* scrawled under the window ledge!

It was eighteen months since he'd written it there, during his first Roseville sojourn. At the time, he'd been glad enough to find a safe haven, free of Prosper English. After living most of his life in something that resembled a stage set peopled with frauds, he'd found the safe house oddly restful; at least it wasn't pretending to be cozy or welcoming. At least it was *honest.* Then he'd moved into a foster home, which (because of the people he'd shared it with) had been far, far worse than the gilded cage in which he'd spent his childhood. From the foster home he'd escaped to Clearview House, where various members of Genius Squad were residing in a curious establishment: half bunker and half boarding school. This address had been a facade, too, with a lie at its very core. Nevertheless, he'd preferred it to the safe house, which had received him yet again after Prosper's escape from prison.

The second visit to Roseville had lasted three months. Three whole months! It had seemed like three years. Yet he hadn't really understood how bad it was, back then. Not in his heart of hearts.

Now that he had a real home, he understood only too well.

Home, he thought. *I want to go home.*

Shutting his eyes, he tried to pretend that he was sitting in his own bedroom. He conjured up a mental image of its silver walls, its blue ceiling, and its checkerboard floor; he remembered carefully filling in those black-and-white squares, one by one, after Fiona had traced their outlines. Together she and Cadel had painted the whole room, working side by side for three consecutive weekends—and it was Cadel who had been allowed to choose the color scheme. "You're the one who has to sleep in here," Fiona had said, cheerfully acceding to his request for a room that felt like "the inside of a computer." She had also bought him a giant plastic chess piece for Christmas (to match the floor), and had helped him to cover the top of his desk with binary-code contact paper, which she had sealed with several coats of clear polyurethane.

Cadel had been impressed by her home-decorating skills. Thanks to Fiona, their humble two-bedroom cottage had been transformed into a warm and colorful nest, full of refinished furniture and recycled objects. Saul hadn't contributed much; he was interested in the house only because it contained his family. If Fiona wanted a cowrie-shell curtain and Cadel wanted a shiny silver bedroom, that was fine by Saul—who didn't feel the need to project his own personality onto the fixtures and fittings. To Saul, the zebra-striped hooked rug and driftwood chandelier were just an extension of Fiona; therefore they met with his complete approval.

He was a quiet sort of person to live with, very neat and restrained. Yet he managed to make his presence felt, despite the fact that he didn't talk much. He would mow lawns, string up fairy lights, and visit garden centers without a word of protest. He would wash dishes and vacuum rugs in the most thorough and painstaking fashion, deriving a peculiar sort of pleasure from every routine chore. Upon walking into the kitchen after a hard day's work, he would immediately put out the garbage or unstack the dishwasher, his tensed shoulders visibly relaxing as he did so.

Though the detective rarely discussed his job, Cadel knew that it couldn't be easy. This much was clear from the look on Saul's face sometimes, late in the evening, when he was carefully unloading his pistol and returning it to his gun safe. There could be no doubt that he savored even the mundane side of married life simply because it wasn't dangerous or distressing.

And now that his tranquil domestic existence was under threat, the strain of it was already carving new lines around his mouth. Fiona's reaction might have been louder and more explosive than Saul's, on being told that she couldn't join Cadel in the safe house. But it was Saul who, in one short day, had aged a good ten years.

Cadel couldn't help worrying about him.

"You should be staying here, too," was Cadel's opinion, offered up to Saul the previous night. "Prosper *hates* you. You're in just as much danger as I am. More, probably."

"No." With a shake of his head, Saul had dismissed Cadel's suggestion. "Prosper wouldn't break cover just to blow a hole in me. He's a practical sort of guy—you know that. I'd have to be standing in front of something he wanted."

"Like me?"

"It'll be all right," Saul had insisted, without specifying how. Then he'd gone off to reassure Sonja and Judith.

Prosper English loathed Sonja. He blamed her for turning Cadel against him. So it was likely that Sonja was also in danger—more so, perhaps, than Cadel. Yet he could understand why the police weren't too concerned about her. Judith's seaside mansion was fully automated, with a wiring system that controlled lights, blinds, sprinklers, TV, air-conditioning, security cameras, and motion sensor alarms. If an intruder was detected in the house while it was empty, the building's central computer was capable of alerting Judith via an e-mail or text message. Furthermore, this computer occupied an air-conditioned closet that doubled as a kind of panic room; Judith could lock herself in there, behind an impregnable door, if she ever felt threatened. "I only wish our safe houses were this safe," Saul had remarked upon first being introduced to what Judith liked to call her "intelligent infrastructure."

The police had therefore decided not to move either Sonja or Judith. Only Saul and Fiona had been forced to camp at a friend's place for the night. "Just until we find Prosper English," Saul had promised with grim determination. "Now that we know he's in town, he won't be at large for long."

Cadel wasn't convinced of this. But he hadn't said anything, because Saul already had enough to worry about.

Tap-tap-tap. The sound of a hesitant knock caused Cadel's eyes to snap open.

"Who is it?" he asked.

"It's me."

Recognizing Saul's voice, Cadel checked his watch. Ten past two seemed pretty early for an afternoon visit. Saul had promised to return around five.

"Come in," said Cadel, wondering what could have brought the detective back to Roseville so soon.

Nothing good, probably.

"I see you've unpacked," Saul remarked as he crossed the threshold. He was surveying the sludge-colored tangle of books and clothes and insulated wiring at his feet.

"Oh. Ah—yeah," Cadel replied. "I'm putting things away."

Saul lifted an eyebrow but didn't comment. Instead he quietly closed the door behind him. "Did you forget anything?" he asked. "Because I can always go back home and get it."

"I'm okay." Cadel flapped an impatient hand. "Just tell me what's wrong."

A lopsided smile tugged at the corner of Saul's mouth. "You're jumping to conclusions," he said, pulling a computer disk from his breast pocket. "I just want you to have a look at this."

"The footage, you mean?" Cadel's heart sank. "Is that the CCTV download?"

"It is, yes."

"All three sightings?"

"All seven. We found some more." Seeing Cadel wince, Saul apologized. "I'm sorry. This must be hard. But we need confirmation. You know Prosper better than anyone. You've seen him disguised as other people. We want to be sure we haven't made a mistake."

Cadel gave a nod.

"This isn't what we agreed to. I realize that." Saul was referring to the decision they'd both made, months previously, about Cadel's role in the ongoing hunt for Prosper English. "And I'm not asking you to participate—far from it. You've got to stay off-line, and keep your head down. All I need is a positive ID. It's not something that Prosper will ever find out about. I'll make a verbal report."

But would that verbal report find its way into an e-mail? Or a phone call? Cadel didn't entirely trust the police—not all of them. He felt that they often underestimated the sheer depth of Prosper's cunning.

For this reason, Cadel failed to respond immediately. He sat for a moment, turning things over in his mind. Then he looked up at Saul, and their gazes locked.

"This might be some sort of test," Cadel said slowly. He was talking about Prosper's reappearance. "Have you thought of that? He might have done this *specifically* to see how I'd react. To see if I'd go after him."

Saul frowned.

"I've got to be careful. *Really* careful," Cadel went on. "He might be trying to flush me out or something."

"But why?" Saul couldn't conceal his anxiety, though he was trying very hard to sound calm. "You haven't so much as Googled his name for the last nine months. You've been as quiet as a mouse. Haven't you?"

"Yeah." Cadel had been taking no chances. He'd been roundly ignoring Prosper, in the hope that Prosper would extend him the same courtesy.

"Then he must *see* you're no threat," Saul argued. "That's if he's keeping tabs on you at all, which is debatable."

Cadel gave a snort. He'd never debated it. He'd never even doubted it.

"And even if he is running a surveillance operation," Saul continued, "it's not as if you've given him anything to worry about. In fact, that might be why he's surfaced now. Because he thinks you're well and truly out of the picture."

Cadel didn't believe this for one minute. Having twice underestimated Cadel—and suffered because of it—Prosper was unlikely to make the same mistake a third time. Unlikely? Hell, the chances were *minimal*. Cadel could offer mathematical proof in support of his opinion; he'd calculated the odds.

He couldn't deny, however, that there was always room for error when it came to probability.

"Anything's possible," he conceded. "I've still got a feeling this has something to do with me, though."

"Which is why you have to sit tight, and not get involved." Saul was firm. "I wouldn't even be asking you for a positive ID if I thought there was any chance of Prosper finding out." He paused for a moment, his forehead creasing as he fixed his attention on Cadel's computer. "What do you think? Should we use your laptop? Would it be safe?"

"I'd prefer to use something else," said Cadel, who had always been paranoid about the health of his hard drive. "You don't know where that disk might have been."

"Good point," Saul murmured. He then opened the door and ushered Cadel through it; together they made their way downstairs, where they found one of the security guards—Angus—sitting in the old dining room. This dark and narrow space had been converted into an office, which contained a couple of CCTV monitors, a computer, a printer, a fax machine, and several telephones. Since most of the equipment on show was either black or gray, instead of white, Cadel preferred the office to any other room in the house.

Angus also brightened up the décor a little. Not that he was very lively, with his bland expression and uninflected voice. Like most of the safe-house staff, he had been trained to keep his distance. But he had red hair and a red face, and his eyes were a deep, vivid blue.

Even in his mud brown suit, he struck a cheerful note.

"Sure," he said when asked if the office computer was available. "But I'm on duty right now. I have to stay here while you're using it."

"Feel free," was Saul's somewhat acid rejoinder. He allowed Angus to insert Saul's disk into the appropriate drive. But once this simple task had been carried out, Angus was promptly banished to the other side of the room.

Cadel soon found himself peering at a list of seven files. Each file bore a tag incorporating a date, a time, and a location, as well as more obscure number groupings that were harder to interpret. He wondered if they might refer to camera specifications or network protocols.

"Each file is a different sighting," Saul explained, motioning at the screen. He was standing behind Cadel, who had laid claim to a wheeled typist's chair. "They're listed in order of appearance."

"Starting three days ago?" said Cadel. And Saul pulled a face.

"Yes. We've been a bit slow off the mark, unfortunately."

According to the list, Prosper had been filmed in Hornsby, Bankstown, Campbelltown, Bondi Junction, Parramatta, and Sydney's Central Business District. In other words, he'd been all over the place: north, south, east, and west. There didn't seem to be a uniformity of times, either: mornings, afternoons, and evenings were all represented.

"As you can see, he's been getting around a bit," Saul continued. "But there's been a double sighting in the CBD, so we're hoping that might have some significance."

"It all has some significance." Cadel planted his fingertip on the third line down. "Look at this. An early start at the railway station. Was he heading in or out?"

"In. Definitely. We've been checking the schedules, and there are three trains he might have caught."

"Yeah, but where did he *come* from, at 5:48 in the morning? That's got to narrow your search parameters." Cadel spun around in his chair, lifting his chin until he was looking Saul straight in the eye. "You know what you need? You need a mathematician. You can apply mathematics to a problem like this. Bayesian theory . . . maybe a Markov chain model. You can look at where Prosper's been and work out where he is now. If you've got enough data."

There was a brief pause. When Cadel didn't go on, the detective finally asked, "*Have* we got enough data?"

"I dunno." Cadel hesitated before adding, "Maybe not. I'd have to give it some thought."

"No." Suddenly Saul shook his head. "No, that wasn't the deal. You should keep your distance. We'll find someone else to do it."

"Sonja could."

"Possibly. But I don't want you asking her. Your job is identification, pure and simple." Saul reached for the mouse, then clicked on the first listed sighting. Immediately, a dim, grainy view of concrete and steel enveloped the computer screen. "Now, what we've got here is a parking lot," he announced. "And this figure here, on the left, *appears* to be Prosper English. We think." He indicated a blurred shape moving briskly past the suspended camera. "Do you want to run it again? We can pause it, if you like."

"Yes, please."

The frozen image showed a tall, thin, middle-aged man wearing sunglasses. His hair was brushed back off his high forehead like a lion's mane; he was clean-shaven, with a long nose and dark eyebrows.

Though the picture wasn't very clear, it sent a cold dart through Cadel's stomach. He had to swallow and lick his dry lips before he was able to speak.

"That's Prosper," he mumbled.

"Are you sure?" Saul was frowning again. "Because you can't really see the face very well—"

"That's him," Cadel insisted, staring at the fuzzy recording like a rabbit caught in the glare of oncoming headlights. "That's Prosper English. I'd recognize him anywhere."

FOUR

Sitting in front of the safe-house computer, Cadel examined the image displayed on its screen.

There could be no doubt that he was looking at Prosper English. Despite the poor quality of the digital video recording, Prosper's high cheekbones and lanky frame were unmistakable. So was his tweed jacket. Prosper had always favored professorial outfits, and Cadel recognized this one—which also featured a matching waistcoat and leather elbow patches. But why had Prosper chosen it? Why hadn't he disguised himself? If he had shaved his head or donned a hooded anorak, he might never have been detected. Yet he'd kept on wearing the same old clothes in shot after shot after shot.

What on earth was he up to?

Cadel couldn't figure it out. Nothing made sense. Though the parking lot sighting suggested that Prosper might have a car, the station sighting suggested otherwise. Though the sunglasses were a form of camouflage, the tweedy jacket was anything but. And the five-second film clips didn't provide nearly enough information. Were there any banks nearby? Any bus stops? Any doctors or pharmacies or Internet cafés? Cadel didn't know. He couldn't even work out if Prosper was following anyone, because there wasn't enough footage. The police had provided only seven brief glimpses of Prosper as he passed seven different cameras. If he was in pursuit of a person who happened to be more than five seconds ahead of him, it wasn't apparent. Not to Cadel, anyway.

What I need, he thought, *is better coverage. Better coverage and proper geographical background.*

But he wouldn't be asking for anything like that. Suppose his request made its way into an official e-mail? Suppose there was a leak? Suppose Prosper had told Dr. Vee to monitor the police network? Cadel wasn't about to take any more risks; keeping the files had been hazardous enough. "I don't know if I can do that," Saul had muttered when asked if he would leave the disk behind. "I thought we agreed that you shouldn't get involved?"

"I won't get involved," Cadel had assured him. "I'm just going to take another look at those files."

"Why?"

"Because I might as well. Because they're already here."

"This isn't your job, though. You should be doing something else."

"Like what? I can't go online. I can't talk to Sonja. I've done all my homework, and I'm sick of watching TV. What else *can* I do?"

It was a good question, to which Saul had been unable to provide a ready answer. So he'd given in. He'd surrendered his disk to Cadel, who had promised faithfully not to download anything off it. "I'll give it back to you when I see you tonight," Cadel had said. "I won't use my laptop, don't worry."

"You have to be careful."

"I know."

"Prosper's not stupid."

"I *know.*" Cadel didn't need to be told how smart Prosper was. Only a smart man could have escaped from prison. Only a smart man could have *stayed* out of prison. Yet suddenly Prosper had resurfaced—in Sydney, of all places—wearing clothes that were bound to be recognized. It was a dumb thing to do, and Prosper wasn't dumb.

So what was he thinking?

Cadel studied the recorded scene in front of him, searching for clues. There had to be a pattern to Prosper's movements buried somewhere inside the captured data. Prosper's timing was important. His choice of route was important. So was his decision to cross the foyer of a multi-storied office block in downtown Sydney. He hadn't used an elevator; he hadn't taken the stairs; he'd simply walked through the foyer.

Why?

Cadel gnawed at his thumbnail, wishing that he could ask Sonja for help. Sonja was good with patterns, just as Cadel was good with systems. She could always spot the numbers lurking within the colors and the shapes. She had an eye for repetition and a nose for anomalies, so she was more attuned to the underlying rhythms of what she saw.

But he wasn't meant to be communicating with Sonja. Not directly. Even an encoded text message was out of the question, because Saul wanted him "off the grid." "No electronic exchanges," the detective had warned. "If there's something important you want to tell her, I'll pass it on myself. In person. It's the safest way." He'd then hesitated before adding, "Prosper might already know where you are. He might have had me followed. But that's okay, because you're in a secure facility. The important thing is that he doesn't find out what you're thinking or doing. The less information he has, the better. Don't you agree?"

It had been impossible to *dis*agree—especially when confronted by Saul's strained expression. Cadel had therefore pledged that he wouldn't use either his phone or his laptop to make contact with Sonja. Instead he'd scribbled an encrypted note, which Saul had delivered to Judith's place.

Cadel sighed. Under the circumstances, he could hardly e-mail the CCTV files to Sonja—and he knew that Saul would *never* agree to give her the disk. Not without official clearance, which probably wouldn't be forthcoming. Someone in the higher ranks of the commissioner's office didn't like the idea of kids becoming involved in police investigations. That was why Genius Squad had folded. That was why, instead of being employed in a useful investigative role, Hamish had been put on probation, Sonja had received an official warning, and the Wieneke twins had simply . . . well, they had simply disappeared.

Cadel wasn't too worried about the Wienekes. They were both pretty streetwise (especially Devin), and Lexi was always popping up on crypt-analysis websites, because she just couldn't leave an unencoded cipher alone. Cadel had established that she was moving between Sydney and Brisbane, using a lot of Internet cafés. He had also spotted her in some-body's Facebook snapshot, which had been taken in a bar full of grin-ning young party animals. So she was clearly getting on with life, despite her disappointment over the end of Genius Squad. And if she wanted to do this without police interference, Cadel could only sympathize. In fact, he had carefully refrained from alerting anyone to her activities—except, of course, Sonja. "If the police are so keen to get hold of the twins, they can do their own legwork," he'd informed his best friend. "It's not *my* job to run online surveillance checks."

All the same, he couldn't help wishing that Lexi and her brother were still around. For the first time ever, he was regretting that Genius Squad hadn't survived. With Genius Squad's help, he would have had no trouble solving the mystery of Prosper's reappearance.

But the squad was now defunct. And Cadel was all alone, with no net-work connection and no access to official databanks.

He might as well have been working blindfolded, with one arm in a sling.

I'm missing something, he decided as he peered at the scene in front of him. He had a niggling sense that the answer—the key, the *pattern*—lay right under his nose; that everything he needed was already there among the blurred figures frozen on the computer screen.

Leaning closer, he tried to interpret the look on Prosper's face. It wasn't easy. It wouldn't have been easy even if the picture had been clearer; Cadel would still have had to fight the nausea that invaded his stomach every time he was exposed to Prosper's chiseled features and loose-limbed form. The last time they'd met, Prosper had been armed and dangerous. He had put a gun to Cadel's head. And Cadel couldn't shake off the memory of that cold, deadly weight sitting against his temple.

Not that Prosper would have pulled the trigger. *I'm not going to shoot you*, he'd once said. *I couldn't bring myself to do anything of the sort. But I'll happily shoot Sonja if you give me the least bit of trouble. You understand that, don't you?*

Cadel could almost hear the smooth, precise drawl ringing in his ears. He could almost see the piercing gaze and wolfish grin—despite the fact that they were both completely absent from Saul's CCTV footage. Prosper wasn't smiling at the camera in any of these shots. If he was even aware of being filmed, it certainly wasn't obvious. His sunglasses concealed any telltale sidelong glances.

He simply walked from one side of the frame to the other, his pace brisk, his hands empty, his expression unreadable.

Defeated, Cadel turned his attention to the other people in the foyer shot. There were five of them: two women and three men. All were dressed in business suits. One was carrying a takeaway coffee cup, while the rest were toting either handbags or briefcases. The smaller woman was talking into her cell phone; she didn't seem to register Prosper's presence at all when he overtook her. Everyone was moving in the same direction, toward the elevators, past an enormous piece of modern sculpture that comprised three giant silver balls hanging from steel wires. Cadel could see one end of a dark leather couch. The floor was pale and glossy; the only visible bit of wall was covered in wood veneer; the front entrance wasn't anywhere in sight . . .

And then, suddenly, it hit him.

The silver ball.

There *was* a pattern, but it didn't have anything to do with timing or movement. Hastily Cadel skipped to the next file, in which Prosper was walking through a parking lot. Sure enough, this scene contained a convex traffic mirror. And in the next scene, at a suburban shopping mall, there was a window display featuring strings of large, chrome-covered balls like overblown Christmas-tree decorations. And at the railway station, a newsstand was hung with shiny, metallic Mylar balloons. And in the harborside hotel lobby, another convex mirror was sitting in a gilded Venetian frame above an elaborate console table.

Not a single shot was without some gleaming little half sphere, its surface a complex web of wraparound reflections.

"Hey, kid," said Angus from the other side of the room. "Your parents have arrived."

Cadel blinked. Spinning around in his chair, he saw that Angus was pointing at one of the security monitors.

Even from a distance, Cadel could identify Saul's car as it glided across the screen.

"They're not my parents," Cadel observed absent-mindedly. "Not yet, anyway." Then he asked the question that was uppermost in his mind. "Does your CCTV network have an IP address?"

Angus's response was a blank, uncomprehending stare. So Cadel tried again.

"Is it connected to the Internet? Is there a central monitoring station?"

"*This* is the central monitoring station," said Angus.

"Yeah, but what if no one's around? Is there remote access surveillance when the place is empty?" Seeing Angus frown, Cadel gave up. "Never mind. I'll check it myself."

"No you won't." The security guard was adamant. "Sorry, mate. You're not cleared to touch any of this equipment."

"But—"

"Work it out with your dad. He might be able to help."

Saul's car was now parked near the front steps; Cadel could see it quite clearly on the screen behind Angus. As for Saul and Fiona, they were already inside, being filmed by the camera in the vestibule.

Hastily Cadel scanned the office ceiling.

"This room doesn't have any cameras, does it?" he demanded. "I can't see one."

"Nope," Angus replied.

"Then I'll wait here. They'll find me."

And they did. Saul, in fact, headed straight for the office, without even pausing at the foot of the staircase. Fiona followed him, looking flustered. Her thick, reddish hair was beginning to escape from all the combs and pins securing it. Her jacket was buttoned up crookedly, and she had forgotten to wear her watch.

When she and Saul arrived on the threshold, Cadel greeted them with an urgent summons.

"Come here! Look at this!" he exclaimed. "You're not going to *believe* it."

The detective sighed. "You haven't even moved since I left, have you?" he murmured. And Fiona said, "I brought your quilt, sweetie. It's in the car."

"Yes—thanks—great. But I might not be needing it." Cadel tapped the screen in front of him. "See this? I think it's a light probe."

Saul and his wife exchanged long-suffering glances. Nevertheless, they both moved forward until they were standing directly behind Cadel's chair.

"I wanted to find a pattern, and I did," he continued. "There's a shiny half sphere in every scene. *Every single one.* I mean, what are the odds?"

"Cadel—" Saul began.

"No, wait. Just listen." Dragging his fingers through his tousled curls, Cadel took a deep breath. "I don't think this is Prosper at all," he announced. "I think this is a piece of malware."

As he'd expected, the reaction was one of total incredulity. Even Angus turned to gape at him. It was Fiona who finally broke the stunned silence.

"What on earth is malware?" she asked.

"An illegal computer program." Saul was shaking his head. "Cadel, that's impossible—"

"What is?" said Fiona. "What are you talking about?"

"It *wouldn't* be impossible. Not if you had the right skills. Not if you were good enough." Cadel began to argue his case. "It makes perfect sense. Why else would Prosper always be wearing the same clothes? Why else would there be a shiny ball in every scene?"

"Coincidence," Saul rejoined.

"Or protocol settings."

"*Cadel,*" snapped Fiona, "could you *please* slow down! You're not making sense. What's so important about these shiny balls, anyway?"

"Nothing. Unless you're doing visual effects." Cadel paused for a moment, his mind racing. *Thank god,* he thought. *Thank god I read all that online SIGGRAPH stuff.* "I only know this because I like to keep up with the latest programming breakthroughs. There's a lot of amazing mathematics that goes into computer graphics these days." Realizing that Fiona was in no way enlightened, he changed tack. "You must have heard of digital doubles," he said. "They're fake people that you stick into real scenes. Computer-generated people."

"Wait a minute." Suddenly Fiona worked it out. Her voice became shrill. "Are you saying that all those pictures of Prosper English are *computer generated*?"

"I'm saying that they could be," Cadel replied. "If you want to create a realistic digital double, you need a light map of the whole scene. And for one of those, you have to use a shiny chrome ball." His heart sank at the prospect of explaining High Dynamic Range Rendering to someone who didn't know what malware was. "I'm not sure how it works, exactly," he admitted. "You'd have to talk to an expert. But a chrome ball gives you the real-world lighting data for a specific environment. Without understanding how the light falls, you can't make it fall properly on your digital double."

"Except that he's not a digital double." Saul nodded at the computer screen, where Prosper's grainy likeness had been caught in mid-stride. "If that guy was a fake, he wouldn't be interacting. He'd be walking through walls."

"Not if he was programmed properly."

"But—"

"This is *all about programming*," Cadel insisted. "You can have a thousand people in a scene, and they can be *programmed* to interact with each other. They can be programmed to fight each other, or run away from each other, or respond to variables like walls or hills . . . It depends what you want them to do." As the detective chewed on his bottom lip, Cadel leaned forward. He felt that he had to make Saul understand. "I don't quite know how you'd pull this off. Like I said, I'm not a computer graphics expert—and neither is Dr. Vee. But suppose he's teamed up with someone who *is*, and they're both working for Prosper English? I mean, Vee's worked for Prosper before. They could have got together and created a security-camera bug."

All eyes immediately swivelled toward the monitors nearby. There was a brief, tension-filled pause.

Then Saul cleared his throat.

"It's a bit of a leap," he said, though he sounded shaken. "Are you sure—that is, can we prove it?"

"I dunno." Pulling at his bottom lip, Cadel considered the matter. His gaze drifted from the troubled faces looming above him to the computer screen sitting in front of him. "If it was me," he reasoned, thinking aloud, "and I was designing this program, I'd have it infiltrating streams of CCTV data where they pass through an Internet traffic point. So you wouldn't see any evidence left on the actual cameras. But there would have to be a whole *library* of really obvious specifications in the protocol before the program could insert Prosper English. You'd have to specify the height of the camera, and the angle, and the tilt, and the type of lens. And you'd have to specify a shiny half sphere and maybe something standardized—something that would give you scale. Like a power point, for instance. Or a manhole cover." He turned back to Saul, inspired by the idea of a protocol checklist.

It was clear, however, that he'd left his audience far, far behind.

"You've lost me," Saul confessed. And Fiona mumbled, "What was that about a library again?"

Cadel felt himself deflate. He realized that he was no Richard Buckland, able to clarify and simplify difficult concepts. Angus looked frankly dazed, as if he'd been knocked on the head with an iron bar.

"Okay, look." Speaking very slowly and clearly, Cadel made one more attempt to hammer his message home. "There are all kinds of different cameras wired up to the Net," he declared. "But if Prosper only shows up on one kind of camera—and if you always see particular things in the shot with him—then it's got to be suspicious. Don't you agree?"

"Oh yes," said Fiona.

"Definitely," rumbled Angus, who by now was completely absorbed in the discussion.

Saul flashed him a sharp glance.

"Aren't you supposed to be watching those monitors?" the detective growled before addressing Cadel once again. "So according to your theory, some rogue computer virus is pasting film clips of Prosper English onto random bits of CCTV footage. Is that it?"

"Umm . . . more or less." Cadel decided not to complicate matters by objecting to the terms "virus" and "film clip," though they weren't really accurate. "I'm not *absolutely* certain," he allowed. "I just think it's possible."

"And worth looking into," Saul muttered.

"Definitely."

"But why?" asked Fiona. When everyone stared at her, she must have realized how ambiguous her question had been. So she expanded on it. "I mean, why would Prosper English want to pop up all over Sydney and cause a commotion? It seems so pointless."

Cadel could hardly believe his ears.

"It's not pointless. It's tactical," he replied. "He wants us to think he's in Sydney because he's *not* in Sydney." As Saul opened his mouth to deliver some cautionary remark, Cadel cut him off. "Which means that I can go home now. Which means that I'll be *safe* back home."

"Maybe," said the detective, who seemed reluctant to commit himself. Cadel, however, wouldn't be silenced.

He had everything worked out.

"I'll be safer at home than I am here," he said. "Prosper might not be in Sydney, but he's obviously got into a whole lot of IP surveillance systems. What if he's monitoring this one?"

"Oh my god." Fiona sounded horrified. "Do you think he is?"

"We don't know," Saul stressed. He was trying to keep things calm. "This is just a theory—"

"Which fits all the facts." Cadel was growing impatient. Why did Saul have to be so stubborn? "I don't want to stay here. It's networked. It's vulnerable. There are too many cameras."

"Cadel—"

"I want to go back home. I'll be safe, at home."

These simple words were enough to convince Fiona, who fixed her husband with an anxious, pleading look. Cadel did the same, widening his enormous blue eyes as he stuck out his bottom lip in mute appeal. (It was a dirty trick, and he was slightly ashamed of himself, but he was also desperate.)

Ambushed on two fronts, Saul quickly buckled.

"Oh, all right," he said, reaching for his phone. "Just let me make a few calls, and I'll see what I can do." *Bip-bip-bip* went the keypad as he jabbed at it with one finger. "But I can't promise anything," he warned. "You know that, don't you? This is going to take a while."

Cadel nodded. Then he smiled at Fiona. Then he spun around to face the computer screen, because Prosper was still pinned there like a moth on a specimen board.

I'll have to tell Sonja, he decided. *She'll have to turn off the cameras at Judith's house.*

As far as he was concerned, they would need to start taking some very serious precautions.

FIVE

By noon the following day, Cadel had been released from protective custody.

He had finally been granted permission to sleep at home, and to attend his computer engineering classes. But the rest of the world was now off limits. He wasn't even allowed to do anything on his own; wherever he went, someone else was supposed to go, too. And that someone couldn't be just anyone.

In the absence of an armed police escort, the job of protecting Cadel would fall on his old friend Gazo Kovacs.

"Gazo has a built-in defense mechanism," Saul explained when asked to justify his choice. "It's more effective than tear gas, and he doesn't need a permit to use it."

He was referring to Gazo's peculiar genetic disability: a stench so overwhelming that it could knock people out. Once upon a time, Gazo had been unable to control his mutant body odor. When Cadel had first met him, at the Axis Institute, Gazo had been wearing a sealed suit that was designed to prevent him from harming his teachers (or fellow students) whenever he became badly stressed. Since then, however, he had learned to manage whatever surge of hormones triggered this unfortunate response, so that it rarely took him by surprise and would only occur when he wanted it to. Regular massages, a change of diet, and an array of special breathing techniques had helped him to live a normal life—as had his job with a firm that specialized in campus landscaping. Gazo now worked three days a week at the University of New South Wales; he was therefore well acquainted with every nook and cranny of the university grounds, and knew quite a few of the staff there, too.

"He's familiar with the layout, he has the means to protect you, and he hangs around with you quite a bit anyway," Saul had told Cadel. "In other words, he's the perfect bodyguard. No one's going to wonder why you're with Gazo."

Cadel wasn't so sure about that. Eyebrows would certainly be raised when he rolled up to his Advanced Programming lectures with Gazo in tow. Even if questions weren't asked, people were bound to wonder—especially if Gazo was identified as one of the men who mowed the campus lawns and clipped the campus hedges.

However, it was pointless trying to argue. Saul was too busy to take time off work, and it wasn't as if Cadel had a better idea. All in all, Gazo's companionship would be preferable to that of a stone-faced, shaven-headed bodybuilder in a pinstriped suit and sunglasses. Cadel could only imagine the sort of effect that someone like Angus would have on a class full of computer geeks.

Not that Angus was available. Not anymore. He and his colleagues had been reassigned; it was their job to protect people who had been classified as "likely targets," and Cadel no longer fell into this category. He didn't qualify for round-the-clock police protection anymore, because Prosper had ceased to pose an immediate and probable threat.

That was the official theory, anyway.

It was based on Cadel's own hypothesis—which had been right all along. Prosper's reappearance was nothing more than an online hoax. This was now proven beyond all doubt, thanks to a very fortunate programming error. While prowling through various CCTV networks, the police had stumbled upon yet another shot of Prosper English. In this one, however, he appeared to vanish halfway across the scene, leaving a black Prosper-shaped hole. Various visual effects technicians had ruled that the hole was a "dropped frame," and that the malware responsible for it had failed to "render the lighting." Clearly some kind of bug was at work, though who had planted the thing was anyone's guess.

According to expert opinion, the person behind the program had to be really, really skilled, because he'd created something revolutionary. But there were many highly skilled people in the computer graphics business, and they were scattered across the globe.

"For all we know, he could be in Russia," Saul admitted, upon relaying this information to Cadel. "It's an international industry now, thanks to the Net."

"But what makes you think this guy's working on his own?" asked Cadel. They were driving toward the university so that he could attend an afternoon seminar; Saul had agreed to meet up with Gazo at the Barker Street entrance. "I mean, this is a breakthrough piece of programming. If one person put it together without any kind of help, why wouldn't he sell it on the open market and make a fortune? Why would he just give it to Prosper English?"

"Maybe he didn't *give* it to anyone," Saul replied. "Maybe Prosper paid for it."

"Maybe." Cadel doubted very much, however, that Prosper English had enough spare cash squirreled away in secret bank accounts to cover the full cost of something so cutting edge. It would take a great deal of money to compensate a bona fide, unsung programming genius for the loss of world domination in HDR environment mapping. "Or maybe Vee helped to design it," Cadel went on. "Maybe there's a whole bunch of people involved, and they can't go public because everyone on the development team is a fugitive of some kind. Like Dr. Vee." After a moment's reflection, he added, "Then again, maybe Prosper had nothing to do with any of this."

Saul flashed him a startled look—just as the vehicle in front of them stopped suddenly. For one horrifying split second, Cadel was afraid that they were going to collide with the back end of a tourist bus.

But Saul stomped on the brake, so hard that Cadel nearly bounced off the windshield. And nothing regrettable happened after all.

"You can't be serious," Saul protested.

Cadel shrugged. "Prosper's a notorious criminal," he said. "If I was some crazy hacker with a grudge and I wanted to get even, I might consider playing a trick on the police." He didn't like to mention it, but this was *exactly* the sort of thing that he himself might have done, once—with Prosper's encouragement. "It would get everyone all worked up over nothing," Cadel finished, "and waste valuable resources. Never underestimate what people will do for kicks."

Saul frowned. He was crawling along by this time, stuck in heavy traffic on Anzac Parade. The sun was glinting on tinted glass and chrome bumpers. The bus ahead of them was belching clouds of black smoke from its exhaust pipe.

"No," Saul said at last. "I don't buy that. One of the computer guys we interviewed was talking about a scan—about running some kind of scanner over a person, to get his exact measurements for a digital double. You couldn't do that with Prosper unless he was in the room with you."

"I guess not."

"You're probably right, though. About this bug being engineered to distract us. Prosper might want us to think he's in Sydney so that we won't look too hard at what he's *really* doing." Saul seemed to be thinking out loud. "I wonder if we're getting too close for comfort? There's a whole team of investigators on this case. It's a global effort. I wonder if he feels like somebody's closing in on him?"

Cadel grunted. He could see the Barker Street intersection coming up, and didn't want to discuss Prosper English anymore. Prosper had a tendency to dominate your life, if you let him. He was hard to shake off even when he wasn't around.

Cadel knew that he shouldn't be speculating, or theorizing, or drawing conclusions about Prosper's activities. The trick was to appear *perfectly harmless*—and that would be impossible if Prosper ever deduced that Cadel was helping the police.

"Did you tell Judith to switch off her security cameras?" Cadel asked, changing the subject as Saul turned left.

The detective nodded.

"Yeah," he rejoined. "Don't worry about that. It's covered."

"Are you going to pick me up when I'm done?"

"No." Saul explained that Gazo would be giving Cadel a lift home. "He'll stay with you there until I get back. Just make sure you check all the entry points before going in."

"But what if you don't get back until late?"

"Then he'll have to eat dinner with you." Catching sight of Cadel's troubled expression, Saul tried to reassure him. "You don't have to worry about Gazo. He's fine with this. He's taken the week off."

"Is he being paid?" Cadel demanded, hoping that the answer would be yes. Saul, however, didn't reply; he had already spotted Gazo, who was up ahead, waiting under a curbside tree. The curb itself was lined with vehicles, so there was no point trying to park. Saul simply braked when he reached Gazo, instructing Cadel to hop out.

"If there's a problem, gimme a call," the detective continued. Then he addressed Gazo, who was approaching the car. "Thanks for this. You're really helping me out, here."

"That's okay." Gazo sounded embarrassed. Instead of his usual overalls, he wore black jeans and a long-sleeved shirt, buttoned at the wrist. His workboots had been replaced by sober black lace-ups, and he had shaved off his wispy goatee. As he leaned toward the driver's window, a strong smell of aftershave hit Cadel like a siren blast or a runaway cement truck.

It was clear that Gazo had tried to dress in a manner appropriate to someone burdened with a grave responsibility. He had even slicked back his hair and slapped on a pair of sunglasses. Cadel didn't think that the result was entirely successful. If Gazo was trying to look intimidating, his long neck, receding chin, and spotty complexion undermined his efforts.

There could be no doubt, however, that outdoor manual work had done wonders for Gazo's physique. His weedy frame had expanded since his days at the Axis Institute. And now that he was sporting a tan—instead of a ghostly English pallor—his spots weren't nearly as noticeable.

From the shoulders down, he made a pretty convincing bodyguard.

"Hi, Gazo," Cadel muttered. He pushed open the front passenger door, clutching his computer bag. "Sorry about this."

"Nuffink to be sorry for," was Gazo's generous response. "*I* don't mind."

"You've got my number, haven't you?" Saul asked him. "And the campus security details?"

"Oh yeah."

"If you're worried about anything, don't hold back. Don't think, 'I wouldn't want to bother him for no reason.' Just call."

"Okay." Gazo inclined his head solemnly. "Whatever you say."

"I'll try to be home by six," Saul concluded, raising his voice as Cadel's door slammed shut. "You got enough money, Cadel?"

"I'm fine." Though he didn't want to appear ungracious, Cadel couldn't help being a little brusque. He wished that Saul wouldn't fuss so much in the presence of someone like Gazo—who, at twenty-one, was already leading a completely grown-up life, with his own job, apartment, and car. The car might be a bomb, and the apartment might be tiny, but they were still enviable accomplishments.

Cadel, in contrast, was living the sheltered existence of a suburban teenager, receiving handouts and obeying curfews. And although he enjoyed being an ordinary kid, he didn't necessarily want to publicize the fact. It made him look like a wimp.

"Bye, Saul," he said. "Don't worry. I'll be fine." Not until he was well clear of Saul's car did it head off, gathering speed; Cadel watched its receding number plate for a few seconds, then cleared his throat.

"I doubt there'll be any problems," he assured his friend. "If Prosper was anywhere *near* Sydney, he wouldn't be trying to pretend he was here."

"Yeah. I know. That's what your dad said." Gazo scratched his neck. "Still an' all, it's best to be on the safe side."

"I suppose so." After a moment's hesitation, Cadel added, "Sonja and Judith want to meet me at Coffee on Campus before my lecture starts. Is that okay with you?"

"Course it is." Gazo's smile revealed jagged clumps of chipped, brownish teeth. His early life in England had been one of homelessness and deprivation; to escape it, he had agreed to enroll at the Axis Institute—where his disabling stench had been regarded as a blessing, rather than a curse. "Why *wouldn't* it be okay?" he asked. "We musta done it a million times before."

"Yeah, well . . . it's different, now. There are security issues."

"Are there?" Gazo stared at Cadel in astonishment. "I didn't know that."

Not for the first time, Cadel had the sense that he and Gazo were trying to communicate through a very thick glass wall.

"Gazo, you're on *bodyguard* duty." Cadel glanced around to check for eavesdroppers. But the footpath was empty in both directions, as far as the eye could see. "Wherever we go there'll be security issues. It's part of the job."

"Oh! Right." Gazo's tone was apologetic. "I fought you was worried about that café, for some reason."

"No. Not especially." Shouldering his computer bag, Cadel headed down the brick-paved route to building K17. This particular road was lined with spindly saplings, parked cars, and clusters of garbage bins; Cadel found himself falling back into his old habits, scanning every face and window and potential hiding place that he passed. With a sinking sense of despair, he realized that he was beginning to behave as if he were still at the Axis Institute. As if he constantly needed to watch for hidden threats.

No, he thought. *Forget it. I'm not going to do this. Not again.* And he made a huge effort to switch off his antennae, deliberately focusing his entire attention on the spruced-up figure beside him.

"Saul told me you were taking a week off," he said to Gazo, who nodded.

"Yeah. That's right."

"Is he paying you?" Cadel wanted to know.

Gazo gave a snort. "Nah," he scoffed, as if the question was utterly ludicrous. "Doesn't 'afta, does he? I still get me 'oliday pay."

"But it won't be much fun. Spending a whole week as my babysitter." Cadel shook his head, trying to shake off the guilty feeling that troubled him like an importunate fly. "This doesn't seem right," he went on. "You're giving up your holiday for nothing. You should ask him if there's some kind of police fund that he can dip into for a little extra cash. There's bound to be."

Gazo laughed.

"I mean it," Cadel insisted. "Informants get paid. Why not you?"

"Because I don't wanna get paid." Gazo flashed him a crooked half smile. "Remember back at the Institute? I wanted to graduate as some kinda stink-bomb superhero and spend the resta me life taking care of people. Remember that?"

"Yes. I remember."

"You fought I was pretty dumb, eh?" As Cadel flushed, Gazo's smile widened into a battered-looking grin. "Well, I *was* dumb. Back then. But now I'm getting a chance to do what I always wanted to do. I'm gunna use me special powers to take care of someone. What could be more fun than that?"

Cadel grunted. It made him squirm when he cast his mind back and reflected on his former, dismissive attitude toward Gazo. Though Gazo wasn't terrifically bright, he certainly wasn't a negligible person. Cadel had come to realize that there were all kinds of qualities just as valuable as intelligence—despite what he might have been taught in the past.

"Maybe you should start a security business," he suggested. "For celebrities and politicians."

"No fanks." Seeing Cadel raise his eyebrows, Gazo elaborated. "I'd end up all over the papers. 'Mr. Stinky,' they'd call me. I'd *never* be able to get any girls."

By now they had reached John Lions Park, which was completely unoccupied; Cadel squinted across a well-worn patch of grass toward Coffee on Campus. There was very little to indicate that even a modest eatery lurked within the computer science complex—just a small sign suspended over a pair of glass doors. And when Cadel approached this sign, he realized that the café was shut.

"Oh god," he groaned, stopping in his tracks. "That's right. They're renovating. I forgot."

"So did I," Gazo admitted. "But you can still phone 'er, can't you?"

"Judith, you mean?"

"Oi! Hello!" A high-pitched hail made them both turn their heads in unison, as if their jaws were being tugged by invisible strings. A few yards to their right, Judith Bashford had emerged from the main entrance of K17. Beyond her, a wall of windows, sheathed in steel mesh, bore the words BIOINFORMATICS, COMPUTER ENGINEERING, COMPUTER SCIENCE, SOFTWARE ENGINEERING. Sonja was nowhere to be seen.

"You're early," Judith announced. She was wearing one of her many-layered, brightly colored ethnic outfits, complete with leather moccasins and beaten-silver bracelets. "We're in here."

"The café's shut," said Gazo, who had never been one to shy away from stating the obvious. Judith, however, didn't roll her eyes or pull a face as Hamish might have done. Instead she shrugged, as if resigned to life's numerous disappointments.

"Someone did tell me, but I forgot," said Cadel, moving past her into K17. On the threshold he was confronted by yet more signage—a white-lettered notice warning him that the area was protected by CCTV cameras—and this made him pause. "Why did you come in here?" he asked.

"Because of the elevators," Judith replied. She then followed him into the building, with Gazo close on her heels; together they all squeaked across a glossy black floor toward something called the Student Office. Cadel couldn't help glancing up at the two security cameras they passed on their way. One was trained directly on the front door, like a sniper's gun. The other was positioned around the corner in a lobby to the right of the main entrance.

It was here that they found Sonja Pirovic. She was sitting opposite a bank of elevators, but she wasn't looking at them. Her gaze was fixed on a wall-mounted "help" button, which had presumably been installed as some sort of security measure.

Cadel knew exactly what she was thinking.

"What's the point of a 'help' button if you can't even push it?" he observed.

The sound of his voice triggered an immediate reaction. Sonja's wheelchair spun around, and her whole face lit up.

"*I-forgot-about-the-café,*" she said.

"So did I. Sorry." After a moment's awkward silence, he jerked his chin at the elevators. "I thought we were going to be running trials on the weekend?"

"*Just-checking-them-out,*" was her synthesized response. Cadel sensed that she was waiting for something—reassurance, perhaps. She was probably worried about Prosper English.

But he couldn't talk about Prosper just yet. Not in such a public place while the cameras were running.

So he tried a more subtle approach.

"I wonder what would happen if I asked for help with my homework?" he remarked, endeavoring to calm her with his breezy, careless tone. He strolled toward the button, which was located right at the top of a very steep staircase. "I wonder if an overdue assignment would count as an emergency?"

Smiling, he glanced over his shoulder—just as Sonja's wheelchair lurched forward. He didn't have time to speak. He barely had time to move. While she hurtled toward him, her face contorted with shock, he stood frozen. Confounded. He literally couldn't believe his eyes.

For a split second, he found himself trying to calculate the wheelchair's impressive rate of acceleration.

"*No!*" screamed Judith.

This scream was like a trumpet blast. It galvanized him. Snapping out of his daze, he threw himself to one side. Then he slipped, stumbled, and fell.

He was still on the ground when Sonja's wheelchair whizzed past him, straight down the stairs.

SIX

Cadel couldn't eat.

He sat staring at the slab of lasagna in front of him: at the thick red sauce and glistening layers of pasta. Red and white. Blood and bone.

He felt nauseous.

"Just a little bit," Fiona urged. She was sitting across the table, nibbling at a caesar salad. "You need to get *something* into you, sweetie. It's going to be a long night."

Cadel nodded. Then he picked up his fork. *Perhaps if I don't look at it while I'm eating it,* he decided, letting his gaze drift as he transferred a sloppy fragment of lasagna from the plate to his mouth. After all, there were plenty of other things to look at. The enormous glass mural on the wall, for instance. The array of cakes under glass. Even the other diners, some of whom were laughing in a fashion that Cadel found abrasive.

He realized that the noisy customers were probably medical staff, while the people who chewed stoically through their meals, grim and silent, were people like him: people whose loved ones were being treated at Sydney Children's Hospital.

Why else would they be having dinner in the hospital café?

"Here he is," said Gazo, who was occupying the seat next to Fiona's. Glancing around, Cadel spotted Saul Greeniaus descending a nearby staircase. The detective had taken off his jacket and tie; his expression was shuttered, and his feet were dragging. Behind him, through a wall of windows, other windows were visible as golden squares in a sea of darkness.

When his eyes met Cadel's, he gave a thumbs-up.

"She must be all right," Gazo murmured. Cadel didn't say anything; the lump in his throat was far too big.

Fiona reached over to squeeze his hand.

"She's in recovery," Saul announced upon arriving at their table. He dropped into the chair beside Cadel's. "She'll be there for a little while, and then they'll be moving her to the surgical high dependency unit for a couple of days. Apparently they've done an MRI scan, because of the head injury, and the results won't be back for another twenty-four to forty-eight hours."

"Where's Judith?" Fiona interrupted, her voice tight with anxiety.

"She's coming." Saul produced a ragged little smile. "She tried to bull her way into recovery, but *no one's* allowed in there. Not even relatives. I told her she should grab a bite to eat while she's waiting." He nodded at the bowl of fries that had been left in the center of the table. "Speaking of which . . ."

"Yeah. Go ahead." Gazo pushed the bowl toward him. "Help yourself."

"Thanks."

Saul reached for a handful of fries. He ate them like someone interested only in refueling, his jaw working mechanically while his shadowy gaze lingered on Cadel.

Fiona said, "So how did the surgery go?"

"It went okay." Though he was talking to his wife, Saul didn't look at her. He continued to study Cadel's face. "I was just speaking to the surgeon, and she seemed pretty happy. No nasty surprises, she said. It could have been a lot worse."

Cadel swallowed. "But—but the head injury . . ." he stammered before his breath failed him.

Saul laid a hand on his shoulder.

"They don't think it's anything really bad," the detective avowed. "Head wounds always bleed a lot. The MRI is standard procedure, just to be on the safe side. They're more concerned about her broken leg."

"Can they fix that up?" Gazo queried, and Cadel had to shut his eyes

54

for a moment. He would never, ever forget the sight that had greeted him at the bottom of those stairs in K17. One look at the strange angle of Sonja's leg had made him sick to his stomach; he'd been retching in a corner when the paramedics had arrived, only minutes after Sonja's fall. He couldn't remember much else about the scene: just her torn skin, her damaged leg, and her bloody face. He couldn't even remember what he'd done to help, though he was sure he hadn't done much. Shock had rendered him useless. It was Gazo who had phoned for an ambulance, and Gazo who had talked to the paramedics—while Judith had stamped around, wringing her hands and threatening to sue the university for constructing such a dangerous flight of stairs.

Luckily the campus and the hospital were right next door to each other. Sonja's trip to the emergency room had therefore been mercifully quick, involving little more than a couple of left-hand turns. By the time Gazo had found a parking place near the hospital's main entrance, Sonja and Judith were already somewhere inside.

After that, it had just been a matter of waiting.

"Her leg's fine now," Saul declared. "That's what the surgery was for. She's in a splint at the moment, but they'll put a cast on her when the swelling's gone down a bit."

"How . . . ?" Cadel began before trailing off. He didn't know how to phrase his next question. How would Sonja's bone ever heal if she couldn't stop jerking around?

Saul's grip on him tightened.

"You don't have to worry," the detective insisted. "It's a broken leg, that's all. The people here are used to dealing with broken legs."

"But she has cerebral palsy!" Cadel blurted out. At which point Fiona seemed to grasp what was troubling him.

"They'll be able to immobilize her somehow," she said. "I guarantee Sonja's not the first person with cerebral palsy who's ever broken a bone."

"Here's Judith." Saul nodded toward the staircase. "She'll have a better idea of what's going on."

Judith didn't look well, even from a distance. Her skin was mottled with patches of red and gray. There were smears of dried blood on her embroidered jacket. She moved heavily, crossing the room and lowering herself into a chair as if her knees were about to collapse beneath the weight of her ample form.

After a moment's silence, Gazo cleared his throat.

"So how's Sonja?" he inquired. "Is she awake yet?"

"No." Judith's retort was crisp, to say the least. It made Saul frown.

"Does she know what happened?" said Fiona.

"Oh, I think we all know *that*." Judith's scowl was aimed directly at Cadel. "I think we all know what *happened*."

Cadel's heart skipped a beat.

"It was Cadel's little *project*," Judith went on, causing the detective's frown to deepen.

"No!" cried Cadel. "It wasn't!"

"What project?" Saul asked him. "What are you talking about?"

But Cadel couldn't answer.

"He's been fiddling with her wheelchair," Judith finally volunteered. "He must have screwed up the command signals."

"I did *not!*" Cadel could manage only a strangled croak. "Do you think I'm stupid? I didn't do any such thing!"

"That wheelchair was out of control!"

"I know," Cadel said hoarsely. "I was there, remember? I saw what happened."

"Cadel." Saul's tone, though calm, was edged with steel. "What's all this about a project? What did you do to Sonja's wheelchair?"

"Nothing! I didn't touch her wheelchair! All I did was add a few commands to the protocol!" As Cadel described his elevator hack, Saul's expression grew darker and darker. "I've *thought* about this!" Cadel finished. "Do you think it didn't cross my mind straightaway? But it can't have been me!"

"No one else has been messing with her wheelchair," Judith pointed out. She spoke so harshly that Fiona winced.

Cadel's reply was just as harsh.

"How do *you* know?" he spat. "You're not a hacker!"

"Shh." Fiona tried to intervene. "No one's blaming anyone—"

"There was a CCTV camera *right there!* On the ceiling!" Cadel spluttered. He swung around to plead with Saul. "I saw the whole thing. It wasn't a malfunction. She came straight at me. She had to swerve—"

"Wait a minute." The detective held up his hand. "What are you trying to say? That this was some kind of attack?"

"Maybe." Hearing Judith snort, Cadel hastened to defend himself. "There's a wireless interface between Sonja's neckband and her wheelchair computer," he said fiercely. "What's to stop someone from hacking into that, and changing the command protocols?"

"It's a *secure signal*," Judith snapped.

"No it's not. Nothing is. Not against a good hacker." Cadel had reached this conclusion a couple of hours previously while pacing up and down in the emergency waiting room. But he still hadn't worked out precisely how the attack had been engineered—or, more important, why. He'd had other things to think about. "Whoever did this was good. Really good," he added, appealing to Saul again. "I can't tell you exactly what they did, because I don't know. All I know is that we need to look at Sonja's wheelchair. And her neckband. Everything."

Saul pondered. Judith sniffed. "Good luck," she said, her voice laced with sarcasm. "Have you seen the state of that wheelchair? It's a write-off."

"Where is it?" Saul asked. Judith, however, didn't seem to know. She hesitated, her rancorous expression yielding to one of uncertainty.

"Roy's got it," said Gazo. When everyone stared at him, he gave a little shrug. "Roy's one of them campus security guards. He showed up when the ambulance came. Don't you remember?"

This time it was Cadel who shook his head.

"No," said Judith.

"Well, he did," Gazo assured her. "And then everybody rushed off, and the wheelchair was all over the floor, and he didn't know what to do wiv it."

"So you told him to keep it?" Saul wanted to know.

"Yeah." Gazo hesitated. "It's pretty smashed up," he said at last.

"And I'm not sure where the neckband is, either," Judith admitted. "I took it off—it was on the floor—it could be anywhere now."

"It could be wiv Roy," was Gazo's suggestion. "Or maybe you left it in the ambulance."

"Don't worry." Despite her creased forehead and puffy eyes, Fiona sounded confident. Confident and reassuring. "We'll find the neckband. It won't have been thrown away. I'll track it down myself."

"No. *I* will," her husband decreed. "If this was an assault, then it's a police matter. And Sonja's neckband will be part of a crime scene." His focus shifted from Fiona's face to Cadel's. "Are you sure about this, Cadel? Are you really convinced that it wasn't an accident?"

Cadel swallowed. Beneath the pressure of that grave, dispassionate regard, he was assailed by doubts. How *could* he be sure, when he didn't know what had happened? Or why? Even if Prosper was capable of remote-control sabotage, there was no obvious reason why he should suddenly have decided to attack Sonja.

Unless he was trying to warn them off?

Prosper knows me better than that, Cadel thought. *If he wants me to stay out of his way, this is the* last *thing he should be doing. It's counterproductive. It's dumb.*

On the other hand, Cadel had seen the wheelchair. It had spun around and headed straight for him. It had virtually locked onto his position, like . . . like . . .

He sucked in his breath.

"What is it?" Saul queried as Cadel rummaged among the textbooks in his bag. "What are you looking for?"

"I just have to check . . ." Cadel mumbled. Not that he was really concerned; he knew better than to walk around with the Bluetooth connection on his cell set to "discoverable" mode. As a seasoned hacker, he had always distrusted Bluetooth, which he regarded as being like a cat flap in a locked door.

Sure enough, when he checked his phone's display screen, Cadel could detect no telltale Bluetooth symbol.

There was, however, a new message.

"What's wrong?" said Fiona, who must have seen him blanch.

Cadel looked up.

"I . . ." He had to lick his lips before proceeding. "There's a message," he rasped. "I had it on mute, for the lecture; it didn't ring . . ."

"What kind of message?"

"A text message." Cadel read it aloud, unsteadily. *"She's got tonsillitis. Bev XX."*

"Who's Bev?" said Gazo. And Judith clicked her tongue.

"It's a wrong number," was her impatient conclusion. But Cadel wasn't so sure.

"It came in at 2:38," he faltered. "That was . . . I mean . . ." His shell-shocked gaze was fixed on the detective. "Could it really be a coincidence?"

Saul was slow to respond. After a long silence, during which he appeared to be deliberating, he finally answered Cadel with another question.

"How could a call to your phone have affected Sonja's wheelchair?" he asked.

"I don't know." Cadel tried to concentrate. "If my Bluetooth had been working, it could have sent a transmission. Sonja's neckband has a Bluetooth interface, so the wheelchair could have fixed on my signal. There could have been a trigger word—like 'tonsillitis.' But my Bluetooth's disabled. It has been since I first got my phone."

"Are you certain of that?" Saul reached for the device. "How can you tell?"

"There's nothing on the display screen." Even as he spoke, Cadel was visited by a sudden misgiving. And he remembered a conversation he'd had, only a few days before, in one of the K17 computer labs. "I could check," he went on, thinking aloud. "Some of the second-year students have been monitoring Bluetooth transmissions as part of an assignment.

They've got multiple receivers around the department for some kind of interactive gaming project." Seeing that Saul was none the wiser, Cadel tried to simplify things. "They might have been logging transmissions. I could ask Richard," he said.

"No. I'll ask him. I'll do it tonight." Instead of passing the phone back to Cadel, Saul began to tap at its keypad. For a moment Cadel thought that the detective must be trying to communicate with Richard Buckland. But when Gazo opened his mouth, Saul shushed him so fiercely that Cadel realized what was going on.

Saul had decided to return Bev's call.

Everyone waited. Cadel held his breath as the detective put the phone to his ear. But gradually Saul's expression soured.

"Damn," he said.

"Nothing?" Cadel inquired, without much hope.

Saul shook his head. Then he switched off the phone and slipped it into his pocket. "All I can do is keep trying," he remarked. "It's a cell phone number, but I can put a trace on it. You never know, the SIM card might not be stolen."

"Even if it was, that doesn't . . . I mean, I can't understand how this could have been done," Cadel fretted. At which point Fiona weighed in.

"Let's not talk about it now," she recommended. "We're all tired, and it's getting late. What we need to do is work out who'll be staying here and who'll be going home."

"I'll stay." Cadel was determined to see Sonja, no matter how long it took. "I can stay here all night if I have to."

"No you can't," Saul countered. And Fiona agreed with him. There was no need to stay all night, she said, because Sonja probably wouldn't be awake until morning. And even if she did wake up, she wouldn't be alone.

"If anything happens, Judith will call us," Fiona added, smiling at Cadel. "We're not that far away. I can bring you back first thing tomorrow because I've taken the day off." She glanced at her husband. "I suppose you'll be working?"

Saul gave a nod. "I need to get hold of that wheelchair," he said.

"And the neckband," Judith reminded him. "Don't forget that."

"I won't," he answered shortly, then turned to Gazo. "If this was an attack, it changes things. Cadel might find himself back in the safe house. But until that happens, we'll still be needing you. So it might be best if you came straight to our place in the morning . . ."

Cadel sat in stony silence as plans were laid and options were discussed without any attempt being made to seek his input. He felt left out. Even worse, he felt *relegated,* as if he were just some ineffectual, messed-up kid, instead of Sonja's best and closest friend.

He was tired. He understood that. He was also deeply traumatized by the events he'd witnessed earlier that day. But he wasn't too shattered to think deductively, or to work out what should be done.

If they *were* under attack, then Prosper English was almost certainly the culprit. And Dr. Vee, or someone like him, must be helping Prosper—because only an infiltration expert could have pulled off either the CCTV hack or the wheelchair hijacking. Cadel knew that the police had been trying to catch Dr. Vee. They had been hanging out in a particular Internet chatroom, waiting for Vee to make contact with one of his own pieces of malware: namely, the program he'd planted in the Corrective Services System almost a year before. Vee liked chatrooms. He liked the way they allowed him to communicate with his malware anonymously by sending encoded messages. No doubt the CCTV bug had a similar command function. No doubt the police would soon be monitoring that chatroom, as well.

But Cadel doubted very much that Vee would be turning up at either site. The Corrective Services bug had been planted for a specific purpose: to get Prosper out of jail. Now that this goal had been accomplished, why would Vee want to revisit a program that might very well be under surveillance? As for the CCTV malware, it was imperfect. There had been a glitch. And the chances that Vee hadn't registered this mistake before abandoning the whole exercise . . . Well, they were remote, to say the least.

No, if Vee was their man, he wouldn't be caught in any chatroom. Cadel knew that the best way to catch an infiltration expert was with a honey trap.

A honey trap containing live bait.

"I want to stay at Judith's," he suddenly announced.

The whole table fell silent. Everyone stared at him. Finally Saul spoke up.

"What on earth for?"

Cadel hesitated. He wanted to explain that he was trying to lure Vee into Judith's Smart Home network.

But he couldn't. Not with so many strangers around.

"I'll tell you later," he promised before appealing to Judith. "Can I please sleep at your house tonight? *Please?*" he begged.

Judith didn't answer immediately. She sat for a moment, her highly colored face a study in confusion. At last she looked to Saul for guidance.

The detective, however, seemed just as perplexed as she was. "I thought you had a problem with fully wired infrastructures like Judith's place," he remarked, pitching his voice very low. "Isn't that why you wanted to leave the safe house?"

"Yeah!" Unlike Saul, Judith seemed oblivious to the surrounding diners. She leaned back, folded her beefy arms, and boomed, "What if you're right, Cadel? What if some hacker's out there gunning for you? Wouldn't it be better to stay away from computerized environments?"

Cadel clutched the edge of the table. For the first time in a very long while, he experienced a sizzling flash of fury that sprang from some deep and poisonous source. It was an ancient anger, and it had the usual effect: his muscles tightened, his eyes narrowed, and his face turned salt white.

"Do you think I'm stupid?" he hissed. "Do you think I don't know *exactly* what I'm doing? Just because I'm worried about Sonja doesn't mean that I'm brain-dead!" All at once, as the red cloud of rage began to recede from his peripheral vision, he became aware of how unnerved everyone looked. Even Gazo was gawking at him in dismay. And Cadel recognized their reaction; he had seen it before. *You start glaring at people like that, my friend, and you're going to get in trouble,* a police officer had warned him long ago.

So he took a deep, calming breath and laced his fingers together tightly. "You don't understand what we're dealing with," he went on, enunciating each word as carefully as possible. His voice creaked with the effort. "But I do understand, because I've dealt with it all my life. If I want to sleep at Judith's, it's because I *have* to sleep at Judith's. For a very good reason that I've thought through. And I won't be sleeping anywhere else."

Having delivered this ultimatum, he sat back and waited—for what seemed like hours. At first no one spoke. Gazo just stared at him, drop-jawed. Judith shifted uneasily. Fiona bit her lip.

At last the detective said, "You might not be safe at Judith's house."

"I won't be safe *anywhere*," Cadel snapped. "Not if Prosper's got his eye on me. There'll be *nowhere* to hide until he's scared off. Don't you understand that?"

Saul blinked. Then he frowned. Then he spent a few moments deep in thought, after which—having reached some kind of decision—he addressed Judith.

"Do you mind if we stay at your house tonight?" he asked.

Judith was slumped low in her chair, her face weary and disgruntled. When Saul made his request, she gave a defeated shrug.

"No," she growled. "I guess not."

"In that case, we might have to impose on your hospitality. After I've made a couple of calls."

As the detective stood up and moved away, he didn't even glance in Cadel's direction.

SEVEN

Judith's house stood two streets back from Maroubra Beach. It was an oversized, two-story building on a very small block of land, with six bedrooms, seven bathrooms, three living areas, and a room fitted up like a private cinema—all black velvet curtains and red plush recliner chairs. There was a chandelier in the vestibule. There was a triple garage. There was a limestone fireplace, with a gas fire controlled by the home automation system. And there was the fancy automation system itself, which had always made Cadel slightly uneasy.

He'd never liked the idea of living in a house with a brain.

This brain, of course, was the central computer. Judith called it "the Wife," because it ran her media hub, security network, climate control, lighting, window shades, and Bluetooth-enabled appliances. Her Smart Fridge could alert the Wife when its contents had to be replenished. Her air-conditioning system could adapt itself to the outside temperature by checking a website that monitored local weather conditions.

"Every woman needs a wife," she'd once said when Cadel had aired his doubts about the wisdom of plugging your whole domestic environment into an Internet gateway. "If I didn't have the Wife, I'd spend half my day drawing blinds and turning lights on." Many of the lights in Judith's house were activated by movement—and for Sonja, this had proved to be a blessing. Freed from the stress of wall-mounted switches, Sonja was able to scoot around at night in her wheelchair on her own. She could also activate the television, DVD player, and stereo system without pressing buttons, because Cadel had reprogrammed the Wife to accept commands from Sonja's wireless communication interface. Through the Wife, Sonja could even send Judith text messages.

Judith's house was the ideal place for Sonja, in all kinds of ways. And for that reason, Cadel had decided to ignore his own misgivings. Instead he had tried to make Judith's place as secure as possible by installing a lot of beefed-up firewalls. He had worked with Sonja to improve the Wife's encryption codes, and had done his best to convince Judith that she should make a point of changing her passwords once in a while.

Inserting a vulnerability into such a well-defended system was going to be difficult.

"I need to give our hacker a weak spot," he explained to his foster parents, after telling them about his plan. "I need to set a trap, so he'll walk right into it without suspecting anything."

Saul grunted. He was driving through a dim suburban labyrinth, heading toward Judith's place; Cadel was sitting behind him, and Fiona was in the front passenger seat. Outside, pools of electric light illuminated bus stops and palm trees, red roofs and corner shops. Narrow slivers of parkland were full of exposed rock and scrubby, seaside ground cover.

The sand-blasted streets were empty of traffic.

"What's going to be really difficult is making this look like a genuine oversight when everything else is so battened down," Cadel continued. But still there was no response from the detective, who remained very withdrawn, as if troubled by an ache in his stomach.

Fiona was also quite subdued, though whether from anxiety or fatigue Cadel had no way of knowing.

"I hope this doesn't mean you'll be staying up all night," she said dully. "Because I really don't want that happening, Cadel."

"It won't," he promised. "If a hacker tries to get in, he'll trigger some sort of alarm. Maybe the fire alarm or the motion sensor alarm—something that'll wake us up. All those alarms are connected to the Wife, so it won't be too hard to manage."

"And what if he gets past your ambush? What if he fills the house with gas while we're asleep?" Saul reeled off a few more worst-case scenarios as Fiona stared at him, aghast. "Suppose he starts a fire with some kinda short circuit? Suppose he locks us in the panic room and turns off the air? If this guy is as good as you make out, don't you think we'll be running a pretty big risk?"

"Oh my god." Fiona was practically hyperventilating. "Is that possible?"

"No," said Cadel. "Because he *won't* get past the ambush. Don't worry. I've thought about this."

"So I gather." Saul braked as he approached a stop sign. "Shame you didn't share those thoughts with us back at the hospital."

Cadel stiffened. He could sense what was coming, and opened his mouth to defend himself. But Fiona was too quick for him.

"Maybe this isn't such a good idea," she fretted. "Maybe we should go back home."

"But—"

"The police can set up an ambush, can't they?" Fiona appealed to her husband. "What about Sid and Steve and all those other computer people? They're *paid* to take risks."

"But Vee isn't after them," Cadel broke in before Saul could reply. "I told you. This is supposed to be a honey trap, and you can't set a trap without bait." It was maddening, the way people kept missing the point— even intelligent people like Fiona. Cadel had to remind himself that she was tired. He had to make allowances for the fact that she hadn't been raised by Prosper English. He had to be patient, even though he felt like thumping the seat with his fist.

I've got to stay calm, he thought. *I can't get too upset, or I won't be any good to anyone.* And aloud he said, "If Vee hijacked that wheelchair, then he's been watching me. And if he's been doing *that,* then he'll find out I'm at Judith's place. But he won't try anything if there's a cybercrime team running in and out. He's much too smart."

There was a long pause. Saul had turned in to Judith's street, and was cruising along at a gentle pace, scanning the dimly lit street numbers. His headlights picked out a parked car here, a letterbox there. Most of the fences were big and solid, made of stone or steel or rendered brick.

"So Vee's your man, is he?" the detective said at last in a neutral tone. Cadel gave a nod.

"Either Vee or someone just as good," he confirmed.

"If he's as smart as you say, what makes you think he'll fall for a honey trap?" Saul pulled into Judith's driveway. "What makes you think he won't get suspicious and stay well clear?"

"He might," Cadel had to concede. "But that doesn't mean we shouldn't give it a go. Because we have to get him. We *have* to. Otherwise he'll try again." Cadel leaned forward, clutching the driver's headrest. A rising sense of urgency—almost of panic—was making him shrill, so he took a few deep breaths to calm himself. "And we can't keep living like this," he concluded. "Not anymore. It's got to stop."

Fiona clicked her tongue. She had caught the note of desperation in his voice and understood why it was there. "Oh, sweetie," she said, reaching around to press his hand. Beside her, Saul activated the garage remote. And as the wide, white automated door in front of them lifted like a portcullis, he guided his car underneath it.

"I'm so tired of the *surveillance*," Cadel went on. "I thought I was through with all that."

"I know," Fiona sympathized.

"It won't stop unless we catch Prosper. We'll never be safe otherwise." Cadel tried to clear away the lump that was blocking his throat. "It could be you next. Or Judith. Or Gazo," he quavered. "It could be anyone. Anyone who has anything to do with me."

"Shhh." Fiona patted his white-knuckled fingers. "We still don't know if this was an accident. And we *won't* know until someone has a really good look at that wheelchair."

"It wasn't an accident." Cadel refused to be comforted. "It was Prosper."

"I don't blame you for thinking that after what you've been through," Fiona said earnestly. "But you mustn't let Prosper dominate your life, Cadel."

At that precise moment, Saul killed the engine—and a sudden, dense silence enfolded them all. Though Judith's garage had been designed to accommodate three cars, there were no other vehicles in sight: just a huge collection of junk. Cadel could see old paint tins and curtain rods, a stepladder, a leaf blower, a collection of plastic storage bins, a spool of cable, a broken chair, a golf bag, and a weed whacker. When Saul extinguished the headlights, this array of domestic debris remained clearly visible, thanks to Judith's sensor-activated lighting system.

"I'm not paranoid," Cadel declared after a brief pause. "You think I'm overreacting—"

"No. I don't." Fiona turned in her seat to address him. "My concern is that you seem to feel responsible for all this. When you're not."

"Of course I am!" he spluttered. "I'm the target, aren't I? And I've got a better chance of tracking down Prosper than anyone else has!"

All of a sudden, Saul spoke up. "You're probably right." He was staring at the exposed brick wall beyond the windshield, his hands at rest on the steering wheel. "And I realize how hard it is for you to trust other people, since it's not the way you were raised. Apart from anything else, other people screw up sometimes. Because they aren't as clever as you are." Saul's gaze shifted to the rearview mirror. "All the same, you can't win this on your own. Prosper has his cronies; you're gonna need your own team. You can see that, can't you? Without help, you'll be fighting a losing battle."

There was an unassailable logic to this argument, which Cadel couldn't challenge. He didn't even try. Instead he slumped back against his seat, gathering up his computer bag as he did so. All at once he felt completely drained.

Saul pushed open the driver's door. "Maybe I'd better check this place out first," he proposed. "You should probably stay with the car."

Cadel sighed. "You don't have to worry," he said. "If Prosper was using hired guns, he wouldn't have bothered to hijack Sonja's wheel-chair."

Saul, however, was adamant. So while Cadel and Fiona waited, the detective carried out a careful inspection of Judith's luxurious abode, from the cable-strewn attic space to the wine-storage cabinet under the stairs. It was a good fifteen minutes before Cadel was given an all clear.

In the interim, he eavesdropped on a call that Fiona made to the hospital—where Judith had nothing new to report on Sonja's condition.

It wasn't until half past nine that Cadel and Fiona finally left the garage, emerging into Judith's enormous, gleaming foyer. Though it boasted a lavish chandelier, this room—like the rest of the house—was almost completely empty; while Judith had spent a great deal on electrical equipment, she wasn't much interested in things like tables or bookshelves. Marooned on vast expanses of parquet and limestone, her few sticks of furniture looked small and cowed, like squatters in a museum.

Only Sonja's ground-floor room was fully furnished. It had originally been designed as a study and was as well supplied with bookshelves as it was poorly provided with built-in hanging space. Therefore, as well as her special bed, her chest of drawers, her desk, her bedside tables, and her elegant ash-veneer entertainment console (supporting a widescreen TV), Sonja's room was crammed with several large wardrobes. It had also been decorated with a colorful assortment of posters, eye puzzles, photographs, patchwork cushions, and mathematical-print lampshades.

Her number-shaped candles, lined up along the windowsill, caught Cadel's eye as he passed her bedroom. And they affected him so painfully that he had to close the door before proceeding.

He couldn't afford to break down—not yet.

Beyond the former library was an open-plan dining area. Next came the kitchen, beside which was tucked the cramped and windowless box (part pantry, part home office) that Judith used as a panic room. The walls of this room were lined with cupboards. A toilet had been concealed in one cupboard; the other was stocked with a sleeping bag, a first-aid kit, a toolbox, a flashlight, a microwave oven, a set of cutlery, and some plastic dishes. All of this stuff had come with the house, along with the emergency food supply—which Judith had been raiding for a couple of years. Only the tinned food was left, and most of that was past its use-by date.

A single wheeled typist's chair sat in front of a built-in desk, flanked on both sides by stacked shelves of technology.

"I hope you're not going to stay up all night patrolling the exits," Cadel remarked as he settled in front of the Wife. He was speaking to Saul, who had dragged a kitchen stool into the panic room and was perched on top of it. "Because you don't have to. If there's an attack, it'll come through the Internet. Not through a smashed window."

"We'll see," Saul replied cryptically.

"I doubt that Gazo will be much good to us, either," Cadel continued, tapping out codes and passwords. Numbers unrolled across the screen in front of him. Panels blinked on and off. Layer by layer, he worked down into the core of Judith's network while he toyed with the idea of tweaking the collision resistance in a cryptographic hash function. Would Vee be tempted to launch a length extension attack? "Gazo could fell an army at fifty paces," he muttered, "but that's not much good if we're up against a hacker in Hong Kong."

"Hong Kong?" Saul echoed.

Cadel shrugged.

"Somewhere that's not Sydney," he amended. "Somewhere that's a long way from here." And then he saw it.

There. Right there, in the backtrace.

"That might be true," Saul was saying. "But until we've established that you need protective custody—" All at once he stopped, having caught sight of Cadel's expression. "What's up? Cadel?"

"Oh shit."

"Is there a problem?"

"Somebody was in here." Cadel couldn't believe his eyes. "Somebody got past my firewalls!"

"Cadel." Saul rose. "Leave it. Don't touch it."

"This is crazy!" Cadel cried, ignoring him. "How could—? Unless Judith's to blame."

"Cadel," Saul repeated. He grabbed Cadel's shoulder, but was shaken off.

So he moved toward the power supply.

"Don't!" Cadel barked. "Just let me do this!"

"It's not safe."

"Yes it is. He can't electrocute me. I have to see what's happened." Peering at the screen, Cadel scowled as he checked Judith's programs. All of them had been hijacked by a piece of malware designed to reroute commands and disable passwords. It had rummaged through bit maps and subroutines. It had seized control of the operating system.

It had turned on the CCTV cameras—and the microphones, as well.

"Oh Christ," Cadel groaned.

"What?" By now Saul was gripping the back of Cadel's chair. "Tell me."

"He's been eavesdropping."

"What?"

"Whoever built this house wanted a sound-recording facility," Cadel explained, frantically jabbing at the keyboard. *Click-click. Click-click-click-click-click.* "Judith told me about it. The original owners were paranoid. They liked to know what their cleaners were saying, and whether they were using the phone or the TV . . . stuff like that." He paused for a moment, glancing around at Saul. "Judith had the mikes disabled, but they're on now. And so are the cameras."

The detective hissed. Then he straightened and yelled *"Fiona!"* before addressing Cadel in a voice that was barely audible.

"Can you switch them off again?"

"You bet," Cadel replied. "I'm pulling the plug."

"Fiona!"

"I might as well, since he's going to find out I've been in here anyway." Grimly Cadel began the process of diagnosis and deletion, without backing up. He simply didn't have the time. "I reckon it's Vee," he muttered. "Because he's using a chatroom bot. And I recognize the privilege escalation exploit." This fact in itself was infuriating. It meant that all his good work had been overthrown by Judith's carelessness. "I mean, how can I possibly patch something like this when Judith comes along afterward and stuffs it up?" he burst out. "I *told* her not to use the same damn password on e-commerce sites!"

"What is it?" All at once Fiona appeared, framed in the doorway. She was clutching a toothbrush. "What's wrong?"

"This system's infested," Cadel replied. And Saul said, "We have to leave."

"What?"

"Not yet." Cadel didn't take his eyes off the data unfolding in front of him. "There's no need to panic. I just disconnected, so we're not exposed anymore. I don't think." (Though that would have to be confirmed to his full satisfaction.) "You should call Sid and Steve," he added. "Tell them there's an IRC bot that Vee might be accessing any minute. Tell them it's fresh."

"Has someone hacked into Judith's computer?" Fiona inquired as Saul picked up the desk phone.

Cadel nodded without looking at her. He knew that Vee's malware had a tendency to recreate itself when threatened; stopping this process would require some pretty nifty footwork. "It's Vee," he revealed absentmindedly. "He's been in here already."

"Oh my god," said Fiona.

"Which makes a lot of sense," Cadel went on, still working away. "I couldn't figure out what might have triggered that wheelchair attack. But if Judith came home and said something to Sonja about turning the cameras off because I'd told her to . . ." Instead of finishing the sentence, he shook his head.

By now Saul was talking to one of the cybercrime team. As he relayed Cadel's message, Fiona ducked out of the room. Cadel barely registered her absence, because he had noticed something very interesting. Vee's malware had been designed to take over a whole range of functions, including some that Judith's house didn't have. There was an application for hijacking a networked fountain pump and a floor-washing iRobot. You could even gain access to a wireless security device specifically tailored to protect firearms. It was as if Vee's program had been created to infiltrate a supersmart home full of bizarre, breakthrough gadgets.

Cadel wondered if the malware's designer was simply being cautious. Perhaps Vee had devised a one-size-fits-all program with a protocol for every possible contingency. But no, that couldn't be it. Because no provision had been included for commandeering a Bluetooth-enabled microwave oven—even though there was a facility for hacking into a Bluetooth-enabled washing machine.

It was clear to Cadel that Vee's malware had been engineered for another house: an actual state-of-the-art, computerized house with guns in it. What's more, the original voltage specifications had been adjusted, from 110 to 240 volts.

Though Cadel couldn't be absolutely certain, he was pretty sure that the program had been written for a house in America.

"Okay. They're on that," Saul announced, hanging up. At the same instant, his cell phone trilled; he grimaced apologetically before answering it.

"Hello?" he said.

Then Fiona stuck her head into the room.

"I've repacked the bags," she reported. When Saul turned away, nursing his phone, she mouthed *Who's that?* at Cadel.

Cadel shrugged. He was far too busy deleting the web browser cache to worry about Saul's phone conversation. Besides, he was interested in the American ghost-house. Surely there couldn't be many homes, even in the U.S., with a networked, toilet-cleaning iRobot? Or a programmable, sensor-driven showerhead? Or a Bluetooth-enabled washing machine? Cadel knew that, given enough time, he could probably even calculate how many rooms were in this mystery house.

If Vee had been hacking into another residence and Cadel could identify it, then maybe—just maybe—it would be possible to work out what Prosper English was up to.

"Uh-huh. Yep. Okay. Yeah, that would be great. Yeah it is. Thanks for that. I really appreciate it." Saul's rumbling commentary was simply background noise for Cadel, who ignored it until he heard the name Richard. Then he spun around as the detective, nodding gravely, listened to whatever recommendations were being fired at him from the other end of the line.

"We're on it. What? Oh sure. No problem," Saul mumbled. "Thanks again. You've been a big help. Okay. Yeah. Bye."

And he broke the connection.

"Well?" Fiona and Cadel both chorused. Cadel added, "Was that Richard Buckland?"

"Yeah." Saul looked up. He was frowning. "I rang him earlier. From the hospital."

"Why?" said Fiona. But it wasn't her husband who answered.

"To ask him about that Bluetooth project." Cadel had forgotten all about it. "What did he say?"

"He said he spoke to the fellow who's been monitoring transmissions," Saul replied.

"And?"

"And there *was* a signal outside the computer labs today." Saul hesitated, his solemn gaze settling on Cadel like something made of granite. Clearly the news from Richard Buckland wasn't going to be good. "A transmission was logged in at 2:38 p.m.," the detective finally revealed, with obvious reluctance. Then, after another brief pause, he concluded, "And it came from your phone, Cadel."

EIGHT

Cadel spent the night under his own roof, after all. But he didn't sleep much.

He had crawled into bed at half past eleven, after two full hours of feverish activity. The cybercrime team had arrived at Judith's house while he was still cleaning up her databanks; Cadel had found himself being consulted about passwords and protocols until Saul had finally dragged him out of the place. Back at home, the detective had made a series of flustered phone calls while Cadel was kept busy answering questions, checking window locks, and helping Fiona to unpack their bags.

Only later, when he was alone in the dark with nothing to distract him, did Cadel at last begin to feel the full, jarring impact of what had happened that day.

Sonja was in the hospital. With a *head injury*.

And it was all his fault.

Lying on his back, staring into the shadows, he couldn't stop thinking about the look on her face. His brain kept hitting some kind of internal rewind button; the same scene replayed itself, over and over again. First came the accelerating wheelchair. Then the look on her face. Then the cry. Then the crash. Then the blood . . .

Cadel covered his eyes.

It wasn't your fault. Fiona had told him this repeatedly. But Cadel knew that he was to blame. Sonja had ended up in the hospital because she was his friend. And Prosper English had almost certainly put her there.

Cadel seemed to hear Prosper's voice echoing around his head: *I'll happily shoot Sonja if you give me the least bit of trouble.* It was a chilling memory—and an instructive one. Had Prosper tried to kill Sonja because Cadel was giving him trouble? Was that it? Or had Sonja simply been the means to an end?

Perhaps she hadn't been Prosper's prime target. Tossing and turning, Cadel forced himself to confront the truth. Chances were good that the attack had been aimed at him. *Prosper wants to hurt me, that's for sure,* he decided. *But is he trying to do it through Sonja? Or am I the one he wants to kill?*

The threat was certainly there. It had always been there. How many times had Prosper placed a gun to Cadel's head in the past? Twice? Three times? Yet the trigger had never been pulled. Always, some kind of warped, possessive, unstable attachment had stayed Prosper's hand. No matter how much he might have deplored his weakness, he had been incapable of harming his own son.

Except, of course, that Cadel wasn't his son after all.

Cadel chastised himself for being such a fool. He knew Prosper. He knew what kind of a man Prosper was: practical, ruthless, manipulative. Yet deep in his heart, Cadel still couldn't believe that Prosper had actually tried to kill him. Deep in his heart, Cadel didn't *want* to believe it. Because that would mean the complete extinction of an ancient, fragile, buried spark of feeling—a tiny, glowing ember that had nourished him for a very long time.

Prosper had been the center of his world once. Prosper had listened to him, and instructed him, and bought him presents. Prosper had *understood* him—or so Cadel had thought.

It was difficult to accept that Prosper might now want to kill him, simply because the connection between them had proved to be a false one.

But why wouldn't he want to kill me? Cadel reflected. *I know enough to be dangerous. I'm smart enough to be a threat. And I betrayed him. I made my choice and I walked away. If I'd been anyone else, he would have killed me long ago.*

He was so torn that he couldn't settle. On the one hand, when he remembered Sonja's bloody face, a vicious rage overwhelmed him; he wanted to smash Prosper's head against a brick wall. But this mental image opened the door to childhood memories of Prosper's commanding profile, indulgent grin, and attentive gaze.

You are my crowning achievement. Prosper had once said that, without a hint of irony. It wasn't something that Cadel could easily forget.

Groaning, he sat up. He threw off his blankets. He swung his feet to the floor. *I'll watch TV,* he decided. *Maybe a glass of hot milk would help me to relax.*

But when reached the kitchen, he found Saul already there.

Even in the middle of the night, the kitchen was a cheerful room, full of yellow paint and burnished copper. Saul, however, looked anything but cheerful; his shoulders were hunched, and there were dark shadows under his eyes. Wrapped in his old plaid bathrobe, he was sitting at the table with several sheets of paper spread out in front of him.

The clock on the stove said 2:15.

"Can't sleep?" Saul asked. When Cadel shook his head, the detective added, "Have I been making too much noise?"

"No." Cadel moved toward the fridge. "What kind of noise have you been making?"

"Oh . . . phone calls mostly. And a couple of visitors."

"Here?"

"There's a team parked outside, watching the house. I pulled in a few favors." Saul sipped from the mug that he was holding. "Fiona took some valerian to help her sleep. Do you want to try that?"

"No." Cadel was nervous about drugging himself. He couldn't afford to lose his edge. Suppose Prosper launched another attack? "I'm getting some hot milk," he explained, removing a bottle from the fridge. "That usually works for me."

"Uh-huh."

If Fiona had been there, she would have asked Cadel how he was feeling. Saul's technique was different. He tended to watch and wait, his dark eyes following his foster son's every move.

"I've been thinking about why this happened," Cadel said at last as he placed a glass of milk in the microwave. "To Sonja, I mean. I know she's the one who ended up in the hospital. But I still don't think she was the main target." Frowning, he hit the "start" button. "That chair was programmed to follow my phone signal," he announced. "I was supposed to get hurt as well."

"Maybe." Saul's tone was very calm. "We don't know enough to be sure yet."

"*I'm* sure. I reckon Prosper's found out that I'm not really his son. He's probably trying to kill me."

"Cadel—"

"It makes sense. Why wouldn't he? I know too much about him. If he ever went to trial, I'd be the star witness. Of *course* he's trying to kill me. Only he's too smart to hire a goon with a gun, because goons with guns always end up talking. Doing it by remote control is much more secure." The microwave pinged; retrieving his glass of milk, Cadel moved toward the table. "He must feel like he's been fooled all these years. He must be furious. He probably wants to wipe me off the face of the earth."

"Cadel." Saul leaned over to grab his wrist. "Don't."

"What?"

"We can't be sure. Not yet. Don't tie yourself in knots about it." In a transparent attempt to change the subject, Saul added, "I had a call from Steve. He told me someone's tampered with your phone."

Cadel's eyes widened.

"One of the wires has been snipped," Saul continued. "To stop that Bluetooth symbol from popping up on the screen." Releasing Cadel's wrist, the detective was quick to offer reassurance. "Steve says it wasn't necessarily a recent job. In fact, it could have been done last year. At Clearview House."

Cadel gnawed at his thumb. He had always been very careful with his cell, carrying it either in his pocket or in the bag that contained his precious computer. The only time he ever let the phone out of his sight was when he came home. Then he might dump it on a benchtop or a bookshelf, along with his wallet and sunglasses.

At Clearview House, he'd always followed much the same pattern. *If the damage was done there,* he pondered, *then who could have been responsible?* He cast his mind back to the day on which he had first received his phone from Saul Greeniaus. At the time, Cadel had been living with another set of foster parents—and since the device had merely been loaned to him, he'd taken very good care of it. But when he was kidnapped by Prosper English, it had been left behind at Clearview House. For a good twenty-four hours it had sat on his bedside table unattended.

Could that have been when the sabotage occurred? Or could the wire have been snipped some time earlier, during his two-week stay in a house full of spies?

The head of Genius Squad, Trader Lynch, had been secretly working for Prosper English. So had Dorothy Daniels, also known as "Dot." Cadel thought about Dot, whose enigmatic presence at Clearview House had always troubled him. Her younger brother, Com, had been one of Cadel's classmates at the Axis Institute; Com had vanished after the Institute's collapse, just as Dot had disappeared after Genius Squad disbanded. Both Dot and Com had shared the same squat build, waxy white skin, and taste for hacking into computer systems. Both had been distinguished by a strangely robotic demeanor, and both had somehow managed to avoid arrest—with the help of Prosper English. Cadel knew that Com had always been a favorite of Dr. Vee's. Could Vee and Com now be working together, on Prosper's behalf?

If Dot had snipped the wire back at Clearview House, then her brother might very well know about it. Especially if Dot herself was still on Prosper's payroll.

"It could have been Dot," Cadel said aloud. "I wouldn't put it past her. She could have done it so she could track my movements somehow, back when she was being paid to keep tabs on me."

"Perhaps," Saul agreed. "I'm gonna be asking Trader about it in the morning." Unlike Dot, Trader was now in jail, and likely to remain there for some time. "If it was Dot, then she was involved in this whole thing somehow. Even if she didn't hijack your phone."

"Yes."

"We need to find out if Bev and Dot are the same person. I've asked for a trace to be put on that call, but the results might not be back for a day or so."

Cadel sighed as he dropped into one of the kitchen chairs. "I doubt you'll find out much," he said glumly. "Whoever Bev really was, she would have stolen the SIM card. *I* would have stolen it. And then I would have destroyed it."

"Maybe."

"You might get a rough idea of where she was calling *from*—" Cadel began, then stopped in mid-sentence. An idea was stirring at the back of his mind.

"But she could have been on the move," Saul finished. "I realize that. Still, it's worth pursuing." All at once, he noticed Cadel's fixed stare. "What is it? What's wrong?"

"She wouldn't have been on the move." Cadel was thinking aloud. "That call wasn't made from a train or a bus. Bev knew exactly where I was. *Exactly.* Which means she must have been plugged into the campus CCTV network *while she was on the phone.*" Lifting his gaze from the steaming surface of his milk, he turned to the detective. "You wouldn't be doing a hack like that in public. Not if you had any sense."

"So—"

"You'd need somewhere private. With a stable Internet connection. Maybe not your own house but a friend's place. Or a hotel room. Or maybe even a parked car with a stolen wireless connection, though I doubt it."

Saul nodded, chewing at his bottom lip.

"You probably won't be able to pinpoint the exact spot," Cadel went on, "but if you could narrow it down to just a few streets—"

"We could canvass them." Saul didn't sound very enthusiastic, and Cadel wondered if it would be worth offering to hack a few customer databases. Probably not. Even if Saul gave him permission to conduct such a hack—even if they managed to secure some kind of official clearance for the procedure—Cadel suspected that "Bev" would be paying her power and broadband bills under an assumed name.

Nevertheless, if she *was* living in the area and she *did* have an Internet connection . . .

"You shouldn't be worrying about this now," Saul was saying. "You must be tired. Fiona will give me an earful if she finds out I've been keeping you up talking about phone traces—"

"You know what might work?" Cadel interrupted. "Wireless mapping."

"Huh?"

"If you can get a rough location, and Bev's still somewhere in the vicinity, we might be able to catch her by wardriving the whole area." Cadel sipped at his milk, considering all the possible scenarios. "We'd need to ask Richard for help," was his final conclusion. "He might agree to do it as a kind of class project. I figure if we could get four or five cars full of wardrivers scanning for access point IDs—"

"Whoa." Saul lifted his hand. "You've lost me."

"I'm not saying we'd hack into anybody's wireless network," Cadel assured him. "But if it's Dot who's done this, or Com, or Vee, I might be able to suss them out." *They could be using old ID signatures,* he thought. *You never know.* "I need to talk to Richard," he said. "Is there some way I could do that? Without using a phone?"

"*I'll* talk to him," Saul promised. And before Cadel could object, the detective plowed on. "I don't want you talking to anyone right now."

"I wouldn't do it *right now.*" Cadel couldn't keep the impatience out of his voice. "It's the middle of the night! I mean in the morning."

"In the morning you'll be going to a safe house," Saul quietly insisted. And Cadel gasped.

"What?" he said. "Oh no."

"Not the one in Roseville. Another one. It doesn't have a networked security system, but it's easy to patrol."

"No." Cadel shook his head. "You're not going to lock me away again."

"Listen—"

"No."

"Cadel. This is serious." The detective spoke gravely and forcefully. "I know how you feel about Prosper English. Deep down, you don't think that he'll ever hurt you. But you're wrong."

"What are you talking about?" Cadel couldn't believe his ears. "Are you deaf? I just *said* that he was trying to kill me!"

"You can say a lot of things without really meaning them."

"But—"

"Prosper got at you once before, and I was to blame. That's not gonna happen a second time. Do you understand?"

Cadel swallowed. As he stared into the detective's taut face, images flashed into his mind: images of a drive through deserted scrubland, with Saul at the wheel of a borrowed car and Prosper in the back. It had been a hijacking, of sorts; the detective had been lucky to escape with his life. And he *hadn't* been to blame. Of course he hadn't. Prosper had simply outwitted them all.

And that, of course, was the point. That was why Cadel couldn't just sit back and let other people take over. He understood how Saul was feeling. They had both been traumatized by the hijacking incident—Saul, perhaps, even more so than Cadel, who had learned to expect the unexpected after years of living in the shadow of Prosper English. But for that very reason, Cadel was better placed to pass judgment.

He took a deep breath.

"Without my help," he bluntly informed the detective, "you're not going to catch him."

Saul's answering smile was little more than a grimace. "It might take us a bit longer," he conceded.

"How long? Six weeks? Six months?" Cadel's voice grew shrill. "You expect me to live in a safe house for *six months*? Doing what? Playing Trivial Pursuit? While Prosper rampages around online, trying to kill people?"

There was a long pause. The detective seemed to be mustering his strength—or perhaps considering his options. It was hard to tell from the pensive look on his face. At last he said, quite gently, "I think you're underestimating us."

"And I think you're underestimating *me*," Cadel rejoined. Then, summoning up all his strength, he fired off his biggest, nastiest shot. "Which isn't something that Prosper would do anymore," he snapped. "Prosper knows not to treat me like a kid. He learned it the hard way. He knows what can happen when people forget how smart I am."

The detective stiffened. Cadel felt awful, but he refused to back down. Because he was telling the truth, and the truth could hurt.

"When it comes to Prosper English, I'm the expert," Cadel insisted, pressing home his advantage. *This is the best thing for everyone*, he told himself. *I can't afford to get sidelined.* "Believe me, I understand why you're worried," he said. "But a safe house isn't going to keep me safe. It really isn't." And by way of a final broadside, he added, "Do you honestly think you could *force* me to stay anywhere? Do you honestly think that I couldn't get out?"

Saul didn't respond immediately. He didn't even move. His gaze had dropped to the papers in front of him; for a while he just sat there, pale and rigid.

At last he glanced up. "So what do you want to do, then?" he asked without expression.

"I want to stay here. I want to talk to Richard Buckland." Cadel found himself quailing beneath the detective's blank-eyed regard. "Don't be angry. Please? Just give me a chance to help."

"I'm not angry." And indeed, Saul didn't sound the least bit angry—just immeasurably tired. "I'm scared," he admitted. "I'm scared you'll end up like Sonja. You're my son now. Protecting you isn't just a job anymore."

Cadel's eyes began to smart. *I need my sleep*, he thought, trying to control himself. *There's nothing to cry about.*

"Would you at least agree to stay inside?" Saul begged. "Away from any CCTV cameras?"

Unable to speak, Cadel nodded.

"Just until I can arrange an escort," the detective continued. Then he frowned. "Are you okay?" he asked.

Cadel cleared his throat. "I'm sorry," was all that he could say.

It was enough, though. And as Saul stretched across the table to ruffle his hair, Cadel saw a holstered pistol tucked beneath the detective's bathrobe.

NINE

When Cadel woke up the next morning, it was after nine. Saul had already left for work. But the kitchen was still full of people.

Fiona was there, shuffling around in a pair of Ugg boots. With her was Gazo Kovacs, who had once again donned his bodyguard outfit: long sleeves, shiny shoes, musky aftershave. Unfortunately, the scrap of toilet paper adhering to a razor cut on his right cheek tended to spoil the overall effect. And he was further diminished by the presence of Angus McNair, a recent arrival from the safe house.

Angus seemed to fill the room. He gave the impression that his scalp was brushing against its ceiling and that the floorboards were sagging under his weight. His partner, on the other hand, was a stocky little man like a short-haired terrier, with hard, flat, poker-chip eyes that scoured the scene in front of him as if they were made of steel wool. "I'm Officer Reggie Bristow," this man informed Cadel, in a voice like the squeak of a rusty gate. "And I'm here to watch your back."

"Oh," said Cadel, who was still on the threshold.

"But I'll be needing your cooperation," Reggie continued. "Which means that you can't leave the premises, you can't answer the phone, and you can't open any blinds or curtains."

Cadel sighed. As he sat down to eat his warmed-up pancakes, the two policemen resumed their "sector patrol," repeatedly checking every access point in the building. What with the steady *creak-creak-creak* of their footsteps, the accumulation of dirty coffee cups on the kitchen table, the locked doors, the screened phone calls, and the stale, bored, muted atmosphere, Cadel couldn't help thinking that his cozy little home had started to feel like a safe house. In other words, it was becoming a prison rather than a sanctuary.

Prosper could be blamed for that, too.

"If I can't leave here," Cadel said to Fiona as calmly as he could, "then how am I supposed to visit Sonja?"

"Oh, we'll work something out," she assured him. "We won't be able to see her until tonight, anyway. That's when she'll be moving out of the surgical high dependency unit."

"Have you heard from Judith?"

"Judith says it's going pretty well. She took Sonja's old Dyna Vox machine to the hospital, which should make things easier for everyone." The chiming of the doorbell briefly silenced Fiona; she set down her cup of tea as Angus's heavy footsteps sounded in the hallway. "Shall I get that?" she asked Reggie, who shook his head.

"Leave it to Officer McNair," he replied.

"But—"

"We can't take any risks."

Cadel bit back a retort. He knew that if there was going to be another attack, it would be launched by a wireless network, rather than by someone who showed up and rang the bell.

He wasn't surprised when the newcomer turned out to be Hamish Primrose.

"You know this guy?" Angus queried, upon escorting Hamish into the kitchen. "He says he's a friend of yours."

"He *is* a friend of mine," Cadel said patiently. And Hamish snorted.

"Some friend!" he scoffed, jerking out of the police officer's grip. "Word is that Sonja fell d-downstairs. I heard she's in the hospital. Is that true?"

Cadel could only nod. The picture that had invaded his mind—of Sonja's striped headband smeared with blood—had rendered him speechless.

"Then why didn't you call *me*?" Hamish spoke through a mouthful of chewing gum. "She's my friend too, y'know."

Before Cadel could think of an excuse, Fiona rose from the table. "It's been a bit hectic," she admitted. "Do you want something, Hamish? Maybe a cup of tea?"

"I left four messages," Hamish went on as if she hadn't spoken. He was glaring at Cadel. "You d-didn't answer them."

"I don't have my phone," Cadel rejoined. "Speaking of which, are *you* carrying a phone? Because you can't bring it in here."

"Huh?" Hamish seemed too stunned to resent this advice. He goggled like a fish, apparently unaware that Angus was already patting him down. "Why?"

"Because someone sent a Bluetooth transmission to Sonja's wheelchair." Cadel explained what had happened while Angus produced a cell phone from somewhere deep within the oversized leather jacket that Hamish was wearing. Only when Cadel had finished did Angus inquire as to whether Hamish had come by car.

"Uh—yeah," said Hamish. "It's parked outside."

"Make and model?"

"It's a green Prius."

"Can I have the keys?"

"I guess so." Hamish fished them out of his pocket. "Why? Are you going to check it for bombs?"

"No." The policeman remained poker-faced. "It's a safe place to put your phone."

"Because we don't want that phone anywhere near us," Cadel broke in. "You and I were both at Clearview House, Hamish, so we might have ended up with the same problem. It's no good hunkering down in an unwired house if you're surrounded by sabotaged cell phones."

Angus, by this time, was on his way out the door; Cadel could only assume that he was heading for the Prius, which Hamish had received from his parents upon finally securing a driver's license after three failed attempts. Cadel had always been slightly suspicious of this unexpected achievement. He couldn't help wondering if Hamish, with his wide knowledge of traffic-related computer networks, might have given *himself* a pass mark on the driving test.

"So you figure it was Dot who messed with your phone?" asked Hamish. He acknowledged Gazo with a careless wave, then threw himself into one of the kitchen chairs. "Or Trader, perhaps?"

"Perhaps." Cadel pushed aside his half-eaten pancake. "Unless *you* did it."

"Ha-ha. Very funny," Hamish snapped.

"It's all part of the same setup," said Cadel as Fiona whisked his plate away. "That, and the CCTV bug, and the malware in Judith's system. It's all connected somehow."

But Hamish wasn't enlightened. "What malware?" he demanded. And Cadel suddenly realized that, in all the confusion, Hamish hadn't been kept properly informed of recent developments.

There was no quick way of summarizing them. It took Cadel at least ten minutes to describe the events of the past two days while Hamish listened avidly and Fiona stacked the dishwasher. By the time Cadel had said his piece, nothing was left on the kitchen table except a sugar bowl.

"So what makes you think you're the main target?" Hamish inquired at last, thoughtfully peeling gum off his braces. "Couldn't Sonja be the one?"

"No." Cadel shook his head. "That chair was programmed to follow my phone signal. I was supposed to get hurt as well."

"Or killed." Hamish seemed almost excited, as if he were engaged in some kind of virtual role-playing scenario. And although Cadel found this attitude intensely discomforting, it also gave him an idea.

"Listen, Hamish," he said. "Remember you were telling me about that computer graphics guy? The one in your gaming group?"

"Warren, you mean?"

"I think so." More than once, Cadel had been invited to join a gang of young tech-heads who met at irregular intervals, in various living rooms, to enjoy a spot of networked computer gaming. "You told me he got hired by a visual effects company."

"That's right," Hamish confirmed. He regarded Cadel in a speculative fashion. "You want me to ask him about that CCTV bug?"

"Not really." As far as Cadel could recall, Warren was no older than Hamish, and hadn't been employed for very long. "I need to talk to someone with a lot of experience. Someone who knows that industry back to front. I thought your friend could give me a name."

Hamish shrugged. "I guess I could call him."

"Now?" asked Cadel, then turned to Reggie. "Have *you* got a phone he could use?"

Reggie blinked.

"It's the safest option, since I've never met you before," Cadel continued. "And I'll pay you back."

Before Reggie could respond, there was a slight disturbance at the other end of the house. A low buzz of voices, a shuffle of feet, and the *bang* of a screen door suggested that someone else had arrived. Hearing the jingle of keys, Cadel wondered if Angus had returned.

But in that case, who could be with him?

"For Chris'sake," Reggie growled. As he hurried across the room, however, Hamish blocked his path with one outstretched hand.

"Phone?" said Hamish.

"Please?" Cadel added.

Reluctantly, the officer reached into his pants pocket. By this time Cadel had identified the voice in the hallway; he glanced at Fiona, who had also recognized her husband's Canadian accent.

"Saul?" she said, frowning. Gazo sprang to his feet. Distracted by the sudden flurry of movement, Reggie allowed Hamish to relieve him of his cell phone.

By the time Saul appeared, with Richard Buckland close behind him, Hamish had already vanished into the laundry to call his friend Warren—and Cadel was the only person in the kitchen still sitting down.

"Don't panic," Saul declared. "It's only me."

He was wearing his charcoal gray suit, which made him look very stiff and formal. Richard, on the other hand, was all mismatched clothes, windblown hair, and frank curiosity. He grinned at Cadel, who stared at him in astonishment.

"Your dad told me you wanted to talk about wireless mapping," Richard said. "How are you, Cadel?"

"Um—okay. I guess."

"This is Richard Buckland," Saul interjected, for the benefit of those (like his wife) who were at a complete loss. In a tired voice he then proceeded to introduce Fiona, Reggie, and Gazo, all of whom stepped forward to shake Richard's hand. Gazo didn't know what to say. Reggie's greeting was flat and dismissive. But Fiona made an effort; she thanked Richard for all his help, and apologized for the state of the kitchen.

"It's been like a wet weekend around here: lots of people stuck inside with nothing to do," she confessed. "Would you like tea or coffee? Or maybe some lemonade?"

"Just water, if that's all right," said Richard.

"Hang on." Cadel glared at Fiona. "What do you mean, 'nothing to do'?" It irked Cadel that Fiona, of all people, should have accused him of wasting time. "*I've* had something to do," he protested. "I've been thinking. And I've worked out how I can travel around safely without worrying too much about CCTV cameras." Uncertain as to how much Richard might know about recent events, he paused for an instant, studying his teacher doubtfully. "Did you hear about this whole camera business?"

As Richard opened his mouth, Saul jumped in ahead of him. "You shouldn't stop worrying about CCTV cameras, Cadel," the detective insisted, ushering Richard toward an empty chair. "I don't care what car you're in; once you leave this house, you'll be running a big risk."

"No I won't. Not if I take a few precautions."

"Like tinted windows?" Saul murmured. Then he peeled off his jacket, tossed it onto the table, and removed his shoulder holster, which he placed gently beside the jacket. "Officer Bristow's car might have tinted windows, but it's also got a Bluetooth GPS receiver. As for the rest of us . . . well, it's possible that *all* our cars are being tracked. Which is why I've swapped mine for a 1999 Corolla." He gestured toward the front of the house. "It's parked two blocks away, and it has no GPS, no car phone, and no E-tag device for tollbooths. Even the radio doesn't work."

Cadel was startled—and impressed. In fact, he was so impressed that he refrained from pointing out that a GPS jammer, attached to the cigarette lighter in Reggie's car, would effectively block most of the tracking devices that might be used to infiltrate the vehicle's systems. *After all*, he thought, *there is a lot of anti-jamming technology about. Who knows what kinds of pluggers or pseudolites Vee might be messing with?* In the final analysis, he agreed with his foster father: an old bomb would definitely be the safest option to drive.

Fiona, however, was appalled.

"What do you mean?" she demanded, gawking at her husband. Though she tried to remain calm, her voice was steadier than her hand; when she placed a glass of water in front of Richard, several drops spilled onto the table. "What on earth has happened to *your* car?"

"It's a temporary switch," Saul replied. "I'll get it back when it's safe to use."

"And mine?" said Fiona.

"Cadel should stay away from your car. And Gazo's. And Hamish's." The detective peered around somewhat irritably. "Where *is* Hamish, anyway?" he wanted to know. "Isn't that his Prius parked out front?"

"He's in there," said Gazo, pointing at the laundry door.

Richard raised an eyebrow. "Are you talking about Hamish Primrose?" he asked, without receiving an answer. Cadel, for one, refused to be sidetracked.

"The Corolla's a good idea," he conceded. "But I don't have to stay inside it."

"Cadel—" Saul began.

"No, wait. Just listen."

Challenging Saul took a lot of courage. The detective's words were infused with a kind of leaden authority, which was even more intimidating than his carefully positioned firearm. But Cadel didn't feel that he could back down.

"I don't care how smart this hacker is," he argued. "No one can watch the feed from *every* camera in Sydney—not for twenty-four hours a day, seven days a week. Not even if he has a team of people working for him. That's why he'll be using video analytics."

Fiona sighed. "Video what?" she said hopelessly. Whereupon Richard kindly translated.

"A computer program will be monitoring the footage being hacked," he informed her. "There are algorithms that can filter incoming video data by looking for specific things. So you can pinpoint exactly what you want to see."

"And this hacker wants to see me," Cadel declared. "But if I'm not in the usual places, how's he going to find me? Unless he gets his software to search for someone with my dimensions, and my clothes, and my movements." His gaze was like a drill bit as he aimed it at Saul. "All I have to do is change those things."

"So what are you saying?" Fiona interrupted. "That you want to disguise yourself? Is that it?"

"Sort of." Cadel hesitated, wondering if "disguise" was really the right word. Perhaps "adjust" or "distort" would be better. "I mean, it might not be much of a disguise," he said. "It might just be a matter of covering my hair . . . wearing oversized shoes . . . maybe a couple of shoulder pads . . ." Seeing Fiona's puzzled frown, he tried to explain. "Computers don't think like us. They're not looking for a complete *person*, they're looking for measurements. Proportions. Spatial relationships. Sometimes they can't see the wood for the trees."

At that point the front door slammed. For a moment everyone stiffened, then relaxed as a familiar, lumbering tread announced that Angus had returned. In the pause that followed, Reggie checked his watch, and Cadel covertly studied the laundry door. Gazo's attention wandered toward a glass jar full of brownies. Fiona, who didn't like to see guns lying around, glowered at Saul's pistol. Richard sipped his water, eyes downcast.

Only Saul remained focused. His dark gaze never moved from his foster son's face.

"I don't understand why you'd have to get out of the car," he finally said. "You told me this project of yours would involve driving around Dulwich Hill scanning for signals. You didn't say anything about doing it on foot."

Cadel's heart skipped a beat. "I didn't say anything about Dulwich Hill, either," was his immediate response. "Is that where Bev called from? Dulwich Hill?"

Saul nodded.

"Well *that's* not a big suburb. We could easily wardrive that." Catching sight of Richard's quizzical expression, Cadel flushed. "I mean . . . if no one objects. To doing it as a class project."

Cadel could feel a prickle of sweat on his upper lip. The idea had seemed like a good one when it had first occurred to him. Now, in Richard's presence, he was beginning to have second thoughts. Was it presumptuous to expect a group of virtual strangers to get involved in such a big and complicated exercise when they had masses of other course work to do?

"Did Saul tell you what I had in mind? About wireless mapping the source of that Bluetooth hack?" Aware that his voice had grown husky, Cadel coughed to clear his throat. "I was thinking we wouldn't need more than half a dozen cars. And if we didn't have enough antennae, we could build some ourselves."

"Mmm-hmm. Yes." Richard had a habit of punctuating his remarks with enthusiastic little murmurs. "Yes, I think I've got a handle on what you want, but . . . who else is going to be involved?"

Although this was a reasonable question, it stumped Cadel—who hardly knew any of his fellow students. And he was about to say as much when suddenly Hamish appeared, triumphantly waving Reggie's phone. "Got it," Hamish announced. Then he caught sight of Richard, and his jaw dropped.

"Hello, Hamish," said Richard.

"What are *you* doing here?"

It was possible that Hamish didn't mean to be as rude as he sounded. Happily, Richard wasn't the least bit annoyed.

"I thought you might need some extra tutoring," he joked as Saul scowled at the dumbstruck Hamish.

"You've been making a *phone call*?" the detective spluttered. "I hope that's not your own phone you're using!"

"It's not," Cadel assured him before turning to Hamish with another question. "Did you get anything?"

"A name. And a number. And a Newtown address," said Hamish. "He's called Andrew Hellen."

"Who's called Andrew Hellen?" Saul demanded. He was interrogating Cadel, who tried to explain as clearly and simply as possible.

"Andrew Hellen is the guy I have to talk to. He's a computer graphics expert. I need to show him that footage you showed me."

The detective sighed. "Cadel," he began, "we've already run those shots past several VFX guys—"

"*You* might have, but *I* haven't!" The words had barely left Cadel's mouth before he regretted their tone. He didn't want to lose his cool in front of so many people. It was awkward, having to discuss the matter in such an overcrowded room; he would have preferred more privacy. Nevertheless, he plowed on, conscious all the while of Fiona's anxious presence, and Gazo's lost look, and Richard's sympathetic regard. "You told me no one knows how this bug even works. Is that right?"

"That's right," Saul admitted.

"Well, did you try to figure it out?" Cadel couldn't entirely banish the impatience from his voice. "Did you ask your CG friends if someone's been making waves with—I dunno—new-generation tone-mapping algorithms or whatever?"

There was a brief silence. Hamish grinned. Reggie rolled his eyes. Saul scratched his jaw.

"Because with any luck," Cadel continued, "only a handful of people in the whole world could have pulled off that CCTV malware. And someone with a bit of inside knowledge might be able to identify who they are."

Saul grunted. He was looking very tired. It was Fiona who began to raise objections. "Couldn't you ask your expert to come here?" she said plaintively. "Instead of going to meet him somewhere else?"

Cadel shrugged. "I guess so. But why should he agree? I'll be taking up enough of his time; he won't want to waste any more of it coming over to our place."

"But what if his office has security cameras?" Fiona seemed surprised that her husband wasn't backing her up. "Saul? What if Cadel gets filmed going in there?"

"As long as I change my dimensions and stay off the beaten track, I should be all right," Cadel argued. "And Newtown isn't far. It won't take long."

"Fine." The detective gave in suddenly. "I believe you."

"And if I'm in the Corolla—"

"Cadel. I said yes." Having made his decision, Saul wasn't in the mood for further debate. "Will you be going this afternoon?"

Cadel hesitated.

"Uh—yeah. If I can set up a meeting," he replied. "The sooner the better."

"Hang on. Wait a minute. Are you sure about this?" Without waiting for an answer, Fiona appealed to Richard. "Are shoulder pads really going to be enough protection?"

For the first time, Richard looked faintly ill at ease. "Oh, I think it might take more than a couple of shoulder pads," he mumbled, at which point Saul addressed Cadel once again.

"Will you be going with Officer Bristow?"

"Sure."

"And how do you intend to disguise yourself, exactly?"

"Oh." Cadel hadn't really thought about that. He had been too busy presenting his case. "Well, let's see," he faltered, glancing at Richard for input. "I guess—I guess I ought to start with my hair . . ."

TEN

Cadel looked like a circus clown.

His bulging cheeks were full of cotton gauze padding. Two pieces of duct tape were dragging back the corners of his eyes. Builder's putty had been placed behind each ear to make them stick out more, and a fluffy white Santa's beard was blurring the contours of his chin. Despite the fact that it was a warm day, a long scarf had been wrapped around his neck, while his hair had been tucked beneath four layers of woolen beanie—not only to conceal his distinctive crop of curls but to increase the circumference of his head.

On his feet were a pair of Fiona's high-heeled shoes, which (being slightly too big) had been stuffed with balls of old newspaper. To give him more bulk, he had donned one of Saul's jackets. And because he wasn't broad enough to fill the jacket, it had been fitted with several sets of shoulder pads. He had a cushion tied around his waist, a folded towel shoved down the back of his running shorts, and a ski glove on each hand.

His striped leggings were designed to mislead, since he'd never worn anything remotely like them before.

"You can't go out in that," Fiona had said upon first laying eyes on his costume. Though barely able to keep a straight face, she had tried to be firm. "You'll get arrested."

"I don't have a choice." Staring into her bedroom mirror, Cadel had been appalled but satisfied. He had managed to give himself the dimensions of a wineglass: the skinny column of his candy-striped legs supported a big, round, no-neck ball. Not a single component of his outfit actually belonged to him, and his face was hugely distorted, what with its chipmunk cheeks, almond-shaped eyes, and brown, cosmetic freckles. "Anyway, nobody will see me."

"Except this Andrew person."

"Yeah, but Saul told him about my disguise." Gazing up at the detective, Cadel had sought confirmation. "You did, didn't you? You warned him when you rang."

"Ye-e-es." Saul's response had been gruff and slow. "Except I didn't realize that you'd be in fancy dress."

Oddly enough, he hadn't been trying to suppress a grin. Though Fiona had bitten the insides of her cheeks, and Reggie had snorted lemonade through his nose, and Angus had laughed until he was doubled over, Saul must have been too tired or worried to find the Santa beard amusing.

Perhaps he would have cracked a smile or two if he'd been allowed to take part in the expedition. He certainly would have felt a little less anxious about it. There had even been talk of letting him make his own way to Newtown, in Reggie's GPS-encumbered four-wheel drive while Cadel went in the Corolla with Reggie. But Cadel had scuttled that idea. Suppose the hacker was scanning CCTV footage for Saul as well? Suppose Saul's measurements triggered some kind of alarm? It was unlikely that even the most sophisticated software would register either of the bodyguards, since they hadn't yet played a big part in Cadel's life. Saul, however, was different—as were Fiona and Gazo.

Cadel didn't want to risk being spotted.

Not that he was exactly inconspicuous himself, wearing high heels and a fake beard. It wasn't his intention, however, to escape the notice of anyone with a functioning set of eyes; he was merely trying to fool a piece of software. And since that meant parading around like a demented preschooler dressed up for Halloween, he had asked Reggie to park Saul's Corolla in the alley behind the house.

Cadel wasn't worried about security cameras. As far as he could tell, there wasn't a single security camera anywhere near his place. His main concern was that, if he left by the front door, he might be recognized (and ridiculed) by one of the neighborhood kids. Having spent most of his early years being picked on by larger, louder, dumber boys who had regarded him as a weird little smart-ass, Cadel wanted to avoid falling back into the same old rut.

He had therefore made his departure through the back gate, with a raincoat over his head. And he had dived into the waiting Corolla like a rabbit into its hole—closely followed by a snickering Angus.

"What the hell is the deal with those shoes?" Angus asked as Reggie pulled away from the curb. "If you're trying to look like a woman, kid, you should lose that beard. It's a dead giveaway."

"It's a bloody joke, is what it is," Reggie snarled. Though Cadel's getup had amused him at first, he now regarded it as something of an insult. Either he didn't like it because he saw it as a puerile, attention-seeking tactic that was bound to backfire or he didn't like it because it made *him* look stupid. "Call that a disguise? You might as well be wearing Mickey Mouse ears."

"It's not meant for *people*," Cadel retorted from behind Angus. "I told you, it's aimed at a piece of software." He was sweating profusely by this time; the scarf and beanies and ski gloves were made for much colder weather. "Could you turn on the air-conditioning, please?" he begged. "I don't want my freckles washing off."

"I dunno if the air-conditioning even works in this bomb," was Reggie's morose retort. However, he grudgingly fiddled with the dashboard dials as the car crawled along in heavy traffic.

Their trip lasted about twenty-five minutes, and ended with an illegal right-hand turn across the path of an oncoming bus. It was an unpopular move, which resulted in a chorus of blaring car horns. "Wish we were in the squad car," Reggie muttered, pulling into a driveway that was blocked by a steel-barred gate. "One blast of a siren would shut 'em all up."

But Angus wasn't listening. He had leaned out of the car to push a wall-mounted button. Meanwhile, Cadel had sunk low in his seat, acutely conscious of the fact that they were now planted squarely across a busy urban footpath. Thanks to his display of bad manners, Reggie had practically ensured that some curious pedestrian would try to peer through the Corolla's rear window. And if that happened, Cadel's Santa beard would arouse widespread interest.

He heaved a sigh of relief when the steel-barred gate slid open.

"Not much room," Reggie grumbled upon rolling into a small parking lot packed tight with vehicles. Beyond it, a low, narrow building lay huddled behind a screen of bushes. No signage was visible near the glass entrance doors.

"Are you sure this is the place?" Angus queried. Then, as Reggie halted in the middle of what was clearly a driveway, he said, "Are you sure we can stop here?"

"No lines," Reggie countered. "No nothing." He switched off the engine. "This is the place. Saul gave me the directions himself."

Cadel remained silent. He couldn't bear the thought of getting out. He dreaded exposing himself to the incredulous stares of complete strangers. *They're going to think I'm mad,* he decided with a sinking heart.

But he didn't have much choice. So he left the car and made his way inside, clutching Reggie's arm for support. (It was hard to balance all the extra padding on top of Fiona's high-heeled shoes.) By the time they reached the reception desk, Cadel was hanging off both his bodyguards like a sack full of tinned groceries.

"Uh—we've got an appointment with Mr. Hellen," Reggie informed the dark-haired receptionist, who couldn't conceal her amazement. Though she promptly picked up a phone, her stunned gaze lingered on Cadel.

"What name is it?" she asked. At which point Cadel took over.

"Could you please tell him we're here with that footage?" he mumbled through his beard. He had forgotten to check whether the building was wired for sound and didn't want to take any chances. It was possible that his name might trigger some kind of online alert. "He'll know who we are. It's police business."

The receptionist swallowed. Cadel was convinced that she was trying not to laugh—and his suspicions were confirmed when she requested, in a wobbly voice, that they take a seat. Clearly she found the contrast between his Santa beard and the words "police business" irresistibly comical. He didn't blame her. He probably would have felt the same way. But there was no telling how many security cameras were lurking in his immediate vicinity, so he wasn't tempted to remove his disguise.

That was why he nearly sprained an ankle as he headed toward the waiting area. Only when he'd collapsed onto the nearest couch did he feel secure enough to take off Fiona's stiletto heels. Sitting down, he didn't need them to increase his height. That was the role of the towel stuffed into his running shorts.

He began to rub his aching toes while Reggie and Angus seated themselves next to him. The room in which they found themselves occupied nearly the entire top floor of an old warehouse, which had been transformed into a stylish space full of steel and glass and exposed brick. Swags of cable spilled from desktops burdened with computer equipment. Row upon row of hunched figures sat hypnotized in front of glowing screens, some with headphones clamped to their ears, some surrounded by half-eaten chocolate bars and greasy paper bags.

None of these young people seemed aware of Cadel's presence, let alone his fake beard. They were all too wrapped up in what they were doing.

Or perhaps, because they worked in the film industry, they were simply used to seeing outlandish costumes.

"Reckon that's him?" Angus observed under his breath. He was squinting at a man who had suddenly appeared at the top of a nearby staircase. This staircase led down to some mysterious lower level. "Doesn't look much like a boss, if you ask me."

"Yeah, but he's the only one old enough to be an expert," Reggie quietly remarked, before jumping to his feet. Angus followed his example while Cadel fumbled to put on his shoes again.

The man approaching them had a lot of black hair and stubble. He wore faded jeans, scuffed sneakers, and a slightly frayed shirt. As he loped across the polished wooden floor, his dark gaze came to rest on the Santa beard—and remained glued there.

He lifted an eyebrow.

"Hello," he said. "You wanted to see me?"

"Mr. Hellen?" Reggie stuck out his hand.

"Yeah." The newcomer's tone was cautious as he exchanged a lackluster handshake. He still couldn't take his eyes off Cadel. "Just make it Andrew . . ."

"Detective Greeniaus wasn't able to come with us," Reggie announced, getting straight down to business. He produced his identification, and would have introduced the rest of his party if Cadel hadn't stopped him.

"Wait," said Cadel. He kept his voice low and husky, just in case. "Would you mind telling me if your security system has an audio feed?" he went on, meeting Andrew Hellen's quizzical stare with a kind of desperate fearlessness. When Andrew's other eyebrow went up, Cadel rephrased the question. "Is this conversation being recorded?"

"Not unless *you're* doing it," Andrew replied. He was beginning to look decidedly ill at ease. "Why? What's the problem?"

"No problem," Angus rumbled. "I'm Officer McNair, and this young man is Cadel Greeniaus, and he needs to ask you something. After which we'll be on our way."

"I realize how weird this must seem, but I'm not a lunatic." Cadel plucked at the white fluff that was hanging off his chin. "This beard is a security precaution."

"Uh-huh." Andrew nodded, though not as if he was wholly convinced.

"I honestly know what I'm talking about. I'm doing a computer engineering degree," Cadel continued. "Did Saul Greeniaus tell you much about this CCTV bug? Because I'm the one who discovered it."

Andrew murmured something to the effect that he employed a few teenagers himself. Then he said, "The guy on the phone mentioned a CG figure popping up everywhere. On DVR networks. Is that what you're talking about?"

"Yes," Cadel replied. Whereupon Andrew shook his head.

"I dunno," he countered. "I can't figure out how *that* would work."

"Let me show you the footage." Having removed one ski glove, Cadel produced a disk from inside Saul's jacket. "Maybe if you see it, you'll be able to help."

Andrew's doubtful expression wasn't encouraging. Nevertheless, he politely capitulated, leading his guests into a cramped, dark, windowless room containing a desk, several chairs, and masses of expensive-looking technology. Dirty cups were strewn everywhere.

Cadel couldn't see any cameras.

"Do you want a coffee?" Andrew inquired as he settled himself in front of a computer screen. "Or a soft drink or something?"

"No thanks." Cadel handed over the disk. "This is clean. Don't worry, it won't infect your system."

If Andrew was at all worried about his system, he kept his feelings to himself. With perfect equanimity, he inserted Cadel's disk into a drive while Angus and Reggie piled through the door, filling the tiny room almost to bursting point. Angus, especially, seemed far too big for such a small space; he kept stealing wistful glances at the coffee cups.

Reggie positioned himself in a strategic manner, radiating distrust from every pore. Cadel wondered if he was put off by Andrew's long hair and unshaven chin.

"That's him." Cadel indicated Prosper's digital double when it materialized on the screen. "He walks across every shot, and . . . see? That's the light probe. You'll find one of *them* in every shot, too."

Andrew grunted. He watched the sequence of images with quiet concentration until he reached the Prosper-shaped hole. Then he grunted again.

"There's the mistake," Cadel remarked unnecessarily. "That pretty much clinched it for everyone." He had been watching Andrew's face, which was long and craggy and well-worn. Experience was written all over it. "So what do you think? Is there anyone who might have done this? Anywhere in the world? I'm pretty sure I know who managed the infiltration side of things, but I don't really understand the whole CG process. Not enough to recognize a signature style or an area of expertise . . ."

"This picture is really rough." Andrew flicked at the screen with one finger. "It's what you'd call degenerated HDRI. The worse the image is, the easier it is to fake."

"But *you* can tell it's fake," said Cadel.

"Nope." Once more, Andrew shook his shaggy head. "Not to look at. Not if the picture's this rough."

"Oh." Cadel was crestfallen. He'd hoped for a telltale clue that might be visible to a trained eye. "But you'd have to be pretty good, wouldn't you? To pull this off?"

"You'd have to be brilliant," Andrew confirmed. "*I* couldn't do it. I don't know anyone who could."

Cadel's heart sank even further. "What, no one at *all*?" He groaned.

Andrew gave a shrug. Then he peered up at Cadel, who was hovering beside him, and said, "Is that what you want? A name?"

"If possible." Taking a deep breath, Cadel tried another approach. "How would *you* tackle something like this? I mean, where would you start, if you wanted to tweak a real-time data stream?"

Andrew sighed as he dragged his fingers through his hair, muttering a few disjointed observations about the need for a "full-on, games-style rendering engine" and how you'd have to "throw it into a sixty-four-bit range." Cadel found it impossible to follow him. "Thing is, though, I'm not a programmer," Andrew finished. "You'd want to talk to somebody with a math brain. A software developer or one of those guys who like tinkering with the software they've already got."

"Like who?" Cadel pressed.

"I dunno. Somebody like Stephen Regulus. He built Massive—have you heard of Massive?"

Cadel gave a nod, almost dislodging his beard. He knew about the revolutionary computer-graphics software called Massive. He had even heard of Stephen Regulus. But Regulus wasn't anything like the culprit they were searching for. Regulus wasn't an outsider. "This malware," said Cadel, taking a different tack, "it's groundbreaking stuff, right? I mean, you could make your fortune with this."

"Right. Yeah." Andrew sounded absolutely definite.

"And it's being used by a crook," Cadel went on. "To sabotage systems." For a moment he let this fact sink in; then he resumed. "Is there anyone in your industry who's smart enough to assemble a package like this but who's a bit of a crook himself? Someone who's got a dodgy reputation? Someone *you* wouldn't employ because you wouldn't trust him?"

There was a long pause. Andrew surveyed Cadel in a pensive manner, as if there was something frankly dubious about asking such questions.

"Well . . . no," said Andrew.

"They wouldn't have to be from Australia. I'm talking about anywhere in the *world*."

"Uh . . ."

"Like America, maybe?" Cadel had remembered the ghostly mansion. "Or Canada?"

"If you can help us, *sir,* it would be a wise decision," Reggie growled from the threshold. He didn't flinch when Andrew regarded him with a palpable air of disbelief. "This is a criminal conspiracy we're talking about."

"Even if you know someone who might know someone," Cadel suggested. At which point, inexplicably, Andrew gave in.

"There's a guy I met in LA once," he said. "Guy called Raimo Zapp the Third. Weird guy."

"*Raimo Zapp the Third?*" Cadel repeated.

"Yeah." Andrew's dry tone spoke volumes. "I think it's a deed-poll name. Which tells you pretty much all you need to know about him."

Nevertheless, he went on to relate what he'd heard about Raimo Zapp the Third. Raimo had been blacklisted by many of Hollywood's special-effects companies because he had been caught stealing scans of famous movie stars. These scans were collections of visual data (amassed by laser scanners) that, when processed, gave filmmakers the information they needed to create digital doubles. Raimo had sold the scans to certain underground directors whose movies weren't the kind that any respectable star would want to appear in. When Raimo was sacked for this misconduct, he had promptly sabotaged his former employer's software protocols. According to Andrew, an entire army of digital robots had started breaking into dance routines whenever it was instructed to engage another army in hand-to-hand combat.

"Like I said, I met this guy in LA, at a SIGGRAPH conference," Andrew revealed. "Way before he messed up. He had a hell of an attitude."

"What do you mean?" Cadel asked.

"Oh . . . chip on his shoulder. He was mad at everyone. Went on and on about CG people not getting the kind of respect they deserve." An ironic smile flickered across Andrew's face as if he was enjoying a private joke that didn't happen to be terribly funny. "It was a big rant," he declared. "I pretty much tuned out."

Cadel bit his lip, thinking hard. It was a long shot. A *very* long shot. There was nothing to indicate that Raimo Zapp the Third had anything to do with the CCTV malware.

On the other hand, he might have connections. Useful, antisocial connections.

"Would you be able to contact him?" Cadel inquired. "Do you know where he lives?"

"No, but I could ask around." Andrew was extracting Cadel's disk from the drive. "You want me to do that?"

"Yes, please."

"Raimo isn't a shy sort of bloke," Andrew offered, handing the disk back to Cadel. "Someone's bound to know where he is."

"If you find out, can you tell me?"

"Sure." Andrew pulled out his phone. "What's your number?"

Cadel hesitated. After reviewing the various possibilities, he realized that Reggie's phone was probably safer than Saul's, or Fiona's, or Judith's. So it was Reggie's number that Andrew finally entered into his electronic phone book.

Then Cadel decided to finish up; he had spotted Andrew's knee bouncing impatiently, and was wondering if they had outstayed their welcome.

"Okay—well—I guess that's all," Cadel said. "Unless you can think of any other names?"

"Sorry." Andrew rose. "Not many sociopaths in this business."

Though his delivery was bland, the gleam in his eye suggested that he was once again enjoying a private joke. But he became more serious as he accompanied his three guests back to the reception area. There, after bidding them good luck, he divulged one final piece of information.

"I just remembered something Raimo told me," he observed. "Guy kept saying he was such a genius that his latest idea would take the world by storm. Which is the *second* reason I didn't take him too seriously."

Cadel frowned. "The first being . . . ?"

"His name."

"Oh. Right."

"Course, he didn't go around wearing a fake beard, but . . . well, you can't judge a book by its cover," Andrew concluded, with a crooked smile and a sideways glance.

Then he pressed a button on the wall, whereupon the steel-barred gate outside slowly began to slide open.

ELEVEN

When Cadel arrived at the Sydney Children's Hospital, he wasn't wearing a fake beard or high heels. He had decided that such a disguise would be useless, since Prosper's surveillance team was probably keeping a very close eye on Sonja's visitors. While pillows and ski gloves might have been enough to fool a computer program, they wouldn't fool anyone watching real-time footage from the hospital's CCTV network.

Besides, he didn't want to appear in public looking like a complete idiot.

So he showed up at ward C3 in his usual T-shirt and corduroys, with a big box of licorice allsorts. Sonja loved licorice allsorts. She loved their geometric patterns and the fact that they were so easy to chew. Cadel figured that, even if she couldn't eat them, they would be something cheerful for her to look at.

He also brought Fiona, Reggie, and Angus with him. Saul had promised to meet them later; he was busy chasing down some kind of lead in Reggie's car, so the two bodyguards had been forced to squeeze into Fiona's little hatchback. On Cadel's advice, they had decided not to take Saul's borrowed Corolla anywhere near the hospital cameras—just in case someone happened to spot Cadel climbing out of the back seat. "That car's supposed to be secure," Cadel had said. "But it won't be once our hacker gets hold of its license plate." He knew that there would be cameras positioned around the parking lot and at many of the drop-off points. That was why, from the moment they swept through the hospital's entrance gates, he felt as if he were being watched.

This feeling strengthened as he approached the front door. It was like approaching a hidden nest of snipers. Things weren't so bad once he had crossed the threshold; he couldn't see much surveillance equipment inside. Nevertheless, he remained jumpy and anxious, despite the presence of his bodyguards.

By the time he reached the third floor, he was drenched in sweat.

Ward C3 South had been set aside for teenagers. Opposite the nurses' station, three large notice boards were covered in snapshots of young people, some wearing bandages and hospital gowns, some decked out in party dresses or hiking gear. Gazing at these photographs, Cadel saw braces and pimples and nose studs. He saw shiny balloons and stuffed animals. It was a vibrant display that somehow made the gray carpet and pus-yellow walls look even sadder.

Sonja's room was at one end of a long, rather dingy corridor. Fiona obtained directions from a nurse, then led the way past glimpses of wheeled beds and drawn curtains and flickering television screens. As he drew nearer to their destination, Cadel found it more and more difficult to breathe. His hands were shaking and his mouth was dry. He felt sick.

"We'll wait here," Reggie suddenly announced. He nodded at Angus, who had already attracted one or two curious stares; the two men then stationed themselves on either side of Sonja's door, standing at ease with their hands clasped in front of them.

Cadel hesitated.

"Go on, sweetie," Fiona urged, giving him a nudge. "Why don't you go in, and I'll get myself a cup of coffee before I say hello."

"But—"

"You're the one she'll be wanting to see."

Cadel wasn't so sure about that. Sonja was no fool. She must have realized that her injuries were somehow related to his presence in her life—unless, of course, she hadn't been well enough to think about anything, lately.

When he stumbled into her room, clutching the licorice allsorts, his heart was pounding like a jackhammer.

The room contained two beds, one of which was empty. The other stood near the window, surrounded by various trolleys and cabinets. Sonja's old Dyna Vox machine was sitting on a wheeled bedside table, and her splinted leg was wedged into a kind of trap or cage, designed (no doubt) to keep it absolutely still. Beneath the bandage wrapped around her forehead, her eyes were sleepy and bruised-looking.

But they brightened when she saw Cadel.

"Gnnn!" she squawked, groping for her Dyna Vox. The sight of her thin, knotted, straining fingers was too much for him. They were so brittle. So *vulnerable*.

His lips began to shake. He had to blink back tears. Seeing this, Sonja became distressed. Her muscles reacted as they usually did, tightening uncontrollably. Her back arched. Her neck twisted. One arm slammed against the Dyna Vox.

Cadel realized that he was going to have to start talking, no matter how big the lump in his throat might be. Otherwise Sonja would thrash about until she hurt herself.

"I'm sorry," he mumbled. "I'm really sorry."

"Naa." Her eyebrows snapped together.

"I've brought you some of these." He held up the allsorts, sniffing hard. The important thing, he knew, was to get her calmed down. "Is there somewhere special I should put them? You haven't got a lot of space."

"Eeh." Sonja flung out a hand, leaning toward him, and he recognized the gesture. She was reaching for his gift. So he placed it on the bed beside her, before leaning down to kiss her, very carefully, on the cheek.

"I guess Judith must have told you what happened," he croaked. "About my phone being hijacked and sending a signal through to your Bluetooth connection." He cast around for a chair. "I didn't even know my Bluetooth was on. Someone sabotaged my phone, somewhere along the line. Dot, probably."

Having located a vinyl-upholstered seat in one corner, he positioned it closer to the bed—while Sonja struggled to spell out a message.

"*The-Wife*," her Dyna Vox finally pronounced in its toneless, electronic voice. Cadel raised his eyebrows.

"Oh," he said. "You heard about that, did you?"

"*Trace*," was her painfully slow response. Then: "*Chatroom*."

"No." He understood exactly what she was talking about. "Whoever hacked the Wife hasn't shown up again. The police have been monitoring his command and control access point, but it's useless, I reckon. He won't come back." In an effort to reassure her, he added, "I'll make sure it's all cleaned up in there before you go home. Don't worry. I'll rip out the cameras if I have to."

He didn't say anything about the hospital cameras, though they were certainly preying on his mind. So, too, was the fact that, without a doubt, there were online systems governing every aspect of the hospital's management: shifts, admissions, medical records, waiting lists. When it came to computerized environments, hospitals were just as heavily wired as banks, or airports, or Smart Homes.

The whole idea made his skin crawl. He felt as if there were mines buried under the floor and peepholes drilled through the light fittings.

"*Not-your-fault*," Sonja spelled out doggedly. "*Stop-worrying-now.*"

Cadel swallowed. "I was the target," he muttered, staring at his feet. "Not you. If I hadn't been there, right at that moment—"

"*Ho-hum. Boring.*" Though she might have been out of practice, Sonja was still able to communicate well enough with her Dyna Vox. As Cadel glanced up in surprise, she went on. "*Not-always-about-you-you-you.*"

Stung, he began to protest. "I'm not saying that. I'm just saying—"

"*Prosper-hates-me-more*," she interrupted, stabbing at the keyboard in front of her. "*So-how-will-you-stop-him?*"

It was hard to judge her mood. The Dyna Vox droned out its messages, and her face was being yanked about by uncooperative muscles. But Cadel thought that he could see a glint in her eye; he sensed that she was being deliberately provocative. To lighten the atmosphere, perhaps? To vent her frustration? He couldn't tell.

All he could do was take a deep breath and hope that no one was eavesdropping on their quiet little exchange.

"The Wife got hacked by a program that was written for another house," he said softly, picking up Sonja's TV remote. After adjusting the volume on her television set (which was tuned to a quiz show), he leaned toward her until he was jammed against the steel bars that had been raised to stop her from rolling out of bed. "Did Judith tell you? When I had a look at the malware, I found all kinds of applications for specific Bluetooth appliances—stuff that Judith doesn't have. We might be able to track down the original house if we can identify someone who's bought all those products."

"America," was Sonja's contribution. And Cadel gave a nod.

"I wouldn't be surprised," he said. Then, shielding his mouth with one hand for extra privacy, he added, "America's a big place, but there can't be *that* many people in the world with a floor-washing robot and a computerized trigger lock connecting their guns to their alarm system. You never know, the manufacturers might have customer records."

"Insurance." It was clear that Sonja's head injury hadn't affected her reasoning skills. *"All-those-things-insured-with-one-company-somewhere? Check-coverage?"*

"I'm not chasing it up myself," Cadel admitted in response to these awkwardly phrased suggestions. "Sid's in charge. I'm not allowed online right now."

Sonja's snort was no accident. It was a voluntary noise meant to convey her disgust. When she rolled her eyes, Cadel felt constrained to defend his foster father. "Saul's just trying to be careful," he murmured. "It's not like I'm on the sidelines, you know. I just have to *look* as if I am, in case somebody's watching."

Sonja blinked. Her gaze flicked around the room, apparently searching for evidence of a bug or a hidden camera. Then her hand moved across the Dyna Vox until it was hovering over the letter V. But she didn't strike the keyboard. Instead she glanced inquiringly at Cadel, who gave a nod.

"Yeah," he confirmed under his breath. "I think it might be Dr. Vee." Aware of how hard it was for Sonja to ask questions, he proceeded to give her the answers she needed without prompting. "If he's in America, though, he's got someone working for him over here. Because 'Bev' made a local call. In fact, tomorrow I'll be part of a wardriver team of Richard's students that's going to be scanning for signature IDs in—"

"*Grah!*" she yelped, so violently that he stopped in mid-sentence. At first he assumed that her squeal must have been a cry of pain, until he saw the anxious look in her eyes. She stabbed again and again at the Dyna Vox, but for some reason she kept missing it. Her fingers never made contact with the keyboard.

"What?" he said. "What's wrong?"

"Dnn! Dnn!"

"Should I call the nurse? Do you need something? Does it hurt somewhere?"

"*Dnn!*"

Still she jabbed at the Dyna Vox without actually touching it.

"Here," he offered, reaching across the bed. "I'll do it myself. Blink twice if I'm on the right letter. A. No? B . . ."

"*NAAH!*"

Her whole body lunged toward him, knocking against the steel frame that separated them. The impact was so unexpected that he jerked back, almost toppling off his chair.

"What the—?" He was stunned. But as he watched her flailing around, swatting at the machine in front of her, something clicked inside his head. "Oh my god," he spluttered. "The Dyna Vox!"

The Dyna Vox had been at Clearview House. The Dyna Vox was a computer.

The Dyna Vox could very well have been bugged—or worse.

"I'll take it," he said, jumping up. When he seized the device, Sonja seemed to relax a little. She fell back onto her pillows with a heartfelt sigh, though her hands kept twitching.

Cadel headed for the door, which he yanked open. Outside, Reggie and Angus were still at their posts. Fiona had parked herself at a more discreet distance, several yards away. Her husband stood beside her, holding a spray of silk flowers.

Judith had warned them that real flowers weren't allowed inside the hospital, because pollen was bad for people with allergies.

"What are you doing?" Cadel demanded. "Why don't you come in?"

"Um . . ." Saul looked to his wife for help. Before she could say anything, however, Cadel thrust the Dyna Vox at Reggie—who received it with a startled grunt.

"We have to get rid of this," said Cadel. "It could be a problem." He turned to address Saul once again. "The Dyna Vox was at Clearview House, remember? Somebody should make sure it hasn't been tampered with."

"Christ." The detective's confused expression slowly yielded to one of alarm. "I never thought . . ."

"But it's Sonja's," Fiona protested as Reggie clumsily scooped up a dangling power cable. "How's she going to communicate without her Dyna Vox?"

"I don't know," Cadel replied, and Saul said, "We'll think of something. Just . . . just take it down to the car, Reg, will you?"

"Which car?" asked Reggie. "Yours or hers?"

Cadel didn't wait around to hear Saul's response. Instead he plunged back into Sonja's room, letting the door swing shut behind him. He was angry with himself for being such an idiot. Of *course* the Dyna Vox could have been bugged. Why hadn't it crossed his mind before?

"I'm sorry," he said, upon reaching Sonja's bedside. "That was stupid. I can't believe it never occurred to me. Thank god *someone's* using her brain." Then he leaned down to whisper in her ear. "If only I knew sign language," he hissed. "This is insane. It's like being back at the Axis Institute."

"Sonja? Hello?" Fiona's cautious greeting interrupted him. She had sidled into the room, bearing Saul's bunch of silk flowers. "Are you all right, sweetie? Are you going to be all right without your Dyna Vox?"

"Of course she isn't!" Cadel snapped. Though he knew he was being unfair, he couldn't seem to moderate his tone. "We have to get her something else! We have to call Judith, right now!"

"Well . . . okay. We can do that." If Fiona was taken aback, she didn't show it. She regarded him with sympathy, and her voice was gentle. "I just wanted to make sure that Sonja doesn't have a problem with this decision you've made—"

"It wasn't *my* decision, it was *her* decision!" Cadel flushed, infuriated by this bald-faced assumption that he was trying to boss people around. "She's the one who thought of it, not me!"

"Oh."

"Maybe they have a spare Dyna Vox here at the hospital," he continued. "Or something *like* a Dyna Vox. There must be a speech therapy unit; couldn't we find out? Couldn't we ask a nurse?"

Fiona frowned. She glanced at her watch. "It's pretty late," she said. "It's after seven. I doubt if any of the clinics or therapists will be available until tomorrow—"

"But we can *ask*, can't we?" he exclaimed, at which point Saul entered the room.

"Ask what?" The detective didn't sound as if he wanted to deal with yet another crisis. "What's the problem?"

"The problem is that Sonja needs to talk!" Cadel cried. "So we need to ask someone if there's a spare Dyna Vox around here!" Seeing his foster parents exchange a pensive glance, he lost patience with them. "*I'll* do it," he barked, before hurrying for the exit.

But Saul was in the way and didn't step aside. On the contrary, he grabbed Cadel's arm.

"Calm down," the detective ordered.

"I'm not—"

"*Calm. Down.*"

Cadel suddenly realized that he was clenching his fists. Subdued by Saul's dark and somber gaze, he made a deliberate effort to relax, taking a deep breath while he flexed his fingers.

"I know you're upset and I know why," Saul declared. "But there's no need to panic, okay?"

Cadel nodded.

"I'll go and see what I can do." Saul straightened, then raised his voice to address Sonja. "Sorry about this," he went on. "I'll be back in a minute to say hello. I just figure it's more important that we fix you up with some way of saying hello back."

From the other side of the room, Sonja gave a squawk that might have been an affirmative response. Fiona said to her husband, "I'll go if you like. I know how these bureaucrats think."

"Yeah," he rejoined, "but I've got my ID on me. And I'm also carrying a gun." As his wife heaved a long-suffering sigh, he turned back to Cadel. "You go and talk to Sonja. That's why you're here. Just leave the rest to me. I'll take care of it."

"How can I talk to Sonja?" Cadel demanded, gesturing wildly around the room. "Even if she *did* have a Dyna Vox, just look at this place! It's all wired up, and I don't know anything about the systems! I don't know if there's wireless medical equipment! I don't know what the security's like!" He started to tug at his hair. "Suppose they have a computerized medication schedule? Suppose someone gets into that and adjusts Sonja's dosage?"

"Cadel. Sweetie. Look over there." It was Fiona who decided to reassure him. She pointed at Sonja's bed. "That's a clipboard. With a chart on it. The people here are still using paper, Cadel; you don't have to worry so much."

"We can look after ourselves," the detective confirmed. "And we can look after Sonja. You're not responsible for our safety; that isn't your job." He put an arm around Cadel's shoulders. "You know what concerns me? That you'll get all worked up and then you'll lose it. Because you're not Superman, son. You're just a really smart kid with a lot on your plate."

"No one expects you to save the world," Fiona agreed. "You can't fix everything, no matter how brilliant you are. You shouldn't have to. I don't want you to."

I don't want me to, either, Cadel thought sourly. *Trouble is, I don't have much choice. Not now that Prosper English is back.*

"You've got to learn to trust other people," Saul remarked as if he'd read Cadel's mind. "Just let it go and get on with your visit."

"But—"

"I know Sonja isn't able to talk right now," the detective continued. "That doesn't mean you can't talk to *her*, though, does it?"

Cadel hesitated. He wondered if he was being paranoid. After all, what were the chances that Prosper had somehow bugged Sonja's room? Was it unreasonable to be so anxious? Was he thinking like a graduate of the Axis Institute instead of a normal human being?

Or was it unwise to discuss anything of importance with Sonja while she was trapped in an environment that he didn't entirely understand?

"Here." All of a sudden, Saul's arm dropped away from Cadel's shoulders. The detective fished around inside his jacket—but he didn't pull his gun out of its holster. Instead he produced a small ring-bound notebook and a ballpoint pen. "If it makes you feel better, you can write things down," he said. "And if you're *really* worried, you can write things down in code. Either way, you'll still be talking to Sonja. And no one can possibly overhear you." As Cadel mutely accepted the notebook, his foster father offered him one more piece of advice along with it. "You're both smart kids, and you've got half an hour left before the ward closes. Why don't you make the most of it while you can? By the time I get back, I bet you won't even need a Dyna Vox anymore. You'll be jabbering away with the TV remote or something."

"With the *what?*" said Cadel. But it was too late. Saul had already spun around, and was disappearing into the corridor.

"Listen, sweetie." Fiona waited until her husband was out of earshot before speaking. "If you don't want to stay, you don't have to," she said. "You're tired. You've had a big day. Just give me the word, and I'll take you home. Sonja won't mind, I'm sure."

Cadel, however, wasn't listening. He was staring across the room at the TV remote.

The TV remote.

There were a lot of things you could do with an infrared remote control . . .

TWELVE

Thi Thuoy lived in a two-story townhouse made of brick. The next morning, when Saul and Cadel arrived there, they noticed several cars parked out front. One of these cars belonged to Hamish Primrose. Another was Gazo's little blue bomb.

Thi answered the door in person. He had dimples, a nose stud, and a big, white, dazzling smile. Over a pair of almost threadbare jeans he wore a Massachusetts Institute of Technology sweatshirt.

Cadel recognized him instantly from the K17 computer labs.

"Hi," said Thi. Though his expression was quizzical, he didn't comment on Cadel's ski gloves, flippers, or padded anorak, having already been warned about them during various phone conversations with Richard Buckland. "Come on in."

"Are you Mr. Thuoy?" Saul inquired from beneath the black Islamic chador that he'd draped over his head. He was dressed from head to toe in a traditional Arabic woman's outfit, which had been a gift to Fiona. Because it was a bit too short, the cuffs of his trousers were clearly visible beneath the hem.

"Call me T," said Thi, his grin widening. "I guess you must be—"

"Detective Inspector Saul Greeniaus. And this is Cadel."

"From the labs," Thi confirmed in a satisfied tone. He was eyeing Cadel. "I *thought* you might be the one that Richard was talking about."

"Is Richard here?" asked Saul as Thi stepped back to admit him.

"Sure is." Thi waved his two guests over the threshold. "Second door on the right. He came with Boyd—you know Boyd?"

Cadel shook his head. The front entrance of Thi's house opened directly into a narrow corridor, which dodged a carpeted staircase and passed several rooms on its way to a big open-plan living area. Cadel caught a glimpse of glossy floorboards, bright paint, and colorful bookshelves some distance ahead, before the detective suddenly stopped short in front of him, blocking his view.

They had reached the second door on the right.

It was Hamish who had once informed Cadel that Thi Thuoy was rich. "You know that guy with the nose stud and the fancy haircut? Well, his dad owns one of those hardware chains," Hamish had said, his expression a mixture of jealousy and awe. "That's why he's got about five computers, and his own house in Leichhardt." Thi certainly wasn't living like most of his classmates; though he was a final-year student with part-time tutoring work, there could be no doubt that he had *some* form of financial support.

This became even more glaringly obvious when Cadel peered through the second door on the right and saw about a dozen computers lining the walls of the room beyond.

"Don't worry," said Thi, who was just behind him. "It's a self-contained system. There's no connection with the outside world."

"It's a *virtual Internet*," Hamish announced from inside the computer room. He was perched on a kitchen stool next to the door. With him were Richard Buckland, Gazo Kovacs, and two other people: a lanky, raw-boned, bearded hippie sporting a rat's nest of blond dreadlocks and a tall, plump, pimply youth whose foot was encased in a plaster cast. This cast was covered in ciphers and mathematical equations, all painstakingly inscribed with a ballpoint pen. The owner of the cast wore a baseball cap over a long, greasy ponytail, as well as a T-shirt bearing the words I'VE BEEN A BAD BOYD.

Cadel realized that he *did* know Boyd—at least by sight. Boyd was a prominent member of Richard Buckland's Advanced Programming class, always spilling soft drinks and tripping over electrical cords. Boyd's high-pitched, nasal voice was as familiar as his fingerless gloves, which he never took off. Hamish had often theorized that "the big fat guy in the baseball cap" must have been born with hairy palms. "He's hiding something," Hamish had repeatedly insisted. "Maybe a really sick tattoo. Or maybe someone tried to crucify him once and the scars are still there."

Cadel didn't know exactly how Boyd had broken his leg but had a sneaking suspicion that it hadn't been done on a football field or a basketball court.

"Isn't this fantastic?" Hamish went on. "I wish *I* had a virtual Internet to play with."

"It has air-gap security," Thi offered, just as the doorbell rang. "Ah," he said. "That must be Vijay." And he went off to admit yet another member of Richard's wardriving team.

"It's a closed circle, this system," Hamish finished. "There isn't any way in unless you're sitting right here. So it's safer than it looks." With a sigh he added, "I wish *I* was rich."

"You *are* bloody rich!" yelped the hippie. "You've got your own car, haven't you?"

"So have you," Hamish retorted.

"Yeah, but I *stole* mine," the hippie pointed out, before erupting into an abrasive cackle.

Cadel decided: *You must be Duke.* He had heard about Duke.

"This is Duke," said Hamish, by way of confirmation. "He b-b-brought a car with him."

"Which he stole," Saul concluded, sourly eyeing the dreadlocks. He had already ripped off his veil, exposing his sweaty, rumpled hair and grim expression.

Duke's answering grin revealed that he had lost at least one tooth.

"Only from my dad," he said. "And it was never reported."

"He's joking," Hamish assured the detective, who sighed. Cadel knew that Duke didn't have a police record. Upon hearing that Hamish intended to bring one of his computer-gaming buddies along on Richard's wardriving exercise, Saul had immediately run a check on Duke, but had discovered nothing sinister about him. Duke was twenty-six years old.

He worked in a warehouse, lived with his two elder brothers, and was trying to pay off several overdue parking fines. According to Hamish, Duke was such a video-game addict that he'd been thrown out by three successive girlfriends—though Cadel doubted very much that this was true. It was hard to believe that *any* girl would be interested in such a scruffy, hollow-chested, rootless obsessive.

Hamish was full of stories about Duke, who had once stayed up for fifty-three hours straight, consuming liters of coffee and cola, as he struggled to defeat an American opponent. Duke often peed into a bottle, rather than getting up from his keyboard. He was known to have lost six jobs because of his all-night, online gaming habit. Cadel felt sure that if any girl had ever let Duke into her home, she would have done so out of pity and would have made him sleep on the living room floor.

"What's with the flippers?" asked Boyd. He was gaping at Cadel, who had already removed four layers of woolen beanie, after spitting out a mouthful of cotton gauze. "No one said anything about going for a swim."

"They're a security measure," Saul explained. "Those flippers affect the way Cadel walks."

"We discussed this, Boyd," Richard gently interposed. "It's all about video analytics, remember?"

"Oh. Yeah. Right," said Boyd.

And Duke said, "Man, you guys look like *total freaks!*"

Cadel bit back the obvious retort—which was that Duke looked like a bigger freak than anyone, with his musty dreadlocks and missing tooth. There was no point taking issue with a person who obviously didn't know enough to go to the dentist occasionally.

Peeling off a flipper, Cadel resolved to stay calm and focused, no matter what.

"So which one are you?" Duke went on, studying Saul with an almost manic curiosity. "Are you the cop, or the stink-bomb guy, or what?"

"He's the cop," said Hamish, causing Duke to raise his hands in an attitude of mock surrender, crying, "It's all right, officer! I'll be good!

I've never had one single speeding ticket in my whole life—you ask anyone!"

"Don't worry about Duke," Hamish declared. "I'll keep an eye on him."

"No you won't." Saul folded his arms and was about to elaborate when Thi reappeared on the threshold, escorting three newcomers. Cadel knew the smallest of them, whose name was Egon and who invariably sat in the front row of Richard's Advanced Programming lectures. Egon had a conspicuously large, beaky nose under an eye-catching crop of fuzzy black curls. He always dressed in the same baggy, stained sweatshirt that hung halfway to his knees; from the rolled-up sleeves of this sweatshirt, his thin and brittle wrists protruded like a pair of ivory chopsticks attached to a couple of disproportionately large hands. But the most noticeable thing about Egon was his grouchy expression. It never changed. He looked permanently dissatisfied, and resentful, and put-upon.

If he was pleased about his invitation to Thi's house, it certainly didn't show. He was wearing a discontented scowl, as usual.

"Okay, everyone—this is Egon," said Thi. "And this is Vijay, and this is Vijay's dad . . . uh . . . Mr. Naidoo."

"I will be providing a car, and also my services as a driver," Mr. Naidoo advised the gathering. He was a solid, balding, middle-aged man in a suit and tie. "Good morning, Mr. Buckland. We met once before, I think."

"Yes," Richard confirmed, leaning over to shake hands. "Thanks very much for coming. We need all the help we can get."

"No problem," Mr. Naidoo said expansively. His son remained silent and poker-faced; unlike the other teenagers in the room, Vijay had donned a neatly pressed shirt, a blue blazer, and dark trousers with a crease ironed into the front of each leg. His hair was beautifully cut, and he had remarkably clear skin. Yet somehow he wasn't memorable. Cadel couldn't recall having seen him in Richard's class.

"All right." Saul abruptly called the meeting to order, glancing around the overcrowded room with quiet authority. "Is everyone here now? Where's your girlfriend, Mr. Thuoy? I thought she was going to help out?"

"She is," Thi assured him. "She had to go to the library, but she'll be back soon."

"In that case, if anyone wants to relieve themselves, you should go now," the detective advised. "Because once this thing gets started, there won't be any rest stops. You'll have to wait till we're through."

"Bathroom's next door," Thi added, at which point Gazo began to make a slightly sheepish exit, muttering apologies as he sidled past various clumps of people. As soon as he'd disappeared, Egon said, in tones of caustic disapproval, "Who the hell was that? Haven't I seen him *mowing grass* somewhere?"

Cadel couldn't help bristling, but it was Saul who answered. After regarding Egon for a moment, the detective said, "That's Gazo. He has high-level security clearance, and he's going to be one of our drivers."

Egon sniffed. "And who might you be?" he asked, with the air of someone determined to be unimpressed no matter what Saul decided to say. "Are you the copper Richard was talking about?"

"That's right. My name is Detective Inspector Saul Greeniaus, and I've been helping to coordinate this exercise with Mr. Buckland, here."

Mr. Naidoo cleared his throat. "Essentially, however, this *is* a university project, is it not?" he said quickly, seeking reassurance from Richard. "It's an extracurricular assignment option delivering additional course credits. Am I right, Mr. Buckland?"

"More or less," Richard agreed. "But we'll be helping the police, as well."

"Does that mean you'll forget all about my parking fines?" Duke joked, energetically scratching his scalp as he addressed Saul. "Since I'm not getting marked on this, I deserve *some* kinda payback."

"Traffic violations aren't my job, Mr. Moloney," the detective rejoined. He was about to continue when keys jingled, hinges creaked, and a screen door banged shut somewhere nearby. Cadel heard footsteps, then a melodious female voice.

"Thi? Are you home?"

"In here!" Thi called, before announcing to the rest of the group, "Snezana's back."

Snezana's appearance caused a sudden hush. Jaws dropped in perfect unison as she paused on the threshold of Thi's computer room, because she was tall and willowy, with enormous gray eyes and long, dark hair that fell to her waist. With her lush lips, fine skin, exotic jewelry, stylish clothes, and high-heeled boots, she could have been a fashion model. Even Mr. Naidoo looked slightly dazed at the sight of her.

Saul raised his eyebrow a fraction.

"Sorry I'm late." Snezana sounded genuinely apologetic. "There was roadwork."

"We haven't even got started," said Thi.

Then Duke butted in. "Are you *really* Thi's girlfriend?" he demanded, goggling at Snezana. "Or did he hire you for the day?"

Boyd snickered. Egon rolled his eyes. Saul said sharply, "Ms. Zivanovic is studying costume design, and has very kindly offered to help us with certain security measures we have to take." Before anyone could question him about these security measures, he turned to Hamish. "For instance, you'll need some extra padding in various places. And so will Gazo."

"Me?" Hamish was dismayed. "Why me?"

"Because you and Cadel are known associates," the detective replied. "I shouldn't have to tell you this, Hamish."

"But I'm not even using my own car!" Hamish protested. "I'll be in Duke's dad's car!"

"No you won't." Saul raised his voice to harangue the entire group. Despite (or because of) his flowing black garments, he cut a very imposing figure. "That's the first thing I wanted to say, before handing these proceedings over to Richard Buckland," he continued. "Mr. Buckland will be in charge of the technical side, but I'll be managing the security of this operation. And if anyone's got a problem with the rules that I'm about to lay down . . . well, let's just say they're nonnegotiable."

"I still don't see why we have to wear idiot disguises," Hamish complained. (Clearly the detective's warning had fallen on deaf ears.) "Why not just sit in the back of a van or something? No one would see us then."

"Unless you had to get out!" Saul bluntly swatted this suggestion aside. "Besides, I've been told that you'll do a better job of tracking signals if you can pinpoint locations visually, as well."

He paused for a moment as Gazo slunk back into the room. Had Snezana not been present, Gazo's return might have occasioned nothing more than a few careless glances. But when Gazo saw Snezana, he flushed, hesitated, then made a rapid withdrawal. Within seconds he was gone.

After a moment, the front door slammed.

"*Gazo?*" Saul yelled after him. Everyone else stared in amazement.

"Where's *he* off to?" Egon finally growled.

Nobody answered. Thi turned to Saul.

"Shall I go and see what's wrong?" he asked.

Again there was no reply. The detective's startled gaze flickered toward his foster son, who suddenly realized what had happened. Snezana must have been too big a shock for Gazo to absorb. He must have ducked outside, just in case he lost control of himself.

He had been trying to protect them all from his unfortunate stress response.

"Just leave him alone," said Cadel. "He'll be fine."

"Are you sure?" Snezana's tone was mildly concerned. "If he's feeling sick, he's welcome to lie down upstairs."

"No." Cadel was adamant. "Gazo has these funny spells. We can always brief him when . . . um . . . when he's a bit calmer."

"Oh! Right." Hamish wasn't stupid; as the penny dropped, he began to smirk. And something about this smirk enlightened Saul. With a start, the detective finally grasped what was going on.

"Oh. Ah. I see." He cleared his throat. "Well . . . as I was saying, it's vital that we take certain precautions. For example, some of us will have to change our appearance slightly, just in case we're being monitored." Anticipating the protest that was almost certainly forming on Egon's tongue (to judge from his outraged expression), Saul added, "This of course applies *only* to people who've had extended dealings with Cadel in the past. People like Hamish and Gazo—"

"And me?" Thi interjected. "We've talked in the labs once or twice."

"No." Saul shook his head. "Passing acquaintances don't count. They wouldn't be subject to the kind of surveillance that we're trying to dodge." He took a deep breath. "Which brings me to my next point. I don't know some of the people in this room, and that's a security risk. So every one of you will be teaming up with a stranger. That way, if anybody feels like deviating from the official plan, it's gonna be reported." Studying the array of astonished and confused faces in front of him, he finished with a firm, "I hope you can all see the sense in this arrangement."

Hamish immediately stuck his hand in the air. "Dibs I get a lift with Snezana!" he said, eliciting a giggle from Boyd, a groan from Duke, and a grimace from Egon. Mr. Naidoo, however, ignored Hamish completely, addressing Saul with an air of concern.

"Excuse me," the troubled parent remarked, "but will I not be permitted to drive my own son?"

"No." Saul didn't beat around the bush. "I'm sorry. I'm sure Ms. Zivanovic will be happy to drive Vijay, though. And I'm sure your son will be happy to let Ms. Zivanovic do the driving."

Glancing at Vijay, Cadel decided that "happy" wasn't really the right word. Vijay looked stunned and just a little lost; when Snezana smiled at him, his gaze fell. He stood rooted to the spot, staring at his feet, while Duke heaved a noisy sigh.

"Man," said Duke, "that is *so* unfair."

"Duke, you'll be driving Thi," Saul went on.

"But—"

"Hamish, you'll be going with Mr. Naidoo. And I *don't* want to hear that you've been messing around." Ignoring Hamish's pout, Saul appealed to Richard Buckland for input. "Do you have any preferences?" the detective wanted to know, glancing from Boyd to Egon. "This one or that one?"

"Oh . . . whatever you think," Richard replied. He seemed reluctant to express any kind of preference when it came to his own students.

Saul grunted.

"All right. Then you can take that one," he decided, jerking his chin at Boyd, "and this one over here can come with me."

He was referring not to Cadel but to Egon. Cadel blinked. Egon muttered, "Terrific," but not as if he really meant it.

Seeing Cadel frown, Saul did his best to explain.

"You'll be with Gazo because he knows you," the detective pointed out. "I'd be worried about his stress levels if he went with a stranger. And he can defend you better than I can, when all's said and done." As Cadel absorbed this oblique reference to Gazo's peculiar problem, Saul proceeded. "He won't be driving his own car. I'll put you both in Thi's, for extra protection."

"Has it got GPS?" asked Cadel. "Because we can't use it if it does."

"I only wish it did," Thi said ruefully, just as Cadel became aware of a general shift in the atmosphere. Boyd and Egon and Vijay all exchanged glances. Then Egon said, "What do you mean, we can't use GPS? How are we going to do this without GPS?"

"We'll have to do it the old-fashioned way," said Richard, coming to Saul's rescue. "With a street directory."

"But why?" Obviously Egon wasn't about to take no for an answer. So Cadel stepped in.

"Because the person we're looking for could hack into anything," he explained. "That's why we can't use our phones, either."

"What?" cried Duke. Even Snezana gawked at Cadel in disbelief. And Egon spluttered, "For god's sake!"

"No phones." Saul was firm. "They can be tracked."

"But I'm a stranger. You just said so," Snezana protested. "Why should anyone be tracking *my* phone if we've never even met before?"

"It's a long shot," Saul had to concede. "But we can't be too careful. *No phones.*"

"This is ridiculous," Egon complained. And the detective smiled a mirthless smile.

"You're just lucky you're not wearing a false nose," he retorted. Then his gaze swept the entire group as he declared that Richard Buckland would now brief everyone on the proposed scanning grid. "Each driver will have an individual route to cover in a specific time frame," Saul announced. "It's important that you don't deviate from your routes, so listen carefully. Once Mr. Buckland is finished, Ms. Zivanovic will be attending to Hamish and Cadel and . . ." He hesitated for a split second before glancing at Hamish. "Will you go and fetch Gazo please? He'll need to hear this."

"Sure," said Hamish, sliding off his stool.

"We should try to be on the road by two and back here by four," Saul added. "If there's any kind of problem, don't call me. I'll hear about it at the debrief. And if you pass each other at an intersection—which is bound to happen—try not to yell or point or do anything else that might draw attention to yourselves, because this isn't a college prank. Okay? This is a *police operation*." After quelling Duke with a stony glare, he nodded at Richard. "Right. That's it from me. Now I'll hand you over to Mr. Buckland . . ."

THIRTEEN

When Cadel and Gazo finally climbed into Thi's car, they had both been transformed by Snezana's skilled hand. Gazo was wearing a fake nose, a pair of slip-on elf ears, and a set of false front teeth that lifted his top lip, distorting his mouth. Cadel had been given false eyebrows, a prosthetic chin (which kept falling off), and a silvery theatrical wig that had changed his hairline, giving him a touch of male pattern baldness around the temples.

"It's an old-man wig, and you don't look much like an old man," Snezana had admitted, upon stepping back to survey her handiwork. "The important thing is that your measurements have changed. I mean, your forehead's a lot higher, for a start."

Cadel had acquiesced to the wig, though it was no cooler than four layers of beanie and made his scalp itch. He had also agreed to pad his upper arms. But he'd refused to don a set of acrylic nails, despite the fact that they made his own nails look wider than they really were. "I'll be using a laptop," he'd pointed out, "and I want to be able to reach the keys."

Of course, he wasn't using his *own* laptop. For safety's sake, he had borrowed one from Thi, who had a couple to spare. This laptop was now linked to a wireless network antenna that Cadel had built himself, quite cheaply, with components donated by Hamish. Boyd had supplied Cadel with various sniffing and scanning programs, while Saul had slipped his foster son a cell phone.

Despite the "no phone" rule, Saul had quietly insisted that Cadel was a special case.

"No one else is taking the same kind of risk," the detective observed while loading Cadel into the back of Thi's car. "Just keep it turned off, and if there's any kind of trouble, dial Reggie. He's on standby in case you need help."

Cadel sighed. He was truly sick of taking precautions, though he knew how necessary they were. "Turning the phone off won't help much," he said. "A roving bug could easily turn it back on." But he promised to remove the phone's battery and to keep his head down whenever Gazo hit a red light or passed a speed camera.

Not that there would be many speed cameras in the back streets of suburban Dulwich Hill.

As Gazo pulled away from the curb, Cadel tried to tell himself that things were looking up. Sonja's condition was steadily improving. The wardriving team also seemed surprisingly competent—though Duke was, without doubt, a weak link in the chain. (Cadel was convinced that Duke would get lost, or stop for a smoke, or run into a tree.) Then there were all the other leads currently being followed: the American Smart House lead, for instance. The chatroom site lead. The Raimo Zapp lead. Though Andrew Hellen still hadn't called with any contact details for Raimo, it was bound to happen soon.

All the same, Cadel couldn't help feeling depressed. His wardriving scheme was a long shot, for one thing; it was unlikely that he'd be able to identify any of the signals collected during the next few hours. What was the chance that Vee or Dot or Com would be using their former access-point IDs? Or that they'd decided to steal an old one of Sonja's, or Judith's, or Cadel's? What were the chances that anyone with any sense would be so criminally careless?

"Minimal," Cadel muttered, causing Gazo to squint up at the rearview mirror.

"Whad's thad?" said Gazo. His voice sounded funny, because of his false nose and teeth.

"Nothing." Surveying the streetscape outside, Cadel calculated that the Dulwich Hill border was approximately five minutes away. "Thanks for doing this, Gazo. It's really nice of you to bother."

Gazo shrugged. "I could be nexd on the lisd, afder Sonja," he replied. "Especially if id's Prosper we're talking aboud. Besides, I god the week off. Ain'd no big deal." After a brief pause, he added, "Anyway, I like helping people."

"It's what you've always wanted to do," Cadel acknowledged. He was busy with his range settings. "I remember you told me that."

"Yeah. I did." Gazo cleared his throat. "I told your dad an' all. I asked 'im if I could join the police."

"You *did?*" Cadel's head jerked up; this was wholly unexpected. "What did he say?"

"He said he'd make some inquiries."

"Wow."

"Problem is . . ." Gazo began, then trailed off. It was Cadel who finally broke the ensuing silence.

"You're worried about your condition?" he hazarded.

"No. *I'm* nod. I mean—well, how many girls look like thad Snezana chick, eh? Nod many." Gazo sighed as he spun the wheel. "Bud now your dad will fink I've god no self-condrol. He'll fink I'm always messing up, when id was jusd thad one girl. I swear, I ain'd been worried for months. Nod for months. And then *she* comes along."

His voice was so gloomy that Cadel began to wonder. Was this merely a case of bad timing? Or had Snezana done more than simply jeopardize Gazo's future career?

Had she left him moonstruck?

"Snezana's very nice-looking," Cadel said at last, "but there are lots of beautiful girls out there. If you were a policeman, you'd have to be sure they wouldn't *all* affect you like that—"

"They don'd," Gazo interrupted. "Id's jusd her."

"Are you sure?" Cadel wasn't. "How much time do you spend with pretty girls, anyway?" The words were barely out of his mouth when he began to regret them. Gazo, however, didn't take offense.

"Are you kidding?" he replied. "I spend 'alf me life on a universidy campus. Thad place is *crawling* wiv lookers." Suddenly his tone shifted; it became rather concerned. "Ain'd you seen 'em, Cadel? All them babes everywhere?"

"Of course." As a matter of fact, Cadel never saw many girls when he was on campus, because Computer Engineering wasn't too popular with female students. There were only four of them in his Advanced Programming class, and one was so quiet and shy, with so much hair, that he hadn't really seen her face yet.

As for all the girls studying law, and business, and medicine . . . well, he had certainly glimpsed them from time to time, on his way to and from building K17. But he hadn't really given them much thought, since most of them were quite a bit older than he was—and taller, too. If they'd noticed him at all, it was probably as a freakish little prodigy with no sense of style.

"I was ad a pardy lasd week, and id were fulla girls," Gazo continued. "Small rooms. Big crowds."

"Really?" Cadel tried not to sound as forlorn as he felt. "How did you get invited?"

"Like I said, I spend 'alf me life on campus. There's always pardies if you keep your eyes open, eh? Even when you're mowing lawns."

Cadel didn't say anything. Instead he flushed. And Gazo must have spotted this, because he hastily added, "I never seen no young kids, mind you. Maybe there's so much booze ad these gigs, people are scared of asking kids who ain'd sixdeen yed."

"Maybe."

"If I join the police, them kids won'd be askin' *me* no more," Gazo observed with a touch of satisfaction, before his mood soured again. "Thad's if I do join the police," he said mournfully. "Thad's if they'll led me in."

"I'm sure they will."

"I dunno. I really blew id back there." Braking at a set of traffic lights, Gazo glanced down at the street directory that lay open on the seat beside him. Clearly, however, he wasn't thinking about his planned route, because he suddenly remarked, "If I do join the police, I'll ged paid more. I could buy a car like this one. And maybe a house like Snezana's . . ."

"That's not her house," Cadel interposed. "That house belongs to Thi. His family's rich."

"Yeah?" Gazo's shoulders slumped. "Figures."

"We're nearly there," said Cadel, who had suddenly noticed a street sign. And Gazo grunted as Duke whizzed across the intersection in front of them.

"There's thad bloke wiv the dreadlocks," Gazo pointed out. "He'll be heading for Marrickville Road, I guess."

Let's just hope he finds it, Cadel thought, but didn't air his doubts about Duke. Instead he focused his attention on the task he'd set himself, logging every access-point ID that they encountered on their journey through Dulwich Hill. Slowly they crawled across a grid of little streets, past rows of Edwardian houses and clusters of aging apartment blocks. Now and then, a speed bump, or a siren, or an angry car horn made Cadel look up from his laptop. For the most part, however, he was too preoccupied to absorb much of the scenery, which dissolved into a kind of background blur.

Nothing untoward happened during that ninety-minute trip. Electronic data flowed in without hindrance. Thi's car purred along, untroubled by mechanical failure. Gazo reached the correct map references at the correct times, commenting briefly whenever he passed a familiar face. "There's your dad," he'd mumble, or "Whad's thad hippie doing here?" But he was careful not to disturb his preoccupied passenger, and barely spoke at all until he arrived at the designated "exit junction," just seventy-eight seconds ahead of schedule. Then he turned to Cadel and said, "I've godda head back now. Unless there's somefink else you need?"

"No." In fact, there *was* something else that Cadel needed. He would have liked a recognizable serial ID signature safely captured in his computer files. The trouble was Gazo couldn't give it to him. "That's okay. I'm finished."

"Did id work?"

Cadel shrugged. "Maybe," he answered. "I won't know until I've checked the other logs."

"Ride," said Gazo. But he waited a minute or so, until it was precisely half past three, before setting off for Thi's house.

Here Richard Buckland was already waiting, having arrived just ahead of Gazo. Soon, however, they were joined by the other wardrivers, reporting back to base. Hopes were high, initially; it was felt that the team had acquitted itself well, despite a few minor hiccups. (Duke had taken a wrong turn, Vijay had suffered a mild bout of car sickness, and Hamish's laptop battery had run out.) At first, Saul's debriefing session was just a noisy exchange of self-satisfied whoops and congratulatory backslaps. Even Duke received a few compliments for not giving up after he'd lost his way. Then an argument broke out as to who might have racked up the largest number of access points. As Boyd and Hamish and Egon squabbled over the final tally, comparing data from six different laptops, Richard pieced together a near-perfect wireless network map of Dulwich Hill, using exactly the same information.

But nothing on this map rang a bell with anyone.

Cadel didn't recognize a single ID signature. Neither did Hamish. "Nope," Hamish finally declared after an exhaustive review of the captured input. He was huddled in Thi's computer room, still wearing his disguise—which consisted of padded leg warmers, a motorbike helmet, and a down-filled ski jacket about three sizes too big for him. "I can't see a thing. Not a sniff. If our guy's in here, he could be any of this lot." Having admitted defeat, he appealed to Cadel. "Unless *you* can think of something?"

Cadel shook his head miserably.

"I knew it was a waste of time," Egon remarked from one corner. He had declined Snezana's offer of afternoon tea and had lapsed into a sulk of epic proportions. "What were the chances? Zero. It was a *dumb* idea."

"It was fun, though," said Boyd, who was peering over Hamish's shoulder. "It would be great to have a map of the *whole city*, don't you reckon?"

"No," snapped Egon. "Why?"

"Because it would tell you things."

"Like what? Exactly?"

"Like where's the b-best place to do your wardriving, Egon—sheez." Hamish rolled his eyes. "You're such a grouch."

As Richard cleared his throat, Cadel suspected that they were in for a lecture about ignoble pursuits, and how wardriving was one of them—except in very limited, fully supervised circumstances. Before Richard could speak, however, Thi suddenly appeared on the threshold with a tray of steaming coffee mugs.

"So," Thi asked, grinning cheerfully, "who won, then? Have we got a score? Who grabbed the most points?"

"Cadel, by the look of it," Hamish replied. "Mind you, I would have done a whole lot better if Vijay's dad hadn't been so bloody *slow.*"

"Shhh." Saul, who was standing directly behind Cadel, reached over to give Hamish a poke in the ribs. "I told you to behave yourself."

"He's not even here," Hamish retorted. It was true: like Duke and Gazo, Mr. Naidoo had wandered out to the kitchen, where he was helping Snezana. But Vijay had remained in the computer room; he stood propped against a rack of hard drives, looking vaguely embarrassed.

He gave an awkward smile as he accepted a cup of coffee from Thi.

"Better to be slow than fast," Richard kindly observed. "If you'd been speeding, Hamish, you might have missed something."

"Not that it would have mattered," growled Egon, "since there was nothing to find anyhow." He sniffed, then glared at Saul. "So can I use my phone yet?" he demanded. "Or is it *still* off limits?"

"You can use your phone," the detective replied evenly. At which point, all of a sudden, Cadel had an idea.

The phones. Of course. The *phones.*

He gasped.

"Wait," he said. "Hang on."

No one heard him except Thi—who threw him a puzzled, slightly apprehensive glance, as if expecting to be told that the coffee was poisoned.

"Wait," Cadel repeated more loudly. Then he swung around to address Saul. "Your phone. What if it *has* been bugged? We could use it to flush him out."

"What?"

"Your phone!" exclaimed Cadel. Excitement propelled him to his feet; as he jumped up, he became the center of attention. "If this hacker is monitoring anyone's phone, it'll be yours, right?" he said. "That's what we decided."

Saul frowned. "Yes, but—"

"That's why we agreed: no phones. Because there's a chance that they might have been compromised. Yours, especially. And his, too." Cadel jerked his thumb at Hamish, who glowered back.

"What are you talking about?" Hamish sounded defensive. "I d–didn't use my phone. You told me not to, and I didn't."

"But if you do, he might hear you. The hacker, I mean." Cadel spread his hands, appealing to the room at large. "Suppose we all go out there again and he's online? Suppose Saul rings Hamish, and says something about a wardrive and the hacker picks it up? What do you think will happen then?"

There was a brief pause. It was Boyd who finally took the plunge.

"If I was him and I was listening in?" he said at last. "I guess I'd log off."

"*Exactly.*" This was the response that Cadel had been waiting for. "And one of us might spot him doing it!"

Peering around, he was disappointed to see nothing but wry looks and creased foreheads. Even Richard didn't try to ease the tension with an encouraging remark. It was as if he'd decided not to interfere.

Thi cleared his throat.

"That's a lot of ifs, Cadel," he said gently. "*If* this guy's online and using a wireless network. *If* he's listening to the call. *If* we spot him shutting down—"

"*If* a dozen other people don't log off at the same time," Hamish interrupted.

"I know," Cadel had to concede. "It's a long shot."

"It's not even that," scoffed Egon. "It's pie in the sky. I mean, come *on*. What are the chances?"

Cadel narrowed his eyes. "Give me a minute and I'll calculate them for you," he rejoined, through clenched teeth. What was wrong with these people? Didn't they understand how *desperate* the situation was?

But of course they didn't. He reminded himself that Egon was just a volunteer, who wasn't acquainted with Sonja and who had never had any dealings with Prosper English. A long shot wouldn't appeal to Egon. He wouldn't understand the need to explore every option. He was only concerned with his course credits.

I've got to calm down, thought Cadel as Saul grasped his shoulder. Though the pressure of that grip was comforting, it also conveyed a hint of reproof. Cadel knew that Saul was telling him, wordlessly, to ease off. There was no point alienating someone who might still be persuaded to help.

"I reckon it's worth a try," Boyd suddenly piped up. When everyone turned to stare at him, he squirmed and scratched the edge of his cast. "You never know, we might get lucky," he continued in his high-pitched voice. "And it's one way of winnowing out the non-contenders."

"I guess so," said Hamish, though not as if he was fully convinced. Thi pulled a face, and Vijay checked his watch. Saul exchanged glances with Richard over the top of Cadel's head.

"Please can we give it another go?" Cadel pleaded. "Just one more sweep? We'll be finished before dinner."

Richard's answering smile showed a hint of strain. "I'm happy to keep going," he murmured, "but I can't speak for anyone else here. It's not my decision."

"I'm in," Boyd said promptly.

"Me too," offered Hamish, adding, "As long as I get Snezana this time." He waggled his eyebrows at Thi, who gave a snort.

"Okay." Despite his obvious lack of enthusiasm, Thi seemed resigned to his fate. "I'll do it."

"So will I," Vijay softly assented, "if my father agrees."

Saul directed a level gaze at Egon, who scowled ferociously. Sensing an imminent fight, Cadel decided to excuse Egon from any further involvement. The loss of one wardriver, though regrettable, would be better than a tedious, time-wasting argument. But just as Cadel opened his mouth, Snezana appeared—and all at once the whole atmosphere changed.

"Are we ready for this now?" she queried, holding up a tray of crackers and dip. "Where shall I put it? On the filing cabinet?"

"Uh . . ." Thi hesitated, glancing at Saul. The detective took a deep breath. Instead of responding, however, he just stared at Egon.

One by one, everyone else followed suit.

"Oh, all right!" Egon finally burst out. "I'll do it! I might as well, since I can't get home unless someone gives me a lift!" Seeing Snezana's wide-eyed astonishment, he flapped an enormous hand at her dip. "You can take *that* away, too!" he barked. "We won't be able to eat it, thanks to the boy genius over here!"

Snezana blinked. She fell back a step, almost treading on Gazo—who was following close behind her with a bowl of chips. As he dodged her stiletto heel, she looked around the room, seeking enlightenment.

It was Saul who came to her rescue.

"I'm sorry," he gravely announced, "but Egon's right. We'll have to cancel afternoon tea. There won't be enough time, I'm afraid." Once again he squeezed Cadel's shoulder. "Not with all the wireless mapping we still have to do . . ."

FOURTEEN

"For god's sake, back off," Gazo muttered.

It was the first time he'd spoken since leaving Thi's place, and he sounded peevish. Looking up, Cadel saw that they were heading down Canonbury Grove, right on schedule. Houses studded with gables and gingerbread fretwork cast long shadows across the peaceful little back street, which was almost empty of life. A woman was pushing a pram along a bumpy stretch of footpath. An old man was walking a very small dog.

"What is it?" asked Cadel, who hadn't said a word for the past twenty minutes. "What did I do?"

"Nuffink." Gazo was glowering into the rearview mirror. "Some bloody fool is tailgading me."

Cadel glanced at his watch. It was 4:48 p.m.: eight minutes exactly since Saul was supposed to have rung Hamish. Yet so far, there wasn't the slightest hint that someone out there had reacted to a carefully scripted message about wardriving. Most of the wireless users that Cadel had logged during his first sweep were still online. And those who weren't had vanished off the grid long before his foster father's call had been made.

Was the detective's phone not bugged after all? Had something prevented him from ringing Hamish? Or was the hacker truly out of Cadel's zone?

It was a long shot, Cadel glumly reminded himself. *There's no guarantee that our target's even* in *Dulwich Hill.*

"Id's a fifdy-kay speed limid, you moron!" Gazo growled, just as the tailgater accelerated, swerving to overtake them. Cadel glanced around in time to see a yellow Toyota Camry roar past; he saw its broken antenna, its dented door, and the BABY ON BOARD sticker plastered to its rear windshield.

He also caught a glimpse of a familiar face: heavy glasses, fat cheeks, pug nose, pudding-bowl haircut—

"Jesus!" he yelped, leaning forward to clutch at Gazo's headrest. "That's Com!"

"Huh?"

"Don't lose him! It's Com! In that car!"

The Camry was now well ahead of them and moving away at a rapid clip. Nevertheless, its license plate was still visible to Cadel, who struggled to memorize it as he fumbled for the phone that Saul had given him.

"Who's Com?" Gazo demanded. "Ain'd we looking for someone called Bev?"

"Hurry up! He's getting away!"

"Thad's because he's doing aboud a hundred," Gazo rejoined calmly. "I'm nod a copper, Cadel. If I stard knocking people down, I'll ged booked." Up ahead, the Camry squealed around a corner. "This car ain'd mine," he added. "I woulden wanna leave ids muffler on a speed bump. You should call your dad."

"I'm *trying!*" Cadel exclaimed. He was desperately stuffing the battery back into his phone. "Can you see him? Is he gone?"

"I see 'im," said Gazo, who was turning left at a sedate pace, having braked at the stop sign that Com had completely ignored. "D'you fink he reckanized you?"

Cadel didn't reply. He was too busy punching out a number on his keypad.

Please don't let Saul's phone be switched off, he thought.

"Whoever he is, he'll ged picked up for sure, driving like thad," Gazo went on. "Hang on—he's hid a red. Look. We god 'im now."

Lifting his gaze, Cadel saw that Gazo was right. A red traffic light was impeding Com's progress. The yellow Camry had stopped behind three other vehicles to let a clutch of pedestrians cross the road in front of them.

Gazo began to speed up a little.

"I can't believe it," Cadel murmured, dazed by his own good fortune. He pressed the phone to his ear. "We've flushed him out. We *must* have. Com must be the hacker!"

"Oh gawd," said Gazo as the red light ahead changed to green. Cadel, meanwhile, was listening to a recorded message: *"You have reached the voicemail of . . ."*

"Damn!" he spluttered. But he wasn't really surprised. Of *course* Saul had switched off his phone. It was what he'd agreed to do: make his call then switch off his phone. For safety's sake. "I can't get hold of Saul," Cadel announced. "I'll have to try Reggie, and he can use his police radio . . ."

Off in the distance, Com was on the move again, almost nudging the rear bumper of a slowly accelerating tow-truck. He was turning left across an intersection that was busy with signage and painted lines; from a quiet suburban avenue he had plunged headlong into a street full of shopfronts, parked cars, and loading zones.

"*Step* on it, Gazo!" Cadel could hardly contain himself. "We're losing him!"

"I'm going as fasd as I can."

The words were barely out of Gazo's mouth when the traffic light that he was approaching changed yet again, from green to orange to red. Bang-bang. Without a second's pause.

"Whad the—?"

Gazo screeched to a halt. He braked so abruptly that Cadel hit his nose on the driver's seat.

"Ow!"

"Whad's goin' on?" Gazo was flabbergasted. "Did you see thad?"

"Quick! Gazo!"

"Id's a *red lide,* Cadel!"

Trembling with frustration, Cadel dialed Reggie's number. He craned his neck as he waited for a response—but the Camry was already out of sight. Then a harsh voice cut across the ring-tone.

"Hello?"

"Reggie? It's Cadel. I can't reach Saul. You have to call him on your radio. You have to tell him that I've just seen Com."

"You've what?"

Cadel took a deep breath.

"It's the hacker," he said, trying to speak very slowly and clearly. "Tell Saul that the hacker is Compton Daniels, and he's in a yellow Toyota Camry, heading north on Marrickville Road." Cadel reeled off the plate number, hoping he'd remembered it correctly. "Have you got that?"

"I think so." Reggie's tone was utterly incurious. *"You've got a fix on some target, and you want him intercepted. Is that right?"*

"Not just any target. Tell him it's Com Daniels. In a yellow Camry—"

"Yeah, yeah. I heard. Heading north on Marrickville Road." Reggie repeated the car's license number. *"Anything else?"*

"It's urgent. You have to be quick—"

"Roger that."

There was a click, followed by the hum of the dial tone. Reggie had hung up.

Cadel felt slightly winded.

"He won'd ged far on Marrickville Road," Gazo remarked. "Id's always jammed up."

Cadel said nothing.

"Your dad's probably coming this way. He mide even see the guy himself—"

"Gazo." Cadel couldn't stand it any longer. "Why don't you take off that ridiculous nose and those stupid teeth?"

"Huh?"

"They're driving me crazy."

Gazo flashed him a reproachful look. "I'm in disguise, Cadel. You said I was under surveillance."

"Maybe. I don't know." Cadel was so distracted, he could hardly keep still. "Oh, why doesn't this *light* change?"

"Id's a long one," Gazo agreed, checking the rearview mirror. Two vehicles were already lined up behind Thi's car, and a third was rapidly approaching. Cadel glanced at his watch. Why didn't Saul ring him? Was the detective worried about the security risk involved? Or hadn't Reggie transmitted Cadel's message?

"So who's this guy we're chasing?" Gazo queried, tapping his fingers on the steering wheel. "Do I know 'im?"

"I'm not sure. He was at the Axis Institute." Cadel saw Gazo wince. "He was in my Infiltration class, but he disappeared when the Institute folded. His sister turned up at Clearview House last year. She claimed that she was looking for him, but she was really working for Prosper English. They probably *both* are now." After a moment's reflection, Cadel added gravely, "They're really smart, those two."

Gazo gave a grunt. "You fink he lives round 'ere, then?"

"I guess so. I mean, it makes sense." Cadel tried to imagine Com's hideout. Was it being shared with someone? Had Com left much behind in his mad dash to escape any wardrivers who might have locked on to his position? "He could even be living with his sister. She could have been in the back of the car, keeping her head down."

"Why?"

"Because she's a fugitive." Cadel shrugged. "Anything's possible."

"D'you fink he'll come back?"

"I doubt it. He'd be a fool if he did." Staring blankly into space, Cadel considered the implications of what he'd just discovered. "I knew it had to be someone like that," he mumbled, thinking aloud. "I knew it had to be Com or Dot or Vee. And now I know who I'm up against, I can work out what to look for. Especially if we find out where Com's been living." He narrowed his eyes. "Especially if he's had to leave any of his stuff . . ."

"Cadel." Gazo swung around. "We've god a problem, here. I don'd fink this lide is gunna change."

Cadel blinked. Emerging from his reverie, he realized that they were still idling at the same intersection, waiting for the same red light to turn green. Eight cars were now sitting behind theirs. Traffic continued to pour across the road in front of them.

"If you ask me, id's blown a fuse," Gazo observed. "Maybe we should go some uvver way."

Cadel squinted up at the glowing red dot. After an extended pause, Gazo tried again.

"Cadel? Did you hear me? I said, should we go some uvver—"

"It's been hacked," Cadel blurted out. His gaze traveled back to Gazo's puzzled face. "Someone's got into the controller box. I should have known."

"Eh?"

"Which doesn't *necessarily* mean we're being watched." Hastily Cadel scanned his surroundings for a camera, a microwave detector, or any other form of monitoring device. But no spyware was visible on any of the poles or walls that loomed overhead. "It might be part of an evacuation plan," he hazarded in a shaky voice. "Someone's probably making sure that if Com's being followed, he'll be protected by an endless stream of red lights."

"Hang on." Gazo frowned. "Didden you say thad *Com* was the hacker?"

"He couldn't be doing all this alone. There has to be somebody else online. There has to be somebody helping him." Swallowing, Cadel glanced over his shoulder. "You're right. We have to turn around. We have to go another way."

"Off we go, then," Gazo said cheerfully. And he executed a rather dangerous U-turn, nosing across the intersection before swerving back to retrace his route. As he whizzed past the vehicles still stuck in the adjoining lane, a lone car horn honked at him.

"I'll head for New Canderbury Road," he announced. "Your guy could be heading there himself."

Cadel nodded. His mind was racing and his heart was pounding; he was trying to calculate Com's likely point of origin, taking into account the Camry's size, trajectory, and maximum speed. And it was hard to concentrate when every car on the road had to be checked for another familiar face. What if Dot was out there, driving around? What if *Prosper* had been flushed from some dark and secret lair?

Cadel suddenly realized that he hadn't been logging his ID signatures. Was there any reason to continue the wardriving exercise? Might he regret it later if he didn't?

Maybe I should stick to our schedule, he decided, dragging his laptop back onto his knees. *Just in case I end up wanting the data for some reason.*

"Oh no." Gazo's impatient groan cut through Cadel's musings. "Will you look ad this? A bloody crash, and id's ride in our way."

As Cadel raised his eyes, he was conscious that the car in which he was traveling had begun to slow. It rolled to a standstill just a couple of yards from another set of traffic lights, beyond which lay a scene of pure chaos. Two other cars had collided at a four-way intersection; one of them had run straight through a red light, clipping the edge of the vehicle innocently heading across its path. The green station wagon had then spun around, leaving a black skid mark on the road. The white hatchback . . .

The white hatchback was Snezana's white hatchback. And the green station wagon belonged to Duke's father.

"Bloody hell!" cried Gazo before Cadel could do anything but gasp. "Thad's nod—is thad . . . ?"

"Oh no." Cadel shoved his laptop aside. He began to claw at his seat belt. "Oh *no.*"

"Don'd move," said Gazo, yanking off his fake nose, his fake ears, and his fake teeth. "Stay here," he ordered. "You're not allowed to get outta the car."

"There's Duke—look!" squeaked Cadel, ignoring him. Even from a distance, Duke's blond dreadlocks were unmistakable. "He's walking around! He must be all right!"

Duke, in fact, was only one of several people milling about at the site of the accident. A fat, middle-aged man with a bag of groceries was patting Duke on the shoulder. Another, much younger man was peering into the station wagon. And a woman in a blue dress was hovering over . . .

"Hamish!" Cadel cried. Freeing himself from his seat belt at last, he reached for the door handle.

"Stay there!" Gazo was already halfway out of his seat. "*Cadel!* You can't be seen like that!"

"Like what?" Cadel gaped at him. "What are you talking about?"

"The wig? The chin? The *flippers?*"

"Oh . . ."

"You look like a freak. You 'afta stay here. Your dad's gunna skin me alive if you don't." By now Gazo was standing on the road; he bent to address Cadel through the open driver's door. "Lock yourself in, eh? I'll be right back."

"Wait—"

But Gazo refused to wait. He slammed the door and bolted, heading straight for the white hatchback. Even as he did so, Snezana emerged from her damaged vehicle, moving very slowly and awkwardly in her high-heeled boots. Skirting a patch of broken glass, she staggered across to where Hamish was slumped. She had a bloodstained tissue pressed against her nose.

Cadel couldn't see what was wrong with Hamish, who was squatting on the edge of the curb, minus his motorbike helmet. *If he's sitting up,* Cadel concluded, *he can't be too bad.* It was obvious that the smash had only just taken place. There were no police at the scene. No ambulance officers were tending to the injured.

Cadel began to peel off his wig just as his phone rang.

It was Saul on the other end of the line.

"*Cadel? Where are you? I got your message.*" Saul's tone was crisp but calm. "*Tell me where you are, and I'll meet you. I don't want you wandering around out there, not with Com Daniels on the loose.*"

"There's been an accident," replied Cadel, who wasn't really listening. He had removed his wig and kicked off his flippers; now he was picking away at his fake eyebrows. "Duke crashed into Snezana."

"*WHAT?*"

"It's on New Canterbury Road. You can't miss it." Tossing aside a strip of acrylic hair, Cadel watched as Gazo approached Snezana and Hamish. Duke, by this time, was fishing around in the glove box of his station wagon. It looked as if Vijay was still sitting in the back seat. "Someone should find Mr. Naidoo," Cadel went on. "Tell him what's happened. Isn't Thi with him? Snezana's hurt. Her nose is bleeding."

"*Cadel—*"

"I think you should come," Cadel declared. "Be careful, though. Someone's been messing with the traffic lights. I think the SCATS regional computer might have been hacked." He was struck by a sudden, dazzling insight. "I wonder if that's what happened to Duke and Snezana?" he exclaimed. "I wonder if both lights turned green at once?"

It was a definite possibility. But how could both cars have been tracked? Though Hamish might have been using a bugged phone (it was certainly possible), neither Duke nor Vijay had been carrying their phones with them. All unauthorized phones had been left back at Thi's house.

Anyway, Com didn't even know who Duke and Vijay were.

"*Cadel? Listen to me.*" Saul's voice had sharpened, the way it always did when he was anxious. "*Where's Gazo? Can I talk to Gazo?*"

"He's not here."

"*What?*"

"He's gone to help." Gazo, in fact, had joined Snezana. Cadel could see them both talking earnestly to the woman in blue, though he couldn't hear what was being said. Snezana seemed to be crying. Gazo was grasping her elbow protectively.

Hamish was still sitting with his head on his knees and his arms wrapped around his stomach.

"I think I'll go and help, too," Cadel decided. "I can't just stay here in the car."

"No! Cadel—"

"I'll be careful. I promise." Though the situation had every appearance of being an ambush especially designed to lure him into the open, Cadel didn't see how another attack could be carried out—not at this particular accident site, anyway. The damaged cars were blocking every approach, so no one could possibly run him down—and he wasn't afraid of snipers, because Com and his cronies were obviously using subtler, more technology-based techniques. In fact, Cadel couldn't help wondering if he himself was the main target after all. If he had been, surely the malfunctioning traffic light would have been aimed at *him*?

At any rate, the risk wasn't big enough to keep him in the car while his friends were suffering.

"I'll see you in a minute," he told Saul. "Don't be too long. Someone needs to come here and organize things."

Disregarding Saul's tinny protests, Cadel broke the connection. He shoved the phone back into his pocket, without removing its battery first. He took off his prosthetic chin, checked his face in the mirror for bits of sticky residue, and pushed open the rear passenger door.

FIFTEEN

Hamish wasn't looking too good. Though he was able to lift his head, his face was ashen, and his glasses were cracked.

"Bloody Duke," he slurred, when he caught sight of Cadel. "B-b-bloody idiot can't drive for *nuts.*"

"We had a green light," Snezana shrilled. "Ask anyone. They'll tell you the same thing."

"Where's Vijay?" asked Cadel, who had been walking very carefully. In his bare feet, with so much glass around, he was afraid of cutting himself. "What's happened to him? Is he still in your car?"

"Vijay's all right." Snezana cast a vague glance in the direction of her hatchback. "He's just a bit upset, I think."

"You shouldn't be out here, Cadel," said Gazo. "Not wivvout your shoes."

Cadel, however, didn't even process this remark. He was too busy studying Hamish, who was breathing in short, shallow gasps. Cadel didn't like the sound of them at all.

"What about you?" he said. "Are you okay, Hamish?"

Hamish gave a grunt.

"Is it your stomach? Does it hurt?"

"It's my chest."

"Your *chest?*" echoed the woman in blue. Her appearance was messy and uncoordinated, as if she'd ducked outside in her cleaning clothes to buy some milk. "That's bad. Your chest? That's *real* bad."

"Has somebody called an ambulance?" Cadel wanted to know. He peered around for confirmation but didn't receive any. Gazo shrugged, in a hapless and hesitant kind of way.

The woman in blue sniffed. "I got no phone," she said sharply, like someone accused of harboring an illegal substance.

Snezana quavered, "You told us not to bring our phones. Remember?" And she fixed Cadel with a plaintive look, which he decided to ignore.

Hamish shook his head.

"My phone got smashed," he croaked. "It was in my pocket. I tried it already."

Cadel stared down at him, aghast.

"It got *smashed?*" he spluttered. "In your *pocket?*" He didn't even want to ask which pocket. A hip pocket might be all right, but a breast pocket . . .

That could be serious.

"Um . . ." Weakly Hamish flapped his hand. "I kind of . . . hit the gear stick."

"Oh boy," said Gazo. Cadel straightened. He was about to suggest that someone call an ambulance right away when a voice behind him bleated, "*My* phone's working. We can use my phone."

It was Duke. Though clearly shell-shocked, he seemed otherwise unaffected by the collision; he wasn't clutching his nose, or his chest, or any other part of his anatomy. He hadn't even suffered a cracked lip or a torn T-shirt. And his grip was steady as he thrust his phone at Cadel—who gaped at him in astonishment.

"*Your* phone?" said Cadel. "What do you mean, *your* phone?"

"Oh, for god's sake." Hamish wheezed. "You scumbag, Duke . . ."

"What?" Duke looked genuinely taken aback—confused that his offer had been so harshly rejected. "I didn't do nothing. I had the right of way," he said, then leveled an accusatory finger at Snezana. "*She's* the one who ran a red light!"

"*I did not!*" she yipped. "*You* did!"

"In your dreams, hot stuff."

"Nobody ran a red light!" Cadel insisted. "It was a malfunction. I think the traffic system was hacked."

"Malfunction my ass," growled Duke.

At which point Hamish made a strained, squeaky, despairing noise. "Shut up, you turkey!" he groaned. "This is all your fault!"

"Eh?" said Duke. By now, he wasn't the only one looking lost. Snezana and Gazo were both exchanging perplexed glances. As for the woman in blue, she'd already given up and had wandered off to find out how Vijay was feeling.

"Why would it be my fault?" Duke demanded, glaring at Hamish. "Your mate just *said* it was a malfunction—"

"They could have *tracked your phone,* dickhead!" Hamish snapped, before he suddenly succumbed to a violent coughing fit. Cadel was the one who had to step in and explain.

"You should have left your phone back at Thi's house," he reminded Duke. "We discussed this, remember? No phones."

"But it was turned off."

"That doesn't make any difference. Not unless you take the battery out." Even so, Cadel wasn't quite sure how the trace on Duke's green station wagon could have been accomplished—if, indeed, it had been accomplished at all. Hamish would have been an obvious target, because he happened to be Cadel's longtime friend. What's more, Hamish had left his phone on (as instructed) to receive the call from Saul Greeniaus. If Com or some other hacker had infiltrated Saul's phone, then the same thing might very well have happened to the phone that Hamish had been using.

But Duke's phone was different. Com didn't know Duke. Cadel didn't know Duke. Could Duke's appearance at the scene have been pure bad luck? Or had he done something amazingly stupid with his phone?

"You didn't try to call Hamish, did you?" Cadel asked him. It was Hamish, however, who replied.

"He didn't have to," said Hamish in a strangled voice. "We b–both signed up for a social mapping service." Seeing Cadel's jaw drop, he breathlessly tried to defend himself. "It wasn't my idea . . . it was a group thing . . . all the other guys wanted to do it . . ."

"Are you off your *head?*" Cadel exclaimed. He couldn't believe his ears. Why would an intelligent hacker like Hamish even consider using a phone mapping service? Especially one that allowed any number of registered friends to pinpoint the exact location of his cell. "You might as well turn on a webcam! Or stick a microchip in your ear!"

"Sorry," Hamish muttered.

"And you didn't think it was important to *mention* this?" Cadel was so appalled, so thunderstruck, that he forgot all about his friend's injuries. "What's the matter with you? Are you brain-dead?"

"I forgot."

"You *forgot?*"

"We signed up ages ago. After we started playing that game . . ."

"Jesus, Hamish!"

"It wouldn't have been a problem, except that Duke had to bring his goddamn phone with him!" Hamish pointed out. Then he began to cough again.

"Cadel—mate—calm down," Gazo remonstrated. "The poor bloke's not well."

"I didn't even know he was linked up!" Cadel cried. He was shaking like a paint mixer. "Anyone locked on to his phone would have been able to hack into the mapping service and get a trace on Duke as well! No *wonder* they collided! It probably wasn't an accident at all!"

"Uh . . . guys?" whispered Hamish. And something about his tone caught the attention of the whole group.

He was staring dazedly at his cupped palm, which was smeared with pale streaks of blood. When he raised his eyes again, they were wide and frightened.

"I just—I . . ."

He couldn't finish.

"Did you cough that up?" Snezana sounded almost as scared as Hamish looked. His nod threw her into a panic. She immediately grabbed Duke's phone, stammering something about going to the hospital. But even as she keyed in the emergency number, a high-pitched *woo-oo* heralded the arrival of a police car.

At the very same instant, Cadel spotted Saul's Corolla approaching from the opposite direction. It came to a sudden halt not far from the hatchback's mangled bumper. Then the driver's door popped open and Saul sprang out, still dressed in Arabic clothes.

Cadel began to pick his way across an uneven stretch of asphalt, doggedly making a beeline for the detective. Saul, however, wasn't in a time-wasting mood. Cadel had barely taken three steps before he found himself toe to toe with his foster father, who had removed his chador.

"Get in the car! Right now!" Saul barked.

"Hamish needs an ambulance." Cadel had just one thing on his mind, and Saul's wishes were of secondary importance. "Is there some way you can get an ambulance? Really quickly?"

But the detective didn't seem to hear. His gaze had dropped to Cadel's bare feet.

"For Chris'sake, Cadel!" he exclaimed. "What happened to your shoes?"

"I wasn't wearing shoes. I had flippers. Remember?"

"You'll cut yourself."

"Hamish needs an ambulance." Cadel refused to be sidetracked, dismissing Saul's fears with an irritable wave. "He's coughing up blood. We've got to do something."

"There's an ambulance on its way here right now."

"Really?"

Saul grunted. He had begun to inspect the scene before him with a kind of measured detachment; his eyes traveled smoothly from one piece of evidence to the next: from the black skid mark to the broken glass to the hatchback's buckled grille. At last he fixed his attention on Hamish, and Cadel heaved a sigh of relief.

Saul would take care of things. He was a police officer. He would know what to do.

"I haven't talked to Vijay," Cadel admitted, struggling to keep his voice steady. "I don't know how *he* is."

"It's all right. Just get in the car."

"This whole thing was a setup. Somebody made them crash. Somebody's hacking the controller boxes—"

"Cadel." Saul spoke firmly but gently. "You can tell me later. Just get in the car, okay? And watch those feet."

Cadel didn't argue. As instructed, he watched his feet intently all the way to the Corolla, not even pausing to glance back at Hamish. In fact, he was so focused on where he was treading that he nearly ran headfirst into Egon, who was draped against the Corolla's front passenger door sullenly watching Saul take charge.

"Hey!" said Egon, fending off Cadel with one arm. "Look where you're going!"

"Oh!" Cadel's chin jerked up. "Sorry."

"I can't believe this. No—actually, I *can* believe this. What I can't believe is that I ever agreed to do it." As Cadel crawled into the back seat of the detective's borrowed car, Egon continued his spiteful monologue. "So who was the idiot driver, then? The bimbo or the Rasta? Wait. Don't tell me. It was the Rasta. Oh dear, and now the bimbo's nose job is ruined."

Cadel didn't bother to reply. He leaned his forehead against a headrest, closing his eyes and swallowing hard. All at once he felt queasy.

"Maybe she can wear that fake nose she gave your friend," Egon continued. "Or get a nose transplant from some supermodel organ donor. Hello—here's Richard. Come to think of it, this street's on his route, isn't it? I bet he's wishing he never got involved in this. I always said it was a stupid idea . . . Lucky for him that copper's responsible . . ."

First Sonja, now Hamish. First Sonja, now Hamish. The words kept banging around inside Cadel's skull like birds caught in a greenhouse. He was very, very frightened. Coughing up blood was bad. He knew that.

It could mean . . . what? A ruptured lung? A broken rib? Hamish was an only child. His parents would be furious. They would blame Saul, and Richard, and Cadel most of all—exactly the way Judith did. You could understand why, too. Cadel was beginning to feel like a radioactive isotope: his proximity was becoming dangerous to people's health. Whatever he did, he left a trail of blood in his wake. *First Sonja, now Hamish. First Sonja, now Hamish.*

Prosper's team of sociopathic geeks seemed to be picking off Cadel's friends one by one.

". . . I said I'd be home by five thirty. At this rate, I'll be lucky if I make dinner," Egon was muttering, apparently unconcerned as to whether anybody happened to be listening or not. "I wonder if Richard will give me a lift back? I mean, I'm in his class. He has a duty. And I don't even *know* most of these people; it's not as if they're going to mind if I'm here or not . . ."

You can say that again, thought Cadel. But he didn't speak, because he felt so nauseous that he was afraid to open his mouth.

He was also afraid to open his eyes, in case he saw something that he wouldn't be able to forget afterward. Like Sonja's fractured leg, for instance. Or the blood in Hamish's cupped palm.

"Oh, great—and here's Boyd," Egon complained. "He's on crutches and I *still* can't get away from him. For god's sake, you big lummox, can't you see there's nothing happening over here? Why don't you go and pick on someone else?"

The howl of a distant siren caused Cadel to raise his head; he saw that Boyd was approaching the Corolla, having apparently extracted himself from the front seat of Richard Buckland's car. Richard had parked at a safe distance from the scene of the accident, well clear of any emergency-vehicle access routes. He had then set off toward the group of people clustered around Hamish, which by now included Saul, Vijay, and a uniformed police officer. Perhaps Boyd found the police uniform off-putting. Or perhaps he didn't feel safe negotiating his way across an obstacle course full of broken glass and potholes on a pair of crutches.

Whatever the reason, he had obviously decided to favor Egon with his company, despite Egon's hostile scowl.

"So what's up?" said Boyd when he was still a good ten paces away from the Corolla. "Did you see it? What happened?"

"What does it look like?" Egon snapped. "The Rasta collided with the bimbo."

"Yeah? Wow. That's no good." Boyd peered around. "Where's Thi?"

Egon didn't answer. Possibly he had decided that the question was too stupid to merit a reply. Boyd therefore addressed Cadel through an open rear passenger door.

"So did you flush anyone out?" asked Boyd. "Because I didn't."

Cadel nodded. For the first time since reaching the accident site, his thoughts turned to Com—and he couldn't help wondering (in a fleeting and distracted kind of way) whether anyone had actually caught up with the fugitive.

"You *did?*" said Boyd. "Really? Cool." When Cadel failed to elaborate, Boyd gave him a verbal prod. "So did you actually manage to identify a particular house or . . . ?"

"No." Seeing Boyd's face fall, Cadel added, "I saw his car. Not his house."

"Because it's not as if this concept actually *worked*," Egon interposed snidely. "I mean, it's not like someone picked up the guy's signal or anything. It was all an accident. An accidental sighting."

"It was *not* an accident." Cadel spoke through clenched teeth. "Our target was flushed out because of the phone call. When Saul mentioned wardriving, Com got so scared that he bolted. And I happened to spot him doing it."

Egon sniffed. "Pity you let him get away, then."

"He hasn't got away! Not yet." Unsure of how much Egon actually knew, Cadel decided to fill him in, reciting Com's license number and describing the fugitive's car. "Every police officer in Sydney will be looking out for a yellow Camry with a broken antenna and a Baby on Board sticker—"

"Yeah, but he won't be keeping *that* car, will he?" Egon interrupted. "Your hacker will have dumped it by now, if he's got any sense. Which he obviously does."

"Hey," said Boyd. Egon, however, wouldn't let him finish.

"You should have had roadblocks set up. Or at least a few extra coppers around. I mean, what did you expect? That your guy would sit tight and wait for you to come charging through the door?"

"*Hey!*" Boyd repeated. "I *saw* that car." As Cadel and Egon both turned to stare at him, he gave a nervous titter. "Yellow Camry? I saw it parked down near the river a little while ago." He jerked his thumb. "It was parked in someone's driveway."

A brief, stunned silence greeted this announcement. Cadel had to lick his dry lips before he could request further details.

"Are—are you sure?" he squeaked.

"Oh yeah." Boyd's tone was sublimely confident. "I saw the license plate and everything. It's the same one."

But Egon wasn't convinced. "Maybe you *think* that's what you saw," he said. "Maybe your memory's playing tricks on you. I mean, what was so special about this car that you ended up noticing its license plate?"

"I always notice license plates," was Boyd's response. "I collect them." Seeing Egon's raised eyebrows, Boyd quickly added, "In my head, not in real life. I collect them in my head." A pause. "Don't you?"

"I've got more important things in my head," Egon said with a sneer.

Cadel, however, wasn't quite so dismissive. He knew that Sonja nursed a weakness for plate numbers. "You play games with them? Is that it?" he asked.

Boyd nodded.

"I can't help it," he confessed with a giggle, "especially since I like cars, too—"

"And when did you see the yellow one?" Cadel cut him off. "How long ago? Five minutes? Ten?"

"Oh no. I saw it when we first started." Boyd had to shift his weight from one crutch to the other before he could glance at his watch. "Maybe . . . I dunno . . . twenty minutes ago? Twenty-five?"

"And you can remember where it was? Which driveway it was parked in?"

"Oh yeah."

"Then you'd better tell Saul," Cadel advised as he slid out of the Corolla. "Because he'll want to get over there right away."

SIXTEEN

Cadel was sitting in the back of a van. He had been sitting there for nearly three hours.

With him were Reggie Bristow and Angus McNair. Cadel wasn't sure exactly where the van was parked, because the only window in sight gave him a restricted view of the driver's cabin, through a screen of steel mesh. All he knew was that they had stopped somewhere in the vicinity of Com's house and that it was already dark outside.

The van had been Saul's idea. He had decided that his foster son should disappear while Com's abandoned residence was being searched, and a van had seemed like the easiest way of shielding Cadel from prying eyes or intrusive cameras. "You can't be seen on the street," Saul had declared. "It's too dangerous." But even he had admitted that Cadel couldn't be sent straight home—not before being given the chance to inspect whatever computer equipment Com might have left behind.

So Cadel had been forced to wait. He had waited while the police established that Com's house was unoccupied and unsecured. He had then waited for the bomb squad to determine whether it was booby-trapped. And he had waited for Saul to check the place out himself, "just to be sure."

After spending so long in such a cramped and dingy box, pissing into an old paint can and staring at Reggie's shoes, Cadel was beginning to feel seriously claustrophobic. He was also suffering from a delayed reaction to the traumatic events of the day—or at least that was *his* diagnosis. Why else would he keep breaking into a sweat while his head swam and his heart fluttered? Surely these passing fits couldn't be the result of a missed meal or lack of oxygen?

I can't stand it, he thought. *First Sonja, now Hamish. I just can't stand it. That's all.*

"You hungry?" Reggie asked. He checked his watch. "Maybe someone should go and get some fish and chips. It must be way past your dinnertime."

"It is," Cadel admitted faintly. "But I don't feel like much."

"You should still eat." Reggie turned to Angus. "You got anything on you? Like a chocolate bar or chewing gum?"

"Nope," said Angus, whose eyes were glazed with boredom. Both officers had been instructed not to read or listen to music while they were on duty. They weren't allowed to make any phone calls unless they were faced with an emergency of some kind. So Cadel had been unable to find out how Hamish was faring.

After being loaded into an ambulance, Hamish had been whisked away to the hospital, with Richard Buckland following close behind. Vijay had also gone to the hospital; his father had decided to take him to the nearest emergency room, even though none of the ambulance officers had considered him to be at risk. Gazo Kovacs had generously offered to drive Boyd and Egon back home, while Snezana had abandoned her car upon being reunited with Thi, who had bundled her off in a taxi.

By the time a van had arrived for Cadel, the only wardriver left at the scene of the crash had been Duke. Untroubled by the fact that his phone had been confiscated (perhaps because he had been putting off the dreaded moment when he would have to call his father for insurance details), Duke had been hovering helplessly on the sidelines. Cadel was convinced that Duke had probably slipped away within minutes of Cadel's own departure. It was hard to imagine someone as feckless as Duke sticking around to organize tow-trucks or help the police with their inquiries. It was even harder to picture him visiting Hamish in the hospital.

Cadel wondered if Hamish *was* still in the hospital.

"Who's that?" said Angus. He raised his head as the sound of an approaching vehicle reached his ears.

Reggie did the same.

Then the engine's purr abruptly stopped. Somewhere outside, a door slammed. Reggie leaned over to address their driver, directing his question through the small window behind the security screen.

"Are we okay?" he rasped.

"I think so," came the reply—followed (after a brief pause) by further clarification. "Yeah, we're good. It's just the DI back again."

Knock-knock-knock! Knock-knock! A sudden rapping on the van's rear end made everyone start. Reggie automatically thrust his hand inside his jacket, but Cadel had already identified the rhythm of the knock.

It was the agreed signal: the all clear. And it was accompanied by Saul's muffled voice. *"It's Saul! Open up!"*

Angus obeyed, though not before producing his weapon. Saul seemed pleased to see it. When he yanked open the double doors and found himself staring down the barrel of Angus's gun, he signified his approval with a nod.

Cadel was the only one who flinched. He didn't like guns—especially when they were aimed at Saul.

"We're good to go," the detective quietly announced. Then he sprang up into the van's rear compartment, pulling its doors shut behind him.

He was moving more nimbly now that he had discarded his Arabic robes.

"Tell Lou we'll head straight for number ten," he instructed. "She can park in the garage, tell her."

Reggie sighed. But he tapped on the communication window and transmitted this message while a space was made for Saul. The detective squeezed in beside Cadel, his long legs folding up like the mechanism on a sofa bed. It had been more than an hour since Cadel's last glimpse of him.

"There's a lot to look at in there," Saul remarked. "A *hell* of a lot. That's why I took so long."

Cadel knew instantly that the detective was referring to Com's house.

"You mean Com left some of his stuff behind?" This was good news, though Cadel was feeling almost too dazed to absorb it properly. "What kind of stuff?"

"Every kind," was Saul's rather cryptic estimation. Though the light was very poor, he seemed to sense that Cadel was staring at him, because he added, "You'll see what I mean. It's strange. No one can work it out."

Cadel pondered this remark as the van began to move.

"How is it strange?" he finally asked. But Saul wouldn't elaborate.

"You'll see," he said. "Just be patient. I can't describe it—you'll have to take a look for yourself." Then, in an obvious attempt to change the subject, he informed Cadel that he'd checked on Hamish's condition. "He'll be in the hospital overnight, to get some tests done. But it looks like he's cracked a rib."

"Is that where the blood came from?" Cadel wanted to know.

"Could be." The detective shrugged. "But he bit his tongue, too, so they're thinking the blood might have come from there. He could have inhaled it."

"Which hospital is he in?"

"Royal Prince Alfred. It was closer than Prince of Wales."

"Oh." Cadel's heart sank as he contemplated visiting both hospitals in a single evening. It would be very difficult—especially for someone who was being pursued by a CCTV stalker. But perhaps by tomorrow Hamish would be at home.

And perhaps Com would stay off the CCTV networks for a while.

"I haven't told Fiona all the details, yet," Saul was saying. "I told her that we've got a result and that we're following it up, but I didn't want to explain everything over the phone. We're gonna have to do that later." The jolting of the van was making his voice shake. "It'll come as a bit of a shock," he admitted. "She'll be worried about you."

Cadel said nothing. His mind was still on the hacks that he'd witnessed.

"You know," he mused, as if the detective hadn't even spoken, "it might have been Com tracking me on closed-circuit TV, but he wasn't the one messing with SCATS. Someone else was in there, and the way they were throwing their weight around, I reckon we have a good chance of picking up their traces."

"Well . . . that's Sid's department," Saul observed. "He'll be looking into the whole traffic-light business, him and his team."

"Yeah, but he's got to do it *now*. Because if Com left a trail of red lights behind him, then that's a good place to start." Receiving no immediate response, Cadel saw that he would have to spell it out. "If we can get into SCATS," he explained, "and figure out where the controller boxes were hijacked, we might be able to see where Com ended up. It would be like a set of footprints."

"Jesus," Angus said admiringly. And Saul stiffened.

"You mean there'll be a record?" His tone was sharp. "Some kind of register that we could check?"

"Well . . . it's certainly something that *I* could check." Cadel racked his brain, trying to remember details of his youthful forays through the SCATS labyrinth. He didn't know exactly how much it had changed since then. "A lot of traffic lights respond to input from loop detectors," he went on. "They're programmed to respond in a certain way to certain conditions. If they don't, there's going to be an invalid signal showing up—unless this traffic-light malware also stops data from getting back to the regional computer somehow."

He considered the likelihood of such a cunning ploy. If Vee were involved, chances were good that the program was as stealthy as a termite. "It's still worth a try," he concluded. "Sid should already be looking at SCATS anyway because of its camera network. That whole system should be *crawling* with fingerprints by now."

The van stopped suddenly, nearly dislodging them all from their seats. Cadel was flung sideways. The back of Reggie's skull bounced off one wall with an audible thump.

"Ow," he said.

"For Chris'sake, Lou!" Angus loudly remonstrated. *"You been boozing it up in there?"*

"Sorry," came the indistinct response. Then the engine died.

But as Saul rose to his feet, Cadel grabbed his arm—because there was a lot more to be said.

"It's time I got back online," Cadel insisted. "You can see that, can't you? I need to tackle this myself."

"Maybe," Saul replied. "I'll think about it."

"There's no point worrying about who might spot me while I'm chasing back trails. Not anymore." Cadel wouldn't let go of Saul's arm. "It's riskier for me on the street than it is in cyberspace. And you need my help. *Sid* needs my help."

"I'll think about it," Saul repeated. "First things first, okay?"

"Like getting out of this bloody van, for instance," Reggie growled. Angus was already leaning toward the rear doors, but Saul stopped him with a peremptory, "Wait."

When the detective's hand disappeared inside his jacket, it became evident that there was no point trying to pursue the subject of Internet access—not while he was fully focused on who might be approaching the back of the van. Saul's tense muscles didn't relax until he heard a familiar *Knock-knock-knock! Knock-knock!*

Lou was giving them the all-clear signal.

Next thing he knew, Cadel was emerging into what appeared to be a small garage. A dusty, dangling light bulb dimly illuminated a framework of wooden beams; though some kind of cladding had been slapped on the outside of the structure, no one had bothered to line its internal walls. Cadel could see cobwebs festooned across stacks of old junk: flowerpots, paint cans, roof tiles, curtain rods. Only the lawn mower and weed whacker looked new.

Two uniformed police officers were murmuring together near a garbage bin.

"Through here," Saul prompted. He nudged Cadel to a side door, which led straight into a small room furnished with a concrete laundry tub and a washing machine. This room opened onto the kitchen, but Cadel wasn't encouraged to stop and contemplate the fridge or the stove. Instead he was hustled into what may have originally been a dining room, since a serving hatch had been cut into one wall.

But it wasn't a dining room any longer. It contained only floor-to-ceiling racks of computer equipment jammed together like books on a bookshelf. Great swags of cabling spilled from these racks, while power boards strewn across the floor sprouted untidy clusters of plugs that were carelessly piled on top of double adapters, clinging together like barnacles or profiteroles.

Cadel had never seen anything like it before.

"Oh my god," he whispered, wide-eyed with astonishment.

"It's the same everywhere, except in the bathroom," Saul revealed. "And the kitchen, of course." He fell silent, watching as Cadel's gaze traveled across the web of technology that surrounded them.

Every screen was dark; every motherboard was silent. That was the first thing Cadel noticed. Nothing was turned on. No heat was being generated at all.

"It was like this when we came in," Saul revealed, as if reading Cadel's mind. "No one's touched it."

"They're so old," said Cadel, wonderingly. A good half of the machines were older than he was; he could tell because they were so big and chunky. There was a Toshiba T4850/500, a Macintosh Color Classic, a Compaq Portable II . . .

Where had Com *found* all these antiques? In the street? On eBay?

"We're concerned that it might be some sort of booby trap," Saul continued. "The explosives dogs didn't sniff out anything, but you can see how all the different components seem to be linked up."

"Do you think they even work?" asked Cadel, as he drifted into the next room. Here a battered velvet couch, a wide-screen LCD television, and a coffee table covered in food stains and burn marks shared the floor with yet more racks of old computers. Beyond an arched doorway at the other end of the room, Cadel could see another, similar display: an NEC PC 8801 on top of a Hewlett-Packard HP-9826 jostling an Amstrad CPC 464.

He could also see two familiar faces, which turned toward him at the sound of his footsteps. Sid and Steve, the forensic computer technicians, were making hushed, awestruck comments about an old model with a built-in dot matrix printer. Steve wore a bleached goatee, a vintage jacket, and a tie printed with winged toasters. Sid had four earrings in one ear and three in the other; his tie featured an eye puzzle of thin, flaring stripes especially designed to confuse and annoy.

"This place is like a museum," Steve remarked without preamble—though he hadn't seen Cadel in months. "There's a lot of new stuff here, but . . . I mean, check this out! An NCR DecisionMate!"

"And not one air conditioner," Sid added. He was shaking his head. "You couldn't turn it all on. I mean, even if everything works—which I doubt—the heat would cook the whole lot in no time."

"That's what I thought," Cadel agreed.

And Saul said, tentatively, "Could that be part of the booby trap? If we turn it all on, will something overheat and explode?"

Sid and Steve exchanged glances before fixing their attention once again on the wall of ancient bytes in front of them. Cadel followed their example, marveling at the work that had gone into the arrangement of so many unwieldy objects. Could they really all be interconnected? Surely there had to be a compatibility problem? Had Com achieved some kind of cascade effect? Or was the entire setup just a blind?

"Computers don't normally explode," Sid said at last. "They have meltdowns sometimes, but they very rarely explode."

"I think this guy is trying to mess with our heads," Steve speculated. "I think maybe he's trying to slow us down like . . . you know, 'Let's devote a hundred billion man-hours to figuring out what we have here.' Which is nothing."

"Not necessarily," Sid rejoined, and Steve gave a snort of derision.

"You think this is some kind of supercomputer? Come *on*, man." Steve appealed to Cadel, whom he had long ago learned to regard as an equal (despite a twelve-year age gap). "There's nothing to be gained from most of the crap in here. You probably couldn't squeeze one megabyte out of it. If you ask me, this is a red herring."

"Or a clever ruse," Sid declared. "Maybe Com's real computer is somewhere in this lot. Maybe we can't see the wood for the trees." A dramatic, sweeping gesture underscored the point he was trying to make. "Where's the best place to hide? In a crowd, of course. And maybe we're looking at the crowd."

A lengthy silence greeted this theory. Cadel, for one, could see the sense of it. Checking every computer in the house would take days, if not weeks—though the sensible thing would be to start with more recent models.

Or would it?

"I dunno," Saul muttered. "Do you really think this guy would leave without taking his computer?" He glanced at Cadel. "Would *you* leave without taking *your* computer?"

Cadel didn't reply. He was too busy pondering.

"I'd take it," Steve volunteered. "But I might not take my backup files. They could still be around." A pause. "Somewhere."

"Did he take anything else?" asked Sid. He was addressing the detective. "Do we know if he packed a bag?"

"I doubt it." The detective shot a quick look over his shoulder to where someone was banging cupboard doors in the kitchen. "He didn't have much time, from what I've heard."

"But have you checked?"

"Not personally. That's not my department." Saul heaved a sigh as he rubbed his jaw. "Let me go and ask."

There were dark smudges under his eyes, and though he left the room briskly, it was obvious how tired he was. Perhaps the gloomy surroundings were having an effect on him; there was something about the matted old carpet, smoke-cured walls, and grubby art-deco light fittings that would have made anyone feel exhausted.

When Cadel sat on the sofa, its springs were so worn out that his knees ended up near his chin.

"If he left without a toothbrush or a change of underwear, he'd have left without his backup files," Sid argued, scanning all the mysterious technology with his hands on his hips. "Maybe this stuff is here to disguise his backup files."

"Or a secret surveillance system," Steve proposed doubtfully.

"You think?" Sid's face fell. "God, I hope not."

"I wouldn't even know where to start," Steve lamented. "You could hide a mike in there and *never* find it again! Not even if you'd put it there yourself!"

At this point Cadel stopped listening. He'd decided to concentrate on a single important question: had Com actually taken his computer with him? On the one hand, it seemed likely that he had; Com, after all, was a supergeek. He was the sort of person who needed his computer the way he needed his pulmonary system. The thought of leaving his computer may not even have crossed his mind.

On the other hand, he wasn't alone. Someone else was working with him—someone who had almost certainly helped to devise his escape plan. And that someone was smart. That someone might have calculated certain probabilities.

What if Com had been caught? Suppose he'd been in possession of a computer packed with incriminating evidence and the police had picked him up? *If it had been me,* Cadel reflected, *I wouldn't have taken my computer. I would have hidden it away so no one could ever find it.*

But not in the yellow Camry. That car wasn't secure enough. With Com in custody, the police would have pulled his vehicle apart to find the missing computer—which was as dangerous to Com as a smoking gun. If Cadel had been the fugitive, he would have hidden his computer somewhere safe but convenient. Somewhere that wouldn't set off an alarm on a metal detector. Somewhere so unremarkable that no one would think of looking there, not even to check for termite damage, or repair a pipe, or replace insulation.

Gnawing his thumbnail, Cadel peered up at the ornate plaster ceiling, which was scattered with patches of mold and wisps of cobweb. Attics were easy to explore but hard to reach in a hurry. An exhaustive police search would soon uncover a hatch in the wall or a cavity under the floorboards. Even if the hatch was concealed behind towering stacks of computer equipment, it would eventually be found once the stacks had been disassembled.

He'd know that he couldn't come back, Cadel reasoned. *Not for a long, long time. Not until the police had stopped watching the house.*

Cadel tried to imagine himself in Com's place. If there were wardrivers around and you had to leave in a hurry, would you want to be fiddling with passwords or safe combinations? If the police suddenly pounded on your front door, would you want to start shifting furniture, or digging holes, or setting fire to your computer? No, you wouldn't.

You'd want to shove your laptop into its predetermined hiding place right away, no fuss. The hiding place would have to be within easy reach: no ladders or flashlights could be required. And once the laptop had been concealed in this secret compartment, no one else would ever choose to look for it there.

"Eric says it doesn't seem like our subject took much with him when he left," Saul announced upon reentering the room. "There's a lot of clothes in the wardrobe and only one empty hanger. The toothbrush in the bathroom might be a spare, because it's in pretty rough shape—but you've gotta wonder if a guy who lives like this would change his toothbrush too often. And the toothpaste is new." Saul's weary gaze wandered over to Cadel, even though he was addressing Sid. "There's no indication that anyone else has been staying here, but we'll have to do a proper search. It would be easy to miss something under all those buttons and wires."

"It would be easy to miss another *room* behind this lot," agreed Sid, whose long-winded commentary on classifying computer models had been interrupted by the detective's reappearance. "There's so much of it, but it doesn't make any sense. If our guy was a collector, his stuff would have to be arranged somehow. Alphabetically or chronologically."

"Or by nationality," Steve chimed in.

"Yeah. That's right." Sid nodded. "And if this whole wall was wired up as one big computer chip, there'd be some kind of system to it as well. The arrangement wouldn't be random—you'd be able to make out a pattern of some kind. But I can't see one." He raised an eyebrow at Cadel. "Can you?"

It took a moment for Cadel to absorb the question. He'd been sitting on the velvet couch, staring blankly into space. Now he blinked, snapping out of his reverie with a little start.

"No," he said. "I can't."

And there was a reason for that, he felt sure. Confusion reigned but not by accident. The house was bursting with computers both old and new. A new laptop might temporarily conceal itself among a host of other new laptops. But what were the old machines for? Had they been used because a house full of new computers would have been too expensive? Were they space fillers designed to distract or mislead?

Then suddenly, like a flash, it came to him.

Of course.

SEVENTEEN

Cadel stood up. He surveyed the vast collection of chips and circuits in front of him, looking for something very big and very old, with very little computing power.

The IBS Beta system? Perhaps. The ICL Quattro? A definite possibility.

"I don't believe this stuff has ever been turned on," Sid was saying. "Not all at once, anyway. The wiring must date back to 1933—just check out the light switches! You'd blow every fuse on the board."

Cadel wandered past him into the hallway, which was lined with more computers. It was like a space-shuttle cockpit, or the business end of a nuclear submarine—except, of course, that a lot of the equipment was much older than any on a space shuttle. There was even a computer with a wooden cover on its chassis, sitting just below eye level.

Cadel stopped in front of it.

It was bigger than a microwave oven.

"Isn't it great?" Steve enthused. He had followed Cadel into the hallway. "That's a Northstar Horizon. I've never seen one before. I've only read about them."

Gently Cadel touched the machine's front panel, which featured two disk-drive slots.

"It's a 1977 model," Steve continued. "Sixteen kilobytes of RAM. It was the first floppy-disk-based system for hobbyists."

"Sixteen kilobytes of RAM," Cadel murmured. These days, you could fit sixteen kilobytes into a matchbox, with room to spare. You wouldn't need more than a tiny fraction of the area enclosed by that walnut-stained casing.

You could tear out its guts, rewire it with a modern CPU, and have a functioning unit with enough space left over to fit whatever else you might want to hide.

Like a laptop, for instance.

"Cadel?" Saul had joined him in the hallway. "I don't know if you should be fiddling with any of this stuff."

"It's okay." Cadel wasn't worried. He didn't believe that Com had installed a booby trap, because booby traps were so time-consuming. For one thing, it was necessary to *arm* a booby trap.

You'd need an extra ten seconds, at least, Cadel decided. *If it were me, I'd rely on camouflage.*

So he kept applying pressure to the most obvious contact points on the Northstar Horizon: the disk-drive buttons, the power switch, the manufacturer's label . . .

Nothing.

"You're not trying to turn it on, are you?" Steve protested. At that moment, Cadel realized that the Northstar Horizon was sitting inside its plywood shell like a drawer inside a cabinet. So he hooked his fingers beneath the lower edge of the front panel, where he found a little catch that yielded with a *click* when he pushed it down. Simultaneously he gave the panel a firm tug.

Just like a drawer, it slid open. But he had used too much force. The steel chassis popped right out of its wooden case, disgorging something flat and square that had been sitting snugly inside.

It was a laptop, and it hit the ground with a *bang*.

"Christ!" yelped Steve.

"Get back!" cried Saul. He grabbed Cadel, who lost his grip on the empty chassis. It was left dangling from a bundle of wires, its front panel almost scraping against the floor.

The laptop lay nearby, looking perfectly harmless.

"It's all right. It's not going to blow up." Cadel tried to offer reassurance as he battled Saul's efforts to drag him into the next room. "It's Com's laptop; it can't hurt us."

Steve began to laugh. "Wow!" he said. "Phew! That was a bit of a shock, eh?" And he regarded Cadel with frank admiration. "You're really something."

"How on earth did you figure out where it was?" asked Sid, who was now standing in the hallway just behind Saul.

Cadel shrugged. "I didn't," he confessed, peeling the detective's fingers off his arm. "I was trying to find the biggest box with the smallest capacity."

"Which was the Northstar Horizon." Sid gave a nod. "Good thinking."

"Now we just have to get into this thing," said Steve. He sounded less than thrilled, and Cadel knew why. Taking the laptop out of its hidey-hole had been easy. Penetrating its defenses, on the other hand, would be very, very hard. One false step and the machine would probably self-destruct, erasing all of its files and possibly even cooking its own circuits.

You could cause a meltdown, Cadel thought, *if you installed a program that overclocked your CPU.*

"I'm almost scared to lift the lid," Steve went on, "just in case we lose something."

"We've got to be careful," Sid agreed. At which point, without warning, the laptop suddenly sprang to life. Its lights began to blink. Its circuitry began to click and purr.

For a moment, everyone stared at it in stunned silence. Then Sid and Steve and Cadel all hurled themselves forward, panic-stricken.

"No!" yelled Steve.

"The battery!" cried Sid. "Get the battery out!"

He reached the laptop just ahead of Steve, snatching it up with such urgency that it almost slipped from his fingers. Cadel was jostled aside as Sid uttered a howl of despair.

"The cover's screwed in!" he wailed. "There's a screw!"

"Here! Quick!!" Sid ordered. Having thrust the machine into Steve's arms, he began to search his pockets. Saul, meanwhile, was hovering in the background, completely lost.

"What is it?" he demanded. "What's going on?"

"Oh, *Christ!*" Sid brayed. He had dropped a jangling bunch of miniature tools and was scrambling to retrieve it. Steve was cursing under his breath.

So Cadel had to answer Saul's question. "The laptop's booting up," he explained.

"Why?"

"I don't know." It was likely, however, that some sort of switch had been thrown when the machine was removed from its hiding place. Cadel suspected that a signal from the Northstar Horizon had been triggered after he'd failed to enter a certain code (or press a particular button) within the correct time frame.

I'm such a fool, he said to himself.

By this time Sid was frantically sorting through his collection of pocket-sized screwdrivers, which hung like keys from an overcrowded key ring. Cadel sidled past him to examine the gutted chassis of the Northstar Horizon.

Sure enough, there was a tiny contact pad inside.

"Cadel. Don't touch anything," Saul pleaded as Sid fumbled to unscrew the laptop's battery cover. It was a fiddly job because the screw was so small—and because Steve kept shifting anxiously from foot to foot, jolting the machine in his arms.

"Hurry!" he begged. "Or we'll lose it all!"

"I *know* that!" Sid snarled.

"Just pull it off! Give it a yank!"

"Will you *shut up,* please?"

At last the cover popped open, allowing Sid to remove the battery. Robbed of its power source, the laptop froze. Its lights were extinguished. Its circuits were silenced.

But Cadel felt quite sure that irreparable harm had already been done. If a self-destruct program had been initiated, it would continue to operate just as soon as power was restored. No matter what Sid or Steve might do to arrest the file-wiping process, something would almost certainly be lost.

And Cadel was to blame.

"It's all my fault," he lamented. "I'm so *stupid*!"

"No, you're not," Steve assured him.

"I am! I shouldn't have pulled so hard! I should have been more careful!"

"You couldn't have known." Sid was examining the laptop with a critical eye. "Anyway, we'll work something out. I bet we can save most of this. All it needs is a bit of lateral thinking."

"Is there anything else we should look at?" Saul asked, watching Cadel intently. "Anything that strikes you as odd, or suspicious? Don't rush. Think about it. Anything at all."

Cadel rubbed his cheek with a trembling hand. His gaze flitted about, alighting on one object after another as he tried to ignore his emotional disarray and concentrate on what he was actually seeing. The big, boxy computers were certainly worth a look; all of them would have to be dismantled, though he doubted very much that Com would have used the same trick twice. The light above was a naked bulb. (Nothing concealed in there.) Moving down the hallway, he encountered a dingy, pale green bathroom, empty except for a frayed towel, a molting toothbrush, and a tube of toothpaste. The bedroom next door contained only a blocked-up fireplace and more racks of computer equipment.

There was, however, a scattering of furniture in the main bedroom, which lay at the end of the hall. Grubby, tangled sheets were flung across a black futon, while the dresser next to it was being methodically searched by a uniformed police officer wearing latex gloves. "Nothing so far," she said upon catching sight of Saul, who had followed Cadel over the threshold. "Just clothes and batteries and extension cords."

Two entire walls were stacked high with technology. The remaining walls were dusted here and there with patches of mold. A desk lamp sat on an overturned bucket. A dog-eared fashion magazine was lying on the bed.

"Com reads *Vogue*?" Saul exclaimed in disbelief.

"It was propping the window open. That sash is busted," the police-woman explained. "I shook out all the pages, but there was nothing."

"Dot's been here," said Cadel. He nodded at the magazine. "And she brought that with her."

"Really?" The detective didn't sound too convinced—perhaps because he was familiar with Dot's bland, conservative, middle-aged clothes, and robotic demeanor. Clearly she had never impressed him as being someone who might indulge in fashion magazines.

But Cadel knew her better than Saul did. He had walked in on her once when she was scrolling through an online lingerie catalogue. He had discovered that there was another, secret side to Dot.

"Com couldn't possibly have a girlfriend," he continued, "and that magazine isn't his. It's only a month old, too, so Dot could have been here quite recently." Contemplating the glossy cover, Cadel decided that at least three people had to be on Prosper's infiltration team. Vee was the one who had hacked into Judith's system. Dot knew all about Cadel's phone. And Com . . . well, the extent of Com's involvement would remain a mystery until his computer files had been examined.

"Ah—Saul?" It was Sid; he'd poked his head around the side of the doorway. "Could I have a quick word?"

"What?" The detective sounded impatient.

"It just occurred to me . . ." Sid hesitated, then took a deep breath. He was no longer nursing Com's computer. "If we threw the switch on that laptop when we moved it . . ."

Another pause.

"Yes?" Saul rapped out.

"Well, I was thinking . . . suppose we turned on something *else*, as well?"

Saul frowned. "Like what?" he said.

"I dunno. Like . . . a listening device. Or . . . or . . ."

"A detonator?" Saul shook his head. "There are no explosives in here. Keith's dogs have already been through the whole place."

"Yeah, but you wouldn't need explosives." Cadel couldn't help butting in. "Not with a gas stove and all this ancient wiring."

Though he didn't really believe that the house was booby-trapped, he had to concede that Sid's reasoning was flawless. And Saul must have realized it too, because his eyes widened suddenly.

"Out," he barked. "Everyone outside."

"What?" The officer straightened. "But—"

"*Now!*"

Saul would brook no argument. He began to bark orders in every direction, chivvying people out of cupboards and corners. Voices were raised. Evidence was abandoned. Angus and Reggie converged on Cadel, who was almost lifted off his feet in the rush for the exit.

Within minutes, Com's house had been evacuated. Cadel found himself squatting behind a police car, some distance from the fluttering yellow tape that now encircled an entire portion of the street. Glancing at his watch, he saw that it was 10:15 p.m. Not very late, really. Yet the windows of the neighboring houses were all dark.

He wondered about the people who had been expelled from these homes earlier in the evening. Would they be allowed to return any time soon? Probably not, if Saul had his way; he was being very, very cautious.

"Where's Sid?" Cadel asked him—because they were both crouched next to the same hubcap. "Has he got that laptop?"

"No," Saul replied.

"*No?*" Cadel was appalled. "You mean he *left* it there?"

"No. Keith took it. I told him to put it in one of his blast containment rings." Despite the darkness, Saul must have sensed Cadel's incredulity. "That laptop could be some kind of fuse, for all we know," the detective added.

Cadel had his doubts. But he didn't say anything—not for a while.

Only after several minutes had elapsed and nothing had exploded, did he hazard another question.

"If the computer doesn't blow up, what's going to happen? Will you let me have a look at it?" he inquired.

"Umm . . ." Saul was craning his neck, scanning the front of Com's house. "Maybe later."

"What do you mean, later? Later when?"

A crunching noise from somewhere off to their right made Saul turn sharply. He relaxed, however, when he saw the shadowy, bent-kneed figure of Reggie Bristow waddling toward them.

"Sorry," muttered Reggie. "I got caught up in all that dog-squad mess. I should have been watching this one." And he gestured at Cadel, who ignored him.

"When can I have a look at the computer?" Cadel demanded. "How long do I have to wait?"

"We'll see." Hearing Cadel's sudden intake of breath, Saul shuffled around to confront him. "There needs to be a risk assessment, okay? That's a dangerous piece of equipment."

"It's not going to blow up!" Cadel protested. "I *know* it's not."

"You don't know anything of the kind," Saul rejoined. "Besides, there are other considerations."

"Like what?"

"Like the fact that it's a primary target." Saul was peering at Com's house again. "If it was *your* laptop, and *you* were our perp, what would you do? Eh?"

"Destroy it at all costs," Reggie volunteered, before Cadel's glare silenced him.

"I wouldn't *need* to destroy it if I'd installed a self-destruct program," Cadel pointed out. But Saul remained unconvinced.

"It would be nice if everyone was as confident as you are," he said. "Personally, I wouldn't wanna take the risk."

"You mean—"

"It's Sid's call. When he's ready, he'll give you what he's got. In the meantime I don't want you anywhere near that computer." Before Cadel could object, Saul turned to Reggie. "Just watch him for a minute, will you? I need to figure something out."

And the detective hurried away, leaving his foster son to fret and seethe. Such an excessive degree of caution was infuriating, though not entirely unexpected. It was the same old story. As a teenager and a civilian, Cadel had to shut up and take orders. His intellect and experience seemed to count for nothing; once again he found himself huddled in the background, waiting for permission to make a move.

He could feel an invisible net tightening around him. After the traffic-light incident, Saul would be reluctant to let him travel. Hospital visits would be curtailed, if not totally forbidden. Every step would be dogged by surveillance teams. Every phone call would be monitored. Every destination would be checked and double-checked.

It would be like the Axis Institute all over again—only worse, of course. Because now he had friends and family to worry about.

Cadel didn't know what to do. Though he felt as if he ought to take matters into his own hands, he was also aware that if he did, he would cause his foster parents a great deal of distress. They wanted to protect him; that was all. Yet in keeping him caged up, off-line, and out of harm's way, they weren't really doing him any favors. He wouldn't be safe until Prosper English was stopped, and how could that possibly happen without Cadel's input?

Things would have to change. Saul needed to understand that. He'd have to be *made* to understand that.

Somehow.

Deedle-ee-deedle-ee-deedle-ee-dee! The sudden tootling of a cell phone made Cadel jump.

"Bloody hell," Reggie cursed. Looking around, Cadel saw him yank the warbling phone from his belt before slapping it against his ear. "Hello? Uh-huh. Yeah. Who's this? Who? Oh."

Reggie locked gazes with Cadel, whose heart skipped a beat.

"Yeah. I guess so. No, he's right here." Reggie offered up the phone. "It's for you," he said.

Cadel swallowed.

"Who-who . . . ?" he faltered, but was unable to finish the sentence. He had been visited by a fleeting and truly horrible thought: could it be Prosper himself on the other end of the line?

No. Of course not. That was ridiculous.

"It's your friend from Newtown," Reggie growled. "The one who needs a haircut."

Cadel took the phone. *For god's sake, get a grip,* he told himself. Then he said, very cautiously: "Hello?"

"Hello?"

One low-pitched, rough-edged word was enough to reassure him. That burred voice wasn't Prosper's.

Almost dizzy with relief, he had to steady himself against the police car with one hand.

"This is Cadel," he croaked. "Can I—can I help you?"

"It's Andrew Hellen here."

"Yes. Hello."

"I've got you some contact details for that guy we were talking about. Raimo Zapp the Third. If you're still interested."

"Oh! Yes. Great. Thank you."

"I don't know if this is still current, but it's the best I could do. No one's had anything much to do with him lately . . ."

And as Cadel cast around for something—anything—to write with, Andrew began to reel off a Los Angeles address.

EIGHTEEN

The next morning, Cadel woke up in something that resembled an armed camp.

Upon first opening his eyes, he was greeted by the reassuringly familiar sight of silver walls, a checkered floor, and a giant chess piece. But he soon discovered that his computer had been taken away during the night. And when he shuffled into the kitchen at around eleven o'clock, he found it occupied by a crew of strange police officers wearing suits and handguns. They kept appearing and disappearing as he ate his breakfast, their movements apparently dictated by some sort of duty rotation.

Once in a while, they would reluctantly admit a couple of technicians with tool belts who would scuttle around, wielding an electric drill or a spool of cable, before disappearing outside again. According to Gazo Kovacs, these technicians were installing a discreet alarm system as well as a set of security floodlights.

"I fink your dad might be worried about you," he observed as he joined Cadel at the kitchen table. "He wants to make sure no one can get in."

Gazo had nobly offered to keep Cadel company while Saul and Fiona were at work. With Reggie and Angus off duty, Gazo's was the only familiar face in the entire house; if it hadn't been for Gazo's undemanding presence, Cadel would have felt utterly abandoned.

Not to mention sidelined.

"Hamish is outta hospital, by the way," Gazo reported, watching Cadel shovel down a large bowl of muesli. "He got out this morning. He's at home now wiv 'is mum and dad. Should be all right."

"What about Sonja?" asked Cadel.

"She's still in hospital. I ain't seen 'er yet. You want some toast?"

Cadel shook his head.

"Sure?" Gazo lowered his voice. "You should. If you don't get in early, them bloody coppers'll scarf all the bread. I already seen 'em polish off your mum's brownies."

But Cadel wasn't interested in food. "What about Com's laptop? Have they got anything off that yet?" he demanded.

"Dunno."

"Have they found his car?"

Gazo shrugged. "Sorry," he said. "I only turned up when your dad was leaving. He didn't tell me much."

"He's taken my computer. Did you know about that?"

Squirming slightly beneath Cadel's unblinking blue stare, Gazo said quickly, "He told me he wouldn't be long. Maybe he'll bring it back wiv 'im. He's probably getting it checked out."

"Listen." Cadel stood up. "Come in here, will you? There's something I want you to see."

He led the way to his bedroom, where he subjected Gazo to a barrage of low-pitched questions.

"Did you drive over?"

"Uh—yeah . . ."

"So you got your car back?"

"No." Gazo sounded apologetic. "It's still at Thi's place, and I've still got 'is—"

"What about Thi's laptop? The one I was using? Is it still in there?"

"Yeah. But I stuck it in the trunk; don't worry."

"I need it."

Gazo blinked.

"What you have to do is go out and buy me a stack of newspapers," Cadel continued very quietly. "Big, thick newspapers. Once you've done that, you can slip the laptop into them and smuggle it inside."

"But—"

"It'll work, I promise. No one's going to wonder why I'm asking for newspapers. It's not like I can surf the Net or anything." Seeing Gazo glance uneasily over his shoulder, Cadel took a deep breath. "I need that computer, Gazo. If you don't get it for me, I'll have to find one somewhere else."

"But your dad—"

"Isn't thinking straight," Cadel finished. He could feel himself slipping into an old and familiar pattern—into the detached, calculating mode that had dominated his early childhood. He knew he was talking to his friend as if they were both still at the Axis Institute, yet he couldn't seem to stop doing it.

"Listen," he said, keeping his eyes fixed on Gazo's troubled face. "Saul's had me locked in a box, and it isn't working. People are getting hurt. First Sonja, now Hamish. What if you're next? I have to do something about it. I have to get online. You can see that, can't you?"

A grunt was the only response. Gazo was staring at his feet in a state of acute discomfort. So Cadel resumed his attack.

"Did Saul actually *tell* you not to bring me a computer?" he pressed.

"Well . . . no . . ."

"Then you're not breaking any promises, are you?"

"He said I should try to keep you safe," Gazo mumbled.

"Which you will be. If you get me that laptop." Aware that his friend wasn't entirely won over, Cadel sighed. "I can break out of here, you know. It wouldn't be so hard. You can tell him I threatened to do it if I didn't get what I wanted."

Something about Cadel's tone made Gazo look up suddenly. The two of them gazed at each other for a few seconds. Then slowly Gazo's expression changed.

"You reckon it's that bad?" he said at last.

"Don't you?"

"I guess . . ."

"It's a war. With casualties. And I can't fight it on my own."

Three minutes later, Gazo was heading out of the house to buy newspapers. When he returned shortly afterward, he found Cadel fully dressed, with clean teeth and brushed hair. Pounding rap music filled the silver-walled bedroom, but Cadel wasn't dancing to this urgent beat. He sat quietly on his bed, waiting.

I don't want anyone to hear me on the keyboard, he'd written in ballpoint pen on a scrap of paper. He waved the scrap at Gazo, who nodded.

"You should return Thi's car," Cadel said aloud, as he plugged the laptop into his modem. "Especially since Snezana doesn't have hers. You should go now."

"Really?" Gazo was surprised. "Are you sure?"

"I'm sure." Cadel didn't want Gazo hanging around. Two people holed up in a bedroom with a bunch of newspapers would be much less convincing than one person holed up in a bedroom with a bunch of newspapers. And Cadel needed to concentrate; Gazo's aimless presence would be a terrible distraction. "Thi will want his car. Especially since Snezana doesn't have one anymore."

"Well . . . okay." There was a pause. "Do you want me to come back?"

Cadel felt a twinge of guilt. Glancing up, he saw that Gazo wore the same lost, glum, bewildered look that had been permanently plastered on his face at the Axis Institute.

"It's up to you," Cadel replied loudly, with an eye on the door. "I'd like it if you could visit Sonja, though, since I can't do it myself. In fact . . ." He reached again for the paper and the ballpoint pen. "You can give her this from me."

And he scribbled a message in the old periodic-table code that he and Sonja had devised so long ago, based on atomic weights and numbers.
27-258-8-158.93-8-232.04-2-167.26-53-14.01-8-91.22-9-16.00-45-126.90-42-14.01-10-180.95-60-32.06-6-210-16-55.85-18-259-2 2-39.1-7-16.00-74-1.00-8-183.85-59-16.00-16-140.91-90-126.90-7-39.1-16-4-74-16.00-7-127.60-23-167.26-32-180.95-7-88.91-5-16.00-66-16.00-7-232.04-53-32.06-52-243-87-16.00-25-16.00-74-16.00-7.

(Com, Dot both heer in Oz for him on Net and SCATS. Fear not—I know how Prospr thinks. He won't ever get anybody on this team from now on.)

Then he passed the paper to Gazo, who slipped it into his pocket.

"If you could stay with her for a while, it would be even better," Cadel added. "She needs you more than I do right now. I mean, this place is like Fort Knox, and I've never trusted hospitals."

Gazo gave a nod. He seemed to have cheered up a little. "You're right," he said. "Okay." And he took his leave, carefully closing the bedroom door behind him.

Cadel immediately plunged into cyberspace the way he would have plunged into a heated pool. He struck out for SCATS, where Com's partner in crime (Dot? Vee?) would almost certainly have left some kind of back trail. Though the music blaring from his CD player was loud enough to make the walls vibrate, Cadel didn't even notice how noisy it was. He was used to shutting out the real world while he went online. As the hours passed and the same songs kept playing over and over again, he became utterly immersed in what he was doing. He forgot to rattle the sheets of newsprint scattered around him. He forgot to lock the door. He forgot that he was a human being, and began to think like a computer program.

In the end, he found what he was looking for. Com's partner hadn't been able to cover his (or her) tracks—not completely. Traffic lights had been tampered with from Dulwich Hill to Burwood, but the process had stopped abruptly at around five the previous evening. *Com left the car in Burwood,* Cadel thought. *He got out and took some other form of transport.* Taxi? Perhaps. Train? Unlikely if there were CCTV cameras at Burwood railway station—though these, of course, might have been tampered with. Cadel wondered just how sophisticated Prosper's CCTV malware actually was. Maybe as well as inserting figures, it could remove them. Maybe there was a program somewhere designed to erase any footage of Com from all the online surveillance networks in Sydney.

"Cadel? What are you doing?"

It was Saul's voice. Cadel jumped; when he turned, he saw the detective.

Though it might have disguised the telltale *clickety-click* of keystrokes, Cadel's rap music had also smothered the sound of Saul's footsteps. Cadel didn't stand a chance. Saul was on top of him before anything could be done to hide Thi's computer.

For a long, tense moment no one said a word. Then Saul reached over to switch off the stereo system.

Their gazes locked as silence fell.

"Com left his car in Burwood," Cadel said at last. "You'll find it somewhere near the shopping center."

Saul processed this news without making a sound. He shifted his attention from Cadel's face to the laptop screen.

"Either someone picked him up in Burwood or he took a cab from there. I doubt he would have caught a train. Not unless the station cameras were interfered with." Cadel couldn't stop a note of defiance creeping into his report, though he tried hard to suppress it. "I'm going to see if I can track down the source of that traffic-light bug. If it's Vee's program, I'll probably find another chatroom, but I might get lucky."

Still the detective didn't speak. He was studying Cadel again, his dark eyes somber, his jaw set.

"Sonja and Hamish are my *friends*!" Cadel blurted out. "And I'm going to do whatever I can to stop anyone *else* from getting hurt!"

"So I see."

"You shouldn't have taken my computer. Not without asking."

"I didn't." Saul pointed. "It's just out there, in the gun safe."

"In the *safe*?"

"I think it should stay there when it's not being used. Especially now that some of Com's programs will be on it."

Cadel gasped.

"What—what do you mean?" he stammered.

"Sid and Steve worked on Com's laptop the whole night," Saul revealed. "What they could save, they're giving to you." He removed a USB flash drive from inside his jacket. "There isn't much, I'm afraid."

"What?" Cadel could feel the blood rising in his cheeks. "Why not?"

"Well . . ."

"It erased its own files, didn't it?" Without waiting for an answer, Cadel drummed his fists on his knees. "I *knew* it would! I *told* you it would! You should have let me have a go!"

Saul shook his head. "Not an option," he said flatly.

"I bet I would have got more out of it!"

"I bet you would, too. But it still wasn't an option." Saul laid the USB drive on Cadel's desk. "Sid wants you to have a look at this."

Cadel snorted.

"What, *now?*" he snapped. "Bit late, don't you think?"

"He's not sure if some of it is corrupted or just encrypted," the detective continued. Cadel, however, was still smarting.

He folded his arms, his expression sour, and said, "You should ask Sonja for help. Or Lexi. They're the real code-breakers."

"You know perfectly well that the Wieneke twins have gone into hiding," Saul calmly replied. "As for Sonja—don't you think she's got enough on her plate?" When Cadel failed to respond with anything but a frosty blue glare, the detective heaved a sigh. "There is one bit of good news," he added. "Sid found that digital-double program. So Com is definitely on Prosper's payroll."

This news hit Cadel with so much force that his jaw dropped. A look of sheer wonder banished the resentment from his face.

"Are you saying . . ." he began, then stopped to clear his throat. When he spoke again, his voice was several decibels higher. "Are you telling me that *Com* was running the computer-graphic bug? Off his own laptop?"

"I'm not sure," Saul had to admit. "I know the program was *on* there—"

"All of it? Nothing was damaged?"

"I don't think so."

"But that's great!" Cadel was surprised to see no answering excitement in Saul's steady regard. "You know what that means, don't you?"

"Uh . . ."

"It means we can turn the tables on them! It means I can go anywhere!"

Still the detective didn't seem to understand. He frowned as he watched and waited.

So Cadel spelled it out. "All we have to do is get a scan of me," he said, "and then use the program to stick me in lots of different places. If I start popping up everywhere, it'll be hard to tell where I *really* am."

Frowning, Saul pondered this suggestion as if he couldn't quite believe his ears.

"Are you sure you could do that?" he finally asked in a doubtful tone.

"Well . . . I'm not *sure*. Not until I look at the program."

A grunt.

"I mean, I don't know much about scans or anything," Cadel went on. "We'd have to talk to that guy in Newtown. We'd have to find out how much it would cost, and how long it would take." He reached for the USB flash drive. "I'd need to look at what's here first."

"And then we'd have to make sure the whole process is legal."

Cadel glanced up from the little cache of precious information in his hand.

"You can't just start interfering with surveillance networks that belong to someone else," Saul gravely pointed out. "Any more than you should start poking around a government-run traffic management system without official clearance." Seeing Cadel narrow his eyes, Saul did the same. "What you've been doing here—it's an offense, Cadel. You could get charged."

"Not if it's police work."

"Since when did you become a police officer?"

"Since now?" Cadel proposed, gesturing at Thi's laptop. "Since you worked something out with somebody so I can do this? I just told you where the Camry has to be. Isn't there some kind of statewide trace on that car?"

Once again the detective sighed. He sat down on the bed, his hands hanging loose. His suit looked crumpled. His shoulders were hunched.

"This is crazy," he murmured. "All of it. Whenever Prosper English shows up, it's like he comes from another dimension. Suddenly we're in the middle of a comic strip. Nothing makes sense. Everything's bent out of shape."

Cadel said nothing. He was keen to start downloading Com's files and felt that Saul was simply stating the obvious. Of course nothing made sense. Of course everything was bent out of shape. Cadel had grown up in a hall of mirrors; didn't the detective understand that?

After a long, uncomfortable silence, Saul pulled himself together.

"Just hold off on hacking into any government databases until I can speak to the right people," he begged. "Can you promise me that? Please? There's plenty for you to do in the meantime."

"I guess so." Cadel was willing to concede that Com's files would probably contain more ammunition than SCATS. "I might need help with this program, though. I might need to talk to a visual-effects person."

"Fine." Saul rose, rather stiffly. "I'll see what I can do."

"And you should send someone to Burwood," Cadel finished, tossing off the suggestion in a careless sort of way. "Maybe do some door knocking . . . talk to some taxi drivers . . ."

"Cadel." There was an edge to Saul's voice. "I've been a cop for more than twenty years. Believe it or not, I know what I'm doing. Okay?"

When he walked out of the room, he slammed the door behind him.

NINETEEN

By seven o'clock that night, there were eight people in the house.

Three of them actually lived there. Three had been formally invited to attend what Cadel described as "a council of war." But the other two were bored-looking men with guns, whose presence Fiona found unendurable. She was already upset about the blazing floodlights in the garden and the temperamental alarm system that now protected every door and window. Men with guns were the last straw.

"They can have their dinner elsewhere," she'd hissed at her husband, "because we won't be cooking for them!"

"There's no question of that," Saul had promised. But despite all the scented candles she'd lit and ambient music she'd played since arriving home from work, Fiona remained edgy and unsettled. Even a warm bath (in a locked bathroom) hadn't calmed her down.

Her reaction to Gazo's reappearance, at about half past five, had been so abrupt—so uncharacteristically tense and distracted—that he'd quietly asked Cadel if it was all right to stay.

"You have to stay," Cadel had replied. "I want to hear about Sonja."

"But I don't fink your mum really wants me 'ere."

"It's not you. It's everyone. This is a pretty small house."

"Is it because of what I done?" Gazo had lowered his voice to a whisper. "I mean—wiv Thi's laptop an' all?"

"No one knows what you did except me. Now what did Sonja say?"

It turned out that Sonja hadn't said very much. Although Judith had been trying to track down a neurological interface device like the damaged one on Sonja's wheelchair, such an advanced speech synthesizer wasn't freely available in Australia. And because Sonja's new Dyna Vox was no more efficient than her old one, she'd been forced to spell out every word, letter by letter, during her conversation with Gazo.

The result had been a long, slow, stumbling exchange spread over several hours.

"But she's doing real good," Gazo had been able to report. "She'll be out soon. Day after tomorrow, they reckon."

"Did she say anything about me?" Cadel had inquired, eliciting a snort from Gazo.

"Are you kidding? You're all she *does* talk about."

"Did you tell her about Com? And his car?"

"Sorta. I didn't know about the car back then. I mean, I didn't know they'd found it."

"Had she heard about the encrypted stuff on his laptop?"

"I dunno."

"Did you ask her?"

"How could I? You only just told *me* about it."

"Oh. Yes. I forgot."

Cadel was missing Sonja more and more acutely, and not just because she was such a brilliant code-breaker. Whenever Sonja was around, it seemed easier to make the right choices. She had a stronger sense than he did of what should and shouldn't be done.

"Well . . . Judith's coming over tonight, so I can tell her all the news, and she can pass it on to Sonja," he'd finally observed at the conclusion of his quiet talk with Gazo. Judith had been asked to join them because she was feeling left out—and because she had lots of money. No one was quite sure how much a full-body scan would cost, but it was bound to be too much for the overstretched police budget. Judith, on the other hand, might consider footing such a monstrous bill—especially if she decided to commission a scan of herself or Sonja. Everyone agreed that Cadel probably wasn't the only one under surveillance; that was why Saul had been forced to don the chador and Gazo, the fake nose. So if

Cadel wanted to avoid detection by scattering his image all over Sydney's CCTV networks, his friends would have to do the same. Otherwise they would be advertising his whereabouts every time they went near him.

Unless, of course, they continued to wear ridiculous disguises.

Judith's disguise that evening was a great big Driza-Bone oilskin coat. She also wore a feather boa wrapped around her neck and a flowery wedding hat pulled so low across her forehead that she could barely see out from under its wide, floppy brim. She had arrived laden down with cakes and fruit, which Fiona had accepted gratefully; the two women had discussed food for a while as everyone waited for Andrew Hellen to show up. Andrew had promised to drop in on his way home from work. He was needed not only because he might have some idea of what a scan would cost, but because he knew things that Cadel didn't.

Cadel was out of his depth. Even after pulling apart the computer-graphic malware, he still couldn't quite understand how its scan component operated. You *could* insert a scan; Prosper's image wasn't an integral part of the program. But his visual data had been manipulated somehow, and Cadel wasn't skilled enough to identify exactly what had been done.

He was satisfied, however, that Dr. Vee must have designed the bug—with a little help from someone else. Vee was an infiltration expert. He couldn't have put together a visual-effects virus all on his own. Like Cadel, he had his limitations. Like Cadel, he would have required the assistance of a highly trained professional.

Unfortunately, there was no telling who that highly trained professional might be.

Andrew Hellen was unable to suggest any more names. Even after examining Com's malware, he could only shrug when asked if Raimo Zapp might be responsible for it. "Maybe," was all that he could say on the subject. But he did request a copy of the program to show to some of his colleagues. And he did remark that it might be possible to flush out the mystery programmer simply because the work itself was so groundbreaking.

"If he hasn't got a patent on it and he's been doing it secretly, then anyone can put up a hand and say it's theirs," Andrew reasoned. "They'll start making a lot of money off it, and your guy might not like that."

"You mean he might try something?" Cadel hazarded, causing Andrew to nod.

Then Saul jerked his chin at the USB flash drive that Andrew was holding. "So you think that program is worth a lot of money?" the detective asked.

"Oh yeah." Andrew nodded again. "Millions."

"Which means that Prosper English must be rolling in dough," Judith declared. "Either that or he's blackmailing the guy who invented this program."

"If it *is* a guy," Fiona weighed in.

By this time they were all sitting around the kitchen table, drinking tea and sampling Judith's cakes. Even Fiona had dragged herself away from the stove, where various pots were steaming and bubbling. The whole room smelled of Bolognese sauce. Yet despite the cozy atmosphere, Andrew was looking slightly uncomfortable—perhaps because there were two armed men hovering in the shadows. Or perhaps he was alarmed that certain people were expecting him to do impossible things. Cadel had already asked him to identify the mystery programmer. Now, as the conversation veered toward the program itself, Fiona wanted to know if Andrew could scan Cadel immediately. "Just in case we decide to go ahead with this whole digital-double thing," she said.

Andrew was forced to explain that he couldn't scan anyone. A specialist would have to be booked and paid for; the price would almost certainly be a five-figure sum. "I can't tell you exactly how much," he confessed, "but it'll be a lot. And then there'll be other costs on top of that . . ."

"What other costs?" Judith said sharply.

Andrew took a deep breath—but it was Cadel who answered. Having already discussed the whole process with Andrew, he understood how difficult and complicated it would be to insert his own digital double into

Com's malware. "The scan is just raw data," Cadel explained. "You have to use it as the basis for a computer model, and then that model has to be rendered—"

"Doesn't the program do it all for you?" Saul interposed.

Cadel shook his head.

"Not really," he replied. "There isn't enough room. You have to use something that's got a fair degree of finish to it." He glanced at Andrew. "Isn't that right?"

"That's right," said Andrew.

"And how long would this refining process actually take?" Fiona wanted to know.

It was a question that Cadel hadn't yet asked; he awaited the answer with as much interest as everyone else. But Andrew seemed reluctant to commit himself.

"It depends on how many scans you're talking about," he murmured.

"Well, let's just say one to start with. One scan." Saul took over the interrogation. "If we manage to get that done tomorrow, how long will it take before Cadel has something he can stick online?"

Andrew hesitated.

"Days? Weeks?" Saul pressed.

"It depends," Andrew finally admitted. "If you've got a couple of people working on the job, flat out . . . I dunno. Maybe three or four days. Maybe more."

Per scan? Judith's tone was so deeply unimpressed that Andrew regarded her for a moment, his expression thoughtful.

"You don't just push a button," he said.

Silence fell. The prospect of shelling out thousands of dollars for something that might take weeks to finish cast a gloom over the entire table. Cadel was especially disappointed. He had been anxious to turn Prosper's own weapon against him. What a perfect solution it would have been!

"I can give you some names if you want to get quotes for a scan," Andrew went on. "But before you do anything, you should talk to me first."

Saul grunted. Fiona sighed. Judith said, "I'll have to think about this." Then she rose, reaching for her feather boa.

"Are you off, Judith?" Fiona sounded surprised. "Don't you want to stay for dinner?"

"No thanks, darl; I've got things to do," was Judith's firm response. She nodded at Saul. "I'll give you a ring tomorrow, once I've made a decision."

"Drive carefully," Fiona pleaded.

"Yes, for god's sake watch yourself on those roads," Saul agreed, pushing back his chair. Soon everyone was standing except Cadel. He sat with his chin propped on his fist, lost in thought.

He snapped out of his reverie only when the visitors began to leave—and even then it was Fiona who thanked Andrew for coming. Before Cadel could utter a word, Andrew and Judith were both heading for the door, with Saul in attendance. And since Judith's departure was so noisy (what with the rustle of her oilskin coat and her strident complaints about parking fines), Cadel abandoned all hope of thanking anyone himself. Had he attempted to do so, he probably wouldn't have been heard.

But as Andrew left the room, he glanced back over his shoulder, acknowledging Cadel's diffident smile with a raised hand.

"Well . . . *he* was nice, wasn't he? Giving up his evening like that?" said Fiona, once the distant squeal of tires told her that Andrew was well out of earshot. She then made for the stove, studiously ignoring her two uninvited, fully armed guests. "So it's not six for dinner, after all. I take it you'll be staying, Gazo?"

"Uh—yeah. If that's okay."

"Of course it is." Fiona began to stir the Bolognese sauce. "In fact, the later you go home, the better. Since there'll be less traffic around."

"I ain't had no problems today," Gazo assured her. "I bin to hospital and back, and no one crashed into me."

"Because you were in Thi Thuoy's car," Fiona reminded him.

But Cadel doubted that the car itself had protected Gazo. "I don't think anyone will be hijacking SCATS for a while," he said, returning his computer to the gun safe. "If they did we'd probably catch 'em, because we're on the alert now. And Vee must realize that."

"All the same—"

"It's like Judith's house." Cadel wouldn't let Fiona finish. "Vee knows we're watching the Wife, so he hasn't been near it. That's why she can still live there." He heard an engine start up in the street outside. "What we *really* have to do is put a stop to that CCTV surveillance," he added. "If we could work out a way of doing that, we wouldn't even need to get any scans done."

"Judith didn't look too keen, did she?" Gazo observed. He was leaning against the back of a chair. "I don't reckon she'll cough up that kinda money."

"I don't think anyone realized it would cost so much," said Fiona. "Did you have any idea, Cadel?"

"No." In his heart of hearts, Cadel had already given up on the digital-double plan. It was the kind of thing that could only be accomplished by people with unlimited funds—people like Prosper English, for example. Despite the worldwide investigation into Prosper's finances, it appeared that he still had access to at least one substantial nest egg.

Unless, of course, Prosper had *blackmailed* the work out of somebody. Judith might have been right about that.

"I don't suppose we could cut some sort of a deal," Cadel speculated without much hope. "Maybe we could get a few scans done in exchange for the rights to Com's malware. Andrew said it was worth money, and if the guy who's responsible starts to kick up a stink, it'll mean that we can pin him down . . ." A faint noise suddenly silenced him; it sounded like the brakes on something enormous. "What's that?" he demanded as a distant yell reached his ears.

Everyone froze. After a heartbeat's pause, all heads turned in the same direction. A high-pitched squeal was growing louder and louder, underpinned by a deep, ominous rumble. Cadel heard clanking. There was a *thump* that shook the foundation. Close by, Saul screamed, *"Look out!"*

Cadel jumped to his feet.

"What the—" said Gazo.

A door slammed. The metallic squeal was deafening. *"Move! Move!"* someone cried from behind Cadel. Gazo grabbed his arm. Footsteps were pounding down the hallway.

Then the house seemed to explode.

Jagged fragments whizzed through the air. Plaster rained from the ceiling. The noise was like a thunderclap as the wall in front of Cadel disintegrated. He fell. *Bang!* One end of a roof beam crashed through the floor, which heaved like a dinghy in open water. Windowpanes shattered. The lights went out.

Clouds of dust enveloped him. He couldn't see. He couldn't breathe. He felt as if he was suffocating . . . The smell was abominable . . .

As he fell into unconsciousness, his last thought was: *Gazo.*

TWENTY

"Cadel? Hey! Cadel!"

It was Gazo's voice, and it seemed to be coming from a long way off. Cadel opened his eyes. The first thing he saw was Gazo's dirty, contorted face. Then the gaping hole behind it came into focus.

The hole was in the ceiling. Huge chunks of plaster had fallen away, exposing beams and wiring and insulation pads. Cadel began to cough.

"I'm sorry," Gazo whispered. "I'm really sorry. I lost control."

Cadel tried to sit up. He felt queasy and confused. The floor around him was covered in litter: broken glass, splinters of wood, sheets of plasterboard. A beam of light was cutting through the dusty air, illuminating a scene like a bomb site. The rear wall of the kitchen was largely untouched, though the fridge had toppled over. But to his left lay sheer devastation. He vaguely recognized his own red quilt, draped across something that looked like . . . could it be . . .

A *windshield*?

"I know it musta bin me, because everyone just dropped like stones," Gazo continued quietly, glancing over his shoulder. "See? Them coppers have woken up now, and Fiona, too. It usually takes about ten minutes."

"What—what—?" Cadel croaked, still staring at the windshield. It had shattered into whitish fragments, most of which had disappeared, but it was still recognizable, set high off the ground.

"It's a bus," said Gazo.

"W-what?"

"A bus hit the house."

Half a brick suddenly slid off the roof of the bus, which had crumpled beneath the weight of falling rafters. One headlight was still working; that was the source of the laserlike beam that shone, straight and steady, across what was left of the kitchen.

There were other lights, too—much smaller and more mobile. Cadel realized that they were bobbing about in the hands of two uniformed men who were busy off to one side of the bus. It was a second or two before he could identify these men as paramedics.

"You called an ambulance?" he said faintly.

"Not me," Gazo replied. "I ain't got no phone."

"Who *is* that over there?" Cadel realized that the paramedics were tending to a motionless figure in a pile of rubble. "Is that—is that *Saul*?"

"Cadel—"

"Oh no."

As Cadel scrambled unsteadily to his feet, someone else staggered into view: a man so caked with dust that it was hard to see what he actually looked like. This man was the source of a high-pitched chant that had been going on for some time, like the nagging, background whine of a power tool. "The ignition cut out and I couldn't turn. The ignition cut out and I couldn't turn . . ." he was saying. Then he swerved toward the paramedics, wringing his hands. "The ignition cut out and I couldn't turn . . ."

"Is that the bus driver?" a familiar voice demanded. It was Judith; she was addressing Gazo from a spot near the kitchen sink, where she had squatted next to Fiona. Though still wearing her voluminous coat, Judith had discarded her hat.

Fiona was now sitting up, coughing and retching.

"Oh—uh—hi," said Gazo, in a dazed fashion. "How did—what are *you* doing here?"

Judith ignored him.

"If that's the bus driver, he must be in shock," she declared. "Someone should sit him down or he'll hurt himself." The distant wail of a siren made her cock her head. "There's another ambulance," she added. "About bloody time."

"Did *you* call it?" Gazo asked her as Cadel shook him off. Other shadowy figures were looming through the dust, but Cadel wasn't interested in them. He stumbled to the two paramedics, who had placed some kind of brace around Saul's neck.

"The ignition cut out and I couldn't turn . . ." the bus driver pleaded. He, too, was making a beeline for the paramedics.

One of them cut him a quick glance. "It's okay, mate. We'll be with you in a minute. Just give us a minute." There wasn't a hint of distress in the paramedic's tone; it remained calm, firm, and kindly. "Is there anyone else still on the bus?"

"I didn't see anyone," Judith butted in. By this time she was on her feet, supporting Fiona. "I watched the whole thing from down the street. There weren't any passengers."

"Did you see what went wrong?" the paramedic inquired.

"Not really. Looked like the brakes failed."

"There's a hill out the front," Gazo volunteered, from just behind Cadel. "You always see buses coming down that hill pretty fast."

"The ignition cut out and I couldn't turn," said the bus driver as Cadel reached Saul. The detective lay unconscious, with a bloody face and torn clothes. A cannula had been inserted into his arm, and a tube threaded into one nostril.

"Is he going to be okay?" Cadel squeaked. "What's the matter with his neck?"

"It's under control." The paramedic turned to Gazo. "Both of you go and sit out the back there, away from the house."

"But what about Saul?" Cadel protested.

"He hit his head. Like you did." The paramedic suddenly raised his voice. *"Everyone get out! It's not safe in here—the roof might come down!"*

"I didn't hit my head," Cadel began. Before he could finish, however, someone grabbed his arm.

A uniformed firefighter had appeared beside him, materializing out of a dust cloud.

"Come on, son," said the firefighter. "This is no place for you."

"Make him lie down," the paramedic instructed. "He's probably concussed."

"No I'm not." Cadel didn't want to leave Saul—not until the detective had opened his eyes at least. "I didn't hit my head. I'm fine."

Clunk! A roof joist dropped to the floor. From somewhere nearby, Gazo said, "We've gotta get out, Cadel." And the firefighter's grip tightened.

"Is that your name? Cadel?" he asked pleasantly.

"Yes, but—"

"I'm Vincent. And I just need to take you outside so someone can have a look at you. Okay? We won't be going far." A nod at Saul. "Is this your dad?"

"No—I mean, yes—"

"Your dad will be coming, too. Don't worry."

"Is he going to be all right?" Cadel quavered.

"He'll be a lot better once he's out of here. And so will you." When Cadel wouldn't budge, Vincent tried another approach. "Where's your mum, Cadel?"

Blinking and coughing, Cadel looked around. He couldn't see Fiona. He couldn't see Judith. Narrow beams of flashlights kept flitting across the rubble, jerking up walls and jumping from surface to surface, distracting him.

"I don't know," he mumbled. "She was over there . . ."

"Don't you think we'd better find her?"

"I saw her sit up."

"Let's go and find her."

Cadel allowed himself to be led outside. Here he immediately spotted Judith silhouetted against the headlights of several vehicles that had apparently been driven into the yard from the rear lane. One of these vehicles was an ambulance. Another was a police car.

Judith was deep in conversation with a uniformed police officer, waving her hands about energetically.

". . . straight through the fence and into the front of the house," she was saying. "Like the brakes failed. Like it was going to turn at the bottom but it couldn't . . ."

"Cadel!"

The choked cry came from Fiona. As Cadel turned, she threw herself at him. He was suddenly engulfed in a hug that was more like a stranglehold.

"Oh my god. Oh my god," she whimpered. "Oh my god, you're all right!"

"Take it easy, love." Vincent tried to peel her off Cadel. "We've gotta be careful till the ambos have a look."

"Don't worry. Saul's alive," Fiona gabbled.

"I know." Cadel's response was muffled by the collar of her cardigan. "I saw him."

"He didn't get crushed," she continued, shrugging off the hands that were reaching for her. Two of these hands belonged to a paramedic. "They're bringing him out right now. There's an ambulance." Annoyed by all the insistent, attentive people hovering in her vicinity, she swung around to snap at the nearest emergency worker. "What is it? I told you! I didn't hit my head!"

"Then where did that bruise come from?" somebody demanded. Meanwhile Fiona's grip had loosened; Cadel found himself being plucked from her arms and deposited onto a bench near the barbecue. A penlight flashed in his eyes. "Just look over here, mate. And up here—that's it. And over this way . . ."

Gazo was dithering about, unable to keep still. The bus driver was being comforted by a woman in a dressing gown. ("The ignition cut out and I couldn't turn . . .") People were shouting, pointing, scurrying.

All at once, a light bulb went off inside Cadel's brain.

Had this really *been an accident?*

There were CCTV cameras on board most Sydney buses; he knew

that. But he also remembered something else—something about computerized data collection. Every bus had its own Tacholink Event Data Recorder, monitoring things like mileage, routes, and working hours. This data could be downloaded by radio frequency or via the Global System for Mobile Communications. And if anyone ever decided to steal a bus, its Tacholink could be configured to immobilize it.

In other words, the ignition wouldn't fire unless the driver had clearance.

"Cadel? Can you wiggle your fingers? Good. That's good. Does it hurt here? No? What if I press this?"

Cadel wondered if Vee was behind the crash. It was possible, surely? Someone like Vee could easily take advantage of the connection between a bus's engine and its Tacholink. He could have used GSM or GPS to disable its brakes or its steering, though Cadel didn't quite know how.

"You blacked out, is that right? Cadel? How long were you out, do you know?"

"Uh . . ." Cadel wasn't paying much attention to the paramedic beside him. He could see a stretcher being maneuvered through the kitchen door and craned his neck to get a better view.

"He was out for ten minutes." It was Gazo who answered. "But I don't fink he hit his 'ead—"

"We'll see. The neurobs look pretty good, but it's best to be on the safe side. In fact, we might stick a neck brace on him." Briskly the paramedic came to a decision. "I think we'll get you to the hospital, matey," she informed Cadel. "Keep you under observation for a bit. Ten minutes is a long time to be unconscious."

"Yeah, but he couldn't breeve, is all," Gazo tried to explain. "It weren't—I mean—the smell's what done it; there was a bad smell—"

"You mean gas?" interrupted Vincent, who had apparently been eavesdropping. "Did you smell *gas* in there?"

"No," said Gazo. "I mean—yeah, but—"

"Jesus." The firefighter shot off like a rocket. Fiona, by this time, was stumbling along beside her husband's stretcher, resisting all efforts to make her sit down. Judith was still being interviewed. The bus driver was having his pulse checked.

Saul hadn't regained consciousness.

"Am I going in the same ambulance as Sau—as my dad?" asked Cadel, rising obediently in response to a hand on his elbow.

"Your mum will be going with your dad, mate, don't worry." The paramedic guided him toward the back fence. "You'll have to go to a different hospital."

"Why?"

"Because we have to take you to the children's hospital. But it's right next door to where your dad will be."

"I want to go with *them*!" Cadel pointed at Saul. "I'm okay! I didn't hit my head; it was Gazo! He stinks so much that he knocks people out!"

"Oh. Really? Well . . . I still want to make sure." From the paramedic's tone, it was obvious she thought that Cadel was babbling. "Why don't you come over here, and we'll get you to hospital, and you'll be able to see your parents after the doctors have had a look at you."

"It's true! You don't understand! Gazo's got a genetic problem!" Suddenly Cadel stopped in his tracks. His stomach was churning. "I'm going to throw up," he bleated, before vomiting onto the lawn.

By the time he had recovered his ability to speak, he was in the back of an ambulance. The paramedics wanted him to lie down; they told him that nausea and disorientation were symptoms of concussion. "But I'm not disoriented!" he cried, his gaze falling on the straps used to restrain injured passengers. That was when it occurred to him: was this *really* an ambulance?

Or was it an attempted kidnapping?

The thought had barely crossed his mind when someone else jumped into the back of the vehicle. Just as the doors were beginning to close, Reggie Bristow wedged himself between them. "Police!" he exclaimed, flashing his identification. Then he wiggled free and vaulted up over the rear bumper, landing beside Cadel.

"This kid doesn't go *anywhere* without a police escort," Reggie announced. He was panting and disheveled but not the least bit dusty. It was obvious that he hadn't been inside the house. "Where are we going?" he demanded, still waving his identification. With the other hand he was fumbling for his radio. "Which hospital?"

"Uh—Sydney Children's," came the reply.

While Reggie was transmitting this news to his colleagues, Cadel agreed to lie down. He felt safe enough doing so, now that Reggie was on board. And it was encouraging to know that they were heading for the Sydney Children's Hospital.

At least I'll get to visit Sonja at long last, Cadel reflected.

Aloud he said, "Tell the driver to be *very careful*. Because someone might sabotage the traffic lights. They might be green when they should be red."

The paramedics made soothing noises.

"I mean it!" Cadel snapped. "I'm not blithering! Someone's out to get me!" When the paramedics kept nodding and clicking their tongues, he appealed to Reggie. "Tell them, will you? That bus was hijacked by remote control."

"You reckon?" Reggie sounded cautious. "How?"

"I don't know. Through the Tacholink. They must have hacked into the GPS or the radio download." Seeing the paramedics exchange a quizzical glance, Cadel lost control. His eyes filled with tears of frustration. "Will you *listen* to me? You have to put on your siren! People will stop for a siren—it won't matter if the traffic lights have been tampered with!"

One of the paramedics patted his arm. "There are guidelines we have to follow when it comes to the siren," she told him. And Reggie added, "Don't worry. Officer McNair is right on our tail." In response to Cadel's startled look, he explained that he had been on surveillance duty with Angus, outside the house. "We were in the back lane, though," he said. "That's why we didn't see what happened."

"It wasn't an accident," Cadel insisted. "Prosper tried to kill us. Saul and Fiona and me."

"Yeah. Well. I guess we'll know for sure after the forensic guys have checked things out." Though Reggie's tone wasn't exactly dismissive, he did seem a bit uncomfortable. "Meanwhile, you should try to relax. You've had a big shock."

"But—"

"Everything's going to be all right," the paramedics chorused in agreement, and Cadel gave up. What was the point of arguing? He would only come across as delusional, and he didn't want to be sedated. Not when he needed to think. Not when he had plans to make.

Desperate times call for desperate measures, he thought. *I've got to launch a surprise attack or I'll never be safe. None of us will. Prosper won't stop until he's brought an airplane down on top of the hospital.*

He won't stop until I'm dead, and all my friends along with me.

TWENTY-ONE

It was after midnight, and Cadel was still in the Sydney Children's Hospital.

For hours he had been lying on a high, white bed, wearing a hospital gown and staring at a blue and yellow curtain. Reggie Bristow hadn't left his side for a moment—not even to pee. The nursing staff had promised to find out how Saul was doing but had so far failed to report back. As for Reggie, he wasn't allowed to use his cell phone inside the emergency area. And since he refused to go anywhere else until his relief arrived, he'd been unable to call Judith or Fiona for an update on Saul's condition.

Not that Cadel had wanted to think too much about Saul. Or Fiona. Or their little weatherboard house. It had been easier to concentrate on the various tasks at hand; conjuring up memories of Saul's slack face, or the devastated kitchen, would have been too much like stepping off the edge of a bottomless pit without a parachute.

Cadel couldn't afford to let his sense of loss overwhelm him.

At one point a cheery little woman with freckles had asked Cadel if his neck was hurting. When told that it wasn't, she had removed his neck brace, informing him that he wouldn't be getting a CAT scan because he had suffered no "overt abrasions."

"You don't look too bad," she'd said after checking his eyes and making him count various things. "We might just send you over to C3 South for the night and take it from there."

Her name was Dr. Jacobson, and she hadn't known anything about Saul, either. But she had been very helpful about the hospital's computer system. Yes, she'd agreed: Cadel's name, ward, admission number, and so forth would soon be in the system if it wasn't there already. His full history, however, wouldn't find its way into the medical record database for another two or three days. That was when the clerical staff would collate all of his charts and paperwork.

"Why?" she'd finished. "Is there a correction you want to make?"

"Oh no. I just wondered." Cadel, in fact, had been wondering how hard it would be to fake his own death. He had studied this subject at the Axis Institute, where his Fraud teacher had once given him an A minus for a phony death certificate. So he was already aware that it could be as long as forty-eight hours before discrepancies between medical and mortuary reports reached the attention of the coroner's office.

The fact that there were processing delays at the hospital, too, was an unexpected bonus.

I could kill myself on cyberspace, and Vee wouldn't know for at least a day, he'd concluded after speaking to the doctor. He had then tried to formulate an escape plan, knowing that, if he didn't keep himself busy and preoccupied, he would go mad with worry. It was now four hours since he'd laid eyes on Saul, and *anything* could have happened in four hours.

Cadel didn't even want to think about the best-case scenario, let alone the worst one.

His main problem was Reggie. He couldn't make a move while Reggie was around. Yet the officer was impossible to shift; he had an iron bladder, displayed no interest in coffee, and was able to sit for hour after hour doing absolutely nothing. Cadel was beginning to despair when one of the nurses stuck her head into his holding bay.

"Somebody called Gazo wants to see you," she informed Cadel. "He says he's your brother." Her tone was slightly skeptical as her gaze roved across Cadel's delicately flushed, perfectly proportioned, heart-shaped face—which certainly didn't look much like Gazo's. "He says he's got news about Saul Greeniaus?"

"Oh! Yes!" Cadel reared up, using his elbows to support himself. "Saul's my dad! The one I was talking about!"

She pursed her lips.

"The dad who's over in emergency next door?" she asked.

Cadel nodded. His heart was pounding in double-quick time.

"I see," said the nurse. "Well, as a matter of fact, we just got a call from radiology, and apparently your dad had some X-rays done before he went to surgery. But I'm not sure if he's in recovery yet." Heaving a sigh, she suddenly gave in. "I suppose a visitor wouldn't hurt. Since it's *family*. But your brother can't stay long; we'll be moving you down to the ward soon."

Then all at once, with a swish of the curtains, she vanished. Cadel heard her shoes squeaking across the shiny floor.

Reggie stood up. "I'll just make sure it's really Gazo," he growled, positioning himself so that he had a clear view of the approach to Cadel's bed.

If Saul was in a bad way, they wouldn't send Gazo, Cadel told himself. *They'd send a priest or a social worker. One of Fiona's friends would come. Or Judith, perhaps, but not Gazo.*

All the same, he was feeling positively queasy by the time Gazo appeared. Shuffling along behind the skeptical nurse, poor Gazo looked tired and cowed; it was obvious that he hadn't even washed his hands since the bus crash. His clothes were filthy and his eyes were red-rimmed. The first thing he said upon catching sight of Cadel was, "They cleaned you up."

Cadel couldn't reply, so Reggie did it for him.

"How's Saul?" asked Reggie as the nurse *squeak-squeak-squeak*ed back to her station. "They reckon he had to have surgery, is that right?"

"Yeah," Gazo confirmed. "They pulled some glass out of 'im, but he's all stitched up now. Judith says they're waiting on a brain scan, because he's got a sore neck. So they put 'im in the surgical high dependency unit." Gazo went on to describe how Judith had been demanding information from every doctor and nurse she could lay her hands on; it was thanks to Judith that Gazo knew as much as he did. "Your mum's been sedated," he warned Cadel. "I guess she'll be discharged pretty soon, since there ain't nuffink wrong wiv 'er." Gloomily he glanced toward the nurses' station. "When I told 'em what really happened, they didn't believe me. Nobody ever does."

"They thought I was disoriented," Cadel concurred, remembering the paramedics and their indulgent smiles.

"They fought your mum was hysterical." Gazo gave a shrug and a sigh before proceeding. "Anyway, Judith says you can both stay at 'er place, seeing as how you ain't got nowhere else to sleep. She says you can go straight there, soon as they let you out." He cocked his head. "Do you *know* when they're gunna let you out?"

"Not yet," answered Cadel, racking his brain. (He *had* to get rid of Reggie!) "I'm supposed to be moving to Sonja's ward first."

"Yeah? Really? That's good," said Gazo.

"No it's not. If I'm a target, I shouldn't be going anywhere near Sonja. Or Fiona. Or Judith." Even as he spoke, Cadel had an idea. He would send Reggie out to make a request for safe-house accommodation over the phone while Gazo served as a stand-in bodyguard.

It wasn't much of a plan, but Cadel was growing desperate.

"Hey, Gazo," said Reggie, just as Cadel opened his mouth, "I need to piss—can you stay here till I get back?"

"Uh . . . yeah. Sure."

"Thanks. I wouldn't ask, except that I dunno what's happened to my bloody backup." Reggie's tone was caustic. "And I figure if Saul let you drive the kid around, you've gotta have something a bit special."

"Special?" Gazo repeated, sounding rather dazed. "Yeah. I guess."

"Won't be a minute," Reggie assured him before hurrying off to visit the nearest bathroom. Cadel could hardly believe his luck. He was so flabbergasted that it took him four or five seconds to collect himself.

Then he flapped his hand urgently, beckoning to Gazo. "Sst! Listen!" Not wanting to be overheard, Cadel kept his voice low. "I need your help. I need to get out of here."

Gazo blinked. "But—"

"Soon. If I don't leave soon, Prosper will do something *really* bad.

Like crash a plane into the hospital." Satisfied that Gazo was suitably appalled (and speechless along with it), Cadel began to fire off a list of demands. "I need you to go back to my house," he whispered, "and get my computer out of the gun safe—the spare key's in the cutlery drawer."

"The *gun safe?*"

"It'll be fine. Safes are tough—they're built that way." After a moment's reflection, Cadel added, "You might want to take a flashlight with you. Once you've emptied the safe, I want you to go to the laundry. Do you know where our laundry is?"

"Yeah," said Gazo. "It's the little room next to the kitchen."

"That's it. Go in there and look in the yellow hamper. You'll find Saul's Arab costume. The black one he borrowed from Fiona. I want you to take that, too."

"Cadel—"

"Shhh. I'm not finished. On your way out, I want you to duck into our garage. Go to the back, where all the gardening equipment is, and on the top shelf you'll find a green bag under a pile of old magazines. *Get that bag.* It's mine. It's important."

"But what if I'm not allowed in?" Gazo protested. "What if the coppers are there?"

"Of course you'll be allowed in." Cadel made an impatient gesture. "The police all know who you are. Just say that you're getting some clothes for me. From the laundry. In fact you *can* get some clothes for me, so it won't be a lie. I'll be needing more clothes."

"All right," Gazo murmured.

"After that, I want you to take Saul's Corolla." Anticipating a flat refusal, Cadel kept reeling off instructions at top speed. "It's parked in the back lane, a few blocks from the house, so no one will see you," he said. "You can do that hot-wiring thing you learned at the Institute, and park it in exactly the same place when you're finished with it. I guarantee, no one will even notice it's been gone."

"But *Cadel—*"

"You're going to need that Corolla!" Cadel argued. "You can't drive *your* car because Vee will recognize it by now. And you'll be coming back here. To pick me up."

"I will?"

"At 4:30 a.m., I want you sitting in the emergency department wearing that Arab costume. With the veil over your face and everything. Understand?" When Gazo nodded, Cadel continued. "I'll meet you at the seats farthest from the reception desk. But you have to come in Saul's Corolla. And you have to make sure you bring the green bag and the laptop."

"Into the waiting room?"

"No. Leave them in the car. Does Saul have any kind of protection?"

"Huh?"

"A guard. You know." Cadel could feel himself growing snappish. He sensed that time was running out and begrudged every wasted second. "Is somebody watching Saul like Reggie's watching me?"

"No."

"Good. In that case, at 3:45, I want you to call the surgical high dependency unit. I want you to ask them if Saul has a bodyguard stationed outside his room. Don't tell them who you are. Just say you're a friend, and ask them that question."

"Why?"

"It doesn't matter. But if they want to know who you are, hang up. You've got to sound *really suspicious.*" Conscious that brisk footsteps were rapidly approaching, Cadel began to count off the crucial six steps on his fingers. "Remember: laptop, Arab clothes, green bag, Corolla, phone call, waiting room," he whispered. "Got that?"

"I—I think so."

"Good," was all that Cadel could manage before Reggie reappeared, looking much more relaxed. Gazo, in contrast, was visibly tense. He mumbled something incoherent when Reggie thanked him and almost fell over his own feet in his haste to get out. Cadel didn't like to see Gazo unsettled. An anxious Gazo was a dangerous Gazo, especially in confined areas like the emergency holding bays.

So his departure was a huge relief to Cadel, who now had nothing to do but wait and hope.

Luckily his move to the ward happened shortly afterward. From the bright, bustling, noisy emergency department he was wheeled up to the dim tranquillity of ward C3 South, where most of the patients were sleeping and most of the night staff were attending to mysterious jobs in little rooms. Cadel's arrival caused a bit of a stir, but it was brief and muted. He was installed in his new bed with a minimum of fuss, largely because another boy was already occupying the bed next to him. Rather than wake Cadel's neighbor, the nurses were careful not to speak loudly or bang things.

Only Reggie raised his voice when he saw what the arrangements were. He demanded that Cadel be put in a room by himself, and upon being informed that no other rooms were available, asked if Cadel could be moved to Sonja's room, around the corner. No, he was told—that wouldn't be possible. Boys and girls didn't usually share.

"Then I'll have to sit beside him," Reggie insisted. "And if you've got a problem with that, you can call the police commissioner."

No one, however, *did* have a problem with that. As one of the nurses pointed out, parents often spent the night with their children. And although Reggie wasn't a parent, he was filling the role of guardian.

So he stationed himself in a visitor's chair next to Cadel's bed and hardly moved a muscle for the next hour or two. While Cadel pretended to sleep, Reggie sat like a carved watchdog. Even when a nurse popped in to change the plastic bag attached to Cadel's neighbor's arm, Reggie didn't so much as glance at her. It wasn't until 3:55 exactly, when his phone rang, that Reggie finally bestirred himself.

Rising, he moved toward the door. Though Cadel couldn't risk taking a peek, he did hear the sound of retreating footsteps.

"Yeah," Reggie muttered. "Yeah, that's right. And I was due to be relieved back at . . . What? When? Shit. No, I didn't make that call." A pause. "Yeah, I can get over there, but what about the kid? Oh. Right. And how long will that take?"

Cadel kept his eyes screwed tightly shut; he had a feeling that Reggie was probably glancing his way.

"Nah, he's asleep. All right. What's his ETA, then?" Reggie grunted. "So I'll tell them . . . what? Twenty minutes? Yeah, it should be. Okay. Understood."

There was a tiny, almost inaudible *beep*, followed by more footsteps. Hinges creaked slightly. A muffled click told Cadel that the door had swung shut, but he didn't open his eyes. Instead he remained perfectly still while several minutes elapsed.

Only when he was quite sure that Reggie had left the room did he climb out of bed and put on his hospital-issue dressing gown. It was now 4:04 a.m. In a quarter of an hour (or thereabouts) Reggie's replacement would arrive; that, at least, was what Cadel had deduced from the bits of conversation he'd overheard. So if everything went according to plan, he would have fifteen minutes in which to get downstairs and meet up with Gazo.

Unless, in the meantime, a nurse happened to raise the alarm.

Cadel tried to reduce the risk of such an unlucky occurrence. First he drew his bed curtains tightly together, screening his empty bed from view. Then he turned on the bathroom light and closed the bathroom door. He figured that, if one of the nurses should look in on him, a light in his bathroom might suggest that he was emptying his bladder. It was a feeble sort of ploy, but it might buy him a minute or two. And a minute could make all the difference.

From his bathroom, Cadel moved into the hallway—though not without first checking that the coast was clear. It was. To his right, the hallway was completely deserted. To his left, the nurses' station was barely visible from where he stood, so he didn't know if there was anyone at the desk.

If there is, he thought, *I'll just say that I'm searching for Reggie. I'll ask where he's gone.*

But he couldn't hear any voices or keystrokes coming from that direction. And when he finally reached the well-lit reception area, no one challenged him—because there was no one in sight. The desk was unattended. The chairs were all empty. And the doctor's office behind the desk was, for the time being, unoccupied.

Cadel didn't hesitate. He knew that there was a computer in this office, having caught a glimpse of it earlier as he was being wheeled past reception. So he ducked straight into the small, shadowy, windowless room, leaving its door only slightly ajar. This, he knew, was his best chance. If he was discovered in any other ward, there would be hell to pay. But if he was surprised in this particular office, he could always claim that he was trying to e-mail someone. Or he could pretend to be a little dazed, from the lingering effects of his head injury. Or he could say that he was looking for his bodyguard. Any one of these excuses would earn him no more than a reprimand. There would be no attempt to call security—of that he was quite convinced.

Sure enough, he found the computer. It was sitting on a desk under a whiteboard, quietly humming to itself. In the eerie glow of its monitor screen, he was able to log on to the hospital system without any trouble; it took him less than five minutes to change his admission details, despite the fact that he was working in the dark, on his knees, with his chin barely clearing the keyboard. For someone like Cadel, the system's firewalls weren't hard to penetrate. He even wondered, for one awful moment, if he was being lured into a trap. But he quickly realized that he wasn't.

He also realized that, if Vee wasn't already rifling through the hospital databanks, he soon would be. They were too tempting a target for Vee to ignore.

Cadel felt so much safer down on the floor that when he'd finished, he crawled out of the office like a rat or a cockroach. His luck was still holding; there was no one else around. So he slunk into the storeroom next door to the office, where he found a cupboard full of bandages. This supply he raided with grim resolve, because he needed bandages—and bandage clips, too. *I'll pay for them later,* he decided, as he concealed several large rolls of gauze beneath his dressing gown. Then he scurried to the exit, which lay at the end of another long, dim hallway.

Not for one moment did he consider doubling back to visit Sonja. He would have loved to say good-bye, but he couldn't afford to waste a second. On the contrary, he had to shut Sonja out of his thoughts so that he could concentrate on more urgent matters—like getting past all the doors that flanked his escape route. There were any number of bathrooms and offices to be passed on his way out of the ward, and each of them might contain people. Padding along a strip of gray carpet, barefoot and damp with sweat, Cadel tried not to look anxious. So what if he was stepping outside? That didn't mean he wouldn't be back again.

If I get caught, I'll tell them I'm going to get a packet of chips from one of those vending machines, he told himself, averting his eyes from the nearest kitchen. Somewhere inside it, an electric kettle was boiling. He could smell coffee and hear the low murmur of a conversation. But he couldn't see anyone—and no one could see him. Yet.

When he reached the big double doors under the exit sign, his stomach turned over. What if Reggie was about to push through them? What if Cadel had miscalculated, and Reggie had simply popped out to buy a chocolate bar?

But no. That was impossible. Cadel had heard Reggie on the phone; Gazo *must* have called the surgical high dependency unit, or why would Reggie have been reassigned? A suspicious call had been made, the police had been alerted, and now Saul had been placed in a high-risk category. Hence Reggie's redeployment. Hence the fact that he had left hurriedly, before his relief arrived.

Taking a deep breath, Cadel pushed through the double doors. Beyond them he could see nothing but a wide, empty hallway hung with children's artwork. Signs pointed everywhere: to the next ward, to the elevators, to something called the Starlight Room. In the harsh electric light, everything had a worn and slightly battered appearance.

Cadel headed straight for the fire stairs. He thought it unlikely that he would encounter anyone in this concrete shaft at four o'clock in the morning, and he was right. He didn't. Having descended two flights, he emerged onto the second floor—where the hallways, again, were deserted. So was the men's toilet. There wasn't even a cleaner attending to the urinals; Cadel had an entire bank of mirrors to himself as he wrapped his head in layer upon layer of bandages, leaving only his eyes, mouth, chin, and nostrils exposed. Bandaging his scalp was enormously difficult, like trying to gift-wrap a football. But he managed it in the end, and used the leftover gauze to bandage one forearm. The result, he decided, was rather impressive. A professional-looking job.

The question was: would it pass muster in the emergency department?

Cadel could only hope so, since his whole scheme depended on it. *All you have to do,* he reminded himself, *is walk straight out of here.* As long as there were swarms of people in emergency, distracting the staff and providing ample cover, he was unlikely to attract too much attention. Because it wasn't as if he'd be walking out on his own—unless, of course, Gazo didn't show up. If that happened, Cadel would have to turn around and go back to bed.

He took a lift down to the first floor. Two bleary-eyed nurses were making the same trip, but they pretty much ignored him. And when the lift doors opened, he found himself face-to-face with a man in hospital scrubs, whose gaze barely flickered as it came to rest on Cadel's bandages. Clearly these were busy shift workers with a lot on their minds; it would take more than a mummy in a dressing gown to spark their interest. Cadel was hugely encouraged by their lack of response. All at once he felt confident that his plan would succeed, despite the fact that he was sweating profusely from every bandaged pore. Though he couldn't hear much through those bandages—and he was becoming very hot underneath them—he knew that if he could just make it to Gazo's car without fainting, everything would be all right.

When he reached the emergency waiting room, he found it stuffed to the brim with crying babies, restless children, and anguished, argumentative parents. Nevertheless, Cadel spotted Gazo immediately. As instructed, Gazo was sitting a long way from the reception desk, wearing Fiona's chador. Only his eyes were visible above the enveloping veil; as they swivelled toward Cadel, there wasn't a hint of recognition in them.

Gazo was staring at Cadel because half the occupants of the waiting room were staring at Cadel. Even among all the fearsome rashes and bleeding lacerations, Cadel stood out like a giant pink gorilla. No one else in the room was wearing a mask made of bandages.

It wasn't until he approached Gazo that the eyes beneath the chador suddenly widened. Gazo jumped up and moved toward Cadel, almost stumbling over his trailing skirts in the process.

"Mummy," piped a little girl in pink pajamas, "what's wrong with that boy's head?"

Cadel ignored her.

"Come on," he mumbled, reaching for Gazo's black-clad arm. "Let's go. Now."

As they shuffled toward the exit, it occurred to Cadel that he should have made Gazo bring Sonja's old wheelchair with him. A wheelchair would have added greatly to the overall effect. Luckily, however, they didn't need one. Nobody challenged them on their way to Saul's Corolla.

Only when they had left the hospital parking lot entirely did Cadel begin to remove his bandages.

TWENTY-TWO

It was almost a year since Cadel had first laid eyes on Clearview House, and even then the place had been run-down. With its rusty gutters, peeling paint, and crumbling chimneys, Clearview House had presented a very misleading facade to the world. Though it had certainly *looked* like an underfunded youth refuge (right down to the bedsheet curtains in the bay window), nothing could have been further from the truth. Tens of thousands of dollars had been spent on computer equipment for the concealed basement; a secret lift had been installed behind a pantry shelf; the entire house had been wired up for a state-of-the-art security system. Disguised as a decrepit old mansion, Clearview House had actually served as Genius Squad's headquarters.

Now, however, it was vacant. Cadel knew this because Saul had discussed it with him; the whole future of Clearview House had been troubling the detective for some time. Apparently the property belonged to Texan oil magnate Rex Austin, who had bought it to accommodate his covert team of hackers and number crunchers. For that reason (and because he had been associating with Prosper English), police in several countries had been trying to interview Rex. But the American billionaire had been uncooperative. After throwing up a wall of lawyers to protect himself, he had pretty much gone into hiding. No one had seen him in months. It was generally assumed that he was moving from one lavish estate to the next, while he threw money at his legal problems in the hope that they would eventually go away.

This had left Clearview House in a kind of limbo. Without the owner's approval it couldn't be leased or sold. No one wanted to repair a house that belonged to someone else. So it was rotting away, its roof sprouting weeds and its lawn turning into a hayfield.

"Which means that I can use the basement and no one will know I'm there," Cadel explained to Gazo as they approached Clearview House along a quiet, tree-lined suburban street. "What's more, if Prosper *does* find me, he won't be able to wreck the basement with a runaway bus. The house might go, but not the basement."

It was now after five a.m., and the sun had risen; empty cars and deserted pavements were tinted with a pale pinkish glow. Luckily there were no early-morning garbage trucks or dog walkers about, so Gazo was able to park unnoticed in front of the big iron gate that barred the way to their destination.

Set in a high brick wall, this gate had once been sensor-activated, swinging open automatically. Now it was chained shut.

"Can you pick that?" asked Cadel, eyeing the padlock on the chain. He knew that Gazo had studied lock-picking at the Axis Institute. "I really don't want to climb over the gate if I can help it."

"Yeah. I guess," said Gazo. He looked decidedly jittery, even though he was no longer wearing his conspicuous Arab outfit. "But what if someone spots me?"

"Like who?" Cadel glanced into the rearview mirror. "The neighbors are all still in bed."

Gazo grunted. Then he yanked at the hand brake, climbed out of Saul's car, and tackled the padlock with a miniature tool kit that he produced from his pocket. It all took a little longer than Cadel had expected. He kept nervously checking the street for signs of life, and was enormously relieved when the chain finally dropped to the ground.

"I'll close the gate behind you," he offered. "Just drive the car around the back of the house—I don't want anyone seeing it."

"Are you *sure* no one's living here?" Gazo nervously scanned the boarded-up windows of the building in front of him. "Maybe we should knock on the door, just in case. There might be squatters. Or junkies. Or neighborhood kids."

"Then you can stink them out," Cadel retorted. "Come on. We haven't got much time—people will be leaving for work soon."

He vacated his seat just as Gazo slipped back behind the steering wheel; within seconds the gate had been pushed open, and Saul's car had rolled past Cadel, heading down the gravel driveway toward Clearview House. Feeling rather exposed, Cadel shut the gate and wrapped the chain around it, loosely. He had changed out of his hospital gown in the car, so he didn't look too peculiar—even though his clothes were rank and crumpled from their spell in Fiona's laundry basket. All the same, he didn't want to be seen. So he quickly followed Saul's car around the back of the house, where Gazo was waiting.

Here someone had been busy breaking windows and spray-painting graffiti. There were shattered bottles in the overgrown flower beds and a shopping trolley had been dumped beside the garage. Grass was sprouting from a chimney pot. The rotary clothesline had been pushed over.

"Why do people write their names on walls?" Gazo wondered aloud. He was still behind the steering wheel but was leaning out of the driver's window. "Why do they want people to know who done it?"

Cadel wasn't listening. Not far from the kitchen door, embedded in the ground, there was a hatch that led to the basement; originally this hatch had been built as a kind of coal chute, but it had been converted into an emergency exit when the lift was installed. To disguise this access point, a doghouse had then been glued to the hatch—but the doghouse had since disappeared.

So where was the hatch?

"What are you doing?" Gazo demanded as Cadel poked around among the weeds and brickwork and bits of discarded rubbish. "I fought you wanted to go inside?"

"I will."

"Then—"

"Hang on." Cadel suddenly realized that he was staring at a patch of brick paving that didn't quite match the surrounding brickwork. One prod revealed that it wasn't made of bricks at all but of polystyrene carved and painted by someone with an artist's eye. Bits of dirt and leaf litter were stuck to the dried paint. A weathered stick, attached to a short length of fishing line, served as a handle.

Had all this been under the doghouse? Cadel couldn't remember.

"There won't be any power," he said, giving the handle a tug. Slowly the hatch creaked open. It was heavy, and the weight of it made Cadel gasp.

"Here." Gazo was suddenly beside him. "I'll go first."

"Did you bring a flashlight? I told you to."

"It's in the car."

"You get it." At Cadel's feet, a flight of concrete stairs led into a well of darkness. "I should have asked you to bring more than one."

"What about the resta your gear?" Gazo had found Cadel's computer in the Corolla's back seat near the flashlight. "What about your laptop and your green bag?"

"Leave them."

Cadel knew that he wouldn't be able to restore electricity to Clearview House until he was able to hack into the power grid. But he wouldn't be able to do *that* until he could find himself a network connection. And since the likelihood of picking up a wireless signal underground was pretty remote, he figured that he'd probably be taking his laptop for another little trip in the Corolla before very long.

"I'll need to do a bit of wardriving before you leave," he told Gazo, who had retrieved his flashlight and was busy locking up the car. "Otherwise I won't have any power. And I can't live in that basement without power."

"I dunno if you can live in it *wiv* power," Gazo replied doubtfully as he rejoined Cadel at the top of the stairs. "It might be full of water or garbage or dead rats or somefink."

"I know." Cadel swallowed. "That's why I didn't do any wardriving on the way. No point if I can't move in."

"Are you sure you wanna do this? It can't be too helfy down there."

"It is," Cadel insisted. "I mean—it *was*. I used to spend hours in that basement. We called it the War Room."

Gazo shrugged. Then he sighed. Then he descended into the shadows, his flashlight beam flitting about like an insect from fuse-box to drainpipe to conduit. There was a door at the foot of the stairs, faintly visible in the wash of pallid daylight flooding through the open hatch. Gazo's beam finally came to rest on a solid steel door handle.

When Gazo reached for this handle, Cadel warned from behind him, "You'll probably have to pick that lock." But the handle turned with a soft *click*.

Gazo froze. He glanced back at Cadel.

"Go on," Cadel muttered.

Taking a deep breath, Gazo gave the door a shove. It swung open on creaking hinges. The air that rushed out didn't smell damp or even stuffy. It smelled of slightly stale fish and chips.

In the halo of Gazo's wandering flashlight beam, Cadel saw a plush-covered beanbag, a stainless steel bar fridge, and a pair of sneakers.

"What the hell . . . ?" a groggy voice complained. Then the overhead lights snapped on as Gazo flicked a switch.

Cadel had to shield his eyes from the glare. Squinting, he realized that the War Room was not the empty concrete shell that he'd anticipated. Nor was it still furnished with all the elaborate computer equipment that had once filled every corner (courtesy of Rex Austin). Most of the technology now on show had quite a frivolous air to it; there were game consoles, and giant amplifiers, and iPhone accessories, and a DVD player, and padded earphones, and a widescreen TV set. Several laptops were also scattered about, among piles of discarded clothing and empty pizza boxes. Over near the elevator doors, a tangle of expensive-looking bed linen had been dumped on top of an old foam mattress.

Cadel recognized the pale, pimply face peeping out from beneath a gold damask quilt.

"*Devin?*" he exclaimed.

"Cadel?"

"What are you doing here?"

"Oh man." Devin grimaced. "How'd you track me down? Was it that bloody sister of mine?"

"No," said Cadel. "I haven't seen Lexi in six months at least."

"Who's that?" Devin had spotted Gazo. "It's not the copper, is it?"

"Of course not. This is Gazo. Don't you remember him?"

"Nuh." Throwing off his covers, Devin revealed a little more of himself. Though he still wore his trademark black beanie and drab sweatshirt, he had definitely lost weight; his cheeks were no longer plump, and there was a sharp edge to his bristling jaw. "Who sent you?" he asked, rising unsteadily. "Did you come to chuck me out? Is that it?"

"As a matter of fact, I came to move in," Cadel replied. "I didn't know you were here already."

"Yeah?" Devin rubbed his bleary eyes, staggering a little.

"I'm on the run," Cadel added. And Devin gave a snort.

"Join the club," he said.

"Not from the police. From Prosper English." Seeing Devin blink, Cadel started to elaborate. "Prosper's trying to kill me. By remote control. He's got a team out there hacking into buses and traffic lights and CCTV cameras—"

"Wait. Hang on. Just give me a sec," Devin pleaded. "I've gotta go have a slash."

As he stumbled off toward the basement bathroom, Cadel turned to Gazo with a question. "You remember Devin, don't you? He was in Genius Squad. One of the Wieneke twins."

"Yeah," said Gazo. He didn't seem very enthusiastic. "I remember."

"Looks like he's got a network connection set up, so I can bring down my laptop after all," Cadel continued. Then the flush of a toilet reached his ears. "Sounds like he's got running water, too."

"I dunno, Cadel." Gazo was gazing around at the general disorder. "Are you sure you wanna stay? This bloke's *gotta* be crooked—he's probably nicked all this gear."

"Probably," Cadel had to acknowledge.

"What if he's working for Prosper English?" Gazo said quietly. But Cadel shook his head.

"I doubt it."

"Why?"

"Because he's squatting in a basement. He can't be getting paid if he's squatting in a basement." Cadel spotted a half-eaten hamburger lying near his feet. "Besides," he concluded, "Prosper wouldn't want to be relying on someone like Devin. He's too . . . I dunno . . . too *teenage*."

"What's too teenage?" asked Devin, emerging from the bathroom. He was fiddling with his fly. "Are you talking about my games, by any chance? You're such a snob, man, you're just like Lexi. I'm allowed to play teenage games. I'm seventeen, for Chris'sake—I *am* a teenager."

"Where did you get them?" Cadel welcomed the chance to ask about the loose clump of DVD cases that lay at his feet. "What are you now, a cat burglar? This stuff must have cost quite a bit."

"It did. But it's all paid for," said Devin. "Except that one. That was a freebie." He pointed to the little USB rocket launcher plugged into one of his laptops. "They sent it to me as a thank-you for buying so much of their other stuff. I should really take it apart—see if I can get any more range out of it."

"But where did all the money come from?" Cadel demanded.

Devin smirked.

"I'm like Robin Hood," he said. "I rob from the rich to give to the poor. Which is me. *I'm* poor."

Gazo pulled a long face. As a former student of the Axis Institute, he had developed a profound aversion to thieves and con men.

Cadel, however, kept his own expression blank. "What are we talking about, exactly?" he asked Devin. "Identity theft?"

Devin shrugged, as if to imply that identity theft was no big deal. "There are plenty of bastards out there who are so rich that they don't even notice they've been robbed," he answered, a little defensively. "Like Rex Austin, for instance. My landlord. Remember him?" A sweeping gesture encompassed the entire contents of the War Room. "A lot of this stuff is courtesy of Rex."

"Account numbers?" Cadel hazarded. "Passwords?"

"Stuff like that."

"Did Lexi help you?"

"A bit." Devin had always been loath to give his sister credit for anything. He quickly changed the subject. "Do you want some breakfast? There's leftover pizza in the fridge."

But Cadel wouldn't be sidetracked. "Where's Lexi?" he wanted to know. "Does she live here, too?"

"In this hole? Are you kidding?" Devin tugged at the waistband of his jeans, which were too large for him, now that he'd lost so much weight. "She lives with her friends, at party central. Still off the grid, but where the action is. Calls herself Jessamine." Devin's tone dripped with scorn. "She's so full of herself."

"I need her help with some encrypted codes," said Cadel. "Do you think she'd come here to see me?"

"I guess so."

"Can you ask her? It's urgent."

Devin was hauling a greasy pizza box out of the bar fridge. "She'd have to do it at night," he rejoined. "Otherwise the neighbors might see her come in."

"That's okay. I need some sleep anyway." Cadel suddenly realized how exhausted he was. "I didn't get a wink last night."

"You can use my bed if you want." Devin was sniffing at a limp slice of pepperoni pizza. It seemed to meet with his approval, because he stuffed half of it into his mouth.

Not wishing to be sprayed with masticated pepperoni, Cadel decided to break off his conversation with Devin and talk to Gazo instead.

"Can you get my laptop out of the car?" Cadel requested. "And my green bag? I'd do it myself, but I have to write a note for Sonja."

"Really?" Gazo perked up a little; he had been gloomily watching a cockroach scuttle across the floor. "What are you gunna say?"

"I'll tell her I'm okay and that I'm sorting things out," Cadel replied. "The message will be encoded. You can take it to her when you visit the hospital then destroy it afterward."

"But—"

"I won't tell her where I am. I'll just ask her to spread the news that I haven't been kidnapped and that nobody needs to panic." Seeing Gazo frown, Cadel offered reassurance. "She can pretend I talked to her on my way out last night, so you won't get in trouble."

"But she's going home today," Gazo reminded him.

"Then you can visit her at Judith's." Cadel looked about him for something to write with—and on. "You'd better hurry, though," he finished. "If you don't return that Corolla soon, someone'll see it's gone. And then you *will* get in trouble."

"Ubusheemamishadee?" Devin gabbled through a mouthful of cold pizza. When the other two stared at him, he chewed, swallowed, and tried again. "Have you seen Hamish lately?"

"A couple of days ago," said Cadel. "Prosper put him in the hospital, too. But he's out now."

"Yeah?" Devin didn't seem particularly disturbed by Hamish's plight. "How did that happen?"

"I'll tell you in a minute. I have to write this note first." Once again Cadel appealed to Gazo. "Please can I have my computer? I'll be done by the time you get back, and then you can take off for good."

"For good?" echoed Gazo, his brow puckering. "But I gotta check up on you, Cadel. Later on. Tonight, maybe."

"No." Cadel shook his head.

"I'll sneak in. I'll be careful."

"Careful isn't enough. Not against someone like Prosper English." Though Gazo's wounded expression was discomforting, Cadel refused to back down. "He's gunning for me, Gazo, and for anyone who's close to me. I don't want you ending up in the hospital like the others."

"Oh. Right," Devin interposed thickly. There was a wad of pizza dough wedged into his cheek. "You don't want *him* ending up in hospital, but it doesn't matter if *I* do."

"You won't," Cadel promised. "I haven't had anything to do with you for months. Prosper won't be watching you, because he's interested in me. He won't even know I'm here."

"Unless he's had you followed," Devin pointed out in a sarcastic tone.

Cadel, however, was adamant. "No one followed me," he insisted.

"That you know of." Devin was obviously relishing the chance to argue; perhaps he was missing Lexi, who was his usual sparring partner. "Didn't you say something about CCTV cameras? What if you were tracked?"

"I'm supposed to be dead," said Cadel bluntly. "And if I'm dead I can't be moving around, can I? So why would anyone be trying to track me?"

There was a stunned silence. Even Devin looked startled.

Finally Gazo found his voice. "What—what do you mean, you're supposed to be *dead?*" he stammered. "Who finks you're dead?"

"The hospital computer system. Which is where Vee will be getting most of his information, now that I've been admitted." Cadel turned back to Devin. "There aren't any CCTV cameras inside that hospital. You only pass them at the access points. And when I left, I was in disguise."

"As what? A body in a bag?" Devin gave a wet snort, like someone trying to suppress a honk of laughter. "What is it with you?" he said. "It's like you're in a weird action movie, with all these Marvel comic crooks constantly on your tail. How come you get to have all the fun while I'm stuck down here in a basement?"

Cadel's jaw tightened. He fixed Devin with a frosty glare, his eyes narrowing, and said, "I'm glad you think this is fun. Personally, I don't enjoy seeing my friends picked off like clay pigeons."

"Yeah, yeah. Whatever." Flapping a careless hand, Devin focused his attention on Gazo. "So if you're leaving now, can I get a lift? Or am I not meant to be associating with a member of the Cadel Piggott support group these days? Seeing as how you've all got big fat targets painted on your butts."

Before Gazo could even open his mouth, Cadel jumped in.

"Cadel Greeniaus," he snapped.

"Huh?"

"It's not Piggott, it's Greeniaus," said Cadel. Then he picked up a novelty Star Wars pen and began to scribble his message to Sonja on the back of an instruction book.

TWENTY-THREE

Cadel was having a nightmare. In it, he was walking down a hospital corridor past one dimly lit room after another. The patients in these rooms were all people he had known at the Axis Institute, and most were badly injured. Clive Slaughter, for example, was burned to a crisp. Abraham Coggins lay bleeding from every pore. Jemima had a fractured skull. Doris was missing part of her face. Adolf had been blown to pieces, all of which had been loosely stitched back together and tucked into a hospital bed.

Though Adolf's tongue was now in tatters, it still worked. He was begging Cadel to get him out—and he wasn't the only one. Hisses and croaks and whimpers followed Cadel down the corridor as he tried desperately to escape. But the corridor opened into another corridor, and then another, and another, until suddenly he hit a dead end.

When he turned around, Prosper English was blocking his path. Prosper wore a tweedy jacket and a wolfish grin. "Come with me," he said, crooking one bony finger. "I'll show you the way."

Behind him, some of the patients were crawling out of their rooms: blackened Clive, bleeding Abraham, reconstituted Adolf. "Cadel," they were groaning. "Cadel . . . Cadel . . ."

"*CADEL!*"

Cadel woke with a start. He was lying on his stomach, and someone was prodding his shoulder. The watch on his wrist said 1:42 p.m.

Twisting around, he saw that the shoulder prodder was a plump, red-haired girl in an apple green suit. Her legs were clad in white stockings and her feet, in a pair of low-heeled brown pumps. According to the embroidered tag on her breast pocket, she worked for C & P Real Estate, and her name was Sandra.

But it wasn't. Not really. Because when Cadel studied her face, he recognized her small dark eyes and her piercings. Though he was used to seeing her dressed all in black, without the wig or the green eye shadow, he still knew who she was.

"Lexi?" he mumbled.

"Sur*pri-ise!*" She dropped onto the mattress beside him, then planted a firm, wet kiss on his brow. "Bet you weren't expecting me!"

Cadel wiped his forehead. He felt dazed and disoriented. "It's not nighttime, is it?" he asked, sitting up.

Lexi giggled.

"No one's going to report me for trespassing, don't worry," she said. "This is the perfect disguise." She glanced down at herself with a grimace. "It's gross, but it's perfect. I borrowed it from a friend."

"So—so you're not a real estate agent?" Cadel stammered.

"Are you kidding? As *if!*"

"She brought her friend's car with her," Devin interjected. He was sprawled across his beanbag. "It's green, like the suit."

"It's a company car," Lexi explained, correcting him. "It's got 'C and P' on the door. I parked it right out front, like I've got nothing to hide." She beamed at Cadel. "Aren't I clever? I couldn't wait around till dark, I was *dying* to see you. You haven't changed a *bit*—my god, you're still wearing that crap fleece hoodie . . ."

"Can you help me with some decoding?" Cadel's fuzzy head was beginning to clear. It occurred to him that he had spent half a day sleeping, and that he shouldn't waste yet more time beating around the bush. "I've got a couple of things off a computer that tried to self-destruct, and a lot of it's just wreckage," he explained, getting straight to the point. "But I'm pretty sure there's uncorrupted text in there—and I can't ask Sonja, because she's in the hospital."

"Oh, is she?" Lexi didn't sound terribly concerned. "I suppose she's in and out of the hospital all the time, being spastic and everything. Best place for her, probably." As Cadel opened his mouth to protest, Lexi plowed on, oblivious. "But what's this about you being in the hospital?" she said. "Devin was talking about Prosper English and CCTV cameras—I couldn't understand *one single word*."

"That's because you're thick," Devin growled.

"No, it's because *you're* thick," Lexi retorted. "You're like an ape or something. Monosyllabic."

"At least I don't have verbal diarrhea. At least it's not blah-blah-blah all day long."

"Just because you don't have any friends to talk to—"

"Hey," Cadel interposed. He knew that if he didn't step in, the twins would start to throw things at each other. "Can we not waste time arguing? Please? I've got enough to worry about."

"Aww," said Devin sarcastically, "izza poor liddle baby gunna cry?"

Lexi was more sympathetic. She draped a pudgy arm around Cadel's neck; the smell of her perfume was almost suffocating.

"You don't have to worry anymore," she cooed. "I'm here now, and I even brought lunch, so you won't get food poisoning from Devin's leftovers."

"Says the person who once tried to feed us hot-dog soup!" her brother yelped. "Says the person who's had maggots in her bread bin!"

"You wouldn't know a bread bin if you fell into one," Lexi scoffed. "You wouldn't know a *fork* if it came up and introduced itself!"

"Would you two just *stop it*?" Cadel staggered to his feet, shrugging off Lexi's arm. "I don't have time for this. Prosper's trying to kill me. If you want to fight, then do me a favor and go somewhere else. I don't need the distraction." He suddenly spotted an unfamiliar computer bag. It was pink and had badges all over it. "Is that your laptop?" he asked Lexi.

"Yes."

"So you're going to stay and help?"

"Of course I am!" Her tone was impatient. "I went to a lot of trouble, you know! Did you think I was just going to blow you a kiss and bugger off again?"

Cadel mumbled his thanks. Though grateful, he was also feeling a bit overwhelmed. It had been a long time since his last meeting with Lexi, and he had forgotten how exhausting she could be. She was always shrieking and bouncing around, intruding on people's conversations and personal space. What's more, she seemed to regard Cadel as a cross between a pet and a pinup. He was constantly having to peel her off him, and that could get quite irritating.

"If you stay here," he said, "Devin will have to go." As Devin opened his mouth to object, Cadel quickly elaborated. "I don't mean that you can't be in the same room together. I just mean that a real estate agent wouldn't be staying here for hours and hours. A plumber might but not an agent."

Devin swallowed. "So you're saying—"

"That you'll have to leave in the green car. Wearing the green clothes," Cadel confirmed. "That's if you can drive, of course."

Lexi snickered. Her brother scowled.

"I'm not dressing up in that," he said, glaring at her suit and stockings. "No way."

"If you don't, someone might get suspicious," Cadel pointed out.

"I don't care."

"You mean you *want* the police to come poking around?" Lexi demanded. "Because they will, Devin. Cadel's right. If that car stays outside for more than an hour, someone's going to think I've fallen downstairs and broken my neck."

"Then you shouldn't have left it there!" Devin raged. "This is all *your* fault, you idiot! You should have waited till tonight! I *told* you to come at night! Why don't you ever listen to me?"

"Because you're not worth listening to, that's why!" Lexi was on her feet by this time and so was her brother. But Cadel stepped between them.

"Stop," he snapped.

"But—"

"*Shut up!*" He turned on Devin, his eyes narrowed, his face white. "Two of the people closest to me are in the hospital. My home has been flattened. I've become a target for every bus and traffic light and CCTV camera in the country. Do you think I'm going to put up with this kind of *crap*?"

"Hey," said Devin. "I'm doing you a favor—"

"Oh, really? How? Since when did this basement belong to you?" Before Devin could respond, Cadel launched into a rapid-fire harangue. "Somebody's got to leave right now. And if Lexi does it, then I'll have to go with her, because I need her help. Which means that she'll become a target. Do you *want* her to become a target?"

"Of course he does," Lexi spat, offending her brother greatly.

"That's a lie!" he exclaimed, flushing. "You always act like I'm some kinda monster, and I'm not!"

"Then get into those clothes and make yourself scarce for a few hours." Cadel gestured at Lexi's disguise. "The wig, as well. You can come back as soon as it gets dark, and then Lexi can go."

"But what am I supposed to do?" Devin whined.

"How should I know? Whatever you normally do. Shoplift. Wardrive. Whatever." Struck by a sudden, disturbing thought, Cadel appealed to Lexi. "You *can* fit into his clothes, can't you?"

Thankfully she could. Devin's clothes had always been several sizes too big for him, even before he'd lost weight; Lexi was able to squeeze into his sweatshirt and camouflage pants without too much trouble, while her twin brother donned her Sandra disguise. Then she plastered Devin with makeup, gave him her keys, and told him to leave via the front door. "That's how I came in," she said, as he tottered toward the lift in her conservative brown shoes. "I just used my old keys. It's weird they didn't change the locks after Genius Squad tanked. Too cheap, I suppose."

Cadel didn't comment. He was already plugged into the Net, trawling through hospital computer systems. Sonja's records showed that she had been discharged that very morning. Saul's details, though scanty, were reassuring; at least he wasn't dead. Cadel, on the other hand, was still as dead as a dodo. That's what it said online, at any rate.

He wondered if Vee would believe it.

"So aren't you going to have lunch?" Lexi inquired after the lift doors had closed on her brother. "I brought a whole bunch of salad rolls. You can have ham salad, chicken salad, or egg salad."

"Whatever you prefer," said Cadel absent-mindedly. He was staring at the screen of his laptop, which he'd placed on Devin's desk. Not that Devin had actually moved any furniture into the basement. His desk was an old wooden door supported by four plastic milk crates, and for a chair he was using another milk crate, topped by two silk cushions. "Do you want to have a look at this?" Cadel asked. "It's the encoded stuff I was talking about. I'm pretty sure it's e-mail–related, but it's got me stumped."

"Where'd it come from?" said Lexi, moving over to peer at the screen.

Cadel told her. He gave her a quick summary of the past week's events as he consumed a chicken salad sandwich. Then, having transferred the relevant files to Lexi's machine, he left her to tackle the salvaged mystery texts while he explored Com's CCTV bug. Somewhere, buried deep inside it, there had to be a clue. A mistake. A chink in Vee's armor. Cadel was determined to pin down his cyber-nemesis, even if it took days and days. He promised himself that he wouldn't leave Clearview House until he had a real-world location for Dr. Vee.

But Vee was clever when it came to covering his tracks. By early evening, Cadel was still floundering about in dense thickets of computer code, with no promising pathway in sight. He had nothing to show for nearly five solid hours of work. It was unbearably frustrating—and mortifying, too. Was he that inept? Had he met his match? Did Vee really outclass him?

I have to start thinking more like Vee, he decided. *Vee doesn't recognize any restraints or boundaries, so it gives him an edge. His thinking might be messy, but it's also left field and lateral.*

Then Lexi cried, "Gotcha!" and Cadel jumped in his seat.

He'd been concentrating so hard that he had forgotten about Lexi, despite the fact that she was noisy and restless even when focused on an absorbing task. She would shift and mutter and sigh, sometimes cursing under her breath, sometimes twanging a rubber band between her fingers. Having made no secret of the fact that she would have preferred a more comfortable place to sit than Devin's beanbag, she'd been wiggling about like a worm on a hook. The crunch of beans had become so annoying that Cadel had blocked it out, using his extremely efficient mental earplugs.

But this sudden yell pierced the cone of silence he'd constructed for himself.

"God, Lexi!" he remonstrated. "You almost gave me a heart attack!"

"I've got it." She thrust her computer at him. "I've got the key."

"Really?"

"Wasn't too hard," she crowed. "Guy's an amateur."

Cadel ignored this veiled attack on his own competence.

"If you've got the key," he said, "I can set up a decoding program. It wouldn't take too long."

"Wouldn't take too long to do it manually, either," Lexi rejoined with a shrug. "It's that *basic.*"

Cadel grunted. He told himself that Lexi was entitled to feel self-satisfied and that he shouldn't take it personally. Instead, he should be glad that she was such an expert decoder.

"What about you?" she asked, for all the world as if she wanted to rub it in. "Any luck?"

"No."

"Oh, well. Maybe his e-mails will tell us something."

Cadel blinked. "You mean these *are* e-mails?" he exclaimed, and Lexi looked confused.

"I thought you knew that?" she said.

"I thought they *could* be."

"Oh."

"Best thing we can do is find out," Cadel decided.

So they did. By half past six, Lexi and Cadel had tweezered some two hundred e-mail messages out of all the corrupted lines of computer code that had been rescued from Com's dying laptop. These messages proved to be a mixed bunch. Some had been sent by members of what looked like a hackers' club; Cadel recognized several tags from his own days as an active, uncontrolled hacker, before he'd decided that most of the phishers, spoofers, and other online con artists weren't really worth knowing. There were also a few ads and alerts in Com's in box, together with one or two cryptically worded questions from a former member of Cadel's Infiltration class. (Cadel made a mental note to pass this information on to Saul as soon as possible, since the police hadn't so far been able to locate many students of the Axis Institute.)

A large number of the messages related to the fact that Com seemed to be a botmaster, controlling hundreds of personal computers all over the world. He had been collecting these machines by e-mailing naïve users who'd often e-mailed back. Saul was bound to be interested in this material, too, and Cadel filed it away for future reference. But he hunted in vain for any hint that Vee or Prosper had been in touch with Com— unless their input was disguised as something else. Perhaps the ads were fake ads, with messages hidden inside them. Perhaps Vee was pretending to be one of the witless bots or the sneaky hackers. It was impossible to say without further investigation. And Cadel didn't know if he had enough time for that.

Only Dot had been communicating under her own name. For the most part her messages were unrevealing, concerned with inconsequential things like integer values or the price of computer cables. Sparse and succinct, these blunt little texts were clustered in three distinct time frames, suggesting that she had never e-mailed Com when she was able to make contact with him by some other means. (In person, perhaps?) Twice, however, she had let her guard down. On one occasion she'd remarked that she was living "just a ten-minute walk from the nearest Borders bookshop," thereby giving Cadel some fairly useful search parameters. And on the second occasion she had stupidly neglected to use an alias or code name when referring to Raimo Zapp the Third.

Zapp fell into a honey trap, her message ran, *set by a psycho Axis graduate who killed her twin sister. She made one attempt on P last year and is trying again, using dumb associate to get to him. Zapp's been warned and has backed off. Question is: how did she find out about association in the first place? Hope you haven't been chasing toxic blonds.*

"Oh my god," Cadel said breathlessly. A psycho Axis graduate who had killed her twin sister? Only one person in the world fit that description. "It's Niobe."

"What?" Lexi looked up; she had been poring over another piece of text. "Have you got something?"

"Niobe's still around. I can't believe it." Cadel noted that the e-mail had been sent two months previously. "Unless she's already dead," he added in a brittle tone. "If Prosper caught up with her, he would have killed her. At least, he would have had someone *else* kill her. He normally doesn't do it himself."

"What are you talking about?" Lexi demanded. "Who's Niobe?"

"Don't you remember?" Cadel turned away from his laptop screen. "Niobe was in my class at the Axis Institute. She and her twin sister were supposed to be psychic. Niobe ended up fracturing her sister's skull, and then blamed Prosper for what happened. She tried to kill him with a poisoned envelope, only she killed someone else by accident—"

"Oh," Lexi interrupted. "You mean that prison guard business? I remember that."

"Well, the same girl's been making a play for someone called Raimo Zapp the Third," Cadel went on. "And she's done it to get close to Prosper."

"*Raimo Zapp the Third?*" Lexi repeated, with an incredulous snort. "What kind of a name is that?"

It was typical, Cadel thought, that Lexi should have fastened on the most minor detail of the whole scenario.

"Are you listening?" he growled. "I said that she was trying to get close to Prosper English. *Through Raimo.* Do you understand what that means?"

"Of course I do! I'm not stupid." She glared at him. "It means you should be looking for Raimo Zapp the Third. Which shouldn't be hard. I bet he's the only Raimo Zapp in the entire *universe.*"

But Cadel was shaking his head. "I don't have to look for Raimo Zapp," he muttered. "I already know where he is."

"Oh yeah?" Lexi sounded impressed, despite herself. "Then why don't you go visit him?"

"Because he's in America," Cadel replied, just as Devin appeared in the doorway.

TWENTY-FOUR

Cadel said good-bye to Lexi at eight o'clock. Four hours later he was still hunched over his laptop while Devin snored away in a tangle of bed linen. It wasn't until half past three that Cadel finally began to flag—and by then he had done almost everything he needed to do.

He had checked on Saul's condition, not once but several times. He had mounted a full-scale search for Dr. Vee, exploring every possible on-line avenue. He had scanned certain Los Angeles County utility data-bases to find out whether Raimo Zapp was still paying his Canoga Park water and power bills. And then, having secured Raimo's e-mail address from one of these databases, he had booked himself a ticket to the United States—after hacking into various airline and bank systems. *I can't help it*, was his rationale. *It's an emergency. And I'll pay them back later.*

His quest to locate Dr. Vee had so far turned up nothing useful. But he wasn't disheartened, because he felt very strongly that Raimo Zapp would lead him straight to Prosper English. As long as Raimo hadn't moved from his old address (and it didn't appear that he had), then Cadel felt confident about being able to trick the American into revealing Prosper's whereabouts.

All it required was a lot of barefaced lying, a forged passport, and a plane ticket to Los Angeles.

Cadel already had the passport. Creating a false identity had been part of his course work at the Axis Institute; his false-identity kit included a phony birth certificate, a forged passport, and a complete, thoroughly tested disguise—all of which were packed into his old green bag. He intended to leave Australia in his old "Ariel" disguise, though not before running some online checks. He wanted to make sure that the girl "Ariel" wasn't flagged as a person of interest in any official database. It was possible (though highly unlikely) that someone might have warned Australia's Department of Immigration or the U.S. Customs and Border Protection Service that Ariel was really Cadel.

On the whole, however, Cadel thought that he would probably be safe. The police knew that he had disguised himself as a girl on several occasions, but they didn't know about his false identity. And although this identity had been constructed at the Axis Institute, under the supervision of Cadel's Fraud and Disguise teachers, there was no reason to think that Prosper had been alerted to Ariel's existence. The forged passport had been one small project among many; what's more, Cadel had been told to destroy the document as soon as he'd received a mark for it. But he'd been far too proud of his work to set it alight or stick it through a shredder. So he'd hidden it away, and now (as far as he could tell) no one else in the whole world was aware that he had it.

Because his Fraud teacher, of course, was long dead.

As he snuggled into Devin's beanbag, Cadel reviewed the coming day's schedule. His flight to Los Angeles would be leaving at 2:30 p.m. He would therefore have to be at the airport by one o'clock at the latest. Before that, he would have to run his checks on Ariel, as well as modifying a particular Trojan Horse program that he'd developed at the Axis Institute. This program would then have to be loaded on to a USB drive—which he would have to borrow from Devin.

But everything can be done before twelve, he concluded, *as long as I wake up early enough.* Devin had left one of his monitors switched on so that its screen would provide a night-light; in its bluish glow Cadel scanned the disarray that surrounded him: the empty cans, the knots of cable, the upended milk crates, the discarded clothes. Somewhere in that mess he'd seen a cardboard box full of USB drives—at least two dozen of them. Surely Devin would be able to spare one?

Cadel's own possessions were neatly stacked on the table. It wasn't a big stack, but he was wondering about airline luggage restrictions when his eyelids began to flutter and his head to droop. *I'm so tired,* he thought, before nodding off.

Next thing he knew, there was a loud noise. A *very* loud noise.

Slowly, reluctantly, he was dragged toward consciousness.

"Hello?" he muttered. Although his eyes were now open, he couldn't see anything. The basement was pitch black. What on earth had happened to Devin's computer screen?

"What's going on?" That was Devin's voice. Cadel recognized it, despite the fact that it sounded rough and groggy. He didn't, however, recognize the loud noise. It was a kind of harsh, grinding roar, with an underlying rumble to it. An engine, perhaps? (Mechanical, certainly.) And there was a smell, too. An odd, swampy smell. The whole floor seemed to be vibrating.

Cadel glanced at his digital watch, which had a glow-in-the-dark function. It was 7:32 a.m.

"Cadel?" said Devin, raising his voice above the chugging drone of machinery. "Are you there?"

"I'm here."

"What are you doing?"

"Nothing. I just woke up."

"What's that noise?"

"I don't know."

"What's that smell?"

Cadel didn't answer. Instead he heaved himself out of the beanbag, heading for the light switch near the elevator doors. He had to grope his way along a wall to do it.

"Did you turn off my monitor?" Devin loudly demanded. "I left that on for a *reason,* Cadel! I *always* leave it on because I don't have a bed lamp!"

"I didn't touch your monitor," Cadel rejoined. But he spoke too quietly.

"What?"

"I said *I didn't touch your monitor*." In the dark, Cadel tripped over a piece of Devin's equipment. "Ow!"

"Where's my phone? Have you seen my phone? I left it just over here . . ."

Cadel ignored Devin, who couldn't seriously have been expecting a reply. (Since Cadel could hardly see his own hand in front of his face, his chances of spotting a tiny cell phone were negligible.) Doggedly he picked himself up and continued to feel his way toward the elevator, until he finally encountered a light switch.

With a sigh of relief he flicked it on.

But nothing happened.

"The power's off!" he cried, just as Devin found his phone. A tiny square of light suddenly became visible; unfortunately, however, it wasn't strong enough to illuminate much more than the fingers holding it.

"Whatever that noise is, it's coming from outside!" Devin squawked. Cadel, meanwhile, had determined that the elevator wasn't working. Though he'd found the up button and pressed it repeatedly, there was no response.

So he made for his laptop, clumsily sidling back along the wall.

"What are you doing?" he asked Devin, who was up and about at last. Cadel could see the cell phone's luminous screen bobbing in midair, as Devin moved toward the fire exit. "Wait! Not yet! We can't go out till we know what's happening!"

The response was a creak of hinges, faintly audible beneath the other, louder noise. Devin had obviously pulled open the fire door, oblivious to whatever threat might be lurking behind it. Half a dozen possibilities had already flitted through Cadel's head: a ride-on mower, for example; or a garbage truck parked outside the kitchen; or a gang of bikers gunning their engines in preparation for a race around the enormous yard.

As long as it wasn't a bulldozer. As long as no one had decided to demolish the building because it was unsafe.

"I can't open this trapdoor!" Devin called from the top of the stairs. At precisely the same moment, Cadel found his laptop's "on" button.

"Come and help me!" Devin cried.

Cadel picked up his laptop. Its screen was already aglow, shedding enough light for him to make out everything that was blocking his path to the fire exit: Devin's mattress, the bar fridge, the TV, the DVD player. But as Cadel threaded his way between all these obstacles, he happened to glance off to his right. And what he glimpsed was so shocking—so unbelievable—that for a few seconds he froze in his tracks, unable even to catch his breath.

"Hurry up!" yelled Devin.

Cadel turned his laptop toward an air vent set high in the concrete wall. Some kind of tube or trough had been pushed through this vent. And from the end of the spout poured a stream of wet concrete, which clumped together heavily as it fell.

So far, the pool on the floor hadn't spread very far. But it was beginning to nudge the edge of a Wii console.

"Hey!" When Cadel tried to shout, he only managed to produce a squeak. So he coughed, swallowed, and tried again. *"Hey!"*

"Cadel," Devin began, from behind him. Cadel whirled around in time to see Devin's jaw drop.

"What do you mean, you can't open the trapdoor?" said Cadel. Upon receiving no answer, he repeated himself at a higher volume.

Devin, however, was speechless. He just stood there, staring at the gray tide that was lapping against all his precious possessions.

Cadel brushed past him. And as the light from the laptop faded, Devin seemed to snap out of his trance. He scurried after Cadel—who set his computer down at the foot of the stairs before adjusting its screen for maximum effect.

The noise was much louder in the stairwell.

"Is that trapdoor locked?" Devin demanded. Cadel shook his head. They both climbed the stairs, then braced themselves against the hatch.

"On the count of three!" Cadel bawled. "One, two, *three!*"

They pushed. Nothing moved.

"Again!" This time, it was Devin who took charge of the countdown. "One, two, *three!*"

Still nothing moved. The hatch remained firmly shut.

Devin began to thump on it with his fists.

"Hey!" he screeched. *"Stop! There are people down here!"*

"Turn it off!"

"Help! Stop! You'll kill us!"

Both of them yelled and pounded for another couple of minutes, until their throats were sore and their hands were bruised. It did no good whatsoever.

Cadel was the first to abandon this tactic. He could see that it wasn't going to work; their shouts would never be heard above the sound of the concrete mixer (or whatever it was), and the impact of their fists was being masked by the machine's vibrations.

Something's parked on top of this hatch, he decided, having caught a whiff of exhaust fumes.

"Use your phone!" He knew from past experience that there was no reception in the basement but was hoping that things might be better at the top of the stairs. "Call emergency!"

Devin thrust his phone at Cadel, who saw from its screen that the signal was practically nonexistent.

"Try anyway!" Cadel urged at the top of his voice. "I'll check the landline!"

He grabbed his computer when he reached the bottom of the stairs, using it to light his way back to Devin's table—which was positioned near one of the many phone jacks scattered around the room. As he picked up Devin's cordless receiver, Cadel's gaze fastened on a piece of Styrofoam that was being pushed toward him by a lava flow of wet concrete.

He couldn't hear any dial tone. The line was dead.

This isn't a coincidence, he decided. Devin hadn't used official channels to supply himself with either power or a telephone service. Consequently, no legitimate construction company would have arranged to have his utilities cut off, because it would have taken a very talented hacker to work out that he was connected in the first place.

A talented hacker like Dr. Vee, for example.

"Oh my god!" Devin exclaimed. He had staggered back into the basement and was pointing at something behind Cadel. Turning, Cadel saw more concrete spilling out of another vent.

Half the floor was now covered in a swiftly advancing gray puddle.

"Isn't the phone working?" Devin shrilled.

"No! It's been cut!" Cadel, by this time, was moving toward the elevator. He remembered that there was an access panel in its ceiling, big enough for a man to pass through. If they could open that panel and climb up the shaft . . .

"Here!" he instructed. "Come and help me!"

Devin obeyed. He reached the lift just after Cadel did, and together they tried to force its doors apart, hooking their fingertips into the crack where the two doors met. Devin pulled one way and Cadel pulled the other; they heaved and strained and grunted, slipping on the shiny floor. But nothing yielded.

"We need a crowbar!" Cadel finally gasped. "Or a lever of some kind!"

"I haven't *got* a crowbar!" Devin protested.

"Anything long and skinny! Think!"

"Is there a way out through here?" Devin wanted to know, and Cadel explained about the access panel as he looked around for a lever.

The only thing that caught his eye was a computer joystick.

"We have to make a really loud noise!" Devin wailed. "Like a big explosion!"

"How?" asked Cadel. He snatched up the joystick, just in time. Two seconds later and it would have been engulfed in concrete. "Do you *have* any explosives?"

"No! Do you?"

"No!"

"There must be something we can use!" Devin peered at the ceiling. "Do any of those pipes have gas in them?"

"You wanna blow us to pieces?"

"It's an *emergency*, Cadel!"

"It will be if you set fire to a gas pipe!" Cadel had retreated to the lift and was trying to insert his rescued joystick between the elevator doors. "Is there some kind of disinfectant in that bathroom?"

"What?"

"Go and have a look for toilet cleaner!" Cadel snapped. "Hurry!"

"But—"

"We'll need whatever foil wrapping you can find, too! And one of those plastic bottles, over there!" Seeing Devin hesitate, Cadel scowled at him. "It's for a bomb, you idiot! Just *go!*"

Devin went. He didn't have to travel very far, because the bathroom was right next to the lift. It was also about the same size as the lift, barely big enough to contain a toilet and a pedestal basin. So the search for cleaning fluids was a short one; Cadel was still struggling with the joystick when Devin returned, wielding a plastic container full of disinfectant.

"What about this?" Devin panted. "Is this any good?"

Damp and red-faced, Cadel paused in his desperate attempt to lever open the lift doors. He brushed accumulated dust and cobwebs off the toilet cleaner's label. Then he checked the list of ingredients printed there, using the pale light from Devin's cell phone. "That'll do!" he said loudly. "Now go and get the foil! The foil and the bottle!"

Devin stared at him in disbelief. "But—but there's concrete in the way!" he objected.

"There'll be even more concrete in the way if you don't hurry!"

Cadel was losing heart. No matter how hard he pushed, the lift doors wouldn't budge. And the concrete had almost reached him. Soon it wouldn't have any more room to spread, and its level would start to rise.

Devin was cursing. "It's sticking to me! It's on my feet!" he howled. *"Help! Yuck!"*

Suddenly Cadel felt something press against his own feet. Glancing down, he saw the concrete surging against the soles of his shoes.

"Jesus," he croaked.

"You'll never do it!" Devin called to him. "We should climb the stairs! It might not get to the top of the stairs!"

Cadel calculated the odds. They weren't good. But if they detonated their toilet-cleaner bomb right under the hatch, they just might get lucky. Especially if they still had space enough to keep away from the blast zone.

He began to follow Devin, slopping through liquid concrete—which was very cold and heavy. The farther he walked, the more difficult it became to pick up his feet. He felt like a mammoth in the La Brea tar pits.

But he broke free upon reaching the stairwell, where Devin accosted him, waving an empty plastic bottle and a piece of foil wrapping.

"We can blow a hole through the trapdoor!" cried Devin.

"Maybe."

"What?"

"*Maybe!*" Cadel wasn't so sure. He'd only once experimented with a toilet-cleaner bomb (when he was still very young), and it hadn't done much more than make a loud noise. Certainly there hadn't been any flames, just some rather toxic fumes. But perhaps a loud noise would be all they needed.

Halfway up the stairs, he sat down to assemble his explosive device, almost deafened by the clamor of the giant gears overhead. When he'd finished, he placed the sealed bottle right under the hatch.

"Aren't you going to light it?" Devin shouted.

"We don't have to light it!" Cadel shouted back. "The chemicals react with the aluminum!" He hustled Devin down the stairs and into a corner of the stairwell. Here they stuck their fingers in their ears, watching wet concrete creep across the floor toward them. They waited. And waited.

WHUMP!

In such a confined space, the noise had an almost physical impact; Cadel could feel it resonating in every bone. Then all at once he was coughing his lungs out. Devin was coughing, too—coughing and pointing. The concrete had almost reached them. The machine's roar hadn't stopped. It was way too dark to see what had happened to the hatch.

Not good, thought Cadel. *There should be light coming in from outside.*

"Maybe . . . *hack-hack-hack* . . . weakened it . . . *hack-hack-hack* . . ." He was so dizzy that he nearly fell as he moved back toward the stairs, stumbling against the wall as he tried to get his bearings. He had to feel his way up to the hatch—which, though hot and charred, didn't break when he pushed it. Instead, it drove a splinter into his hand.

"Ouch!" he cried. Overtaken by another coughing fit, he didn't have the strength to keep pushing.

"They must have heard!" Devin sobbed beside him. "They must have!"

Cadel shook his head numbly. It occurred to him that the situation was very, very serious. He was trapped, and couldn't think of another escape route. There was no phone. No power. The water supply was useless. A smoke signal? It would choke him to death long before it escaped through enough chinks to alert the people outside—who might, of course, already *know* that he was trapped.

He tried to calculate how swiftly the concrete would rise. How long before it reached the top step? It was already at the bottom step; he could just make out a faint, wet sheen. Devin was shaking him. The smell was terrible.

Then, all at once, the noise stopped.

TWENTY-FIVE

There was a moment's stunned silence.

Devin was the first to collect his wits. *"Hey!"* he bellowed. *"Hey! Stop!"* He began to thump on the hatch—until Cadel grabbed his arm.

"Shhh!" hissed Cadel, who was listening intently. He could hear a scuffling noise. Something creaked overhead. A light dusting of soot fell onto his upturned face as the charred timber above him vibrated; he had to turn away, coughing.

At last a muffled voice said, "Cadel? Is that you?"

"Gazo?" Cadel wheezed.

"Hang on." Gazo sounded flustered. "I've gotta move this truck."

Almost immediately, an engine roared to life again within yards of where Cadel was sitting. He slapped his hands over his ears. Then, as heavy wheels rumbled across the hatch, a sharp *crack* sent him scurrying to the bottom of the staircase.

He had a horrible feeling that the damaged trapdoor might cave in if the weight on top of it shifted. And he didn't want to be squashed by the rear tire of whatever monstrous vehicle had been blocking their way out.

"Keep clear!" he shouted at Devin, who ignored him. Devin was so desperate to escape that he kept shoving at the hatch, apparently oblivious to the fact that a huge weight was rolling across it. An ominous crunching sound, which made Cadel wince, didn't trouble Devin in the slightest. When the wood split and sagged, Devin simply pushed harder.

He gave a whoop of triumph as daylight suddenly flooded into the stairwell.

"Yay!" he cried. "Done it!"

Cadel scrambled up the stairs, so eagerly that he almost tripped. But he managed to reach the hatchway without falling, and followed Devin through it. Meanwhile, Gazo had parked the truck and switched off its engine.

"See?" was the first thing that he said to Cadel. "Ain't you glad I decided to check on you?"

Cadel had to crawl out onto the brick paving. His knees were like cotton; they wouldn't hold him up. He sat gasping for breath, squinting in the bright light.

Gazo squatted beside him, exuding a faint, foul odor.

"Christ!" Devin squawked. "What happened to *them?*"

He was on his feet, though he reeled slightly as he glanced around, shading his eyes with both hands. Cadel lifted his head. Not six yards away, a man wearing an orange safety vest lay face-down in the high grass. His hard hat had rolled off, and he had dropped his cell phone.

Gazo must have seen Cadel's gaze fasten on this motionless figure because he said, "I had to stop 'em somehow. They wouldn't listen. They kept talking about this pumping job they had to do."

Another man was lying on his back, not far from the first. He had been dragged some distance along the ground, to judge from the marks that his muddy boot heels had made. He, too, was dressed like someone off a construction site, in a tool belt, overalls, and a reflective safety vest.

"I had to pull 'im outta the truck," Gazo volunteered, as if he could read Cadel's mind. "I couldna moved it uvverwise."

"You mean you *stank* them to death?" Devin exclaimed, causing Gazo to stiffen.

"They're not dead!" Gazo snapped. "They're out cold!"

"For how long?" Cadel inquired, and Gazo shrugged.

"I dunno. About ten minutes?"

"Then we'll have to be quick." Cadel rose unsteadily, using Gazo's arm as his support. Nothing else moved. The vehicles were silent and still. The supine figures could have been discarded shop dummies.

Cadel looked from one piece of evidence to the next. He noted that the white pickup on the grass had GREENING LANDSCAPES painted on its door, whereas the much bigger truck parked near the hatch was labelled CORLUCCI CONSTRUCTIONS.

"Is that your pickup?" he asked Gazo, who nodded.

"Yup," said Gazo. "I were on me way to work, see, and I figured if I brung a gardener's truck, people would fink I come 'ere to cut the grass—"

"Are those sandbags in the back?" Cadel interrupted.

"No. They've got gravel in 'em."

"We'll need some of those." Cadel stumbled slightly on his way toward the pickup. "Two sacks each will probably do it."

"Do what?" Gazo sounded worried. "Cadel, we gotta get out. Before these blokes wake up."

"Hang on. There's something I have to do first."

"For god's sake!" Devin protested. "Could someone please tell me what's going on? Why the hell are these guys even *here?*"

"Because Prosper English sent them." Reaching the pickup, Cadel began to tug at its tailgate. "Come and help me, will you? We need about six of these sacks down in the basement."

"What do you mean, *Prosper English sent them?*" Devin's voice was shrill. He had to raise it over the shriek of rusty metal, as the tailgate was lowered. "What's Prosper English got to do with it?"

"Prosper must have gotten someone to cut off your power and phone," Cadel explained. He began to yank at the topmost bag of gravel before Gazo gently pushed him aside. "Then he would have organized a hack into Corlucci Constructions, to get this job booked in. Either their booking system is based on computer readouts or Prosper did it over the phone, with a bit of social engineering. He's good at that. He's good at manipulating people."

"But how could Prosper English even know you're here?" Devin demanded. "I thought you were supposed to be dead?"

"I am."

"Then—"

"Later. We'll talk later." Cadel turned to Gazo, who was pulling a two-wheeled trolley from the back of the pickup. "Can we load some of these sacks onto that pushcart thing?"

"*I* can," Gazo replied. "But not you. You ain't trained for it." He dumped a bag of gravel onto his trolley. "So where do you want 'em, anyway?"

"I need to get my laptop," said Cadel.

"Your *laptop?*"

"And my green bag."

"But—"

"I can't leave without them," Cadel insisted. "We have to throw these sacks into the concrete downstairs, like steppingstones. That way I can reach my computer without getting stuck."

"But this gravel ain't mine!" Gazo paused, a second bag cradled in his arms. "I can't just frow it into wet concrete; I'll get fired!"

"No you won't."

"Yes I will!"

"Not if I pay for it. You can buy some more."

"Cadel—"

"Would you please *hurry?*" Cadel was fast losing patience. "We haven't got much time!"

For a moment Gazo hesitated. Then, slowly and reluctantly, he dropped the second bag onto the first.

Devin, however, wasn't so accommodating.

"This is crazy," he spluttered. "Why the hell do you need your laptop? *My* stuff's all down there, and *I'm* not going back for it. No way."

"Your stuff's all over the floor," Cadel rejoined. "It'll be trashed by now. My stuff's up high."

Thud! Another bag of gravel joined the pile on the trolley.

"Well, I'm not hanging around for the sake of your bloody computer," Devin decided. "I'm off. Right now. Before someone blows the whistle on us."

"Fine," said Cadel. His tone was flat. "Good. Off you go, then."

Thud! went the next bag.

"And no offense, or anything," Devin added, "but don't come after me, okay? Because I can do without the hassle."

Cadel sniffed. "If it wasn't for you, there wouldn't *be* any hassle," he muttered. Whereupon Devin's eyes narrowed.

"What's that supposed to mean?" he said sharply.

Thud!

"It means that Prosper found out where I was. And not because of anything *I* did," Cadel retorted. He could feel a familiar tide of hot rage creeping up into his throat. "I've been *really, really careful*, Devin. I haven't made a single slip."

"And you're saying I have?" Devin barked. "Is that it?"

"I'm saying someone has."

"Up yours, Cadel!"

Thud!

"It might have been Lexi," Cadel had to concede. "She's always shooting her mouth off."

"Screw you," Devin snarled. "You really are a jerk, you know that? I've lost all my stuff, and now you're blaming *me!*"

"It wasn't your stuff." Cadel regarded him with icy contempt. "You stole the money that paid for it."

Devin gasped. He turned bright red. When he raised his fist, however, Gazo stepped in.

"Hey," said Gazo. "That's enough."

"What you gunna do, fart on me?" Though Devin sounded defiant, he was already retreating. "Well, screw you, too! I hope you *both* get caught, you freaks!"

"Hey—come on . . ." Gazo made a halfhearted attempt to stop him. "Don't be like that. You're all shook up. So's Cadel. You gotta pull it togevver."

But Devin wasn't listening. He had already bolted, heading for the front gate. Cadel watched him go without regret. There was no point getting sentimental about the Wieneke twins. They were loose cannons, and Cadel was quite sure that one (or both) of them had somehow tipped off Prosper English. Not deliberately, perhaps; Cadel doubted very much that they had *consciously* betrayed him. Nevertheless, they were unreliable—and he couldn't afford to get mixed up with unreliable people.

They'll be better off out of the way, he told himself. *Prosper will leave them alone, if they're not with me.*

"Come on," he said to Gazo. "Let's do this."

Ignoring his friend's doubtful look, Cadel returned to the hatch—where Gazo soon joined him. Together they stood for a moment, contemplating the sludge at the foot of the stairs.

"Are you sure it ain't too deep?" Gazo queried.

"It ain't. I mean, it isn't. You stopped it just in time." Before Gazo could raise any further objections, Cadel pushed the topmost bag off the trolley. *Thud!* A single hard shove then sent the bag rolling downstairs until it hit the congealing concrete.

"There's the first one," Cadel declared calmly. "You should go down and stand on that, so you can throw the next one in."

Gazo didn't say another word. He simply hoisted a second sack onto his shoulder and began his descent, moving very slowly and carefully. When he reached the lowest step he placed one foot gingerly on the discarded bag of gravel, which didn't sink, or tip over, or slide out from under him. As Cadel had promised, the bag made an excellent steppingstone.

Gazo was able to position both feet on top of it before relinquishing the next bag.

Unfortunately, however, he had to keep doubling back for more—because he refused all help. "Them bags are too heavy for you," was his blunt assessment of the situation. Though the minutes were ticking by, he refused to give in; with dogged persistence he single-handedly built a path to Devin's table while Cadel kept an anxious eye on the comatose construction workers.

One of these men was starting to twitch by the time Cadel's personal effects had been retrieved from the basement. It was Gazo who noticed a telltale fluttering of eyelashes on his tallest, burliest victim. "We've got about a minute to get out of here," he informed Cadel, who immediately began to sprint toward the pickup. As he flung his laptop and green bag onto the front seat, Cadel heard a groan. As he climbed in after his luggage, he heard somebody else coughing. And as he slammed the door shut, he saw movement over near the house: a hand was reaching limply into the air.

"Step on it!" he squealed.

Gazo didn't need to be told. His key was already in the ignition; there was a very nasty *chugga-chugga-chugga* before the engine suddenly fired and the pickup surged forward. Gazo spun the wheel, executing a high-speed U-turn. Bumping and skidding over uneven ground, they charged toward the gate—which Gazo, luckily, had left standing open.

Glancing back, Cadel was reassured to see that no one had yet sat up.

"Do you think they'll remember you?" he asked breathlessly.

Gazo shrugged. "Hope not."

"If they remember anything, they'll remember this truck. They'll remember Greening Landscapes on the side."

"Yeah. I guess."

"I don't see how you could get arrested, though." Cadel was thinking aloud. "Not for having toxic body odor. I mean, it's not *your* fault, is it? How can you get charged for assaulting someone when you couldn't help yourself?"

Gazo flicked him a look. "It weren't no accident, Cadel," he said drily.

"Of course not. *I* know that. But you can pretend it was an accident if anyone tries to blame you."

Gazo grunted. By this time they were several streets away from Clearview House, heading for the anonymity of a busy main road. Gazo kept checking the rearview mirror, as if he expected to see a cement truck on their tail. Cadel was nervously watching for unmarked police cars and sabotaged traffic lights.

"So where d'you wanna go?" said Gazo after a long pause.

Cadel checked his watch. It was still quite early—too early to make for the airport.

Besides which, he had things to do first.

"Where were you taking this load of gravel?" he inquired. "To the university?"

"Nah. It's for a private job. New driveway out in Vaucluse."

"Is it a new driveway for a new house?" Cadel wanted to know. "I mean, is anyone living there?"

"Not yet."

"What about the builders? Will they be around?"

"I dunno. Probably not." Gazo's tone was cautious. "The house is pretty much done—except there ain't no hot-water system. That's coming on Tuesday."

"Do you have the keys?"

"Only to the garage."

"Then we'll go there," Cadel decided. "I need to download something. *And* get changed. And maybe send an e-mail, if I can do a bit of wardriving on the way."

"But—"

"I'll need a USB drive as well. Maybe we can swing by a computer shop, and you can go in and buy one for me."

"Listen—"

"And after all that, you can drop me at the airport."

"The *airport?*"

"I'm going to America." Cadel frowned as the pickup swerved. "Keep your eyes on the road, Gazo."

But Gazo was already pulling over. He braked in front of a doctor's office without switching off the ignition. Instead he left his engine idling as he turned to confront Cadel.

"You gotta be kidding me," said Gazo. "America? Are you mad?"

"I don't have a choice."

"Of course you do!"

"I don't. There's a lead I have to follow." Seeing Gazo open his mouth, Cadel quickly forestalled him. "If I stick around here, Prosper will find me. My job is to find him first."

"Yeah, but—"

"I'll be getting help from Kale Platz," Cadel went on. "Remember Kale? He's an FBI agent."

Gazo's brow puckered. "Uh—"

"He came here from America a couple of years ago. He was the one who arrested Prosper, that time when Vadi knocked you out."

"Oh. Yeah." Gazo hadn't forgotten the night he'd escaped from police custody. "So Kale Platz—he was the one who locked me in the van?"

"That's him."

"And does he know you're coming?"

"Not yet. I'll tell him when I arrive."

"Cadel—"

"I've got his address and phone number. There won't be any trouble. All you have to do is help me get on the plane."

But Gazo was shaking his head.

"If Saul finds out I done all this . . ." he began, then sighed.

Cadel tried to reassure him. "If Saul finds out, I'll be the one who gets in trouble," he insisted.

Gazo gave a derisive snort. "Are you joking? He'll have me for dinner."

"He won't."

"He *will*."

"Then disappear!" Cadel was rapidly losing patience. "You've done it before. If you're that scared, lay low for a while. You'd be better off vanishing anyway, with Prosper on the warpath."

"And lose me job?"

"You'll get another one," said Cadel—at which point something else occurred to him. "Speaking of jobs, do you have any money? I can't go anywhere near my bank account in case Vee's keeping an eye on it." When there was no immediate response, Cadel pressed Gazo further. "I'll pay you back. I need to exchange it for some American dollars."

Still Gazo didn't speak. He was staring straight ahead, his lips pressed tightly together.

"What? *What?*" Cadel demanded. "Tell me what the problem is! I can't mess about, Gazo. If you're not interested, just let me out right here and I'll find an Internet café. I can always get the money from Sonja's account; I know *she* won't mind. She'll understand how important it is."

At last Gazo turned his head. "You know what?" he mumbled. "You sound just like Prosper."

"Huh?"

"When he used to boss people around, I mean. Sometimes he'd be firing off orders like no one else had a brain in their 'eads. He talked like that to me all the time." There was a quiet dignity in Gazo's rebuke. "I know I'm not real smart—not like you, Cadel. But you'd still be in that basement if it wasn't for me. You got no call to be acting like whatever I say ain't worf listening to."

Cadel swallowed. All at once he felt dizzy.

"Sure, I'll let you into that garage. And I'll take you to the airport, too, since you're probably right. You usually are," Gazo admitted. "All I'm saying is, you should watch yourself. Because nobody likes a smart-arse bullyboy, and most people don't know you like I do. They might take it wrong. Same as Devin did."

"I'm sorry," Cadel whispered. He was horrified. Stricken. He suddenly looked so white—so ill—that Gazo hastily tried to make amends.

"It's okay. It's just because you're scared, I reckon. You didn't really mean it, eh?"

"I'm so sorry."

"Don't fret. I ain't mad or nuffink." When Cadel seemed to derive no comfort from this, Gazo offered up more in the way of reassurance. "You're only a kid. You've had a tough time. When *I* get scared, I stink the place out. So I can't exactly blame you, can I?"

"I'm sorry," Cadel repeated. "I'm so sorry."

"Hey—no harm done. Forget about it." Gazo reached for the gear stick. He flicked on his indicator and checked for approaching traffic.

Before he could pull back onto the road, however, Cadel squeaked, "Stop!"

Obediently Gazo braked. The pickup jerked to a standstill. Cadel pushed open the passenger door and leaned out.

Because he hadn't had any breakfast, there wasn't much to throw up. Even so, it wasn't a pleasant experience.

TWENTY-SIX

Cadel had never been on a plane before. At least, he couldn't *remember* having been on a plane before. As a two-year-old he'd been smuggled into Australia from the U.S., but he wasn't quite sure how this had been accomplished—whether by plane, boat, or submarine. He had no memory of the trip, and Prosper English hadn't provided any details.

So he was quite nervous as he approached the airport, despite the fact that he knew what to expect. He'd been briefed by Gazo, and he'd watched countless television documentaries over the years dealing with things like air safety, thrombosis, and customs officials.

Nevertheless, he couldn't help worrying. It was hard not to, because he was traveling under a false name, with a forged passport, as a member of the opposite sex.

The main problem was that Ariel didn't quite fit him anymore. Though he hadn't grown much since first donning her snap-on earrings and Indian cotton skirt, there had been a lot of minor changes in his appearance—so many that they were beginning to affect the overall impact of his disguise. He was still small enough and cute enough to pass as a girl, but only if he was exceedingly careful. It couldn't be done unless he took various precautions: plucking a few mustache and chin hairs, wrapping a scarf around his Adam's apple, wearing sleeves so long that they covered not only his arms but most of his hands as well. (His knuckles were no longer the knuckles of a teenage girl.) His jumper had to be very baggy, and his makeup had to be very thick.

He also had to do as little talking as possible. Though his voice wasn't exactly a booming baritone, it had well and truly broken; no matter how high he pitched it or how softly he spoke, it wasn't entirely convincing as a girl's voice. So he'd decided to pretend that he had laryngitis. If he kept coughing and sniffing and squirting saline spray up his nose, people were unlikely to question his hoarseness, or his reluctance to answer questions.

"They might stay away from me on the plane, as well," he'd observed, "if they're afraid of catching the flu."

"They might," had been Gazo's response. "Or they might be shoving cough drops and aspirins and neck pillows at you the whole time. Blokes on planes always chat up young girls. I seen 'em do it on my way here from England."

"You think?" Gloomily Cadel had surveyed himself in the pickup's wing mirror. He'd looked good, but not *that* good. Surely even a pair of enormous blue eyes wouldn't be enough to make up for a hacking cough or a volley of wet sneezes? "Maybe I'll pretend not to speak English," he'd decided.

He had taken a taxi to the airport, having come to the conclusion that Gazo's pickup was too distinctive. A Greening Landscapes gardening truck was exactly the sort of vehicle that might stand out on CCTV footage of the airport's busy drop-off zone—where there were bound to be dozens of security cameras. And although Gazo had wanted to come with him in the cab, Cadel had scotched this idea, as well. In many ways, Gazo was just as distinctive as his truck. It was possible that Vee or Com or Dot might be keeping an eye out for Gazo, whereas it was much more unlikely that Ariel would trigger any online alarms.

Unlikely, but not out of the question. Despite his enveloping scarf, high heels, and baggy jumper, Cadel's measurements might still rack up enough matches to alert a video analytics program. So he kept his head down on his way to the check-in line, using his handkerchief to shield his face as he pretended to blow his nose repeatedly.

The taxi trip hadn't been much of a challenge. After receiving his instructions from Gazo, the driver hadn't uttered a single word during the entire half-hour journey. This might have been because Cadel was posing as a foreigner who couldn't speak English. Or it might have been because the driver himself hadn't been exactly fluent in the same language. Whatever the reason, they had parted without exchanging more than a halting sentence or two.

But the check-in counter was different. A cheerful Qantas representative asked Cadel question after question. Did he want an aisle seat or a window seat? Had he packed his bags himself? Were there any sharp instruments in his carry-on luggage? Cadel answered hoarsely, sucking on a cough lozenge as he sniffed and mopped his nose. He was hoping that the cold symptoms might explain his grumpy, monosyllabic demeanor. He was also hoping to distract the attendant with his wet noises and eucalyptus smell while she checked his passport, which hadn't really been used before. He was concerned about his passport. He didn't know if it was convincing enough.

He needn't have worried, though. After about three minutes, he came away from the check-in counter with his boarding pass, his departure card, and instructions about where to go next. The security checkpoint was a breeze; having briefly surrendered his watch and computer bag, he stepped through the metal detector and was quickly on his way. No one asked any questions. No one wanted to search his baggage. He was surrounded by busy, preoccupied people who weren't the least bit interested in who he might be, or what he might be up to.

It was still possible, however, that he was under surveillance. The airport was honeycombed with electronic security systems, and there were cameras mounted everywhere. For that reason, during his ninety-minute wait in the departure lounge, Cadel spent most of his time glued to one carefully selected spot. He had chosen it because it gave the cameras a restricted view of the top of his head. As long as he remained there and didn't look up, his face would stay off the airport's CCTV footage. In fact, he was so anxious to avoid being filmed that he moved only once, to go to the toilet (in the ladies' bathroom). Otherwise he sat with his head down, either reading or pretending to sleep, until his flight number was called.

And all the while he was sweating bullets, afraid that the police were going to pounce on him. Even after he'd boarded his flight and the hatches had been firmly secured, he didn't feel entirely safe; it was still possible that a last-minute delay might ruin everything. Only when his plane had finally taken off did he stop worrying about police interference—and start worrying about Prosper English instead.

Planes were vulnerable things, run by complicated computer systems. What if Vee had worked out how to invade the navigation program on this particular flight? What if he'd done it to another plane as well and the two aircraft were heading straight for each other? What if Prosper knew *exactly where Cadel was,* and had decided that a midair collision would get rid of him once and for all?

If Prosper wanted to crash this plane, he would have done it when it was taking off, Cadel reasoned. The most dangerous sections of any flight were the takeoff and the landing; he had heard this over and over again, from any number of sources. If Prosper hadn't sabotaged the jet during takeoff, when so many things could go so terribly wrong, then he was unlikely to do it over the Pacific Ocean.

That was what Cadel told himself, anyway. It was something to cling to during the fourteen-hour trip, which he didn't enjoy very much. Apart from the hovering threat of sabotage, he had to endure all kinds of other discomforts—like the constant attentions of the woman wedged in beside him. She was a fat, friendly, gray-haired grandmother named Jan, who wasn't at all put off by his sniffing and coughing. On the contrary, she seemed worried about him and kept trying to make him comfortable. She would offer him her serving of cheesecake, for instance, or show him where his airsickness bag was, or kindly explain away various frightening phenomena. "You always get a bit of turbulence when you're flying through clouds," she would say; or "That's just the undercarriage retracting; isn't it, Vern?"

Vern was her husband. He didn't talk much, but he had a bladder problem. After he had climbed over Cadel four times in one hour to go to the toilet, Cadel agreed (in a hoarse mutter) to swap seats with him. So Vern ended up on the aisle, and Cadel found himself trapped by the window, unable to escape Jan's endless chatter about swelling feet, sore ears, and dehydration. "You should get up and walk around," she suggested more than once. "Otherwise you'll get a blood clot."

Cadel dodged this steady stream of advice as best he could. He buried himself in a glossy magazine. He slapped on a pair of earphones and stared hard at the miniature TV screen in front of him. He pretended to fall asleep—and then he *did* fall asleep, only to be wakened two hours later by Vern's reverberating snores. After that, he didn't sleep again. He was too cramped, and worried, and miserable. There were so many things to keep him awake and fretting, apart from the air-safety issue and the fragile nature of his own disguise. He was anxious about Saul and Sonja. He was concerned that his plan to trick Raimo Zapp might fail. He was nervous about getting through U.S. Customs, and even more scared about what might await him outside Los Angeles airport.

Most of all, however, he was troubled by what Gazo had told him. To be accused of talking like Prosper English . . . what could be worse? For years Cadel had been actively rejecting the lessons he'd learned as a child. Yet he seemed to be reverting to his old patterns of behavior. Was Prosper's influence impossible to eradicate after all? Was it like a clinging vine, rooted so deep in Cadel's past that no amount of hard work could rip it out?

It's because I'm stressed, he decided. *When I'm dealing with Prosper, I end up acting like Prosper. Which is another reason why I'm better off on my own just now.*

God forbid that he would ever find himself using and abusing other people the way Prosper did.

Breakfast was served about two hours before the scheduled end of the flight. Although he wasn't hungry, Cadel forced down a small wad of scrambled egg and half a sausage. Then, as the plane gradually descended, he pressed his nose against the window and watched California unfold beneath him. Jan kept asking him if he could see Disneyland or the Hollywood sign, but he ignored her. He wasn't much interested in the scenery. Instead he focused his attention on the plane itself: on its speed, its heading, its hydraulics. He watched its flaps rise and its wheels drop. He listened for any telltale bangs and checked the air crew's faces for signs of panic.

The landing, however, passed without incident. A smooth touchdown was followed by an uneventful trip along the runway. Cadel didn't leap up when the seat belt signs were extinguished. Instead he chose to disembark with the stragglers, sensing that the first passengers to go through customs might endure closer scrutiny than the last ones off the plane. He waited until Jan and her husband were well ahead of him, then joined the tail end of the crowd that slowly made its way down corridors and along moving walkways, until it reached a forbidding row of glassed-in booths.

Here, at last, were the U.S. Immigration officials.

Cadel's heart began to pound as he surveyed these stone-faced men and women. He couldn't help thinking that they would be more suspicious than the staff at Sydney airport—if only because he was arriving, rather than leaving. What's more, each booth was fitted with equipment that scanned both eyes and fingerprints, and Cadel wasn't sure about his status in America. The chance that he'd left his fingerprints behind as a toddler was almost nonexistent; nevertheless, he approached his designated booth with a dry mouth and sweaty hands.

The woman behind the counter accepted his passport without comment. As she studied his photograph, he sniffed glumly, trying to look as sick as possible.

"Here on vacation?" the woman suddenly fired at him.

Cadel nodded.

"Visiting family?" she asked.

"A family friend."

"Is that who you're staying with?"

"Uh-huh."

Cadel had declared on his immigration form that he would be living at Kale Platz's house during his trip to America. It wasn't a complete lie, because Kale was still part of the investigation into Prosper English. The FBI had been monitoring Prosper's activities for years, and Kale had visited Australia at least twice since rescuing Cadel from Prosper's seaside mansion. Kale and Saul Greeniaus were in regular contact, frequently exchanging tips, warnings, and personal updates. What's more, the FBI agent had sent the Greeniaus family a Christmas card with his home address printed clearly on the top left-hand corner of the envelope.

So Cadel was quite sure that Kale would be happy to hear from him. In fact, it was possible that the FBI had already been warned about Cadel's disappearance. And if that was true, then he didn't have much time—because Kale Platz had seen him dressed as Ariel. Two years before, when Cadel had walked out of Prosper's house into police custody, he had been wearing exactly the same skirt and earrings and hairstyle. It wouldn't be long before Kale remembered that. It wouldn't be long before the FBI started checking passenger manifests and CCTV footage.

All I need is a couple more hours, Cadel thought. *Just a couple more hours, and then I'll turn myself in.*

His plane had touched down at 9:15 a.m. He was therefore convinced that he would be enjoying Kale's hospitality by mid-afternoon—and if Kale decided differently, then U.S. Customs and Immigration could take it up with the FBI.

"Yeah," he added, in husky but confident tones. "I'll be staying at my friend's place."

"Could you place your right index finger on the screen, please?"

Cadel obeyed. He had his photo snapped, his eye scanned, and his fingerprints taken before he was waved on. No electronic alarms were triggered. He wasn't asked to step into a back room. Clearly his biometric details weren't on file in the United States.

And if the woman who interviewed him had any niggling doubts about his gender, she kept them to herself.

Cadel proceeded toward the baggage claim carousel. Here he picked up his green bag, which he'd checked as a precaution. (He'd decided that it might look a bit odd if he went all the way to America with only carry-on luggage.) There was a queue to get through the Customs checkpoint, but no one wanted to inspect *his* meager possessions, and he soon found himself waiting in a taxi rank, surrounded by cars and concrete.

The cabs didn't look like Australian cabs. The drivers didn't have Australian accents. Everything seemed intensely foreign, yet oddly familiar; Cadel felt as if he were in a Hollywood movie. He was so dazed and disoriented that, when asked where he wanted to go, he forgot to disguise his voice. He forgot about coughing and sniffing and mumbling into his handkerchief, and blurted out Raimo Zapp's address without making the slightest attempt to sound like a girl with the flu.

It didn't matter, though, because the cab driver was completely uninterested in his passenger's true identity. There was only one thing that concerned him: whether Cadel had enough money to pay for a trip to Canoga Park.

"Thassa long way," he warned Cadel. "That will cost you—oh, more'n fifty bucks."

"It's okay." Cadel had three hundred and seventy-five American dollars in his wallet, courtesy of Gazo's bank account. "I'll need you to wait for me at the other end, too. Can you do that?"

"Yeah. But it might be a hundred. A hundred plus."

"That's fine."

"You got the money?"

"I've got it. Could we go?"

Cadel was growing nervous. He didn't want to linger near the camera-infested airport. He was also worried about his appearance, which seemed to be having a bad effect on the cab driver. Did Cadel really look so untrustworthy? Was there something dishonest about his face or his clothes or his voice? Why did he give the impression that he couldn't pay his bills?

It was only later, after they had traversed Los Angeles, that Cadel realized what the problem really was. Canoga Park lay in the San Fernando Valley, more than thirty miles northwest of the airport. To get there, the cab had to cut through endless stretches of suburban sprawl, passing strip malls and shopping centers, parks and schools, bridges and construction sites. Though he didn't see any beaches or movie stars, Cadel did see all kinds of things that he'd never laid eyes on before: billboards ten stories high, advertising new television shows; a white church the size of a parliament house, occupying an entire hill; block after block of stores that were covered in Spanish signage. He saw diners and pet salons, yellow school buses, and black and white police cars. It was all so new and dazzling that it kept him confused and off-balance for quite some time.

But as the meter ticked away, he gradually began to understand one all-important fact. In Los Angeles, the wealthy people were so immensely rich that, by comparison, the poor people seemed somehow poorer. And after taking such a long tour through neighborhoods where every house looked like a miniature Greek temple, or Renaissance palace, or Georgian country seat, Cadel quickly realized—upon reaching Canoga Park—that he had arrived in one of the less prosperous parts of town.

Suddenly, he understood his driver's concern. The problem wasn't Cadel's youth, or his cheap clothes, or his lack of luggage. The problem was his destination.

Gazing out at dusty yards and peeling paint, it occurred to Cadel that a lot of people in Canoga Park wouldn't be able to afford a one-hundred-dollar cab fare.

TWENTY-SEVEN

Raimo Zapp's house came as a big surprise.

It was a small, shabby place that seemed to be cowering behind a two-car garage. The front yard was unfenced and badly in need of a mow; apart from the neglected lawn, it contained only a shaggy palm tree and a letterbox. The aluminum windows were all firmly shut, as were the venetian blinds that hung rather crookedly behind them. Pale stucco walls were streaked with gray stains, and paint was peeling off the shutters.

Cadel had expected something a little more flashy, despite the fact that Raimo's neighbors were all living in similar houses, on a street that had a dusty, depressed air about it. Surely a visual-effects genius didn't have to scrape around for spare cash? Surely Prosper's bribes must have been temptingly substantial?

Only later did it occur to Cadel that Raimo had probably been spending his money on the latest computer graphics equipment—which could cost hundreds of thousands (if not millions) of dollars. All over the world, techno-geeks were constantly skimping on things like food, clothes, and deodorant so that they could buy the latest gadget or game. Cadel could understand this compulsion perfectly.

"I'm going to leave my stuff in the car," he said to the driver. "If you wait here, I'll be back in about fifteen minutes." Seeing a mistrustful frown reflected in the rearview mirror, Cadel added, "There's a laptop in this bag. It's worth a lot more than my fare, so I'll definitely be coming back for it. Okay?"

A grunt was the only response from the man behind the wheel. Now that the money issue had been resolved, nothing seemed to perturb him; on his way to Canoga Park he hadn't so much as blinked when a monstrous truck had veered into the lane just ahead of his cab, almost clipping its front fender. The bewildering tangle of freeways hadn't fazed him in the least, and he hadn't asked a single question during the entire course of the trip.

Nevertheless, Cadel had decided not to push his luck. Changing clothes in the taxi might have been a little too weird for the driver to stomach. And although Cadel could have changed in a big shopping mall somewhere—ditching his old cab as a girl before hailing a new one looking more like himself—he was pretty sure that an American shopping mall would be full of cameras.

As for using a more isolated bathroom, it simply wasn't an option. Deserted football fields weren't usually supplied with working taxi stands, no matter what city you were in.

So he had decided to approach Raimo as Ariel, despite being extremely concerned about a prolonged, face-to-face encounter. Would all the sniffing and coughing be enough to disguise his voice? Was Raimo the kind of computer jockey whose inexperience with girls would leave him so dazzled by a display of jewelry and makeup that he wouldn't see through them? It was difficult to say—especially since Niobe was part of the equation.

Cadel didn't know if she was still around. If she was, it was doubly important that he conceal his true identity. And even if she wasn't, she might very well have told Raimo about him. Or *Prosper* might have told Raimo about him. Either way, it was possible that Raimo might recognize him if he turned up as Cadel, in his usual sneakers and T-shirt.

On the whole, Ariel was a safer bet. Therefore Cadel marched up Raimo's driveway in Ariel's high heels, with Ariel's ponytail bobbing against the back of his neck and Ariel's skirts swishing around his ankles. He tried to remember what he had learned at the Axis Institute about disguising himself. *Transformation isn't as hard as you might think, if you've got the right attitude,* his teacher had once told him. *Whether you're mak-*

ing yourself visible or invisible, the thing about a disguise is that half the time you can hide behind just one prominent feature. A big nose. An awful tie. Even a giant pimple. People will be so busy noticing whatever it is that they won't pay much attention to the rest of you.

Cadel decided that his fake cold might serve as a distracting focal point. And as he pushed the doorbell, he wiped his nose on his handkerchief, aware that someone might be inspecting him through the peephole in the front door.

At last he heard footsteps from somewhere inside. They grew louder and louder, before stopping abruptly. There was a scraping, jingling noise, which he identified as the sound of a security chain being fastened.

The door opened a few centimeters, revealing two luminous brown eyes magnified by a funky pair of orange-rimmed glasses.

"What do *you* want?" a reedy voice inquired.

"Oh—ah—are you Raimo?" asked Cadel. His own voice was so shrill with nerves that it had a convincingly feminine pitch to it.

"Why? Who wants to know?"

"I'm Ariel."

"Who?"

"*Ariel*. I'm Warren's friend? He told me he sent you an e-mail."

"Oh." There was a pause. "Okay . . ."

"He wanted me to give you something."

The orange glasses disappeared for a few seconds. There was more scraping and jingling, then the door creaked open farther. Cadel found himself staring at a man of about his own height, who was dressed in a black T-shirt, tight black jeans, and pointy-toed snakeskin boots.

"Ah'm Raimo," said the man. His short body and long limbs made him look vaguely like an insect. So did his all-black outfit and his small bony skull, which was clearly visible beneath a close-cropped layer of peroxided hair. Despite the bags under his eyes, he didn't seem to be very old—perhaps in his mid-twenties. "You better come in, ah guess."

Cadel obeyed, trying not to look as scared as he felt. It was like walking into a freezer, thanks to the power of Raimo's cooling system. With every step, old candy wrappers crunched beneath Cadel's shoes; there were hundreds of wrappers strewn across the shag pile carpet, which was a bright, almost fluorescent green. The house reminded him of Com's place, because it had stale-smelling air and grubby paint. Com's place, however, had been damp and moldy, with small windows and high ceilings, whereas Raimo's house was a 1960s box, cramped and unadorned and full of filtered glare. What's more, there were no walls of old computer equipment. Raimo's technology was all cutting edge, except for his collection of antique pinball machines. Cadel was hugely impressed by those—and by the more modern arcade games, as well. He couldn't believe how many of them had been jammed into the front room, which otherwise housed only a bar fridge, a wall-mounted flat-screen TV, and a novelty chair shaped like an enormous red hand.

Raimo sat down on the palm of this hand, leaning back against its fingers.

"So what's the story?" he inquired, folding his arms and crossing his legs. His tone was imperious; he had a southern accent. "Suddenly ah get an e-mail outta the blue from someone ah never met, saying he works for Andrew Hellen and asking if ah kin place a body scan. Like ah'm some sorta distribution point. What is this, a setup? Huh? Are you trying to finger me—is that it?"

Cadel played dumb. From the very beginning he had cast himself in the role of ignorant messenger, sent on a mission that he didn't understand. "Hey!" he squeakily protested. "I'm just doing Warren a favor. *I* don't know what it's all about."

This, of course, was a lie. Though the e-mail sent to Raimo had supposedly been written by Hamish's friend Warren, it had actually come from Cadel—who had secured Raimo's e-mail address from a certain Los Angeles County utilities database. While impersonating Warren, Cadel had offered Raimo a scan of Nicole Kidman, feeling sure that such a prize would be irresistible. Cadel's message had also warned Raimo that a friend would bring the scan to Los Angeles and collect payment for it; there could be no question of dispatching such an enormous file through cyberspace, where it was bound to go astray. *I know there must be a market out there I just don't know where it is*, Cadel had written. *I figure you can pay me a percentige of the Fee & I can keep a look out for more good scans we could have an arangemint.*

He wasn't sure whether Raimo would take the bait, so he'd tried not to sound too crisp and professional. The spelling mistakes had been deliberate—as had the somewhat grandiose style. In striving to come across as a greedy teenager, Cadel had even used various computer-gaming terms, describing Ariel as his avatar, and commiserating with Raimo for having been "seriously ganked" by the computer graphics industry. *Andrew Hellen says you got XP with black market scans*, Cadel had explained, *and my friends going to LA so why not?*

Ariel herself was another convincing element in his plan. No self-respecting police force would send a sick teenager to entrap a suspect: at least that was Cadel's theory. He knew that his age was a definite plus. For that reason, he adopted the fretful whine of a spoiled suburban princess—the sort of girl who would be utterly clueless when it came to any form of computer technology other than Facebook and iPhones.

"All Warren did is give me this," he continued, coughing piteously as he produced a USB drive. "I'm supposed to give it to you once you pay for it. That's all he told me. Apart from the name and address."

Raimo's lip curled in a sneer. "Are you kidding?" he scoffed. "You think ah'd hand over money for something sight unseen?"

"That's what he *told* me."

"Well, you kin forget it," said Raimo, nodding at the sliver of metal in Cadel's palm. "That could be anything. Hay-ell, it could be *nothing*."

"But I'm supposed to get the money!" Cadel's voice cracked as it mounted toward a squeal. "Can't you just call him?"

"Why don't *you* call him?" was Raimo's uncooperative response.

"Because my phone doesn't work over here."

"Are you from Australia, too?"

"Of course I am!" Cadel was careful to sound affronted. It was easier to stay high-pitched that way. "Can't you tell?"

Raimo shrugged. He was watching his visitor with bright, unblinking eyes, and something about the way he sat there—a dark little dot in a giant red hand—made him look like a squashed mosquito.

"What about *your* phone?" Cadel suggested. "We could use that."

Raimo said nothing. Instead he uncoiled his limbs and stood up. *Crunch-crunch-crunch* went the soles of his boots as he strode through a sea of candy wrappers. Cadel nervously followed him down a narrow hallway, past a room fitted out as a home cinema. The screen in this room was gigantic; it faced two rows of raked, adjustable seats, which were upholstered in plum-colored velvet and fitted with cup holders and footrests. It seemed obvious to Cadel that Raimo had blown all his money on the most luxurious home cinema known to man.

And then they passed the room next door.

Confronted with rack upon rack of eye-popping computer technology, Cadel realized that he was mistaken. The greater part of Raimo's wealth must have been poured, not into home cinema wiring, but into the kind of equipment that NASA would have envied. All at once, Raimo's arctic air-conditioning made perfect sense. It was clearly for the benefit of his machines, which exuded a lot more heat than your average suburban family. Hovering on the threshold, Cadel saw that several holes had been punched in one wall so that cables could be run from an adjoining room. The only trace of human occupation was the layer of wrappers on the floor.

"Here," said Raimo up ahead. He was standing just inside the doorway of the rear bedroom. When Cadel joined him, Raimo gestured at one of three desks that had been wedged into this rather cramped space, which was also occupied by a king-sized waterbed. The bed was unmade, and its black satin sheets were littered with more candy wrappers. The desks supported an array of computers, printers, modems, USB drives, mikes, speakers, and phones. "You kin use the Star Trek phone," Raimo instructed, "but you gotta call collect."

Cadel hesitated. The Star Trek phone was on the other side of the room; to reach it, he would have to turn his back on Raimo. Had Raimo engineered this maneuver for the sole purpose of attacking him from behind? It seemed unlikely, but Cadel couldn't afford to take any chances. He was all alone, in an unfamiliar environment. If he never emerged from this house again, no one in Australia would ever know what had happened to him.

Then suddenly his gaze fell on the floor—and he realized that there was no way in the world that Raimo could launch a surprise assault. Not with so many wrappers strewn around. The crackle of plastic underfoot would be a dead giveaway.

"Well . . . all right," Cadel agreed, crunching past the bed. "Just don't blame me if he gets really mad at being woken up."

As he punched his own number into the keypad of Raimo's Star Trek communicator phone, Cadel surreptitiously scanned the room for traces of Niobe. But there was nothing: no photographs, no jewelry, no discarded underwear. If she was around, she was keeping a very low profile. Perhaps she had learned to do that, over the years; Cadel didn't know. At the Axis Institute she had never been a retiring sort of person. On the contrary, she and her sister had been loud, exuberant, and messy. It was possible, however, that she had changed since then. It was possible that she had learned not to leave a trail of hair accessories and feather-topped pens in her wake.

Cadel could see no evidence that *anyone* had been in the house apart from Raimo. Certainly there was no sign of Prosper English. When given the choice, Prosper had always tended to live a rather elegant life, full of silk shirts and marble bathrooms. Grotty project homes ankle-deep in rubbish weren't his style. Had Prosper ever set foot in this place, he would have done something about the wrappers. And since there appeared to be several months' worth of wrappers on the floor, it was unlikely that he had been a visitor for at least that amount of time.

On the other hand, it was perfectly possible that he had been communicating with Raimo, who had an eerily familiar quality about him. Raimo was exactly the sort of employee who had always ended up on Prosper's payroll—and not for the obvious reasons, either. Sure, Raimo looked a bit odd. Sure, he was an obsessive loner, just like so many members of the Axis Institute staff. But it was his strangely disconnected air that was so unnerving. Again and again, Cadel had encountered the same sort of thing at the Institute: a sense that the person in front of you wasn't truly engaged with you or with anyone else. A feeling that you were being regarded as an inanimate factor within some utterly self-centered scheme, conspiracy, or distorted worldview. Brendan, Max, Luther, Vee . . . they had all shared this characteristic. They had all suffered from the same tunnel vision.

At one stage or another, they had all studied Cadel the way Raimo was studying him now—with a gaze that was both wary and calculating, yet fundamentally dismissive.

"The number you are calling is not currently available . . ."

Hearing a recorded voice, Cadel was hugely relieved, though he hadn't really expected anything else. As far as he knew, his cell phone was sitting somewhere in the wreckage of his demolished bedroom, without a battery.

"No answer," he informed Raimo, who seemed unimpressed.

"Too bad."

"I could try again. In a couple of minutes."

"Nuh-uh." Raimo shook his head. "If he ain't picking up his phone at four a.m., he won't be picking it up at four fifteen."

"But—"

"You wanna show me something? Then come back when you kin show it to me. Ah'm a busy man. Ah got work to do. You're wasting mah time."

"But I *can't* show it to you!" Cadel lamented. "I don't have a computer to put it on!"

"Ah do," said Raimo. Despite his bored and patronizing tone, there was something about the way he kept his attention fully focused on Cadel that betrayed a quickening interest. "You kin upload it onto one of mine. Then ah kin check out what's on it, and pay you if it looks good."

Cadel had a hard time controlling himself. He was both delighted and astonished; who would have thought that his disguise would prove to be *this* successful? Apparently Raimo had sized him up as a complete bimbo unable to understand that once the contents of the USB drive had been uploaded, the actual drive would lose its value. Raimo thought that Ariel was stupidly trying to sell the drive, rather than the information on it.

And Cadel was happy to go along with this misconception.

"So if you don't want it, you'll give it back?" he asked plaintively.

"Yeah. Like with a jacket. If ah try it on and it don't look good, ah'll put it back on the rack."

"Which means it wouldn't get ruined or anything?"

"Ruined?" Raimo's scorn was almost palpable. "How could it get ruined?"

"Oh, *I* don't know!" Cadel whimpered. He was fiddling with his handkerchief, trying to convey the agony of his indecision. "This is all too hard for me! I should never do favors, I always get screwed!"

Raimo tapped his chunky gold wristwatch with one finger. "You got thirty seconds," he declared. At which point Cadel capitulated.

"Okay," he said, thrusting the USB drive in Raimo's direction. "You take it. What do I care? It's not like I'm being *paid* for this."

The little device was promptly plucked from Cadel's grasp. Holding his breath, he watched Raimo sit down in front of the nearest computer—which was already turned on. All Raimo had to do was shove Cadel's USB drive into the appropriate port.

As the connection was made, Cadel scanned his immediate vicinity for some means of defending himself. Though he could rely on Raimo's computer to behave in a predictable way, he couldn't tell how Raimo himself would react. At best, there would be recriminations. The worst-case scenario might involve thrown chairs or black eyes. Cadel didn't know Raimo well enough even to hazard a guess; the safest thing was to be prepared for anything.

He braced himself for the coming explosion.

"God day-um!" Raimo suddenly exclaimed. "What *is* this?"

"Huh?"

"Ah cain't get nothing off this piece of junk! Cain't even read it!"

"What do you mean?"

"There ain't no scans on this here." Raimo turned in his seat to glare at Cadel. "What are you trying to pull? Huh?"

"Nothing!"

"You must think ah'm some kinda dim bulb!"

"Is it broken?" Cadel tried to sound disoriented. "Maybe you need a special password—"

He broke off, dodging the USB drive. Raimo had hurled it at him.

"Git!" barked Raimo.

"But—"

"Ah'll count to three. If you ain't outta here by then, ah'll go git mah twelve-gauge." Rising, Raimo stood with his shoulders hunched and his teeth bared. Despite his small size, weedy build, and kitsch glasses, there was something extraordinarily menacing about him. Perhaps it was because he looked so much like a wasp; there was even a waspish buzz to his voice, which grew more and more noticeable the angrier he became. "It's legal to shoot burglars in these parts," he hissed, "and since you're just a thief who's trespassing on mah property, ah guess no one'll blame me if you leave here with a load of pellets in your ass!"

With a frightened yip, Cadel bolted. He ran down the hallway while Raimo shouted after him.

"ONE!"

Cadel skidded to a halt, blocked by the front door.

"TWO!"

He yanked the door open.

"TWO AND A HALF . . ."

Pelting along the concrete driveway, Cadel risked a fleeting glance over his shoulder, just in time to see the front door bang shut behind him. But he didn't slow down. Though he doubted very much that Raimo was about to shoot him on the street, in broad daylight, Cadel was glad of an excuse to run. He wanted to reach his cab as quickly as possible.

"Quick!" He slammed into the side of the cab, then jerked open the nearest passenger door. "Let's go!"

"Where to?" the driver asked as Cadel flung himself into the back seat.

"Just go," said Cadel. "I'll tell you when to stop."

The driver shrugged but didn't argue. Cadel began to fumble in his green bag, feverishly searching for his antenna. Only when his laptop was on and his various scanning programs were fully engaged did he look up to inspect the scenery gliding past.

It was more of the same: stucco houses, bearded palm trees, patchy lawns. The driveways were full of vehicles—two or three per house. A parked car had its hood up, so that someone could tinker with its engine.

"Stop!" Cadel exclaimed. "Pull over! Right here. That's it."

The cab rolled to a standstill. Cadel peered at his computer screen. He had managed to infiltrate somebody's wireless connection and wasn't entirely proud of the fact. But it had to be done. He couldn't waste time. If he didn't act quickly, he might lose his only chance.

The *clickety-click* of his fingers on the keyboard finally seemed to rouse the impassive driver, who went so far as to look around.

"You gettin" out here?" the driver asked.

"In a minute." *Click-clickety-click.* "In a minute I want you to take me to the nearest public phone."

"You mean this isn't where you wanna get out?"

"Not yet. Hang on. Let me finish." Sensing an unexpected degree of restlessness in the front seat, Cadel wondered if his driver might actually know what was going on. "I can't take notes in a moving car," was the first excuse that popped into Cadel's head. "Just let me finish this letter, would you?"

The driver gave a grunt. And at that precise moment, Cadel found what he had been looking for.

"Gotcha," he crowed. A few more keystrokes was all it took; soon data was gushing into his laptop, which absorbed the invisible flood silently, without pause or complaint.

At last Cadel raised his eyes from the screen in front of him.

"All right," he announced. "Five more minutes, and then we can go. Maybe to a shopping center. There must be plenty of public phones in a big shopping center."

"A mall, you mean? You wanna go to a mall with pay phones?"

Cadel nodded.

"That's it," he said. "Take me to a mall with pay phones."

TWENTY-EIGHT

Raimo's computer files contained a scan of Rex Austin.

Cadel sat back, staring at his laptop screen. Around him the buzz of the food court was almost deafening. Bright lights bounced off sleek plastic and shiny chrome. Dozens of people were lined up at counters ordering fried chicken, hamburgers, tacos, sandwiches, noodles. Dozens of other people were sitting at tables chewing away at doughnuts or sandwiches or slices of pizza. Here and there, cleaners were pushing mops around, or picking up rubbish.

Cadel had bought himself a bag of chips with the change left over from his very expensive taxi ride—though not before getting rid of Ariel. Her skirt, shoes, jewelry, makeup, and undergarments were once again stuffed away in his green bag, which lay on the floor between his feet. Changing back into his ordinary clothes hadn't been easy. Though he had entered the ladies' toilet with complete confidence, he'd found that walking out again—as a teenage boy—had required a lot of nerve. But he had managed to do it (thanks to some split-second timing) and had then marched straight to the nearest pay phone, trying to ignore the pounding of his heart.

All the while he'd been conscious of the security cameras overhead, tracking his every move.

"*Hello?*" Kale had answered on the very first ring.

"Uh—is that Kale Platz?"

"*Yes.*"

"It's Cadel. Cadel Greeniaus."

The ensuing pause had told Cadel everything he needed to know. So had Kale's eventual reply, which had been crisp and to the point.

"*Where are you?*"

"Los Angeles."

"*What?*"

"Could you come and get me?" Though he'd sensed that Kale was already aware of recent developments in Australia, Cadel had nevertheless started to sum them up. "Prosper's been trying to kill me. He nearly killed my friend Sonja—"

"*I know. Just tell me where you are.*"

"I'm at the Beverly Center. I can wait for you in the food court."

"*Then that's where we'll meet. Just stay right there, okay? Don't go anywhere with anyone else.*"

"I won't," Cadel had promised.

"*Do you have a cell phone?*"

"No."

"*I'll be there as soon as I can.*"

"Wait. Before you hang up—"

"*What?*"

"How's Saul?"

Kale's response had been tinged with exasperation. "*He'll be feeling a lot better now that he knows you're all right.*"

Something about Kale's tone had suggested that a lot more would be said on the subject, at the appropriate time, in the appropriate place. Not that Cadel was particularly concerned. Compared to all the other threats that hung over him, a tongue-lashing was the least of his worries.

Anyway, when Kale sees this scan, it'll make up for everything, Cadel decided. He himself knew that the scan of Rex Austin was incredibly important. For one thing, it meant that Raimo—or someone he knew—had been in physical contact with Rex. It also meant that Cadel might have been unfair to Lexi. Maybe she hadn't told anyone that he was at Clearview House, after all. Maybe the leak had occurred because of Devin.

Devin had been stealing money from Rex. According to Devin, it had been easy to siphon a few thousand dollars out of the billionaire's electronic bank accounts without triggering any alarms. But suppose Devin had miscalculated? Suppose he *had* been noticed?

As Cadel pieced together a possible scenario, he blocked out all the distractions in his immediate vicinity. There was a pattern emerging; he could feel it. Raimo Zapp had been associating with Prosper English, who in turn had helped Rex Austin to set up Genius Squad. Raimo had a scan of Rex on file. Devin had been preying on Rex's bank accounts. And as soon as Cadel had moved in with Devin, Prosper had found out about it.

Could Rex and Prosper still be cooperating? Cadel thought it very likely. He had never met Rex Austin, and neither had Kale Platz or Saul Greeniaus. Rex was a hard person to get hold of; he could buy enough lawyers, security guards, and personal assistants to keep the rest of the world at bay. But what if Prosper English had wriggled his way through Rex Austin's defenses? What if the two men were in cahoots?

And what if Rex had somehow identified the thief who was preying on his bank deposits?

Devin's name would certainly ring a bell with Prosper, who might have decided to keep an eye on him after all—despite the fact that Cadel hadn't met with the Wienekes for months. Of course, Devin didn't get out much. And when he did, it was usually at night. Plotting his movements via local CCTV networks would have been next to impossible. So how had it been done? Online, perhaps? Did Vee have Devin's passwords?

And then, suddenly, Cadel recalled the USB rocket launcher that Devin had received as a thank-you for buying so many other gadgets. Perhaps it hadn't been a gift at all. Perhaps it had been a Trojan horse: a bug disguised as a generous gesture. Cadel could easily imagine someone like Dr. Vee keeping track of Rex Austin's money as it moved from the billionaire's bloated coffers to Devin's false accounts to the online cash registers of Apple and Microsoft. Perhaps Vee had noted Devin's purchasing habits and faked a delivery to match them. Perhaps Devin's greed had been Cadel's undoing.

If so, then Prosper could have been listening to every word uttered in the basement of Clearview House. The thought made Cadel feel quite faint. He blinked and shook his head, trying to expel a rising sense of panic. Lifting his gaze from the computer, he sought to comfort himself with an everyday suburban scene: the bustle and clatter of a busy food court.

That was when he saw that something had changed. Around him, the tables were empty. A breathless hush had replaced the murmur of conversation. No one was hovering behind the steaming displays of hot food.

His heart seemed to do a backflip. *Oh my god,* he thought. *What's happened?*

"Cadel," a lone voice said. "Are you okay?"

Cadel looked around. Kale Platz stood about nine yards away, small and slim and dressed in a rumpled gray suit that was exactly the same color as his eyes. He'd grown a mustache since his last visit to Australia, but otherwise his sallow, long-jawed face hadn't changed much. What remained of his mousy hair was still cut very short.

His tense demeanor didn't do much to calm Cadel's fears.

"He-hello," Cadel stammered. "What's going on?"

"You tell me." Kale was watching him intently. "Is there anything I should know?"

"Yeah. Lots. I've got some really interesting stuff here." But even as he spoke, Cadel knew that he'd misinterpreted the question. Several large men in dark suits were positioned around the vacated food court. A uniformed police officer had joined two security guards in front of a pizzeria outlet. "Is this . . . ? Are you . . . ? I'm not carrying a bomb, if that's what you're worried about."

"Did you come here with anybody?"

"No."

"Where did you get that computer?"

Cadel swallowed. It dawned on him that the food court must be in a state of lockdown. Somehow this particular wing had been cordoned off while Cadel had been wrapped in a daze of calculations.

I've really got to stay more alert, he told himself. *What if Kale had been Prosper English?*

"This isn't a trap," he assured the FBI agent. "No one kidnapped me. It was my own idea."

"What's in the bag?"

"Clothes. Oh—and a wardriving antenna, but—"

"Push it toward me. With your foot."

"But—"

"Do it."

Seething, Cadel did as he was told. He surrendered his green bag. He lifted his hands from the keyboard. He stood up to let Kale pat him down.

But when Kale reached for the laptop, Cadel said, "Wait. Hang on. I have to show you something on that."

"Later," the FBI agent rejoined. He shut the computer with a *snap* before carelessly tucking it under his arm. Several of his colleagues were converging on Cadel, who didn't like to see his precious laptop being treated in such a cavalier fashion.

"Please be careful," he begged as Kale hustled him to the nearest exit. Other agents closed in around them, to form a protective barrier. "That computer has some really important stuff on it. Stuff that needs to be backed up. I put a special virus on a USB file that went into the computer of a guy called Raimo Zapp."

"Has anyone else been using it?" Kale asked.

"Using what?" said Cadel. "*My* computer?"

"Has anyone else had access to it? Either directly or indirectly?"

"No."

"Are you sure?"

"I think I would have noticed if it had been interfered with," Cadel retorted. By now they were heading toward a service lift, down a corridor that hadn't been decorated with consumers in mind. There was a lot of bare concrete and scratched paint; clearly, this part of the mall was for staff only. "You've got it all wrong," he continued. "Prosper doesn't know

I'm here. At least, I don't *think* he knows. I'm one step ahead of him now. I've got some good data; I just have to work out what it means."

Kale, however, wasn't listening. He was too busy coordinating Cadel's transferral from one floor to another, using a walkie-talkie to communicate with various unseen colleagues stationed around the mall. So Cadel gave up. He stopped trying to explain and allowed himself to be delivered, like a prisoner or a parcel, into the custody of the FBI. From the service lift he obediently followed Kale across an unpopulated strip of parking lot, until they arrived at a small cluster of dark, shiny four-wheel drives. One of these cars had been earmarked for Kale and Cadel; its driver lurked behind a heavily tinted windshield. Half a dozen armed escorts piled into the other two vehicles, which were supposed to be shielding the front and rear of Cadel's car.

"Where are we going?" he inquired as soon as they were on the move.

"Westwood," said Kale, from beside him.

"What's that?"

"It's where I work," Kale replied. "In a secure facility."

"Is it very far?"

"No."

"It's not a jail, is it?"

The FBI agent slowly turned his head. He studied Cadel with a piercing gaze as their vehicle jolted over a speed bump and swerved onto the street. There was a brief pause.

"No," Kale said at last. "Why?"

Cadel shrugged. "I dunno," he muttered. "That's what secure facilities usually are, aren't they?"

"Not this one. The Federal Building was designed to keep people *out*."

"Oh."

"On the other hand," Kale drawled, "maybe jail is the best place for you, after the stunt you've pulled."

Cadel's heart sank. He'd been hoping for a short respite before the reproaches started flying about. But he took a deep breath and tried to defend himself.

"I was going to pay back the money," he quavered. "Just as soon as I could."

Kale's eyebrows jumped. "What money?"

"Uh—"

"There's *money* involved?"

"I had to buy a plane ticket," Cadel pointed out. "It was a phony deposit—"

"From where?"

"From nowhere. It didn't *belong* to anyone. It wasn't *real* money."

Kale clicked his tongue. "This gets better and better," he growled. "A false passport, an illegal entry, and now a fraudulent transaction."

"I told you, I was going to pay it back!"

"You think that makes everything all right?" Kale said roughly. He fixed Cadel with a baleful glare. "What the *hell* is the matter with you? Huh? I thought you were meant to be some kinda genius?"

Cadel bristled. He'd been expecting condemnation but nothing quite so harsh. "You don't understand—" he began, before Kale interrupted him.

"No. *You* don't understand," the agent snapped. "You are in deep shit, kiddo. Not only with your poor old dad, but with the Department of Homeland Security, and with the Federal Bureau of Investigation, and with the entire Australian police force—"

"*I had to do this!*" Cadel cried, flushing. "Prosper English is trying to kill me! I have to track him down!"

"*You* have to track him down?"

"Yes! *I* do!"

"Because no one else can? Is that it?"

Cadel flinched away from the sneer in this question, but it didn't silence him. "Yes. That's right," he confirmed quietly, lifting his chin and squaring his narrow shoulders. "Because no one else can do what I can do."

The FBI agent uttered a wet, scornful noise. "You might want to listen to yourself," he rapped out. "You might want to consider what you sound like when you say something like that. The word 'megalomaniac' springs to mind."

Cadel gasped. "I'm not a megalomaniac!"

"No?"

"I'm a *realist*."

"Yeah," Kale scoffed. "I've heard that before. From inside traders. And insurance scammers. They all say 'Let's be realistic, here. Who really loses out?'" He thrust his flattened nose and beetling brows at Cadel. "They all seem to think the law doesn't apply to *them*."

Cadel was beginning to falter beneath this barrage of accusations. He felt winded, as if Kale had kicked him in the solar plexus. He also felt bewildered. Surely his motives were obvious? He'd been trying to *save lives*. Prosper had knocked his house down, for god's sake!

"You can't talk to me like that," he said at last, hoarsely. "Everyone I care about is ending up in the hospital. I'm living like a fugitive because the police can't catch Prosper English. And you're blaming *me* for doing what it takes?"

"Lying? Stealing?"

"It's got me a whole lot closer to Prosper English than *you* are!"

"So what you're saying is: the end justifies the means." Kale's tone was dry and flat as he flipped open a packet of chewing gum. "Wasn't that Stalin's excuse? You still got a ways to go, son. Looks like Saul hasn't beat all that Axis Institute crap outta you, just yet. Maybe it's because he doesn't always play by the rules himself—especially where his family's involved. Personally, I wouldna let you anywhere *near* this case." He popped a blue stick into his mouth. "One thing I do know, after so many years on the job: by acting like the guys you're after, you end up just the same," he concluded. Then he leaned forward to address his colleague. "Keep it tight, Chuck, or some A-hole's going to cut in ahead of us."

Cadel turned to stare out the window. His hands were shaking. His stomach was churning. His eyes were glazed with tears. *It's because I'm so tired*, he assured himself. *If I wasn't so tired, I wouldn't be so upset.*

He knew it was more than fatigue, though. Kale had touched a sore spot. He had tapped straight into one of Cadel's greatest fears—just as Gazo had.

What if Prosper English had left a permanent brand? What if Cadel's default setting would always be the one that Prosper had programmed into him so many years ago?

"I guess it could be worse," Kale suddenly remarked. "At least you had the sense to call me. That's gotta count in your favor. What we need to do now is make sure there's nothing else I should know about. Nothing that needs to be squared away with the right people." *Chomp-chomp-chomp* went his jaw. "You'd better give me a full debrief. Every detail, from the time you left police custody."

But Cadel shook his head.

"I can't," he croaked, thinking of Gazo and Lexi and Devin.

"Cadel—"

"I'm not a snitch."

Kale sighed. "Okay—how about this?" he said. "Anyone else involved, you call 'em X or John Doe. Whatever."

"You might still know who they are."

"I might," Kale conceded. "But there's nothing I can do about it. This won't be a formal statement. You're not making any admissions relating to these people. And it's not like they're in my jurisdiction."

Cadel hesitated.

"I'm not lying to you. I don't make a habit of lying. Like I said before, there's a right way and a wrong way." Cocking his head, Kale fixed Cadel with a steady, searching look. "If you want me to watch your back, I've gotta know what kind of trouble might be heading straight for you. And I can't do that without information."

It was a perfectly valid point. Cadel could see the sense of it. And he wasn't feeling strong enough to stand firm, what with his queasy stomach and his growing fatigue.

"All right," he said. Then he launched into a halting account of the previous two and a half days.

TWENTY-NINE

"Hey. Buddy."

Cadel jerked awake. He had been dreaming that he was in the Beverly Center food court and that someone was sitting across the table from him: a gray-haired man in a tweed jacket. At first glance this man had looked like Prosper English—but only at first glance. Closer inspection had revealed that his pale skin was growing browner and more leathery; his dark eyes were beginning to turn blue; his mobile mouth was hardening into an iron trap. "What's wrong with you?" he'd said crossly, in Raimo's voice. "You know who ah am. Just think about it."

Rex Austin, Cadel thought as he sat up. He was on a couch, in an office. The office was on the tenth floor of the Federal Building, at 11000 Wilshire Boulevard, Westwood. He remembered that now. He remembered where he was. Kale had brought him to the Los Angeles headquarters of the FBI, which occupied several floors of a huge white tower set in a vast expanse of asphalt parking lot. After passing through all kinds of security checks (scanners, metal detectors, code-locked doors), Cadel had finally arrived at Kale's workspace, which looked just like any other workspace with its array of desks, cubicles, computers, telephones, and ergonomic chairs. There was also an office with a couch in it; Cadel had been invited to use this couch once he'd finished telling Kale all about recent events involving Raimo Zapp, Rex Austin, and the basement of Clearview House.

Upon consulting his watch, Cadel saw that he'd been asleep for four hours and twenty-eight minutes.

"There's a call for you," said the strange man who'd woken him, holding out a cordless phone. "You wanna take it?"

"Uh—"

"I think it's your mom."

Cadel rubbed his eyes. Then he reached for the phone, which he placed gingerly against his ear. "Hello?" he mumbled.

"Cadel?" It was Fiona, all right. She sounded strained. *"Is that you?"*

"Yeah." He coughed. "I'm here."

"What's wrong? Are you sick?"

"No. I've been sleeping." An awkward silence ensued; Cadel finally broke it with a question. "How's Saul?"

"He's good," Fiona replied. *"The MRI results came in, and they're good. He's got a big lump on his head and a fractured collarbone, but that's about it. He'll probably be discharged tomorrow morning."*

"Great." Cadel would have liked to say something a little more heartfelt, but Kale's colleague was standing nearby, listening to every word. "That's fantastic."

"I'm not sure where we'll be living." Fiona's voice was dull, as if she felt too exhausted to be anxious. *"My mother's offered to put us up, but there's really no room for you at her place."*

"Don't worry about me," Cadel said quickly. "I can't live with anybody right now." That much, at least, was blindingly clear to him—even in his groggy condition. "I'm too much of a target. They'll have to put me in a bunker or something."

"Is that why you ran away?"

Cadel swallowed. He couldn't answer immediately. At last he said, "I had to disappear. I didn't have a choice."

"It wasn't your fault, Cadel. The house. The injuries. No one's blaming you for those." When Cadel didn't respond, Fiona added, *"Saul's here. He wants a chat."*

"Hang on." Cadel covered the mouthpiece. He gazed up at the man who was hovering over him and said, "I need to talk to my dad. Could you . . . I mean, can I do it in private?"

Kale's colleague considered this request for one carefully measured beat then nodded. "Sure," he replied.

"Thanks." Cadel waited until he was alone in the office before addressing the phone again. "Okay. I can talk now."

"Cadel?"

Cadel's heart skipped a beat. "Uh—hi," he said hoarsely, having recognized Saul's voice. It was a touch weaker than usual, but otherwise unchanged. There was no slurring or hesitation.

Cadel's feelings were mixed. On the one hand, he was braced for a scolding. On the other hand, he was almost sick with relief and gratitude.

Because Saul was alive. Alive and alert.

"Kale tells me you're okay," the detective remarked.

"Yes."

"He tells me you managed to decode some of that stuff we lifted off Com's laptop." Quite unexpectedly, Saul got straight down to business. Cadel had been expecting a preliminary reprimand. *"He tells me Raimo Zapp was mentioned in one of Dot's e-mails. Along with Niobe and Prosper English."*

"Yes." Cadel eagerly pounced on this chance to explain the thinking behind his recent conduct. Could Saul have decided to skip his lecture about willful recklessness and move on to a tactical discussion instead? "When I saw that e-mail, I realized how important Raimo Zapp's files would be. And they are. I haven't looked at them all, but he's got a scan of Prosper English. *And* one of Rex Austin. Did Kale mention that?"

"He did. Yes. He also mentioned that they might not be admissible as evidence in a court of law, thanks to the way you got hold of them."

Cadel caught his breath. Then he let it out in a sigh of resignation. So he wasn't going to be let off the hook, after all.

"I know the law isn't your area of expertise," Saul went on. *"But you'll have to factor it into a few decisions if you're determined to take the lead on this. Which you obviously are. Against all advice."*

"I had to come. I didn't have a choice." Hearing no response from the other end of the line, Cadel began to defend himself.

"Prosper found me at Clearview House. He sent a bunch of builders to pump the basement full of concrete."

"*I know.*"

"He must have told them where to park. So they would block the emergency exit. He had it all worked out."

"*I know. Kale briefed me.*"

"I got scared. I mean, I got *really* scared." Only in hindsight did Cadel realize how scared he had been. At the time, he'd been too busy planning his next move to focus on the welling fear in his gut—which might very well have affected his ability to think things through. "Maybe I should have asked Fiona to buy the plane ticket," he allowed. "Maybe I panicked a bit too much. But I did have to come here. I couldn't have stayed."

Saul muttered something inaudible. Before Cadel could ask him to repeat it, however, the detective said wearily, "*At least you'll be safe enough at an FBI field office.*"

"I'm sorry I didn't tell you." No matter how feeble it might sound, Cadel knew that he had to apologize. For everything. "And I'm sorry about what happened. About your head and . . ." His voice trembled slightly. "And the house . . ."

"*That WASN'T YOUR FAULT.*"

"I should never have moved in with you. I should have known that Prosper would come after me one of these days—"

"*Okay, listen.*" Saul cut him off. "*I didn't call up to give you hell or listen to a load of garbage about this being all down to you. I called because you're in trouble.*" There was a brief silence, as if the detective was husbanding enough strength to proceed. At last he murmured, "*I can't help you, Cadel. I'm stuck here in bed, my arm's useless, and I . . . I'm no good to you right now. What you need is a lawyer.*"

"But—"

"*Kale's a good guy. I trust him. I like him. And he likes you. Trouble is, he's not in charge over there.*" The sound of labored breathing suggested that Saul was either close to tears or—more probably—trying to adjust an injured body part without hurting himself. *"Fiona and I both think that you should have proper legal representation,"* he concluded, a little raggedly. *"So we're sorting it out with the FBI. Kale's got no problem with that. He thinks it's a good idea."*

But Cadel didn't. On the contrary, he was aghast. "I don't want you paying for a lawyer!" he yelped. "You'll go bankrupt!"

"Cadel—"

"No way! No *way!*"

"You're a juvenile. Someone has to be there for you."

"No they don't. Because I'm helping the FBI. I'm going to break this case wide open for them." Cadel hurried to back up this extravagant claim, knowing that Saul was probably skeptical. "When Kale talks to Raimo, we're going to find out a whole lot more. We might even find out where Prosper's living! Don't you think they'll go easy on me if that happens?"

The detective's sigh came gusting down the line. *"It won't happen,"* he said.

"What do you mean?"

"Raimo's not talking," Saul pointed out. *"He's lawyered up and accusing you of gaining unauthorized access to his computer. He wants you charged, Cadel."*

"How—how do you know that?"

"Because I talked to Kale. Before I talked to you. He told me what's been going on."

Cadel felt slightly winded by this unexpected blow. He had to collect his scattered thoughts before speaking again. "You mean Raimo's in custody?" he asked. "You mean Kale got him while I was *asleep?*"

"That's right," a sharp voice interrupted. It was Kale himself, walking into the room with a couple of dark-suited colleagues. "We went straight over and picked your guy up for questioning," he said. "But I don't know how long we can hold him. Not on one e-mail pulled off Compton Daniels's laptop." As Cadel opened his mouth, Kale anticipated his question. "Your dad had a *warrant* to confiscate that machine. Zapp's files are another matter. We're still working on the legalities."

"Who's that?" Saul buzzed into Cadel's ear. *"Is that Kale?"*

"Yes," Cadel replied. "Do you want to talk to him?"

"Could I?"

"Saul wants to talk to you." Handing over the phone, Cadel noticed that Kale's companions had identical looks on their faces: calm, mild, unresponsive looks. He wondered if all FBI agents were trained to look like that when dealing with people they didn't know.

"Yeah. Oh, yeah. Uh-huh." Kale seemed to be answering Saul's questions. "Yeah, about an hour ago. Nothing so far. Whole place is empty. What?" A pause. "Yeah, I wouldn't be surprised. I'll have to check it out myself. Yeah. Yeah." Kale glanced over at Cadel, then quickly averted his eyes again. "Yeah, I *was* thinking that. Now we've got an all clear. Wouldn't be any risk—I'd be going myself. Okay. Sure. Mmm-hmm."

Cadel sensed that he himself was being discussed but couldn't work out the context. What whole place was empty? Why did Kale need an all clear?

"No, I'll do it now. Okay. Yeah. Don't worry. Sure. It's taken care of." Abruptly Kale broke the connection. "A nurse just came in to see your dad," he informed Cadel. "But he'll call again later. You okay with that?"

Cadel nodded.

"Good." Kale surrendered the phone to one of his companions, who whisked it out of the room. "Meanwhile, there's something you can help us with. It's a long shot, but I think it's worth a try. Since you know Prosper English better than anyone." He turned to his remaining colleague. "Have we heard from Gus yet?"

"No, sir."

"Well, go and see what the trouble is, will you? I want to be out of here in ten minutes." Having dispatched his messenger, Kale leaned against the nearby desk, arms folded, ankles crossed. "I'm still not sure what you know," he said, fixing his hard, bright, speculative gaze on Cadel. "I guess someone must have told you we've been keeping a lookout for Rex Austin? He's wanted in connection with the Genius Squad bust. But he's a hard man to get hold of."

"Yes. I heard about that," Cadel replied cautiously.

"In fact he's *so* damn hard to get hold of that we're starting to wonder," Kale confessed. "I mean, the guy's always been paranoid. He's always been security conscious, on account of all the dough he's got. He was never one to fill his house with staff or go anywhere on foot. When he wants to meet somebody, he does it by Skyping or video conferencing. He's a loner," Kale added. "Kinda guy who doesn't trust people. Like me."

Cadel waited.

"But there's paranoid and paranoid," Kale went on. "And when a guy sacks the personal assistant he's had for twenty years, you can't help taking notice. Especially when he sacks his butler, too. And his accountant. Not in person, mind you. Just leaves a message."

"You've had him under surveillance?"

"Not exactly. Like I said, no one's laid eyes on him for months. But we've been monitoring his activities, and he's been making some pretty big changes. In his business life as well as his personal life."

"You mean—"

"Closing accounts. Selling companies. Firing staff." Kale cocked his head. "And now this body scan crops up. Sitting in Zapp's computer, alongside a scan of Prosper English."

"So it could be one of two things." Cadel's brain had been working furiously. "Either Rex wants to do what Prosper's been doing and make it look like he's somewhere he's not—"

"So we won't be searching in the right place. Yeah. That's one explanation."

"Or Prosper's impersonating Rex," Cadel finished. Although the first possibility had already occurred to him, the second was entirely new. It hadn't even crossed his mind, owing to a dearth of background information. "Maybe Prosper's trying to take over the whole Austin business empire," he posited. "Maybe the scan is for security footage. Or videophone messages. Maybe they've got some kind of voice transformation technology as well—so people will believe it's Rex who's ordering them around instead of Prosper."

"Maybe."

"Because that would make sense, wouldn't it?" Cadel was thinking aloud. "If the police have been cracking down on Prosper's bank accounts, then where's he been getting his money from?"

"Good question."

"He could have been stealing it off Rex. Or maybe the two of them are working together, and Rex has been *giving* Prosper the money." As far as Cadel could see, there were two acceptable scenarios: either Prosper had persuaded Rex to revamp Austin Enterprises—and elude the police with the help of fake CCTV footage—or Prosper had gotten rid of Rex, and needed a scan to take over the dead man's property. "What do *you* think? Do you think Rex Austin is still alive?"

Kale shrugged. "It'll be hard to prove he isn't unless we find a body," was his oblique response. He hadn't taken his eyes off Cadel. "That's why we've raided his place in Laguna Beach."

Cadel blinked. The look on his face seemed to amuse Kale, who cracked a sour little smile.

"What do you mean?" Cadel demanded. He sensed that he was missing a very important piece of the puzzle. "When did that happen?"

"Oh . . ." Kale glanced at his watch. "About two hours ago."

"Two *hours* ago?"

"We've got reason to believe that Prosper English might have moved in."

A sudden tapping at the door interrupted this exchange. As Cadel gaped like a fish, speechless with confusion, Kale turned to field whatever inquiry might be heading his way.

But it wasn't an inquiry. It was an announcement, delivered by the same agent who'd been sent to find out what the "trouble" was. "We're set to go," he reported from the threshold. "I was just talking to Gus. He says the car's ready, and it's all clear at the other end."

"Okay. Thanks," said Kale. "You wanna round everyone up?"

"Sure."

The obliging agent vanished again, so swiftly and silently that he might have been a genie disappearing in a puff of smoke. Kale turned back to Cadel.

"A while ago, your dad sent us some interesting data," said Kale. "It was a set of applications designed to infiltrate all the Bluetooth appliances in a networked house. An *American* networked house."

"I know about that," Cadel interposed—then caught his breath. "God!" he exclaimed. "Don't tell me it was written for *Rex Austin's* house?" But it must have been. He could see that now. It made perfect sense.

It also settled one particular matter, once and for all.

"I don't think Rex is alive," he declared. "Or if he is, he's being held captive."

"Whoa. Hold on." Kale lifted a hand. Cadel, however, wouldn't be silenced. He found himself babbling enthusiastically, as the complete picture began to take shape in his mind's eye.

"Someone as paranoid as Rex Austin would be hard to get at, *unless* you infiltrated the security system in his house. I mean, you could sabotage one of his appliances so he'd call a repairman. And you could send your *own* repairman. And that would be the end of that. Especially if you shut down all his alarms at the same time." Cadel could imagine the whole sorry spectacle. He could practically see it playing out in front of him. "It must have been Vee who designed that program," he mused. "Somehow he must have got hold of the house specs. Do we know who the architect was? Or the electrician? They might be worth talking to."

"We haven't found them yet," said Kale. "But I tracked down the insurance policy on that house, and every item listed there matches the applications in the program you dug up. When you told me about Austin's scan, I put two and two together. I suddenly remembered his beach house—because I've been to that house. I went there months ago to see if he'd talk about Genius Squad. It was some spread, I've gotta tell you."

"You went inside?" Cadel exclaimed. Kale, however, shook his head.

"Couldn't get past the lobby," he admitted. "Your dad hadn't sent me those applications back then, so I didn't have a case that would *get* me inside."

"But now you do?"

"Since we saw the insurance policy. It's a match, all right. Looks like Austin wanted a staff-free house. He wanted a fridge that would order his food, and a robot that would clean his floors, and heating that he could turn on before he got home." Kale snorted. "Like I said, he didn't trust people. And the more staff you have, the riskier it gets."

"I guess so." All the same, Cadel couldn't help wondering if computers were riskier than people in the long run. "So when you dug up the insurance policy, and saw that everything matched the hack from Judith's house—"

"I sent a team down to Laguna Beach," Kale concluded.

"Right."

"And now I want you to check out the place yourself." Upon receiving no answer, Kale frowned. "Cadel? Did you hear me?"

"Mmm?" Cadel was distracted by vague memories of what he'd read about voice cloning. Was speech-synthesis technology advanced enough nowadays for Prosper English to imitate Rex Austin on the phone? Or had Vee devised yet more breakthrough programming—perhaps with the aid of a rogue sound engineer, instead of a computer graphics expert like Raimo Zapp?

"Earth to Cadel? Did you hear what I said?"

"Huh?" Cadel snapped out of his reverie. "Oh. Sorry. What?"

"I said I want you to check out Rex Austin's place," Kale repeated. "The one in Laguna."

"*Me?*"

"I've got a team down there right now, with a search warrant. But they haven't found anyone. There's no sign of Austin—*or* English. That's why I figure you could help." Cadel's lack of response drew from Kale a more detailed explanation. "See, if we've missed something, you might pick up on it. Since you know Prosper English better than anybody."

Cadel grunted. Though he'd said much the same thing on any number of occasions, the thought that it might be true suddenly seemed unbearably depressing. For one thing, it implied that he and Prosper were somehow alike.

"I doubt I know Prosper better than you," Cadel mumbled. "You're the one who's been investigating him all this time. You must know him pretty well by now."

"Yeah, but you've had breakfast with the guy—and lived to tell the tale. None of *us* have done that. You've been up close and personal." Seeing Cadel's vinegary expression, Kale tried to adopt a wheedling tone (without much success). "It's perfectly safe down there. We've made sure it's not bugged or booby-trapped. The way we've got it staked out, it's probably safer than the Pentagon."

Cadel said nothing. He was too busy swallowing the bitter taste in his mouth.

"It's up to you," Kale grudgingly had to concede. "If you don't wanna go, you can bail out. Or we could put it off for a couple of days while you make up your mind—"

"I'll go. You're right. I should go." Cadel stood up. He had decided, abruptly, that there was no point fretting over the past. Not when the future seemed so uncertain. "When are we leaving? Now? Will I have time to go to the toilet?"

"Uh . . . yeah. Sure." Though taken aback by this apparent change of heart, Kale clearly welcomed it. He clapped Cadel on the shoulder. "Do you wanna bite to eat first?"

"No, thanks."

"Did you bring a toothbrush? I can send Chuck out to buy one. And there's a shower downstairs if you feel like freshening up."

"I'm okay. Don't worry about me," said Cadel, whereupon his companion pulled a wry face.

"I *have* to worry about you, kid. You're not sixteen yet." Kale began to nudge Cadel toward the door. "In fact, I've fixed up a lawyer for you, but I guess she'll have to meet us in Laguna Beach. Since we don't wanna be waiting around for the whole afternoon—"

"A *lawyer?*" Cadel stopped in his tracks. "What lawyer?"

"Don't look so scared. She's good. She specializes in juveniles."

"But—"

"You're not under arrest. You're just underage." Kale couldn't stop a hint of impatience from creeping into his voice. "You need someone to take care of your interests. I'd do it myself if I could."

"But a lawyer . . ." Cadel protested. "Lawyers cost money! And I don't *have* any money!"

"We'll work something out," said Kale. "There's a reward posted, remember? Fifty thousand dollars, for information leading to the arrest of Prosper English. If we catch him, you'll be eligible for that reward." He dredged up another acidic little smile, so lacking in mirth that it was more like a scowl. "Hell," he added, "fifty thou should buy you at *least* two days with a third-rate lawyer. And you'll have enough change left to treat yourself to an ice cream sundae!"

If this was meant to be a joke, Cadel didn't find it very amusing. Nor was he particularly reassured. In fact, he began to wonder, on his way downstairs, whether Kale had told him everything he needed to know. The FBI wasn't famous for its transparency. Cadel couldn't help feeling that somewhere in the bureau's archives, a big, fat file probably had his name on it.

I just hope they understand where I fit into all this, he fretted. *I hope they understand which side I'm on.*

He told himself to stop thinking like Prosper English as the elevator doors slid open.

THIRTY

Cadel fell asleep in the car. When he woke up again, about forty minutes later, it was still moving.

"Are we there yet?" he drowsily inquired, peering out the window. A distant oil refinery was visible, ominous and imposing against a backdrop of dark clouds.

"Not yet," said Kale, who was sitting beside him.

"It's funny seeing all these gum trees," Cadel observed. "It's like we're in Australia." Then he had second thoughts. "Except in Australia there aren't so many oil derricks all over the place," he added.

No one replied. The two FBI agents in the front seat—Chuck and Feliz—hadn't yet opened their mouths. As for Kale, he was tapping out a text message on his phone.

When he'd finished, he turned to Cadel.

"Are you hungry?" he said. "We can pick up a burger if you like."

"No thanks." Cadel's stomach was screwed into a tight little knot; the prospect of forcing food into it made him feel queasy. "Does Rex Austin have a wife?" he asked. "Or children?"

"Not anymore," Kale replied. "The wife divorced him about twenty years ago. She lives in the Bahamas now. And his heir apparent's dead, of course."

"Oh. Right." Cadel remembered something he'd learned back in Genius Squad—something about Rex's murdered son. "There weren't any other kids? Just the one?"

"Just the one," said Kale.

"So no one's been living with him?" Cadel wanted to get things straight in his head. "Not even a girlfriend?"

"Only the faithful butler. Who got sacked." Kale suddenly began to reel off facts and figures, as if Cadel had hit some kind of command button. "Austin owns three domestic properties: an apartment in Texas, a cabin in Oregon, and the house in Laguna Beach. The beach house is his biggest expense. It was built three years ago, at a cost of eleven million dollars. A gardening service takes care of the grounds and the pool. A maid service comes in once a week—"

"Why does he need a maid service?" Cadel interrupted. "What about the cleaning robots?"

"Maybe they don't do windows or baths," Kale said drily, before continuing with his report. "Austin also owns a lot of commercial property in LA, New York, Dallas, and Seattle. He leases a couple of private jets. He doesn't belong to any social clubs, but he's associated with a lot of business bodies. He owns four cars, and one's an old pickup. He smokes, drinks, and takes several prescription drugs for cholesterol and high blood pressure." As Cadel's jaw dropped, Kale offered up a slightly crooked grin. "Like I said before, we've been monitoring his activities."

Cadel was impressed. But then something occurred to him. "Has Rex filled any of his prescriptions lately?"

This question elicited a honk of laughter from Feliz. Kale's grin twisted sideways.

"You're really something," he said obscurely. "No. Rex Austin has *not* filled any of his prescriptions lately. Not as far as we know. But you don't really need a prescription to get drugs—not if you have enough cash. And he might be wanting to keep a low profile."

"I guess." Cadel wasn't convinced. "All the same . . ."

"All the same, it's a red flag," Kale agreed. At which point his phone buzzed, and he had to answer it.

Once more Cadel gazed out the window. They were still cruising along an enormous freeway, past endless tract housing. The sea was nowhere in sight, though signs kept indicating a series of invisible beaches: Hermosa

Beach, Huntington Beach, Newport Beach. Cracking towers and heavy industry were giving way to houses clustered along scrubby ridgelines. A lowering sky made Cadel wonder how bad the thunderstorms could get in California. Would they be worse than the ones in Sydney?

For a moment, his thoughts turned to Sydney, as he wondered if he was still officially dead back there. Probably not. It was fifty hours at least since he'd altered the hospital records; any discrepancies would surely have been identified and corrected. By now, in fact, Dr. Vee would almost certainly have discovered the truth.

But Cadel didn't want to dwell on Dr. Vee, or the hospital records, or Sydney in general. Such gloomy reflections would only trigger feelings of guilt and loss, which Cadel couldn't afford to entertain. Not if he wanted to keep his wits about him. So he banished all traumatic memories from his mind, focusing instead on the passing landscape.

As the road turned west, it hit a collection of yellow, sunbaked hills. Signage informed Cadel that he was traveling through the Laguna Coast Wilderness Park. A toll had to be paid at one point; when Cadel spotted the Nix Nature Center, he experienced a fleeting sense that if he'd come here on vacation, he might have had quite a lot of fun.

And still they kept going, until a wooded valley closed in on them, shady and verdant and sprinkled with evidence of genteel tourism: art galleries, glass blowers, even something called the Plectrum Dulcimer Company.

"There's a taco wagon," Kale finally announced, breaking the extended silence. "You wanna taco?"

"No thanks." Cadel had spotted a crowd of men in a parking lot. "'Day Laborer Hiring Area,'" he read aloud as they zipped past an official-looking sign. "What does that mean?"

"It means that if you pay a buck and stand there all day, someone might come along and ask you to trim the beards on their palm trees," said Kale. "Or not."

"Around our place, they hang out at the Home Depot parking lot," Chuck suddenly remarked, in a surprisingly high-pitched voice.

Feliz said nothing.

As Laguna Canyon opened into Laguna Beach, Cadel began to sense money in the air. The canyon had puzzled him. With its quirky businesses and untamed growth, it had seemed like the sort of place that might be inhabited by aging hippies—and Rex Austin wasn't an aging hippie. Laguna Beach, on the other hand, was all glamorous shops, lush trees, and clipped lawns. Cadel could easily imagine a bunch of billionaires hanging out in Laguna Beach. Not billionaires like Rex, perhaps, but the other kind: billionaires with yachts and miniature poodles and bikini-wearing girlfriends.

"Does Rex have a dog?" Cadel wanted to know. Again it was Kale who answered.

"Nope."

"Not even a guard dog?"

"He's got a couple of horses in Oregon," Kale revealed. "That's about it."

He glanced up from his phone to scrutinize Cadel. "We haven't noticed any suspicious dog deaths, if that's what you're wondering. And no one's canceled any subscriptions, either. But his private jet hasn't left the ground in two months."

By this time they were heading south, along a cliff-top road. To the left rose a line of steep hills, looming over terraced suburban sprawl. To the right, lots of high-density coastal architecture blocked out most of the ocean view—though here and there Cadel caught a glimpse of white caps on dark and restless waters. Palm trees whipped about in a gusty wind.

"Normally you can see Catalina Island from here," Kale remarked. "But not with all these low clouds and sea spray." He leaned forward suddenly. "Take the next right," he told Feliz.

The next right was a short road lined with impressive dwellings: Spanish-style adobe villas, glass-and-concrete boxes, overblown half-timber cottages with river-pebble chimneys. All were oriented toward the sea, and all looked slightly too big for their yards. The street itself ended at the edge of a sandy cliff, but Feliz didn't go that far. Instead he turned left onto a narrow lane, which ran between high fences until it reached a lofty, steel-barred gate hung with CCTV equipment.

This gate was set in a stone wall, and protected by a car like the one in which Cadel was sitting. After a brief consultation with Kale, the driver on guard duty moved his vehicle, allowing Feliz to guide his own car through the gate and into the grounds of Rex Austin's beach house. By this time, Cadel had grasped that "beach house" was hardly an adequate description of the home that Rex had built for himself. To begin with, it wasn't on the beach. It was a cliff-top mansion surrounded by several acres of ecologically sensitive landscaping. Patches of grass and low scrub alternated with spiky palms and paved areas. Reflected in the serene surface of a tiled swimming pool, the main building was a beautifully integrated expanse of tinted glass, bleached wood, and gray stone.

Around it were huddled a flock of smaller structures, including a pool house, a six-car garage, an elaborate toolshed. They seemed to be bracing themselves against the wind.

"Oh man," said Feliz, his tongue loosened by surprise. "I sure could live in this place."

"Just park over there by the door," Kale instructed. He then turned to Cadel, who was eyeing Rex Austin's luxurious spread with ill-concealed misgivings. "It's got a familiar sorta feel to it, don'tcha think?"

Cadel swallowed. It was as if Kale had been reading his mind. The Austin estate did, indeed, bear a striking resemblance to the house that Prosper had once inhabited on Australia's east coast, along with his strangely fishlike manservant, Vadi, and his black-toothed secretary, Wilfreda. Of course, Prosper's house hadn't been quite so big or so carefully tended. It hadn't boasted a pool, a rooftop viewing platform, or a floor-cleaning robot. Instead of being shoehorned into a popular and expensive suburb, Prosper's residence had been perched on a bushy headland, at least ten minutes' drive from his nearest neighbor.

All the same, there were enough similarities to make Cadel's heart sink. Even the FBI's presence struck a chord, because the last time he'd seen Prosper's cliff-top hideaway, it had been surrounded by a heavily armed squad of police.

"Takes me back," said Kale, who had been a member of that very squad. "One thing you can say about Prosper English, he has a good eye for real estate."

"You think he's been here?" Cadel asked.

Kale shrugged. "I think it's the sorta place he likes, put it that way." Unbuckling his seat belt, he pushed open the nearest door. "Anyway, we'll have a better idea when we look around."

There was a CCTV camera mounted outside the main entrance and another one in the vestibule. Cadel winced as he passed them. He could no longer spot a networked camera without wishing he was in disguise. "Have you disabled the security system?" he queried in a hushed voice that nevertheless echoed around the cavernous, galleried space just inside the front door.

"Yup," said Kale. He put his hands on his hips as he surveyed the giant white pillar at the other end of the room. A staircase was wrapped around this pillar, and a lift was tucked deep inside it. "I see we got a real *artistic* layout here," he declared sarcastically. "Some architect musta been stoned off his face on peyote buttons when he designed this place."

"It feels like the ceiling's going to fall in on us," Cadel agreed. The ceiling, in fact, seemed to be tumbling toward them, swooping from the top of the two-story pillar to a low spot just above the front door, its surface all jagged and broken up. Cadel couldn't help thinking that the whole interior had a weird, distorted quality to it, with walls that were stepped and textured like the soundproof walls of a recording studio and parquet floors set in patterns that played tricks with his eyes. Corners jumped out unexpectedly. Skylights were scattered overhead in careless clumps, as if jagged bits of glass had become embedded in the roof after a terrible explosion. There didn't appear to be a single right angle in the entire house.

"I'd get seasick if I had to live here," Kale remarked. "What's the point of it all?"

"Maybe it's eco-friendly," said Cadel.

"Maybe."

"Maybe it's *meant* to make you feel seasick. Because the sea's outside."

"Whatever." Kale shook his head. "I thought Austin was a hard-line conservative. I never thought he'd hole up in a carnival ride like this."

Cadel wondered how Prosper might feel about holing up in a carnival ride. Pretty happy, no doubt, since Prosper's entire life had been one big hall of mirrors.

"Right," said Kale. "Let's get started."

Their first stop was a colossal open-plan room that wrapped around three sides of the ground floor, rather like a horseshoe. The outer wall of this room was made of glass, affording panoramic views of the California coast. Though it was hard to ignore these views, Cadel tried to concentrate on the room's contents. The couches were huge leather blocks. The dining table was big enough to seat eighteen people. The rugs on the floor had been peeled off the carcasses of endangered wildlife.

Casting his mind back to Prosper's Australian cliff-top hideaway, Cadel recalled bronze sculptures and wing chairs, wrought-iron lamps and tapestry wall hangings. Although there *had* been a fur rug, it had been made of kangaroo hides.

Rex Austin seemed to favor zebra skins.

"According to the insurance records, this stuff is all Austin's," Kale observed. He was peering at the screen of his cell phone, scrolling down some kind of text message. "Barcelona chair," he read out. "Swarovski crystal chandeliers (two). *Untitled* by Mark Rothko . . ."

"None of it looks like the stuff at Prosper's house," Cadel volunteered.

"Let's try the kitchen."

The kitchen and butler's pantry were located well away from any panoramic vistas. No expense had been spared in fitting out these rooms, which contained—among other things—an eight-burner stove, two ovens, a commercial-grade dishwasher, and a wall-mounted television screen. Many of the appliances were Bluetooth-enabled.

When Kale pulled open the Bluetooth-enabled fridge, he found it almost empty except for a couple of condiment jars and a six-pack of imported beer.

"Hmm," he said.

"This fridge is the type that tells you what needs ordering," Cadel pointed out. "We can check when the last order was filled."

"Not now. We'll get to that later." Kale moved past one of the other FBI agents into the pantry, which was well stocked with long-life food in packets and tins. "You once told me that Prosper drinks his coffee black," he remarked. "Do you know what brand he likes?"

"No," Cadel admitted. He picked up a box of raspberry-flavored Pop-Tarts. Once, to distract Prosper, he had set some curtains on fire with a raspberry-flavored Pop-Tart.

The memory made his blood run cold.

"What's up?" asked Kale.

"Nothing."

"Does Prosper eat Pop-Tarts?"

"I'm not sure." Cadel returned the box to its shelf. "When I saw him last time, he didn't know much about them."

"This must be the wine cellar," Kale deduced. He was standing over a hatch in the floor. "Is it all clear underground?" he wanted to know, raising his voice to address the agent in the kitchen.

"Yes, sir. We've been through there."

"Nothing to report?"

"Nothing except some real nice champagne."

From the hatch, a circular staircase led down to a subterranean room; movement-activated lights flicked on as Kale descended into a long, low basement lined from floor to ceiling with wine racks and glass-fronted refrigerators.

"Wow," Kale muttered. He turned to Cadel, who was bringing up the rear. "Do you know what Prosper drinks?"

Cadel shook his head.

"Pity," said Kale. "If Austin's wine merchant has started supplying something different, it might be another red flag."

"I don't know if Prosper *does* drink," Cadel had to confess.

"Oh, he drinks, all right. He was a sommelier when he was young. Before he figured out there wasn't any money in it." Seeing Cadel's puzzled expression, Kale translated. "A sommelier's a wine waiter."

"A wine waiter?" Cadel couldn't believe his ears.

"He was straight out of school, training up. Had some kind of apprenticeship in a fancy London restaurant. But it was one of those places where all the major crooks used to hang out, so he got in with some bad company." Kale frowned, scanning row upon row of dusty bottles. "Maybe we *should* check with Austin's wine merchant," he said. "If the orders have gotten classier, lately, Prosper could be responsible."

"What else do you know about Prosper?" Cadel demanded. Somehow he couldn't picture a young Prosper English in an apron wielding a corkscrew. The whole image was too surreal. "Do you know where he went to school?"

"Sure."

"You *do*?"

"Cadel, we've got a file on the guy that's about a billion gigabytes." Kale glanced at him curiously. "I figured Saul would have shown you most of it."

"No."

"Well . . . maybe when we get back to headquarters, I can let you see the unclassified stuff. Meanwhile, I want you to concentrate. Is there anything here that makes you wonder?"

"Not really." Cadel did wonder why one man would need so much wine, but understood that such a question was irrelevant.

"All right. We'll keep trying, then." Kale checked his watch. "I don't know when this lawyer of yours is gonna show. She's taking her sweet time getting here."

Cadel followed him back up the stairs and into a library, which was furnished with a generous supply of leather-bound books, a massive wooden desk, and all the very latest computer technology. The home theater next door was almost as lavish as Raimo's had been; leading off it was a marble bathroom with a spa bath. There was also a game room (containing a full-sized pool table) and a small gymnasium where Rex stored his fishing rods and other sports equipment. A utilities cupboard contained his floor-cleaning robot, which looked a bit like a giant hubcap. The toilet-cleaning robot was nowhere to be seen. "Must be upstairs," Kale hazarded.

Cadel was amazed at the sheer size of the house, which seemed monstrously big for one person. But he wouldn't have wanted to live there himself. For a start, he didn't like all the cameras and sensors and Bluetooth-enabled devices, which made him feel incredibly exposed. And as he moved through the house, its odd proportions began to disturb him more and more.

He couldn't put his finger on exactly why they were so troubling. It wasn't as if they were affecting his sense of balance. Despite Kale's earlier complaint about seasickness, Cadel wasn't sick or dizzy. He was simply conscious of a nagging discomfort that was mental, rather than physical.

"Where's the panic room?" he finally asked. Maybe *that* was the problem: an unaccountable absence. "If Rex is paranoid, there should be a panic room."

"There is. Somewhere," said Kale. After making a few inquiries, he discovered that the panic room was on the floor above—so he and Cadel headed upstairs. By this time the sky was slate gray and the choppy sea beneath it even darker; Cadel could see this quite clearly when he reached the main bedroom, which had a sweeping coastal view. But he wasn't interested in the view. He was interested in the panic room, and the contents of the walk-in wardrobe, and the book that was perched on a bedside cabinet.

"Don't touch that," Kale warned as Cadel reached for *The Collected Short Stories of Edgar Allan Poe.* "We'll see if it's got fingerprints on it."

Cadel withdrew his hand.

"We'll dust the phone, as well," Kale continued. "And bag the sheets. There might be hairs or DNA." He watched as Cadel's gaze traveled slowly around the room. "I don't suppose Prosper's a big Poe fan, is he?"

"You should know that better than me," Cadel retorted. "You're the one with the billion-gig file on him." Without waiting for a response, he added, "Are you checking the phone records for this place?"

"It's in the works. Takes a while to get something like that—more than a couple of hours." Kale narrowed his eyes. "What is it?"

Cadel was staring at the king-sized bed. It was all made up, with sheets and blankets and about twenty cushions of different shapes and sizes. But it didn't look as if anyone had ever slept on it.

After a moment's hesitation, he bent his head to sniff at a pillow.

"Prosper English had some Trumper cologne at the other place," Kale observed.

"Then he won't be wearing it anymore," said Cadel, straightening. The pillow had smelled of laundry detergent. No one, he felt sure, had used it since it was last washed. "What kind of aftershave does Rex wear?"

"That we've gotta check." Kale whipped out his phone. "What's in the bathroom now?"

Cadel went to look. He found quantities of fluffy blue towels, a glass jar full of soap, a comb, a toothbrush, a bottle of Old Spice, a tube of shaving gel, and an unopened packet of disposable razors. The shower stall was bone dry.

"No Trumper cologne," he said. "Maybe Prosper's switched to Old Spice."

"We'll dust it for prints," promised Kale, before returning to his phone call.

The bathroom itself was smaller than Cadel had anticipated. He didn't understand why its dimensions surprised him so much. Could the enormous size of everything else have given him inflated expectations? The walk-in wardrobe beside the bathroom was also quite small; Cadel noted this with an increasing sense of perplexity as he surveyed the racks and shelves and drawers full of clothes.

Surely there was no need to cut corners in such a house?

"We'll have to check all the sizes," Kale remarked from the door, flicking his phone shut. "See if they correspond with Rex Austin's measurements." He made a face. "No tweed jackets," he pointed out.

"No," said Cadel, who doubted very much that any of the checked golf pants, yachting caps, or safari suits belonged to Prosper English—unless Prosper was trying to disguise himself. "No waistcoats, either."

"Yeah. Prosper English never did favor sportswear, did he? He went more for your classy collegiate stuff."

"Did he really go to university? I mean, was he a *real* psychologist?"

"We think he went to college under an assumed name. In South Africa." Kale suddenly became aware that Chuck was hovering behind him on the threshold. "Yeah? What is it?"

"We can't find any old surveillance footage at this end," Chuck reported. "But we're contacting the firm that monitors this place. They might have something on file."

Kale grunted. Cadel spun around.

"You haven't reconnected, have you?" he exclaimed. "I mean, is the system back online?"

"Uh—no . . ." Chuck seemed startled. His eyes flicked toward his superior, as if seeking guidance.

"Good," said Cadel. "Because that means we can set a honey trap."

The idea had come to him while he was contemplating the lack of movement-activated sensors in Rex Austin's wardrobe. He'd thought to himself: *This would be a great place to hide from a nosy hacker.* Then a light bulb had gone off inside his head. Of course! This was a house just like Judith's. And just like Judith's, it could be used as a honey trap . . .

"Someone's been watching me via web-based CCTV networks," he explained. "Whoever it is, he might have figured out where I am by now. And if the system here goes back online, it'll be really tempting." Cadel wasn't discouraged by the silence that greeted this suggestion. On the contrary, his tone became more urgent. "If the hacker takes a risk and tries to see what I'm doing, I might be able to pin him down."

Kale was scratching his jaw. "You're talking about an online ambush," he said flatly.

"That's it. Only I'd have to do it myself, because I know what to look for."

"Mmmph." Kale grimaced. "Your lawyer won't like *that*," he opined.

"My lawyer's not here yet."

"I guess not . . ."

"I won't let any hackers start messing with the house," Cadel insisted. "There won't be any malfunctioning doors or exploding fridges, I swear."

Kale pondered. Then he sighed. Then he turned to Chuck and said, "Is Larry here?"

"Larry's in the panic room," Chuck replied, cocking his thumb. "He's the one who's been searching for security footage."

"Okay. Good." Kale nodded before addressing Cadel once again. "Agent Domenico is our computer expert, and he'll be in charge. But if you talk to him about this and he says it's workable, then you can try it out. *Together.* Is that clear?"

"I guess so," Cadel reluctantly agreed. "Except that it might waste a lot of time, explaining what I want to do—"

"I said, *is that clear?*"

Though Kale wasn't tall, he could be very imposing. It had something to do with his banked-down impatience and the way he used his voice. He gave the impression that he had lots of energy to spare.

Cadel swallowed.

"Yes," he mumbled.

"All right," said Kale. "Then let's have a look at this panic room, shall we?"

THIRTY-ONE

Rex Austin's panic room was exactly like Judith's. It had the same kind of concealed toilet, a similar bank of cupboards, and an almost identical built-in desk. Even the light fittings looked familiar to Cadel.

And it's no bigger than Judith's, either, he thought, his gaze coming to rest on a small collection of monitor screens. They were mounted over a computer keyboard, and all were blank save for the one in the middle, which seemed to be displaying some kind of directory.

A short, solid, swarthy young man was peering at this directory through a pair of rimless spectacles. He had clipped black hair, bright green eyes, and the kind of vigorous stubble that needs to be shaved twice a day if it's to be kept under control.

Kale introduced him as Agent Larry Domenico.

"Larry's in computer forensics," Kale explained. "Larry, this is Cadel. He's got an idea you might want to consider."

"Hi," said Larry. He shook Cadel's hand.

"You guys can discuss things while I step outside and make a phone call," Kale suggested. "It's a little cramped in here for three people, anyway." He then addressed himself exclusively to Cadel. "If I were you, I'd take a look at those cupboards. Just so you don't miss anything."

"All right," Cadel agreed.

"They've been searched already, haven't they?" Kale asked Larry, who nodded. "Good. Okay. I'll leave you to it."

There was a brief silence after Kale had gone. Larry seemed to be waiting for input. Cadel didn't quite know how to begin. At last he said, in a hesitant tone, "I know quite a lot about computers. Did—did Kale tell you that?"

"I've been briefed on it," Larry confirmed. He wasn't unfriendly, just unforthcoming. Cadel wondered if this blank-faced demeanor was some kind of FBI interrogation technique.

"Well . . . I was thinking that I could set up an ambush for the hacker who's been spying on me," he continued. "If we log on to the Net again, he might try to get back in. And I might be able to catch him doing it."

Larry took his time answering. It was as if he wanted to consider the notion from every possible viewpoint.

"This is the same guy responsible for that tailor-made infiltration program?" he finally asked. "The one designed specifically for this house?"

"Yes." It was a relief to discover that Larry was so quick on the uptake. "I'd have to be ready, though. I'd have to get everything set up before we reconnected."

Larry pursed his lips. Again he appeared to be weighing his options.

"I wouldn't let anyone get into the systems, here," Cadel added. "If that's what you're worried about."

"I'm not worried," Larry said calmly. "How were you wanting to proceed?"

Cadel explained how. Larry absorbed this information without comment, nodding occasionally when he judged that some sort of feedback was required. At one point he even vacated his chair so that Cadel could have easy access to the computer. And when Cadel had finished, Larry's "mmm-hmm" somehow conveyed that Cadel's plan had been fully absorbed and understood.

"I think it's worth trying," was Larry's final assessment, delivered after the usual period of careful, almost painstaking consideration. "As long as Agent Platz alerts the rest of the team."

"We'll need to switch everything back on," Cadel advised. But Larry didn't hear; he had already left the room to consult with Kale Platz. Therefore Cadel got up and yanked open the nearest cupboard door, behind which he found a selection of tinned foods. The next cupboard contained sheets, pillows, a first-aid kit, and an inflatable bed. The cupboard after that was full of toilet paper. There seemed to be nothing noteworthy in any of the cupboards. Cadel certainly couldn't see any Trumper cologne or silk waistcoats.

Only the cramped dimensions of the storage space puzzled him. In fact, they puzzled him so much that he wandered out into the bedroom, past Kale and Larry, until he'd retraced his steps to the bedroom door. This door opened onto a short passage lined with linen cupboards. Turning left at the end of the passage, Cadel entered another bedroom that was slightly less impressive than the main one; it had a less imposing view, a less expansive bed, and much less floor space. But it did have its own bathroom and walk-in wardrobe, which appeared to share the same wall cavity as those opening off the main bedroom. As far as Cadel could judge, both bathrooms were probably set back to back.

Or were they?

The second bathroom was even narrower than the first. Cadel measured it with his feet. He did the same in the second wardrobe, which was empty. Then he returned to the passage, where he tried to pace out its length. Unfortunately, all the stepped floors, curved walls, indented corners, and irregular alcoves made judging distances very hard.

Kale joined him as he was inspecting the linen cupboards.

"What's up?" asked Kale.

"I don't know . . ." Cadel surveyed the beautifully laundered, carefully folded sheets and towels. They told him nothing. "Have you ever seen a plan of this house? I mean, something that shows you the ducts and plumbing and elevator shafts?"

"No. But I'm sure we can find one. Why?"

Cadel hesitated. He felt slightly embarrassed by his own suspicious nature; clearly he had reached the point where he couldn't even trust his own eyes.

Thunder rumbled in the distance.

"It must be this weird architecture," he ventured at last. "I can't make the connections."

Kale frowned. "What do you mean? What connections?"

"It feels like it doesn't fit together. Like it's not systematic." Cadel scratched his scalp, wondering if he was being bamboozled by a clever design. "You don't have a measuring tape, do you?" he said impulsively, just as a cry rang out from the panic room.

"Sir? *Sir!*"

It was Larry's voice. Galvanized by its urgency, Kale hurried back to the monitor screens, with Cadel close behind him. All of the screens were now operating; they showed a selection of views from across the entire house, in full color and real time.

Larry was pointing at one of them. "Look," he said.

Kale gasped. Cadel froze. They stood gaping at an angled shot of the toolshed's exterior filmed by a camera that must have been mounted near its door. This camera was tracking the progress of a man wearing orange overalls and a baseball cap. He crossed the visual field at a brisk pace, leaving it behind just as Cadel croaked, "That's Prosper."

Kale leaned forward. He grabbed Larry's shoulder, saying, "Where's he gone? Find him! Hurry!"

"It might be a trick," Larry warned. He skipped from one view to the next, his fingers fluttering, his gaze fixed on the screens. "Didn't you say there was some kinda CCTV bug that inserts a fake Prosper English into the footage?"

"There!" Cadel exclaimed. "Stop!"

There were multiple shots on each screen: shots of the main gates, the pool, the garage, the front entrance (from several angles), the wine cellar, the driveway, the viewing platform. Every window was protected by a camera—as was every exterior door. And the yard contained more cameras than the house.

One of these cameras was focused on the shrubbery behind the toolshed, where a fleeting glimpse of orange was visible before it disappeared behind a cluster of large, gray, spiky plants.

"Did you log on to the Net?" Kale asked Larry, whose brows were knitted in consternation.

"No," Larry replied. "If it's that CCTV bug, it must be in the system already."

"It's not the bug," said Cadel. When his two companions blinked at him, he jerked his chin at the closest monitor screen. "There were no shiny spheres in either of those pictures. You need a shiny sphere to make it work."

Silence fell. For a couple of seconds no one spoke or moved. Then Kale whipped out his police radio.

"Okay—who's near the toolshed?" he snapped at Larry, his eyes scouring the screens in front of him. Some half a dozen agents could be seen in various locations, either patrolling the grounds or stationed at strategic vantage points. "Show me, dammit!"

"Umm . . . let's see now . . ." Larry murmured, jumping from shot to shot. But Kale couldn't wait. He charged out of the room, throwing a few last instructions over his shoulder.

"Stay here and keep the door locked. Don't open it to anyone but me," he barked. "If you see the perp again, call it through *pronto*. I want his exact position."

"Roger that," said Larry.

"There might be more than one," Kale added, before slamming the door shut behind him. Cadel then locked it. He thought that Kale was probably issuing a general alert, but couldn't hear anything through all the layers of reinforced steel that protected the panic room.

"Bingo," said Larry. He'd hit upon a stretch of gravel path, which was pinched between a high hedge and the perimeter wall. For some reason, Prosper English had decided to use this path. Cadel couldn't help wondering why, since gravel was such a noisy substance to walk on.

"Now that would be . . . what? The southeast sector?" Larry wondered aloud. "What are the camera coordinates on this?" He fumbled for his own walkie-talkie. "There's gotta be a network map in here somewhere."

"Look." Cadel pointed at another scene. "There he is. In the distance."

"That's southeast, for sure," Larry decided, then promptly made his report to Kale.

Cadel, meanwhile, had spotted something. One of the cameras seemed to be focused on a narrow lane that ran between a high stone wall and a patchwork of fences. It took him a moment to work out that he was looking at the outer edge of Rex Austin's property, where it hit a line of neighboring backyards.

Cadel's gaze only snagged on this obscure corner because a small steel door in the stonework was stealthily opening.

"Look! Quick! There might be a car!" he yipped. On the screen, Prosper was pulling the door shut behind him, in a leisurely kind of way. Then he moved west, out of the visual field.

"That's an access point," said Larry. "Goddammit, someone should be covering that!"

"Is there a cliff-top walk of some kind?" asked Cadel, but received no answer. Larry was firing an update into his walkie-talkie as he searched the CCTV network for Prosper's orange overalls. Cadel noticed a flurry of movement on the monitor screens; FBI agents were rushing past cameras, guns drawn.

"Maybe it's not a car," he continued anxiously, thinking back to the jetty at Prosper's Australian hideout. "Maybe he's got a boathouse down there."

"Not possible," Larry rejoined. "There are no private beaches in California. It's all public land along the coast."

"Oh." Cadel wiped his sweaty palms on the front of his T-shirt. "Well . . . maybe he hasn't been living here at all, then. Maybe he's been living nearby and paying visits." After a moment's reflection, he added, "Maybe someone's hired him as a gardener. He's certainly *dressed* like one."

Larry said nothing. After skipping around for a bit, he had managed to refine his search by concentrating on shots of an area around the southwestern corner of the estate. Agents were converging on this spot from all directions, surging through the steel door and spilling out onto the lane, clumping into pairs before they disappeared off camera. From one angle, Kale could be seen talking and gesturing—but he stopped abruptly when a call came through on his police radio.

It was Larry's call.

"I haven't got a fix on our target," Larry declared. "I think he's moved out of range."

"Roger that." Kale's voice sounded fuzzy and distorted. *"Keep your eyes peeled. Just in case more of 'em start coming out of the woodwork."*

"Woodwork is right," muttered Larry. "Where in hell was he hiding? That's what I want to know."

"You could check the footage," said Cadel. "There might be something we missed."

Larry's grunt signified approval. He began to call up various review menus while the screens that he wasn't using continued to jump automatically from viewpoint to viewpoint. Vacant room succeeded vacant room. Wind-tossed glade succeeded wind-tossed glade.

As he stared at the swaying trunk of a distant palm tree, something pricked at Cadel's subconscious like a hot needle. That palm tree, he knew, was delivering a very important message. That palm tree was bugging him. It was practically *waving* at him. "Hey! Hey! Look!" it was saying. "Can't you see what's wrong?"

But he couldn't. Not yet. And before he could solve the puzzle, he was distracted by another movement.

Someone was walking down an upstairs hallway, wearing a gray tweed skirt and blood-colored twinset. Cadel recognized her instantly.

Weak-kneed, he had to grab at the edge of the desk.

"Wilfreda!" he croaked.

"What?" Larry didn't even glance up. He probably didn't know that Wilfreda had worked for Prosper English back in Australia. After Prosper's arrest, she had disappeared; no one had ever been able to discover her whereabouts.

Until now, of course. Now Cadel knew exactly where to find her.

She was walking briskly into the bedroom next door.

"It's Wilfreda! She's in the house!" he squawked. And this time he made an impression. Larry looked at Wilfreda, caught his breath, and jumped to his feet.

"She's in the next room," Cadel whispered. He didn't know if she would be able to hear him through the wall that divided them, but he didn't want to take any chances. "What if she can get *in* here? What if she has a key or a code?"

"Is she armed?" Larry, too, had lowered his voice to a hiss. For a moment they watched Wilfreda open all the drawers in a bedside cabinet, one by one, as if she was searching for something.

Cadel couldn't hear the drawers slam shut. "There must be some kind of insulation," he said hoarsely. "I don't think we need to keep quiet. I think this room is soundproofed."

"Maybe. Or maybe not," Larry murmured. Without taking his eyes off Wilfreda, he pulled a handgun from the shoulder holster beneath his jacket. "You know how to use a walkie-talkie?"

"Huh?"

"You press this button to send and this one to receive." Shoving the police radio into Cadel's damp palm, Larry edged toward the door, his attention still fixed on Wilfreda's blurred image. Having briefly disappeared into the wardrobe adjoining the second bedroom, she had re-emerged to peer under the bed. "She doesn't seem to have a gun," Larry continued very quietly. "And she might try in here, if she doesn't find what she's looking for out there."

"Yes, but—"

"As soon as I've got her in my sights, you can call Agent Platz. Okay?"

"Okay, but—"

"There's no one outside, is there?" Larry's shifting gaze fastened on a shot of the main bedroom before Cadel could even answer. "No. It's all clear. Make sure you lock this door behind me." Under his breath he added a fierce, final directive. *"Don't come out.* Not until you hear from Agent Platz."

Then he ducked into the next room, closing the door behind him with a soft *click*.

Cadel immediately engaged the lock, as instructed. When he turned back to the monitor screens, he saw a foreshortened Larry sidling out of the main bedroom, poised for action. Meanwhile, in the bedroom next door, Wilfreda had finished rummaging through the walk-in wardrobe. She was now standing with her hands on her hips, surveying her immediate vicinity with a dissatisfied air.

Thank god Rex Austin's so paranoid, Cadel thought. Without access to such an intrusive CCTV network, he would never have been able to follow Larry's progress out of the main bedroom and into the hallway outside. It looked very much as if Wilfreda was about to enter the same hallway. She shook her head, spun around, and . . .

Suddenly the screen went black.

Cadel was startled into an exclamation. "What the—?" He leaned forward, fruitlessly jabbing at switches. He squatted to check for loose cables beneath the desk. Then—upon seeing nothing untoward—he straightened again, examining the radio in his hand. What had Larry said? Press *this* button to send and *this* one to receive? Or was it the other way around?

"I'll take that," a crisp voice remarked behind him.

And Cadel dropped the radio onto the floor.

THIRTY-TWO

Prosper English stooped to pick up the walkie-talkie.

"Dear me," he said. "I think you might have broken this. But I'll turn it off, just in case."

He wasn't wearing orange overalls—or a tweedy jacket, either. Instead he was dressed in shapeless corduroys and a knitted jumper so shabby that it was beginning to unravel at the hem. Both garments looked too big for him. Though he had always been thin, it was obvious that he'd lost even more weight; his cheeks were hollow, his hands were like claws, and his long nose seemed beakier than ever. As for his complexion, it was dull and pallid, as if he hadn't been out in the sun for months.

Behind his gold-rimmed spectacles, his eyes were still as black as a snake's and as sharp as a hawk's. But they were also pouchy, bloodshot, and ringed with dark smudges.

When Cadel opened his mouth, no sound emerged.

"Don't bother. They can't hear," Prosper drawled. A wolfish smile crept across his haggard face. "As you so insightfully remarked, this room is soundproof."

Cadel flung himself at the door. He wasn't fast enough, though; Prosper yanked him back, hauling him by the collar. Choking and gasping, Cadel was dragged through a dark hole that had opened up in one wall. Only later did he realize that this hole had previously been concealed by the cupboard full of toilet paper. For the moment, his only concern was getting air into his lungs again.

Suddenly he was released. Dropping to the floor, he coughed and spluttered, vaguely aware that Prosper was pulling the cupboard shut behind them both. Something went *click*. Something else jingled.

Cadel began to crawl away. He staggered to his feet just as Prosper caught his elbow.

"Calm down," said Prosper. But Cadel pulled free.

"Get off!" he yelled, kicking out wildly. They were in a small, narrow, windowless space with a door at each end. Fluorescent tubes overhead illuminated nothing in the way of potential weapons: no stools or lamps or fire irons. The walls were lined with yet more cupboards.

When Cadel lunged for the nearest doorknob, he was grabbed again.

"Calm down." Prosper spoke sternly, his fingers clamped around Cadel's wrist. "There's no need to panic . . ."

"Let go! Let go of me!" Cadel swung at Prosper, who promptly seized his other wrist. No matter how furiously Cadel jerked and tugged and wriggled, he couldn't loosen the iron grip that restrained him.

"Help! *Help!*" he bellowed, and Prosper sighed.

"For god's sake, boy, use your head. I just told you this place was soundproof."

Cadel barely heard. He was hysterical with fear, pumping adrenaline and deaf to all arguments. He tried to bite one of the psychologist's bony hands.

"STOP IT!" With a single shove, Prosper slammed him against a cupboard. Cadel found himself squeezed between a hardwood panel and an arm like an iron bar.

Then Prosper lowered his head until they were eye to eye.

"I'm not going to hurt you. Is that clear? Cadel?"

"You're lying!" Cadel sobbed. "You tried to kill me!"

"What?"

"You've been trying to kill me!"

Prosper blinked. As he withdrew his face a little, Cadel tried to escape by sliding toward the floor. But it didn't work. Prosper simply applied more pressure.

"What are you talking about?" he demanded.

"You *know* what I'm talking about!" Confronted by raised eyebrows and pursed lips, Cadel lost his temper. "You tried to push me downstairs! And run over me! And drown me in concrete!"

"I did *what?*"

"Of course you did! I *know* you did! Do you think I'm *stupid?*"

"Okay, listen." Prosper took a deep breath, adjusting his hold so that one elbow was wedged painfully into Cadel's sternum. "We're going to discuss this, but not right now. Right now I need to get you downstairs so you can address yourself to a little problem I'm having." His bright, black gaze bored into Cadel's skull. "Are you going to be sensible? Are you going to be smart? Or am I going to have to truss you up like an Egyptian mummy?"

"You'll never make it downstairs!" Cadel spat. "There's an agent right outside!"

"Who can't get in again. And by the time he works out how to un-lock two sets of reinforced doors, we'll be long gone." Seeing Cadel's brow crease in perplexity, Prosper grinned. "My dear boy, I won't be using the *outer* staircase, I'll be using the *inner* one. That panic room out there is just the tip of an iceberg."

Distressed and distracted, Cadel stopped fighting. "What do you mean?" he asked.

"Haven't you worked it out yet?" Prosper seemed surprised. "When I heard you ask for a measuring tape, I thought you must have hit on it. That's why I was forced to take action." He grew impatient when Cadel continued to stare at him blankly. "Isn't it obvious? A panic *room* wasn't enough for our friend Rex. He built himself a panic house, as well."

"A panic *house?*"

"Concealed inside the other one. There's a hidden staircase. And a hidden kitchen between the pool and the basement. And a hidden bed-room behind the chimney flue—"

"Why?"

"*Why?* Because Rex was paranoid. He was afraid of kidnappers. *And* escaped convicts. *And* former employees. The list goes on and on." Prosper's tense frame relaxed a little as he mulled over Rex Austin's peculiarities. "In my opinion, the whole panic-house concept was a failure. It made him overconfident. And men of his generation simply don't understand the kind of things a hacker can accomplish nowadays."

Cadel winced. He knew enough about Prosper to understand that the word "overconfident," when used in this context, was very bad news. "Where *is* Rex? What did you do to him?"

"Oh, we'll discuss that in a minute. When we get downstairs," Prosper replied. Then he stepped back, gesturing gracefully toward the nearest door. "Shall we go? It's not far. And it's really quite interesting."

Cadel hesitated.

"I swear I won't hurt you. Unless you kick up a fuss," Prosper assured him. "Believe me, if you've been having trouble, it wasn't my doing."

"Yeah, right," Cadel scoffed. "Are you saying it was *Com* who tried to run me over?"

"If it was, he'll answer for it."

"Don't give me that rubbish!" Cadel said harshly, rubbing his wrists. "Why would Com want to kill me? Why would *anyone*, except you?"

Again Prosper sighed, in a long-suffering manner, as if unreasonable demands were being placed on him. "I'm hardly in a position to answer that," he pointed out. "It's not as if I've had any direct contact with my Australian team recently."

"So you admit it!" Cadel pounced on this confession like a cat on a bird. "You admit you hired Dot and Com!"

"Well, of course," Prosper said mildly. "I had to keep track of you somehow."

"And Vee?"

"Ah. Well." A smile tweaked at the corner of the psychologist's mouth. "Let's just say that Vee's not in Australia at the moment."

"But he's been tracking me, hasn't he? With security cameras?"

"I believe that *is* one of his more ingenious techniques, though I gather the grunt work is usually done by Com—"

"Was it Com who stuck you into the CCTV footage?" Suddenly Cadel was ravenous for information. Suddenly he was desperate to know if he had miscalculated somehow. "Why would he do that? When I was minding my own business? It was *stupid*!"

For the first time, Prosper looked puzzled. He frowned, and seemed to forget that there were more urgent matters to attend to.

"What footage?" he asked, narrowing his eyes.

"You know. Around Sydney."

"Around *Sydney*?"

"Don't try and pretend you don't know all this. You *must* know all this."

But even as he spoke, Cadel began to wonder. Prosper's face wore a grim look.

"Perhaps you'd better tell me what's been going on," he said.

Cadel eyed him, torn between terror and suspicion. "Your digital double kept popping up all over the place," he quavered. "And then I worked out it wasn't really you."

"I see."

"After that, Sonja's wheelchair was hijacked. It nearly killed me, and Sonja ended up in the hospital. Naturally I thought you did it."

There was a brief pause. At last Prosper said, "Naturally."

"And then I tracked down Com, but he got away. And then someone destroyed my house by remote control. And when I hid in a basement, it was pumped full of cement." Realizing that this litany of horrors seemed to be having very little effect on the psychologist (who was nodding thoughtfully), Cadel blurted out, "Why would *Com* do all that?"

"Because you tracked him down, I suppose." Prosper's tone was casual. "It sounds as if he was trying to protect himself."

"Yeah—by *that* time, maybe. But I didn't start it! *You* started it, when you stuck yourself into all that footage! Of *course* I was going to get involved after you turned up on my doorstep!"

"That wasn't my idea."

"Ha!"

"Listen. Use your head for a moment." Prosper placed a hand on Cadel's shoulder—and kept it there, despite the way Cadel flinched and squirmed. In a dry, pleasant, precise voice, the psychologist then proceeded to hammer home his argument, apparently ignoring the fact that outside, not far away, all hell might be breaking loose. "Do you honestly think that, if I'd wanted to kill you, you wouldn't be dead already?" he murmured. "There are any number of trained assassins I could have hired to do the job, and they wouldn't have messed it up with overcomplicated things like concrete."

"Yes, but—"

"That CCTV program was built so that I could pretend to be in Stockholm, or Capetown, or Montreal. The possibilities are endless. So why would I pretend to be in Sydney and get *you* all stirred up?"

"I don't know," Cadel mumbled. "It never did make much sense."

"Of course it didn't. Because you were no kind of threat at all." As Prosper continued, he couldn't suppress an undertone of sneering disdain. "I mean to say," he said, "there you were, acting like a little angel, all wrapped up in your quiet little suburban life, with your homework and your wholesome friends and your charitable projects." He stopped suddenly; no doubt it had occurred to him that blatant contempt might alienate the very person he was trying to win over. After clearing his throat, he proceeded in a gentler fashion. "Why do you think I hired Dot and Com in the first place? I did it because I wanted to make sure that you were behaving yourself. I needed to know that you weren't—how shall I put it?—collaborating with the police?"

"I wasn't!"

"I know."

"Then—"

"You must have made them nervous somehow." Prosper was adamant. "You must have done something to make Dot or Com really nervous."

"I didn't, though!"

"You must have. And they, in turn, must have thought that if *I* showed up—or appeared to show up—my presence would scare you into minding your own business."

"But that's stupid!"

"Clearly."

"Why on earth would they think that? Couldn't they see it would have the opposite effect?"

Prosper smirked. He appeared to be genuinely amused. "My dear boy," he said, "we're talking about *Compton and Dorothy Daniels*. Those two weren't born; they were assembled. So they're not exactly the most sensitive, insightful pair when it comes to human motivation." For one fleeting instant, he gave the distinct impression that he was savoring a private joke. Then the glint in his eye was abruptly extinguished. "I don't know what part Vee might have played in all this," he concluded, with an evenness that chilled Cadel, "but I intend to find out. Because I really don't approve of employees who take matters into their own hands. For that reason, I also intend to locate Dot and Com and . . . well, have a quiet word, shall we say?"

Cadel shivered. He had broken into a sweat, and his knees felt like cotton wool. It was shock, he decided: shock and jet lag. Now that the immediate effects of his adrenaline boost had worn off, he was beginning to experience his usual reaction to Prosper's physical presence: an insidious, deeply rooted, clutching sense of dread that always left him numb and disoriented.

Nevertheless, he found the strength to utter a feeble retort.

"Good luck," he bleated. "You'll have a hard time getting out of this *house*, let alone the country."

"Oh, I think not," Prosper replied. His swift changes of mood were startling, and more pronounced than they had ever been before. All at once the hissing snake had turned back into the suave and genial professor. "Not if you can help me, dear boy—and I'm sure you can. So let's just step this way, shall we? And I'll show you something that you'll really enjoy."

Cadel didn't protest. He allowed himself to be pushed into a narrow passage, which followed a circuitous path—up a step, down a step, under a pipe, around a corner—until it reached the bedroom that Prosper had been talking about. Though cramped and windowless, this space had been nicely decked out with a plush fitted carpet, muted wallpaper, and nests of silk cushions. There was a TV and a bar fridge. Elegant lamps cast tranquil pools of light onto polished cabinetry, illuminating a clutch of dirty dishes here, a stack of empty boxes there.

The single bed hadn't been made. Cadel noticed that at once. He also noticed the enormous number of unwashed wineglasses scattered around.

"Not bad, is it?" Prosper remarked. "Can't say I admire Rex's taste in Rieslings, but it would be oafish to complain."

Cadel said nothing. As he was hustled out of the room into another passage, he tried to keep himself calm and focused by tackling an important question that had so far been left unanswered: namely, what in the world he might have done to spook Dot and Com in the first place. It didn't make sense. He hadn't been searching for either of them, back before the appearance of Prosper's digital double. In Prosper's own words, Cadel had been "behaving himself." There had been no attempt to re-convene Genius Squad since Prosper's reappearance, no halfhearted monitoring of Vee's old command-and-control chatrooms. Instead, Cadel had turned his back on the past, stayed off the hacker sites, and concentrated on his studies.

Of course, he'd continued to mix with a few former members of Genius Squad but never once had he asked Judith about her police work. Never once had he expressed the slightest interest in going after Prosper English. Like a model student, Cadel had been keeping his nose clean—except for the modest amount of hacking he'd done to connect Sonja's wheelchair with a certain elevator management system. And even *that* had been more of a noble undertaking than a piece of industrial sabotage . . .

All at once Cadel caught his breath.

"SCATS!" he exclaimed.

Prosper blinked. "Come again?"

"I was about to start hacking into the Sydney traffic system!" Cadel was thinking aloud; he couldn't help himself. "I wanted to make sure that Sonja didn't have to push any buttons at pedestrian crossings!"

But Prosper wasn't enlightened. "You've lost me, I'm afraid," he said.

"Com was *already in SCATS!*"

"Ah."

"He must have been scared that I'd find his trail! What a *fool* he is!"

"Yes. Well. The real world was never exactly his forte, was it?" Prosper didn't seem terribly interested. He nudged Cadel forward, adding, "There's a staircase round the next corner. Just watch your step."

Cadel briefly considered breaking free and heading for the nearest exit, then dismissed the idea. For one thing, he didn't know where the nearest exit actually was. For another, he had a feeling that Prosper might be armed. And although the psychologist had refrained from shooting him on previous occasions, it had since been established that the two of them weren't really father and son.

Cadel wasn't sure exactly how far this news had spread. But he was afraid that, if the truth *had* filtered through to this dim little bolthole, it might have changed Prosper's outlook on certain things.

"Not far now," said Prosper as they reached the top of a circular staircase. "When you get to the bottom, turn right."

"Where are we?" Cadel asked, before experiencing a sudden flash of insight. "Are we inside that big pillar? In the vestibule?"

"Very good." Prosper poked him between the shoulder blades. "And it's a long way down, so don't try my patience."

The walls of the stairwell were probably soundproofed. Even if Kale was running up the outside stairs, it seemed unlikely that he would hear raised voices coming from inside the pillar.

Nevertheless, Cadel decided to make a bit of noise.

"Have you been in here ever since you escaped?" he said as loudly as he dared.

"Not quite," was Prosper's terse response.

"Where's Wilfreda?"

"I've no idea."

"So she's not in the house, then?"

"My dear boy, surely you've worked *that* out?" Prosper didn't trouble to hide his exasperation. "Wilfreda hasn't been near this place for a week. All of the footage you saw was recorded. It's old. I just played it back on some of the external monitors."

"The *external* monitors?" Cadel echoed.

"You'll see what I mean in a minute."

At the bottom of the stairs, another door led into a curving passageway. This passageway (which had a chilly, clammy, subterranean feel to it) opened onto a large, low room divided into several well-defined zones. There was a kitchen zone, with granite benchtops and a full complement of plumbing and appliances; a dining zone, which contained one small table and a single chair; and a zone occupied by an enormous amount of computer technology.

Cadel stared in amazement at the monitor screens, which outnumbered the panic room's array by two to one. Every screen displayed several views of the house or yard. There was even a shot of the empty panic room itself, taken from above.

"I see your friends haven't got in yet," said Prosper. "That buys us a bit of time. With any luck, they might think you've collapsed. Or that you can't get the door open."

"I didn't see any camera in there." Cadel was confused. He couldn't understand how he had missed something so important. "I'm sure there was no camera on the ceiling . . ."

"Of course not!" Prosper snapped. "It's *inside* the ceiling. Aimed at an air-conditioning vent." He pointed at another screen, where five or six agents were gathered outside the panic room. "There they are. See? Looks as if they've tried shooting a hole in the lock." With a snort, he added, "Much good it'll do them. That's steel plate; it was built to withstand a bomb blast."

Cadel was putting everything together in his head. He was so impressed by the ingenuity of the setup that he almost forgot to be frightened.

"So this here is the *master* system?" he demanded. "This one controls the other one?"

"Clever, isn't it?"

"And there are microphones, as well." It wasn't a question; it was a deduction. Cadel recalled that Prosper had been quoting his own remarks back to him. "You can listen to people talking."

"Oh yes. Every room is wired for sound." Prosper gave a satisfied nod, evidently pleased that Cadel had inferred this from the available evidence. "Speaking of which, I should tell you that I would *never* use Old Spice, no matter *how* desperate I was—"

"Did Vee design all this?" Cadel interrupted, gesturing at the bank of screens.

"Good god no!" said Prosper. "It was Rex's doing."

"So his architect knows about it." Cadel remembered that Kale had been looking for the architect. It was an encouraging thought. But before Cadel could derive any comfort from the prospect of imminent rescue, his hopes were dashed.

"Believe me," Prosper declared, "whatever that architect knew, it was buried with her." As Cadel glanced up, eyes widening, Prosper raised both hands in an attitude of injured innocence. "Not my doing, I assure you. That was all down to Rex."

"What—what are you talking about?" Cadel stammered, though he already knew. He just couldn't accept what he was hearing.

"Rex killed the architect." Prosper spelled it out matter-of-factly. "He took a contract out on her because she knew too much about this place. All the other construction workers were from Mexico. Illegal immigrants. God knows what happened to *them*."

Cadel was appalled. But he reminded himself that he was listening to a very accomplished liar. "I don't believe you," he croaked.

The psychologist shrugged.

"Believe what you like," he rejoined. "I've watched hours of old security footage, and it's all there." Laying a heavy arm across Cadel's shoulders, he adopted the light, gentle, soothing accents that he had customarily employed when counselling troubled adolescents, back in his days as a Sydney psychologist. "So you see, dear boy, Rex Austin was no great loss to the world. I've always said that there's nothing more dangerous than a rich old plutocrat with rampant paranoia."

Cadel swallowed. The time had come to ask, so he asked. Through dry lips he muttered, "What did you do to him?"

"Ah. Yes. Now that's what I want to discuss with you." Prosper steered Cadel toward the computer keyboard. "It seems that Rex caused a bit of a problem when he tried to escape. But I've got a feeling that you might be able to reverse that problem. And if you do, we'll all be much better off . . ."

THIRTY-THREE

Prosper explained his predicament, calmly and succinctly. It appeared that Rex Austin hadn't entirely trusted the panic house. Frightened that it wasn't secure enough, he had also built himself a hidden escape route. According to Prosper, an underground tunnel led directly to the base of a nearby cliff, where a small motorboat was concealed.

"The door in the cliff is a masterpiece," he said. "It looks just like a rockfall. I suppose it must have been prefabricated and then installed overnight."

Prosper had personally gone to examine this door, wearing orange overalls and a baseball cap. Though footage of his excursion was more than two months old, it had still fooled Kale and Larry—and Cadel, too. In fact, Prosper hadn't set foot outside since visiting the cliff face, because he'd decided that it wasn't safe to do so.

"I was afraid you'd notice that there wasn't a breath of wind in those old shots," he added. "But you didn't."

"I did. I mean, *subconsciously* I did." Cadel remembered the niggling sense of unease he'd felt upon viewing a wildly tossing palm tree. "Something was bugging me—I just didn't have a chance to work out what."

"Mmm." Though clearly not convinced, Prosper continued his narrative. He explained that Rex had tried to escape from Prosper's team by hiding in the panic house. When that tactic had failed, Rex had retreated into the tunnel, never realizing that its automatic locking mechanism could be compromised. "Vee disabled the doors at both ends, so they wouldn't open," said Prosper. "He hacked into the system and changed a set of protocols. I should have asked him to change them back, but I never did. Too squeamish, I suppose." As Cadel gasped, Prosper wrinkled his nose in disgust. "I mean, what was the point? Rex was already underground; why go to the trouble of interring him somewhere else?"

Cadel closed his eyes. *This is a bad dream*, he thought. *I'll wake up soon.*

"It was his own fault," Prosper insisted. "I kept asking him to cooperate and he wouldn't. He must have thought he could hold out forever, because there were emergency supplies on that boat of his. But something went wrong. It must have been a heart attack."

Cadel's eyes flew open. "You killed him. I knew it. I *knew* you killed him!"

"I didn't kill him. He killed himself." Prosper's tone was oddly peevish, as if he were discussing a lazy gardener or an especially stupid pet. He seemed to be expecting a measure of sympathy from his audience. "Do you think I wanted him to die? It would have been *so* much easier if he'd cooperated, but he wouldn't. And as a result, I had to do all kinds of tedious and expensive things. I had to get his voice cloned from old recordings, with something called concatenate speech synthesis. I had to commission a digital double, and that wasn't easy: I didn't have a body scan, you see, because a *dead* body's no good in these cases—especially one that's been dead for a while. His measurements had to be recreated from existing footage, which cost a *mint*. I must have lost half his estate already, paying off technical support. As for the time involved . . . well, all I can say is, thank god I had the sense to target a recluse. With someone like Rex, no one worries when he disappears off the radar for a couple of months . . ."

As Prosper rambled on, Cadel stared at him, dumbfounded. Prosper never rambled. It was completely unlike him. Was he losing his mind? Had two months inside a windowless rabbit warren driven him mad?

Checking the monitor screens, Cadel saw that Kale had made no visible progress. The panic-room door remained tightly shut.

". . . but of course you're not interested in any of this," Prosper was saying, having spotted Cadel's sidelong glance. "You're interested in how you're going to get out. Well, I can help you with that—providing you help me first." He tightened his grip on Cadel's hunched shoulders. "You see, my original plan was to wait here, snug as a bug, until your FBI friends finally gave up and went home. Which they would have done, I'm sure, if you hadn't started making pointed remarks about the size of this building. That was when I realized the tunnel would soon be my only option."

By now Cadel was as tense as a bowstring. His fists were clenched so tightly that his fingernails were hurting his palms.

He knew what was coming.

"Unfortunately, I can't get hold of Vee at the moment," Prosper continued, "which is why *you'll* have to open up the tunnel instead. I'm sure you're quite capable of doing that." He reached out with one hand to grab a wheeled typist's chair, which he dragged toward the computer keyboard. "And since we don't have much time, you'd better get started."

Cadel didn't speak. He didn't move. He was too busy thinking.

If Prosper let him onto the system, would it be possible to warn Kale somehow? Without alerting Prosper at the same time?

"Oh, and I wouldn't try to open any *other* doors," the psychologist smoothly remarked, right on cue, "because if that happens, someone's going to get hurt." He fished around beneath his jumper before pulling out something that he pressed against Cadel's skull. "I'm not saying it'll be you, necessarily. It might be one of your FBI friends. All I'm saying is that there *will* be bloodshed. And I'm sure you don't want that."

Cadel couldn't see the gun, but he recognized the feel of it. His scalp seemed to burn where it touched the barrel. His skin crawled. His stomach heaved.

"You always end up waving guns around," he said hoarsely.

"Because they're effective."

"It always comes to this, doesn't it? You point a gun at me and tell me what to do." Cadel's voice was shaking with fear and despair. "I'm *so sick* of it. Do you know that? I'm so sick of you and all your *crap*." Memories flashed into his head, one after the other: memories of Sonja's bloody face, of Saul's unconscious form, of a house collapsing and wet concrete rising. "Why don't you leave me alone?" Cadel cried, tormented beyond endurance by these images. "Why don't you change the script for once?"

"Oh, I have," said Prosper, through his teeth. "In *this* script, I'm not your dad anymore. In this script, I'm just a well-disposed friend who could easily run out of patience." When Cadel recoiled, Prosper gave a snort of derision. "Did you really think I hadn't heard? I might be in hiding, dear boy, but I still manage to catch up on all the latest news."

Cadel swallowed. *Oh god,* he thought. *Oh god, oh god, oh god.*

"So let's remind ourselves at this point that I no longer have a stake in your survival," Prosper snarled, with the kind of venom that he'd formerly reserved for people like Saul Greeniaus and Sonja Pirovic. "I mean, it's not as though you're carrying my DNA, is it? There's no genetic imperative to stop me from blowing your brains out. Which is why we're going to skip all this silly posturing and proceed to the business at hand." He applied so much pressure to the gun that Cadel's head was pushed to one side. "Open that tunnel. *Now.* Before I lose my temper."

Cadel's heart was in his throat. He was convinced, by this time, that something had changed. *Prosper* had changed. His cool facade was beginning to crack. The controlled menace of his speech and the hard glint of amusement in his eye were both giving way to something wilder and more vicious.

What would he do if Kale managed to get in? Bullets would fly, certainly. Gas might be used. At best, there would be some kind of siege; Cadel might be stuck in an underground cupboard with Prosper for days. For *weeks*, if the emergency supplies held out.

Such a prospect was unimaginable.

"Even if I do this, what makes you think you'll get away?" Cadel faltered. "What makes you think someone won't shoot your boat full of holes?"

"Because *you'll* be in it," Prosper replied. "I'm going to need you."

"Which is why you won't kill me now," said Cadel with as much defiance as he could muster. He braced himself for a violent reaction but wasn't the least bit surprised when it didn't come. Once again, Prosper's mood had changed. In a matter of seconds, he'd reverted from a red-eyed beast to a suavely bantering professional.

"Oh, I think we've already established that," he drawled. "Right now I won't shoot you, for any number of reasons. But if the FBI come busting in here . . . well, who knows?"

Glancing up, Cadel found himself trapped in the force field of Prosper's regard. They stood staring at each other. Then Prosper sighed.

"The thing is, Cadel—and I'll be frank with you on this, because it's an important consideration—the thing is that I've been stuck inside here for several months, and it's not been easy. Not at all." The strain of it, in fact, was roughening Prosper's voice and drawing harsh shadows across his face. Suddenly he looked much, much older. "There's no way on God's earth I'm going to let anyone lock me up for another twenty years. It's just not going to happen. Do you understand what I'm saying?"

Slowly Cadel nodded. He understood, all right.

"So it's up to you," Prosper concluded. "Either we stay here and go through ten kinds of hell, culminating in god knows how many casualties, or you accompany me on a quiet little marine jaunt, which might very well end when we agree to split up and go our separate ways. What do you think?" When Cadel remained silent, Prosper added, "I mean, you're supposed to be a genius, aren't you? And it doesn't take a genius to work out what ought to be done here."

Cadel couldn't concentrate. Not with Prosper's anthracite gaze drilling into his eye sockets. Only by wrenching his own gaze firmly away from Prosper, and training it on the multiple views of busy FBI agents, was Cadel able to focus clearly on the dilemma confronting him.

He noticed that someone was disassembling a fuse-box—and he wondered if the panic-room door might be booby-trapped. Suppose it blew up if you tried to force it?

I'll have a better chance outside than I will stuck in here, he decided. *Outside will be full of variables. Inside, there's only one way things can go.*

"All right," he said. "I'll do it."

Then he dropped into the typist's chair.

With the passwords that Prosper gave him, Cadel found it easy to isolate the automatic door locks. It was quite a relief to be working with computers again; by fixing his attention firmly on source codes and file format identifiers, Cadel was briefly able to forget where he was and how he was feeling. He was even able to forget Prosper, who remained very quiet as Cadel wriggled his way past Vee's rather sloppy checkpoints. Vee hadn't put much effort into his door-disabling protocol. It was obviously a rushed job, which hadn't been treated as something that required much of a defensive shield.

In just a few minutes, Cadel had repaired the original program. He didn't restore its biometric subroutine, but he did scrub out Vee's numerous modifications, which were really quite ugly and far too elaborate. For the first time, Cadel realized how much Richard Buckland had influenced his opinion on such things. Though Vee's programming was effective, it could have been *more* effective. It could have been cleaner, leaner, and harder to mess with.

"Okay," Cadel finally announced, resisting the temptation to stray into any other parts of the system, "that's done." He spun around in his chair. "There's a new password now. If you enter that manually, the tunnel doors will open up."

Prosper narrowed his eyes. He had been standing behind Cadel, silently watching the monitor screens.

"The new password is 'Sonja,'" Cadel added without expression.

Prosper seemed to accept this. He certainly didn't comment on it.

"So the locks still work?" was all he said.

"They have to. The doors won't open unless the locks work."

"Right." Prosper grasped Cadel's arm, pulled him out of the chair, and guided him toward the kitchen cupboards. To Cadel's amazement, Prosper then dropped to one knee and removed a portion of kick plate beneath the dishwasher. Without a kick plate to restrain them, two parallel stainless steel rails immediately sprang across the floor.

Prosper used them to pull the dishwasher out from beneath the benchtop.

"It's got wheels," he explained as the appliance rolled forward about a yard or so along the rails. Behind it, in the wall, was a hatchway. And beside the hatchway was a small touchscreen interface device.

"Now," he said, waving his gun, "get down there and key in that password."

"Do you—" Cadel began, then hesitated.

Prosper frowned at him.

"What?"

"Do you know where . . . um . . ."

"Where Rex is?"

Cadel nodded.

"He's nowhere near the hatch, if that's what you're worried about." Prosper sounded impatient.

"How can you be sure?"

"Because I've seen the footage. That tunnel has cameras in it." When Cadel continued to stand there, unconvinced, Prosper yanked open a pantry cupboard. There was a brief and noisy interlude as cans and jars were pushed around. Then Prosper shoved a plastic bottle of dishwashing liquid under Cadel's nose. "There. Just keep your face shoved up against that," Prosper advised. "It'll mask the smell."

Cadel cleared his throat. "It's not the *smell* I'm worried about," he said plaintively. But before he could point out that he had never seen a corpse, and was scared of what Rex might look like, Prosper interrupted him.

"Well, you *should* be worried about the smell. Because there's bound to be one. And if you feel like throwing up, kindly refrain from doing it all over me." Using the gun for emphasis, Prosper gave Cadel a sharp prod. "Go on. Hurry. We haven't got all day."

Cadel forced himself to kneel. In a rather pathetic delaying tactic, he then removed his bottle's screw-top lid, surreptitiously placing the little plastic disk to one side, on the floor, where Kale might see it.

"Nice try," said Prosper. The lid quickly disappeared into his pocket. "And don't start throwing that detergent around, either, or I'll make you eat it."

With Prosper breathing down his neck, Cadel had run out of options. There was only one way to go. Cadel therefore did as he was told; clutching his bottle, he squeezed under the benchtop, shuffling forward on his knees and elbows until he was able to key his revised password into the touchscreen security device.

As soon as he hit "enter," the hatch in front of him swung open—releasing a faceful of damp, fetid air.

"Oh man . . ." he muttered.

"Go on," said Prosper from above him.

Cadel started to crawl. Luckily he wasn't crawling headfirst into a pitch-black hole. Beyond the hatchway, fluorescent lights were flickering on. (Had they been triggered by an infrared movement sensor?) He could see gray concrete walls and some cable ducts running off into the distance. His detergent bottle was wedged uncomfortably into his chest.

"Hurry up," snapped Prosper.

The smell wasn't as bad as Cadel had expected. In fact, with the sharp scent of artificial lemons filling his nostrils, he could barely detect even a whiff of corruption. It was Prosper who grimaced upon emerging into the escape tunnel.

But he didn't let the smell slow him down. And he didn't for one instant take his eyes off Cadel.

"What are you doing?" Cadel asked. He couldn't understand why Prosper was still crouched on the floor, reaching back through the hatchway with one hand while aiming his gun with the other. "Are you stuck or something?"

Prosper shook his head. Then he gave a heave, pulling at some invisible weight, and the ensuing *clunk* told Cadel what had happened. Prosper had been dragging the dishwasher back into place. Cadel could only assume that the two rails had retracted automatically.

After kicking the hatch shut, Prosper scrambled to his feet.

"Right," he snapped. "Off we go."

The tunnel was actually a wide corridor lined with reinforced concrete. It contained nothing but lights, cabling, and a handful of CCTV cameras—several of which had been smashed with a heavy object. Cadel didn't ask if Rex had done this. It was the sort of thing an imprisoned man might do, but it didn't bear thinking about.

Instead, as he was propelled down the tunnel, Cadel tried to concentrate on what he should do when he finally got out. There weren't any private beaches in California. Did Prosper realize that? Did he understand how dangerous it would be trying to launch a boat on a public beach? What if someone was standing nearby when the tunnel door opened?

I could shout for help, Cadel decided. *A neighbor might hear. Or a surfer. Or a fisherman.* Of course, Prosper had his gun—but could he actually risk firing it? A gunshot would be noisier than a shout. A gunshot would bring all the FBI agents running.

"God help us," Prosper croaked. They had turned a corner and hit a stench. Even Cadel could smell it, very faintly, through the clean, chemical odor of fake lemons.

He stopped in his tracks, reluctant to advance around the next corner.

"We must be close now," Prosper remarked. He was obviously holding his breath. "The boat's been left where you can push it straight down to the sea."

"He's not *in* the boat, is he?" Cadel demanded, struck by a sudden, terrible thought. And he felt the gun quiver against the back of his neck.

"God," Prosper growled. "I hope not."

"You don't *know?*"

"No. I don't know."

"But you said there were cameras!" Cadel protested.

"He smashed most of the cameras down this end. With an oar. He didn't want us watching him." Sucking in another gulp of air, the psychologist laid a hand on Cadel's shoulder. "You can close your eyes if you want to. I'll steer you in the right direction."

"But what if he *is* in the boat?"

"Then we'll have to bail him out, won't we?"

Cadel nearly threw up. He had to swallow several times before thrusting his entire nose into the bottle of dishwashing liquid.

Prosper seemed to relent a little.

"I'll take care of it," he promised in the tight, creaky, rapid-fire voice of someone trying not to breathe. "Just close your eyes and do what I say. All right?"

Cadel nodded.

"All right." Prosper gave him a push. "Start walking and I'll tell you when to stop . . ."

THIRTY-FOUR

Cadel stood absolutely still, his eyes squeezed shut and his nose rammed into the bottle of dishwashing liquid. He sensed that he was in a large space, though he couldn't have said why. Perhaps it was the way Prosper's coughs and curses echoed off the walls.

"Okay. It's safe to look now," Prosper said at last, breathlessly. "I've covered him up."

"Was he—is he—?"

"He's not in the boat." After a brief pause, occasioned by a fit of coughing, Prosper added, "It was better than I expected. Must be all the salt in the air."

Cadel didn't want to think about what *that* meant. So he opened his eyes. The first thing he spotted was an aluminum dinghy sitting directly in front of him. Its bow was pointed at a big metal roller door, and it had an outboard motor attached to its stern.

Beside this vessel, a green tarpaulin had been spread across the concrete floor. There was a lump beneath the tarpaulin.

"For god's sake, what are you gawking at?" barked Prosper. "I told you, there's nothing to see!"

"I—I—"

"Now bring that oar over here and stick it in the boat. We might need it."

There was already an oar in the boat, but Prosper wasn't pointing at that. He was indicating a second oar, which lay at one end of the large, triangular space in which he and Cadel both stood. The space itself was about the size of a three-car garage; it was where the last stretch of tunnel widened out, like the top of a martini glass, upon approaching the inside of the cliff face.

Damp and cold and lined with rough gray cement, it was one of the most inhospitable places that Cadel had ever experienced.

"On second thought, what am I saying?" Prosper suddenly remarked. There was an undertone of amusement in his voice. "I don't want you anywhere *near* that oar. The last thing I need is a fractured skull." He turned away from the wall-mounted computer screen near the roller door, closing the distance between himself and Cadel in just a few, long strides. "Stay right where you are. I'll take care of this myself."

Cadel hesitated. A picture had flashed into his mind: a picture of himself throwing detergent into Prosper's face before snatching up the oar and bringing it down on the psychologist's head.

But this whole notion was pure fantasy. For one thing, Prosper had a gun. And as for the inevitable impact . . . the *crunch* of wood on bone . . .

Cadel shuddered. He couldn't bear the thought of it. He was paralyzed by fear and doubt.

Then Prosper passed by, and so did the moment.

"What's that over there?" Cadel asked, squinting at the wall-mounted screen. "Is that a CCTV monitor?"

"Of course it is." Prosper picked up the discarded oar. "Do you think Rex would even *consider* going outside without checking that the coast was clear first?"

He tossed his oar into the boat with a *clang*. Meanwhile, Cadel peered harder at the flickering screen, which wasn't big enough to display more than a single image. Either there was only one camera on the other side of the roller door or you had to flip from camera to camera using the keypad under the screen.

"You might want to put this on," said Prosper, who had been inspecting the dinghy's contents. (He was holding his breath again.) "It looks a bit wet out there, and I know what a sheltered life you've been leading since I saw you last . . ."

Cadel glanced around, just in time to get an oilskin coat full in the face. He nearly dropped his bottle.

"The weather should work to our advantage," Prosper continued, "because there won't be anyone out and about. And even if your friends are scouring the cliff-top, visibility will be *very* poor."

With a growing sense of panic, Cadel edged closer to the CCTV screen until he could clearly make out the spray-flecked view of what lay just beyond the roller door: whitecaps, scudding clouds, a narrow stretch of shingle. Waves were breaking high over a pile of rocks.

The storm. Cadel had forgotten about the storm.

"We can't go out there!" he squeaked.

"Of course we can."

"But—but—" Staring in shock at the turbulent sea, Cadel let his bottle drift downward, away from his face. Almost immediately, a foul smell rushed up his nostrils and set him coughing. *"Oagh—aagh—cakk..."*

"The fresh air will do us both good," Prosper added. He had scooped up the oilskin coat again; his consonants were blurred and his vowels snubbed because he was trying not to breathe through his nose. "Put this on if you're worried."

Once again the coat took Cadel by surprise. This time, however, he didn't drop it. Instead he dropped his bottle, which he didn't dare retrieve. He was afraid that, if he bent down, he would throw up.

By now Prosper had returned to the CCTV monitor. Jabbing at its keypad, he skipped from scene to scene, scrutinizing a sequence of bone-chilling pictures: roiling white surf, rain-lashed boulders, a heaving horizon.

"Good," said Prosper.

"Good?" Cadel wheezed.

"There's no one in sight."

"We'll *sink* out there!"

"Don't be ridiculous."

"It's blowing a gale!"

"It's a bit of rough weather." Prosper seemed genuinely unmoved—

and mildly diverted by Cadel's alarm. "Weather like this isn't hazardous. Not for a seagoing vessel with an outboard motor and a bilge pump."

"How do *you* know?" Cadel cried. "You're just a wine waiter; you're not a fisherman!"

Prosper blinked. He had been studying the CCTV footage, but Cadel's accusation caused him to glance down, eyebrows raised. There was a moment's silence.

"I used to sail my own yacht," Prosper rejoined at last. "It was a hobby of mine. Naturally that was some time after I had abandoned my fledgling career as a sommelier." Suddenly, without warning, his mood changed. He jammed his gun hard against Cadel's upper lip and said, "Put that coat on. Now."

The way Prosper spoke, through clenched teeth, scared Cadel far more than the *click* of the gun being cocked. There was no arguing with that whiplash voice, or those narrowed eyes. So Cadel hurriedly thrust an arm into one sleeve, expecting his hand to emerge from the other end. But the sleeve was far too long; so was the second sleeve. Cadel had to push both of them up until they were concertinaed around his wrists. Then he tackled the zipper, which wasn't a hard thing to manage as long as his arms were raised. When he let them fall back toward his knees, however, each cuff slid over his knuckles, flapping and dangling like empty windsocks.

"Lift your arms straight out to your sides," said Prosper, frowning.

Cadel obeyed. He did so automatically, staring up at the monitor screen and wondering what on earth he was going to do once he hit the beach. An oilskin coat wasn't a flotation device. It wouldn't save him if the boat sank. How was he supposed to swim in sleeves that were overshooting the tips of his fingers by a good hand's length?

"Hmm," said Prosper. He began to circle Cadel, who vaguely expected him to make some stupid comment about folding the cuffs back. Instead, Prosper pounced. He grabbed both sleeves from behind.

"Hey!" Cadel protested. But before he could pull away, a sharp prod to the back of one knee made him buckle.

Next thing he knew he was kneeling on the floor, and Prosper was tying his sleeves together. It was like being handcuffed.

"I'll drown!" By now Cadel was seriously frightened. "I can't swim! Not like this!"

"You won't have to swim."

"Help! *Help!*"

"Oh, shut up." Prosper placed a foot between Cadel's shoulder blades, pressing down hard. At the same time, he reached across to push a few buttons on the wall-mounted keypad.

Doubled over, with his chin almost touching his thighs, Cadel heard a crunching sound. When he turned his head, he saw the steel roller door begin its slow ascent. He also caught a glimpse of the rough plaster surface behind it.

He could hardly breathe.

"Right," Prosper said briskly. Removing his foot from Cadel's back, he seized a handful of oilskin collar. Cadel was then jerked upright and propelled toward the boat. With his hands tied behind him, he couldn't really fight back—though he resisted every effort that was being made to pull him along. He dug in his heels and hung like a dead weight. Upon reaching the boat, he wedged both feet against its gunwale and pushed hard.

"Help! *Help!*"

"Jesus," hissed Prosper, who was trying to bundle him over the side. "Don't be such a *fool!*"

"*Lemme GO!*"

"This is completely irrational." Prosper adjusted his grip, hampered somewhat by the need to keep his gun pointed at the ceiling. "How can I *possibly* let you go if you won't calm down?"

At that instant, a gush of crisp, salty air invaded the room. Cadel realized that the outer door was swinging open and bucked so convulsively that Prosper nearly lost his footing.

"*Stop it,* damn you, I've got a *gun!*"

"Help!"

"There's no *need* to panic like this!" Prosper snapped. "I know you can swim; I paid for the lessons myself!" As the whistling wind hurled sea spray into his face and his captive kept thrashing about hysterically, Prosper's tone took on a frantic edge. "Why the hell are you so worried about a bit of water," he demanded, over the pounding of the surf, "when you've survived a bus crash and a runaway wheelchair? This will be like *summer camp*, for god's sake!"

Cadel froze. His muscles clenched, rigid with shock. Even his tongue wouldn't move.

"I'll untie you when we're out to sea!" Prosper said loudly. "You can man the bilge pump!" Then he lifted Cadel into the boat, before scurrying behind the stern and throwing himself against it. Slowly, as Prosper pushed, the vessel began to slide forward. "Don't even try to stand up, you'll just hurt yourself!" he advised between grunts.

Cadel was sprawled at the bottom of the boat among various bits of maritime equipment: a rope, a distress flare, a life jacket, a couple of oars, a manually operated bilge pump. Above him, the ceiling seemed to be rushing by at a rapidly accelerating pace. But although he saw the concrete beams, and the strip lighting, and the furled roller door, they didn't fully register. He didn't really absorb them because he was too busy processing what he had just heard.

The bus? he thought. *I didn't mention that bus.*

Suddenly he found himself looking directly up at the sky, which was low and dark and full of movement. Rain splashed into his eyes, making them sting. He rolled about, head bouncing; beneath him sand and rock scraped roughly against the keel until, with a swelling heave and a loud *slap*, the boat hit water.

"I didn't say anything about a bus," he croaked.

Prosper wasn't listening. Perhaps he hadn't even heard. What with the wind, the waves, and the clatter of loose oars, it wasn't easy to hear such a small, weak, wobbly voice. Certainly Prosper didn't reply. Instead he gave the dinghy a huge shove, leaping into it before it could get away from him.

The impact was tremendous. For one nasty moment, it felt as if the vessel was about to flip over. But it remained buoyant, despite Prosper's wild scrabblings.

Cadel was nearly kicked in the head as Prosper tried to get the outboard motor started. Already, their boat was being pushed back toward the tunnel's entrance by a tumultous surf.

"I didn't—" Cadel began, at which point the two-stroke engine roared to life, drowning out his second attempt to speak.

Chugga-chugga-chugga-v-r-R-O-M-M.

Prosper laughed. He was wet and dirty, and his skin was gray with cold, and his long hair whipped across his spray-flecked glasses with every gust of wind. Nevertheless, he looked exultant.

"God, it's good to be in the open air!" he exclaimed, steering the boat out to sea. Hitting swell after swell, the little dinghy rocked and lurched. Cadel couldn't sit up—not with his hands tied behind him. The bucking of the keel kept throwing him from side to side.

It was Prosper who finally leaned across and dragged Cadel into a sitting position, before glancing back over his shoulder.

No activity was visible on the edge of the receding cliff-top. The hole in the cliff was gone, replaced by polyurethane rockfall that looked just like genuine rockfall. The only sign that it had ever swung open were two semicircular lines that had been scored in the sand. And they were quickly being expunged by the rain.

"I don't see anyone up there, do you?" Prosper inquired at the top of his voice. But Cadel didn't choose to answer this question. Instead he asked a question of his own.

"How did *you* know about the bus?" was his response, pitched high and loud over the swishing of raindrops, the *clop* of water hitting aluminum, and the engine's throaty *putt-putt-putt*. "I thought you hadn't been told what was going on?"

This time Prosper heard. His smile evaporated. The sparkle in his eyes was snuffed out. But he didn't say a word as he locked gazes with Cadel—whose own eyes widened in horror.

"You knew all along." It was suddenly, blindingly obvious. Prosper had been lying. Of *course* he had been lying. He was a habitual liar. "You—you did this," Cadel stammered. "You tried to kill me."

Prosper frowned. "What?" he said, straining to hear.

"You tried to kill me!"

"No." Prosper shook his head.

"You did! It was *you!*" Cadel found himself gasping like someone being punched in the chest. "*You* were the one, right from the start! *You* gave the orders! *You* kicked things off!" The dinghy bounced over the crest of a very large wave, but Cadel hardly noticed. He had forgotten his bruises, and his nausea, and his fear of drowning. His whole attention was fixed on the hunched, lanky, sodden figure at the helm. "Why did you do it?" he wailed. "I was *minding my own business!*"

Prosper took a deep breath. "This is hardly the time or the place—" he began. Cadel, however, interrupted him.

"I was leaving you alone! I was perfectly happy! I was leading my own life!" bawled Cadel. "Why did you have to mess it all up? Why do you *always* have to come back and mess it all up?"

Prosper lowered his chin. Though his glasses were covered in smears of salt, there was no mistaking the anger that flared in the inky depths of his eyes. With his long yellow teeth bared in a snarl, and his hair billowing wildly around his head, and his bony frame folded into origami angles, he looked like a cornered beast.

"I didn't mess anything up!" he shouted into the wind. "*You* made a mess of your life, not me!"

"What are you *talking* about?" Cadel was almost hysterical with disbelief. "I was fine! Everything was fine until you came along!"

"Pottering around in the suburbs with a bunch of cripples and gardeners! Wasting your time at school surrounded by simple-minded wage slaves!" Practically retching with disgust, Prosper couldn't contain himself. A faint flush was staining his hollow cheeks. The veins were standing out on his temples. "What's the matter with you? Where's your self-respect? How can you stand that kind of *servitude?*"

Cadel's jaw dropped.

"It's pitiful!" Prosper railed. "All the work and money and time that went into raising you, and this is the result! This pettiness! This mediocrity!" He leaned forward, white-knuckled, to drive his point home. "Can't you see what you've *become?* You're throwing your life away!"

Oh my god, thought Cadel. Suddenly he understood. And he said, in tones of wonder, "You're jealous."

Prosper's head jerked back as if he were recoiling from a blow. But his reply, when it came, was scornful. "Don't be a fool!" he barked.

"You wanted to screw up my life because you've screwed up your own." The truth of this was so painfully clear. Prosper was stir-crazy. He'd been trapped in an underground bunker for months and months, skulking like a sewer rat while Cadel enjoyed a carefree, sunlit existence. "You couldn't bear to see me happy," Cadel cried, "because you don't know how to be happy yourself!"

Prosper grinned. But it was a rictus of a grin, like a jagged cut gaping open to reveal white bone.

"You weren't happy!" he retorted.

"I was!"

"You weren't! Not until I gave you something to do with yourself!" Prosper's sudden laugh was like a shutter banging or shots being fired. "Hasn't life been more exciting since I forced you to flex your muscles a bit? I wasn't trying to kill you; I was trying to set you free! I was teaching you to make use of those God-given talents that no one else seems to appreciate! And I was right—do you see? Because here you are, really *living!*"

Cadel opened his mouth. He wanted to explain that he was no longer a warped little puppet with a blinkered view of the world; that a normal life was all he needed; that he now had a family, to which Prosper didn't belong. He wanted to slam a door in Prosper's face by rejecting their shared past. He wanted to point out that Prosper was deluded, and maladjusted, and caught in a trap of his own making.

Before any of this could be said, however, the outboard motor sputtered, choked, and died.

THIRTY-FIVE

"Goddammit," said Prosper.

He tried to restart the engine but wasn't successful. Again and again the result was a discouraging *ugga-ugga-ugga*. Meanwhile, the boat began to drift.

"Untie me!" Cadel shrieked, almost dislocating his shoulder as he struggled to free himself. "Quick! Or I'll drown!"

But Prosper was fiddling with the outboard motor. He swore as the keel beneath him pitched and tossed helplessly.

"This is ridiculous," he protested, turning to peer at all the loose supplies that were sliding around underfoot. "There must be a spare can . . ."

"Please! Oh, *please!*" Cadel could see the rocky shoreline inching nearer and nearer. "You've got to help me; we're running out of *time!*"

"Why the hell would you have an escape boat with an empty tank?" said Prosper, who seemed to be talking to himself. He certainly gave no indication that he had heard Cadel. "Rex thought of everything else, for god's sake—why not gas?"

"*Because he used it all up trying to attract attention!*" Cadel screamed. The answer was so obvious that he couldn't understand why he hadn't thought of it before. Rex must have run the engine for hours, hoping that its throbbing rumble would spark the curiosity of passing beach-combers. But the noise hadn't been loud enough—and the fumes had probably killed him. "If we're out of gas, we're going to crash! You've got to untie me!"

Again Prosper didn't respond. He was squinting at the cliffs that loomed to his left, a pensive frown on his face. Then all at once he reached for the oars.

"Please," Cadel sobbed, "*please* let me go, I don't want to drown!"

"Oh, stop it!" snapped Prosper. "You're not going to drown!" Having fitted each oar into an oarlock, he began to row. He did it very well, with smooth and powerful strokes that did a lot to stabilize the storm-tossed dinghy. Cadel, however, wasn't reassured. By this time the bottom of the boat was awash, and the rain-veiled cliffs looked awfully close.

"There's a distress flare in here!" he cried. "We should light it!"

Prosper shook his head.

"Do you still have that police radio?" Cadel demanded. "Maybe you could call for help!"

"No." The strain of exertion was clearly evident in Prosper's voice as he swung back and forth. His cheeks were flushed and his breathing labored.

"I could do it myself!" pleaded Cadel. "You wouldn't have to stop rowing! It won't take a minute to untie me!"

"That radio is back in the house," said Prosper, stubbornly plying his oars. So Cadel tried another tack.

"You're not going to get away! Not without an engine! Can't you see that?" No reply. "There'll be a statewide alert! Even if we *don't* capsize, the police will pick you up as soon as you hit solid ground!"

Finally Prosper found the breath to speak. "Not in Mexico they won't," he rejoined into the teeth of the wind.

"*Mexico?*"

"We can do it." *Cre-e-eack* went the oars in their oarlocks. "I'll call Wilfreda when we get there."

For a split second, Cadel was distracted. For one fleeting moment, he forgot all about the jolting waves, the threatening cliffs, and the water sloshing around his ankles. "You said you didn't know where Wilfreda was!" he exclaimed.

"I don't," Prosper admitted. "But I do have her number."

At that instant, a wave broke over the bow, dumping several bucket-loads of water into the wallowing dinghy. Cadel gasped.

Prosper scowled. He turned to peer at the nearby cliff-top, his profile colorless against a darkening backdrop of slate gray sea and sky. Though he was trying to head south, the swell was pushing him eastward, straight toward land.

Cadel could see this with perfect clarity. And he was quite sure that Prosper couldn't have missed it.

"Let me bail out the boat! I *promise* I won't do anything else!" Sitting in a puddle of bilge, Cadel realized that hysterical ranting wasn't going to get him anywhere. He had to argue his case, calmly and firmly. He had to *reason* with Prosper. "I'd be stupid to hit you," he went on in a far more subdued fashion. "I can't row this boat by myself. I swear to god, I'll do whatever you tell me, just *untie my hands!*"

The psychologist kept rowing, lunging forward and pulling back, his muscles braced against the boat's far more erratic movements. But his hooded gaze was now fixed on Cadel—rather than on the surrounding scene of stormy chaos—and something about that unreadable gaze was oddly encouraging.

Had Prosper decided to see reason, at long last?

Suddenly the oars lifted. They swung back on board, as if the vessel were folding its wings. Instead of reaching for Cadel, however, Prosper bent and grabbed the distress flare.

"No point taking any risks," he said, tossing it over the side. Then he began to pluck at Cadel's knotted sleeves.

Cadel didn't cry out. Though he saw the flare vanish with a *plop*, he didn't utter a word of protest. What was the point? Prosper had gone mad. It was almost as if he *wanted* to die. Either that or he genuinely believed that he was invincible.

Cadel knew better. He also knew that, if he was going to survive, he would have to choose his words with care. It was important that Prosper not be angered or alarmed. He had to be lulled into a false sense of security.

For that reason, Cadel made his eyes very big (and his voice very small) as he thanked the psychologist for untying him. Furthermore, despite the fact that a serviceable handgun was still tucked into Prosper's waistband, Cadel made no immediate attempt to arm himself. The time wasn't right for a frontal assault. *I'll wait until he's rowing again,* Cadel decided.

Almost on cue, their boat spun around in a circle, like a leaf going down a drain.

"Jesus!" Prosper exclaimed. He snatched at the oars and wrestled them back into position while Cadel frantically tore off his oilskin coat. The bilge pump was rattling around nearby; it looked a bit like a bicycle pump, except that it was bigger, with an attached hose. After a moment's intense contemplation, Cadel pushed one end of the hose over the side.

The other end was attached to the top of the pump, near its handle.

"How well can you swim?" Prosper asked unexpectedly. Though he was short of breath and straining to be heard, his tone was almost conversational. "I'm a pretty strong swimmer—are you?"

"No," Cadel replied, furiously working the pump. It wasn't very efficient. Though it did suck up brine from the surging, splashing pool in which he crouched, the volume of water being moved was dangerously small, in Cadel's opinion—especially in view of the fact that he was being constantly interrupted. Every roll of the boat threw him off-balance. He would bounce off the side or fall on his face.

"So after all those lessons, you're still not much good?" Prosper sounded more amused than annoyed. The way he was talking, he could have been steering a paddleboat across a pond. "I should have strangled that coach of yours with her own silver whistle!"

Cadel lifted his gaze. He licked his salty lips. "You think we'll have to swim? Is that what you're saying?" he inquired hoarsely.

"Not at all. I'm just wondering who should get the life jacket." Prosper fell silent for a moment, panting as he rowed. He had to fill his lungs a few times before proceeding. "I certainly don't think it'll do *you* much good if you're a weak swimmer anyway. But it might make a world of difference to *me.*"

Another pause. Another stroke. Prosper seemed to be expecting some kind of reaction, to judge from the smirk that was tugging at the corner of his mouth. Though Cadel stiffened, however, he didn't speak. He didn't try to contend that the weaker swimmer deserved the most help, because he knew that Prosper would only make some barbed comment about the survival of the fittest.

"Trouble is," Prosper added, pitching his voice high above the wind, "I don't know how I can put that life jacket on unless you take the oars." Though his lips were blue, and his teeth were chattering, and his hands were shaking as he dragged at the oars' slippery shafts, he seemed almost to be teasing Cadel. "What a conundrum, eh? Should I give you the life jacket or should I give you the oars?"

Cadel swallowed. "The life jacket," he retorted.

"Oh, really? Why?"

Because the oars aren't going to save either of us, Cadel thought. But aloud he said, "Because I'm not strong enough to row."

Suddenly a huge wave slammed into them. It nearly flipped the dinghy over, and it sent Cadel reeling. He was pitched straight into Prosper's lap as the psychologist lurched sideways. Then the boat righted itself. A loose oar slipped into the sea. Prosper stretched an arm over the side, reaching desperately.

He had to lean past Cadel, who was now sprawled at his feet—and as he did so, Cadel spotted the gun-butt. It was protruding from Prosper's waistband, right under Cadel's nose.

"Got it!" yelped Prosper, seizing the oar.

At that very instant Cadel grabbed the gun.

"Freeze!" he shrilled.

The boat rolled again, steeply. To prevent himself from sliding into the stern, Cadel had to hook one arm around an oarlock and hold on for dear life. The bilge pump bounced off his ribs. Seawater slapped him in the face.

Then Prosper caught at his free hand, pushing it upward. With his wrist immobilized, and his gun pointed at the clouds, Cadel couldn't do a thing. In fact, he probably would have been overpowered if Prosper hadn't been tired out—and if Prosper's own free hand hadn't been occupied with the rescued oar.

For what seemed like hours, but was probably only a few seconds, the two of them remained trapped in a stalemate. Prosper couldn't afford to drop his oar, while Cadel couldn't risk letting go of the oarlock. Neither could achieve any kind of ascendancy—not while they were both throwing every ounce of strength they had into a bout of elevated arm wrestling.

Finally Prosper began to laugh.

"I should have known this is how it would end," he brayed. "You dragging me down for the third time in a row." Grinning like a skull, he narrowed his eyes. "So what was all that about not trying anything?" he said. "It's good to see that you still can't be trusted. I'd hate to think you'd *completely* rejected your upbringing."

Bang! Bang! Bang-bang-bang!

A volley of gunshots rang out as Cadel fired into the air. He knew that Prosper couldn't shoot him without bullets. It was also possible that someone, somewhere, might hear the shots. Though he realized that he would be left defenseless, Cadel had calculated that an unloaded gun would be a safer option than the alternative. So he kept squeezing the trigger until it produced nothing but a sad little *click*.

If Prosper was surprised, he didn't show it. Nor did he fly into a rage. On the contrary, he dropped Cadel's wrist and picked up the life jacket.

Cadel didn't know what to think. He stared in confusion, wet and breathless and freezing cold. The gun was now just a useless lump of metal, weighing him down. He wondered, fleetingly, if he and Prosper should each take an oar. What if they rowed together, sitting elbow to elbow? Would there be any advantage in that?

"Maybe this time it'll be different," was all that Prosper had to say. "Maybe this time, I'll drag *you* down *with* me."

But then a wave broke like thunder nearby. White froth cascaded over them. The boat reared like a startled horse, nearly pulling Cadel's arm out of its socket as he clung to the oarlock. Prosper didn't have a choice; if he hadn't grabbed the gunwale, he would have been hurled backwards.

Rather than relinquishing the life jacket, he let go of his oar—which was promptly snatched away by a surge of water.

"If I were you," he loudly suggested, "I'd hit me with that gun and take this life jacket!" He was wearing a strange, lopsided grin, and there was a wild look in his eye. "It seems like the obvious solution, don't you think?"

"Wh-what?" Cadel's own teeth were chattering now. His shoulder was killing him. The whole world seemed to be moving in slow motion, spinning off course. Or was it the boat? The boat was spinning, too—and a dark, heavy, towering threat loomed somewhere off in the middle distance. But he couldn't focus on that. He didn't have the energy. He was still trying to work out what to do with the gun.

"Didn't I teach you *anything?*" Prosper thrust his face into Cadel's, bawling out advice over the boom and hiss of breaking waves. "When it comes to survival, it's every man for himself! Forget the common good! Forget the bleeding-heart crap that all those coppers and social workers have been feeding you! I *know* you, Cadel—you're a pragmatist! You think with your head! *You should hit me with the gun and take the life jacket!*" He laughed again—the craziest, most despairing laugh that Cadel had ever heard. "If you do that, dear boy, I'll die happy!"

The words were snatched away by a howling wind. Then a huge jolt yanked Cadel from his seat. He felt the impact through his entire body. His head snapped back. The breath was knocked out of him. Turning somersaults, he saw the dinghy's crumpled bow soar up to block out the sky—and knew instantly what had happened.

They had hit submerged rock.

Suddenly he was buried in water. The gun was gone. His lungs were bursting. He thrashed and kicked and dislodged one shoe. Something nudged him, but bobbed away when he tried to grab it. He surfaced, gasping, and caught a glimpse of the boat. It had flipped over. He couldn't reach its exposed keel, though he tried to swim in that direction. The swell, however, was dragging him away, around and around, pushing and tugging. There was no sign of Prosper. A broken oar flashed past. Sea spray lashed and stung.

Then a huge wave lifted Cadel like a cork, before submerging him again. Dumped in a trough, he was propelled down, down, down by massive forces, as tons of water piled up on his head. He said to himself, *I can't drown. Not now. This is impossible.*

An overwhelming sense of disbelief snuffed out his panic. He wasn't thinking about Saul, or Fiona, or his friends. He was thinking about the boat and how he might reach it. Kicking off his other shoe, he struck out for the greenish light overhead, away from the darkness beneath him. *Swim. Swim. Swim.* The word beat a tattoo inside his skull. His whole life had been narrowed down to that one, simple procedure. *Swim.*

All at once he was gulping down air. The relief was so great, it was almost excruciating. But his arms felt so weak. His chest felt so sore. He couldn't see the boat—in fact, he could hardly see anything, because his eyes were full of salt water. And a terrible realization was creeping up on him. He asked himself: *Is this how it's going to end? Am I going to die off the coast of California?*

The third time he went down, he wasn't pushed; he was pulled. A rip dragged him under, twirling him like laundry in a washing machine. And when he struggled toward the surface, it seemed to recede. The pale, submarine light grew fainter and fainter. The blackness crept up on him, on every side, like the walls of a tunnel. He was suffocating—his chest was burning—he *had* to breathe!

What happened next was a jumble of vague impressions: darkness, then a blank period, then a solid presence and a loud noise. A sensation of acute urgency was followed by one of immense relief. But never once did Cadel break through into consciousness. His mind was adrift, detached from everything firm, proven, and understood; he let his own identity slip away. The world dissolved. There was nothing left. He was floating . . . floating . . .

. . . and coughing. He was coughing. *Hack-hack-hack.* Slowly he reconnected with his arms and legs. They were pinned down. He couldn't move.

Hack-hack-hack. He struggled for air.

"He's breathing!" someone shouted. And someone else said, "Thank you, Jesus."

Cadel opened his eyes. A face was hovering over him, against a backdrop of dark cloud. The face was long and brown and damp, with very white teeth. Cadel didn't recognize it.

"Are you okay? Can you hear me?" the lips enunciated.

Cadel didn't reply. He retched, then tried to roll over. Immediately the weight on his chest and arms lifted.

He heard someone say, "It's a miracle."

By this time, the edges of his vision were clearing. He could see things—and make sense of them, too. He was lying on sand. He was wet. He was alive.

It was raining.

As he threw up, something was placed across his shoulders. A jacket? It nearly blew off again, before an eager pair of hands tucked it around him like a shawl. More people were talking, high above his head. He couldn't look at them. He couldn't move. He had to lie there in his own vomit, because the effort involved in bringing up a bellyful of seawater had exhausted him.

Gradually the murmur of voices became clearer. They all seemed to be male voices, with American accents. He heard "phone" and "shock" and "ambulance." Then he started to cough again.

"Jesus! Cadel! Oh my god . . ."

"Kale." The word sprang into his mind, followed by a flurry of other words: "Prosper" and "boat" and "life jacket." Meanwhile, someone had squatted beside him.

He craned his neck to look up at the hunched figure.

"Kale?" he croaked.

"Are you sore? Can you move? Is anything broken?" It was Kale, all right. He raised his voice sharply before Cadel could ask about Prosper. *"Where's the ambulance? Did someone call an ambulance?"*

"I did."

"They're on their way."

"I've done a first-aid course . . ."

"Should we shift him? Before they get here?"

"He needs to be kept warm . . ."

This babble of responses was reassuring. There had to be six or seven people standing around in the rain—and it occurred to Cadel that some of them might be police officers.

Kale certainly was. His jacket was flapping open in the wind, exposing the gun tucked into his shoulder holster.

Prosper doesn't stand a chance, thought Cadel, slumping with relief.

"Prosper," he rasped, and Kale leaned down to listen.

"What's that?" asked Kale. He laid a hand on Cadel's sodden curls. "Can you sit up? If you can sit up, we'll carry you. We'll get you up the stairs."

Up the stairs? Briefly distracted, Cadel raised his chin again, peering through the forest of legs that surrounded him. Across an expanse of sand and rocks he saw a crumbling orange cliff face with a flight of steps hanging off it.

Though he didn't recognize these steps, the tightly packed mansions perched above them rang a bell.

"We won't take you back to that goddamn house," Kale assured him, at which point Cadel understood that the "goddamn house"—Rex Austin's house—must be quite close. It had to be close or Kale wouldn't have turned up so quickly.

Unless it hadn't been quick? Cadel didn't know. He couldn't tell how long he'd been lying on the beach like a stranded whale.

Minutes? Hours?

"Where's Prosper?" he muttered. And this time Kale heard.

"Prosper?"

"He was on the boat with me . . ." As Cadel strained to peer back over his shoulder, Kale started firing orders at the men clustered around them both. Clearly many of these people were also FBI agents; Cadel registered the fact in some remote corner of his brain, though he didn't really listen to what was being said. It was happening too far above him, and he didn't feel well enough to concentrate.

He did notice, however, that the churning, thundering surf had to cover a lot of ground before it was able to lick at his toes. And he thought, *Did I get all the way up here by myself?*

There were no drag marks that he could detect—but then again, there were no marks of any description. No footprints, no tire tracks, no nothing. The sea would have washed everything away.

"Cadel. *Cadel.*" Kale squeezed his arm. "Can you hear me?"

"Of course I can hear you," said Cadel, feeling vaguely annoyed. "I don't have water in my ears."

"You told me you were with Prosper. In a boat. Is that right?"

"Yes."

"What happened? Did he throw you overboard?"

"No." A fit of coughing intervened before Cadel could finally gasp out, "The boat capsized."

"Jesus."

"I took the gun, but I dropped it. Prosper got the life jacket." As he tried to organize his scattered memories, Cadel made a feeble attempt to sit up. His head swam with the effort. He was starting to shake. "There was hardly any gas in the engine," he continued. "Rex must have turned it on, to make a noise. He's under a green thing now."

"Take it easy," Kale begged. "Don't force it. You can tell me later."

But Cadel couldn't seem to stop talking. The words kept spurting out of him, like the seawater he'd swallowed. "We hit a rock," he continued. "The boat was upside down. There's a house inside the other house— that's where Prosper was hiding. Wilfreda was there, too, but she's gone to Mexico, I think."

"Shhh. It's okay. Can you hear that siren? That's the ambulance."

"Prosper's a good swimmer. He told me so." Cadel was flagging. His eyelids drooped. His muscles wouldn't hold him up anymore. "You'd better be careful," he murmured, sinking back onto the sand, "because Prosper took the life jacket. If I made it, then he made it. He wasn't scared. He wouldn't have drowned."

"Down here!" Kale shouted. *"Over here!"*

A radio crackled nearby.

"He'll be heading for Mexico, too," Cadel added, before his tongue decided, of its own volition, to stop working. His lips wouldn't move. His eyes wouldn't focus.

He felt so tired . . .

THIRTY-SIX

They were waiting at Sydney Airport: Fiona and Saul, Sonja, Judith, Gazo . . . even Hamish. When Cadel emerged from Customs and Immigration, he spotted them at once.

What with Sonja's wheelchair, Saul's bandaged head, and Judith's neon-pink glasses, they were very hard to miss.

"Christ," muttered Kale, transfixed by Hamish's leather jacket. It was so heavy with studs and chains and rivets that it must have weighed as much as Hamish did. "What is this, a three-ring circus?"

Cadel didn't respond. The sight of all those eager faces had rendered him mute; he could hardly manage the stiff little smile with which he greeted the flurry of waving triggered by his sudden appearance. Next thing he knew, he was engulfed in a knot of people as Fiona threw her arms around him and Gazo relieved him of his green bag.

Saul and Kale shook hands, awkwardly. It wasn't an easy maneuver, because Saul's right shoulder and arm were imprisoned in a complex arrangement of bandages. But the two men did their best, without dislodging anything. Then Saul thanked Kale, and Kale apologized to Saul.

Meanwhile, Cadel was being bombarded by questions.

"Are you feeling okay? How was the flight?" said Fiona. "Did you manage to get any sleep?"

"D-did you hear about Dot and Com?" said Hamish. "They were picked up in Melbourne. *Boy*, are they in trouble!"

"Do you want to go straight to my house? Or is there some kind of police business you need to get through first?" Judith asked Cadel, in a voice that was just a fraction too loud. And Fiona hastened to elaborate.

"We're all living at Judith's—you and me and Saul," she explained. "Just for the time being."

Sonja remained silent. But her brown eyes strained toward Cadel, and her taut, quivering neck told him how keyed up she was. He would have liked to say something nice to her. He would have liked to compliment her on her tartan skirt and matching hairband. He even opened his mouth. The words, however, wouldn't come.

And he couldn't give her a kiss. Not in public, surrounded by people like Kale and Hamish.

"We're blocking the exit," Saul suddenly observed. Though he looked terrible, with bruising and grazes all around his right eye, he seemed to be coping pretty well with the heaving bustle and reverberating noise of the arrivals hall. "Let's get out of here. Who's going with Judith? Sonja, of course . . ."

"Do you want to go with Sonja, sweetie?" Fiona turned to Cadel, who nodded. Saul threw him a quick, speculative glance but didn't speak.

Judith boomed, "I've got room for two more—the rest of you will have to pile into Gazo's car."

It was decided that Judith would take Sonja, Cadel, Fiona, and Saul, while Kale and Hamish would ride with Gazo. Both cars would be driven to Judith's Maroubra mansion, where a bed would then be found for Kale.

"It's a bit crowded at my place," Judith confessed, as they all trooped off to the airport's multilevel parking lot, "and I don't have much furniture, but I'm sure we can work something out."

"Is it properly secured?" Kale wanted to know. Though bleary-eyed and unshaven after the long flight, he was still on full alert. "Are we talking about a fully operational alarm system?"

"It's safe enough now," Saul replied. "There was a problem, but that's been solved." Laying a tentative hand on Cadel's shoulder, he quietly added, "Sid and Steve have been terrific. They've cleaned out Judith's whole network for us."

"And they've been pulling a whole b-buncha stuff off Dot's computer," Hamish chimed in, "because she didn't get a chance to wipe her files. So what with that, and Raimo Zapp's data, and whatever they can get out of Niobe, I reckon Vee won't stand a chance." He sidled up to Cadel as the whole group stopped in front of an elevator. "You heard they found Niobe, didn't you? She was hiding out in San Diego. And it looks like Vee might b-be holed up in New Zealand somewhere, so—"

"That's not for public discussion!" Saul interposed sharply.

And Kale clicked his tongue. "You got a big mouth, kid," he informed Hamish, before addressing Saul once again. "I figure Cadel should use the stairs. Just in case. Like the kid said, we've still got a certain hacker perp at large."

"Right," Saul agreed. There followed a general discussion about who should go in the lift (with Sonja) and who should use the stairs, but Cadel didn't take part in this debate. He was still dazed and reeling, though whether from jet lag, fatigue, or emotional shell shock he wasn't sure. Physically, he had fully recovered from his near-death experience in the Pacific Ocean. After a very short spell in the hospital, he had been released into Kale Platz's custody, with a prescription for anti-diarrhea medication and a pamphlet about post-traumatic stress. He had then spent most of the subsequent two days—before his flight back to Australia—eating and sleeping and watching the two hundred and thirty cable TV channels to which the FBI agent subscribed. No demands had been placed on Cadel. Everyone had tiptoed around him. And on the trip home, he had flown business class, courtesy of Judith Bashford.

So it wasn't as if he had suffered any kind of injuries or periods of deprivation. And he was pleased to see everyone—of course he was. *Extremely* pleased. Why, then, couldn't he scatter smiles and hugs like confetti? Why did the parking lot staircase feel like a mountain when he started to climb it? Why did he dread the prospect of a long drive in a crowded car, even though the people who would be sharing it with him were his nearest and dearest?

Perhaps it was sheer cowardice. Perhaps he was scared that someone would raise the subject of Prosper English long before they reached Maroubra. It was inevitable. It was even understandable. Yet the thought of it made Cadel feel sick.

"Do you want to sit in the front, sweetie?" Fiona inquired. "You're not looking very well."

Cadel shook his head. Then he found his voice, at long last.

"I want to sit next to Sonja," he mumbled.

"Okay." Fiona sounded faintly relieved—perhaps because Cadel had decided to talk. She turned to her husband. "Why don't *you* sit in the front?" she suggested. "It'll be easier for you."

Saul concurred. He was quite pale by this time and had to lower himself gingerly into the seat beside Judith's, taking care not to bump his bandaged head or jolt his broken collarbone. It took even longer to get Sonja properly settled; shifting her about had always been a complicated job, and the cast on her leg made it more difficult than usual.

Finally, however, the car was fully loaded. The last door slammed. The last seat belt was fastened. As Judith pulled out into the sluggish traffic, Saul twisted around to peer at Cadel.

"We can talk in here," the detective announced. "It's not exposed like that parking lot." A brief silence ensued; when Cadel didn't ask any questions, Saul went on. "I don't know how much Kale's told you, but things have been moving very fast at this end. Hamish was right: Dot and Com are both under arrest, and we're closing in on Vee. So you don't have to worry anymore. Okay? *There's no need to worry.*"

"Our house was fully insured, and there won't be any legal repercussions," Fiona added, backing him up. "The lawyer over in Los Angeles is taking care of that, and we've got lots of good people working on the case over here. I'm *convinced* you won't be charged—especially since the cost of that ticket was repaid so quickly."

"Still, it's good you're not sixteen yet," was Judith's unexpected contribution, which elicited a frown from Saul.

"Age is only one factor," he reminded her in a reproving tone. "There are lots of other considerations, too."

"Like the extreme stress you were under, Cadel," Fiona weighed in. "And the fact that you were so cooperative with the police."

"It'll be okay," Saul insisted. "Like I said, there's no need to worry."

Cadel swallowed. His gaze slid sideways, toward Sonja, but she couldn't offer any reassurance. All she could do was roll her eyes.

Though he didn't want to upset her, he couldn't help himself. He had to ask. He *had* to.

"What about Prosper?" he croaked.

A weird kind of stillness descended on the car. For a split second, even Sonja stopped moving. Fiona cleared her throat. Judith's knuckles whitened on the steering wheel.

"I don't think . . ." Saul began, then paused and took a deep breath before remarking, very gently, "I don't think *anyone* has to worry about Prosper anymore."

"Except maybe the Prince of Darkness," said Judith. When Saul flicked her a warning look, Judith seemed taken aback. "What?" she demanded. "It's a fair comment!"

Fiona sighed. "Judy, we've talked about this—" she began but was interrupted by Cadel.

"Prosper might not be dead," he murmured. "Have you thought of that?"

Another tense silence fell. Fiona pressed his hand. The car jerked forward.

"If he's dead, then why hasn't anyone found him?" Cadel continued weakly. "Why hasn't he been washed up?"

"It can take weeks for that to happen," Saul replied. "What with the currents and the sharks . . ." Somehow he must have sensed his wife's dismay; perhaps he heard the upholstery creak beneath her as she flinched, because he abruptly abandoned the subject of sharks and their feeding habits. "Didn't Kale discuss this with you? I thought he did. He *said* he did."

In fact, Kale had discussed the subject endlessly. Upon hearing Cadel's first (and somewhat garbled) account of the dinghy accident, he'd concluded that Prosper might have faked his own death. But then Cadel had recovered enough to provide more details, and Rex Austin's boat had been found—along with a flare, an oar, and one of Prosper's shoes. From that moment on, Kale's opinion had altered. The fact that the life jacket was still missing had cut no ice with Kale. He was convinced that Prosper was dead, despite the absence of any remains.

Like Saul, Kale had mentioned things like sharks and tidal currents. He'd insisted that *no one* could have swum to Mexico from Laguna Beach—not in the middle of a storm. And he'd dismissed Cadel's objections about the missing life jacket.

"I'll agree, Prosper could have been wearing it," the FBI agent had conceded at one point. "But that doesn't mean he survived. The bilge pump is missing, too, remember. And that length of rope you were talking about." According to Kale, the fact that Prosper hadn't washed up along the coastline of Southern California within twenty-four hours of disappearing was pretty conclusive. "Of course there'll be an inquest, but if he didn't crawl up onto a beach somewhere, he's dead for sure. He would have been spotted. I don't care how fit he was—he would have been knocked around so bad, they would have had to scrape him off the rocks."

This was more or less what Saul was saying as Judith drove beneath a boom gate, out of the parking lot. Gazo was ahead of them somewhere, on his way to Maroubra. Everything looked slightly strange to Cadel, even though he hadn't been out of the country for long. He wasn't used to seeing cars on the left-hand side of the road.

"You barely made it to shore yourself," Saul argued, "and you were lucky. I mean, it's a miracle that the waves pushed you straight onto the beach. If that hadn't happened, you would have drowned."

"Maybe that *isn't* what happened," Cadel replied dully. "Maybe it wasn't the waves that pushed me onto the beach."

Fiona gasped. Saul said, "What are you talking about?"

But Fiona was way ahead of him.

"You surely don't think that *Prosper* saved you?" she protested. "Oh no. No."

"People have been going on and on about how lucky I was—" Cadel began, before Judith cut him off.

"Are you kidding?" she said scornfully. "Prosper took the bloody life jacket! Why the hell would he have done that if he wanted to save you?"

"Because he's a better swimmer than me," Cadel rejoined. For days he had been searching his memory for hints and contradictions. There had been a solid presence—he could certainly recall that. But had it been Prosper or the boat?

According to Kale, it had been the boat. According to Kale, Prosper couldn't possibly have saved Cadel. And Saul shared this opinion.

"If Prosper had dragged you onto dry land, he would have left footprints," the detective pointed out.

"Not necessarily." Cadel refused to budge. "Not if he stayed below the tidemark."

"Are you serious?" Judith scoffed as she spun the wheel.

Then Fiona weighed in with her own objection. "He wouldn't have gone back into the water, sweetie," she demurred.

"I'm not saying he did." Cadel could feel himself growing more and more defensive. He could feel his heart pounding and his muscles clenching and his mouth drying up. "For all we know, he could have walked over to the rocks *through* the water. There were rocks at the end of that beach. He could have climbed those rocks until he reached the top of the cliff."

"And then what?" asked Saul. "He would have been spotted, Cadel. A wet guy in a life jacket? He would have stood out like a sore thumb."

"It was raining," Cadel retorted. "And he probably got rid of the life jacket."

"In that case, it would have been found."

"Not if he threw it into the sea. You just *said* it was probably lost at sea."

"Yeah, sure—if it was wrapped around Prosper!" By now Saul's irritation was beginning to show. Staying twisted around in his seat couldn't have been easy; it must have hurt his shoulder, because he was red and shaky and damp with sweat. For some reason, however, he'd decided that demolishing Cadel's arguments should be done face-to-face, and eye-to-eye. "If that life jacket was thrown off a cliff, it would have washed ashore again," the detective declared.

"You don't know that."

"Cadel, the place was crawling with police. Where could he have gone, with only one shoe? Did he have any money? Did he have a functioning phone? It's not like he caught a cab."

"Have you checked?" asked Cadel. When he received no answer, he realized that he'd scored a point. "Wilfreda's still out there somewhere," he continued. "For all we know, she might be living in Laguna Beach. He might have gone to stay with her. It's possible."

Saul gave a startled grunt. "I thought you said she was in Mexico?" he exclaimed.

Cadel colored. "I did," he had to admit. "That's what I assumed. But it isn't what *Prosper* said." Hearing Judith snort, he became more strident. "Prosper said that *we* were going to Mexico: he and I. He said he'd call Wilfreda when we got there. Which might just mean that he wanted her to drive down and meet us."

"Sweetie . . ." Suddenly Fiona spoke up. She squeezed Cadel's hand again, gazing into his eyes with anxious compassion. "Listen to me for a minute," she said. "I realize that you've spent your whole life in Prosper's shadow. I realize that in the past, whenever you've started to feel safe, he's always come back to spoil things. And I understand why you can't let go of the feeling that he'll *keep* coming back no matter what." As Cadel stiffened, she took a deep breath. "But this time, I swear to you, he won't come back," she promised. "He won't. He's gone. You're free now."

"Because he's not bloody Superman," Judith agreed. "If he'd made it to shore, he would have been found. And since he wasn't found, then he must be dead."

No, thought Cadel. *No, no, no. That can't be right*. There was a bitter taste on his tongue.

"If Prosper drowned, why didn't I?" he snapped. "Prosper was a good swimmer! He had a life jacket! Why would *he* drown and not me?"

"Because you were lucky," Saul replied. His voice roughened a little as he added, "Because we were all lucky. Incredibly, unbelievably lucky."

"Or because Prosper saved my life!" Cadel blurted out. When Saul turned to face the windshield, it was as if he'd passed judgment. Cadel felt panic-stricken, and close to despair. "It makes sense!" he cried. "It does!"

"It does *not*," said Judith. She glanced up into the rearview mirror. "Prosper took the life jacket. He tried to kill you. What about Sonja's wheelchair? What about the runaway bus?"

"I—I—"

"He was going crazy, Cadel. You said it yourself. I've read your state-ment." Saul's tone was deep and weary. "He practically confessed when he mentioned that bus. He had it in for you."

"Yes, but—"

"He was using you as a hostage. That's why he didn't shoot you in the house," Saul went on, much to Fiona's annoyance. She shot a fierce look at her husband, then placed a comforting arm around Cadel's shoulders.

"We'll never know what *might* have happened," she said, soothingly. "All we know is what *did* happen. Which is that you're home safe, with your family, and that the danger is well and truly past."

"No thanks to Prosper," Judith added. "He didn't save you, Cadel. I mean, why on earth would he have done that?"

"Because he loved me," Cadel whispered. The words came unbid-den; for an instant he thought that they'd simply crossed his mind and hadn't been uttered aloud. But then he heard Judith hiss, and Sonja squeak, and he realized that he must have spoken after all.

"You don't believe it because you don't understand," he said hoarsely. "Prosper was different. He wasn't like other people. He might have hated me, but he loved me, too. In his own way. He couldn't help it; not after raising me for all those years." When no one responded—when he saw nothing but expressions of disbelief on the faces around him—Cadel wailed, "He *did*! He did! I know he did! He only wanted to wreck my life because he wasn't a part of it!"

And as sympathetic hands reached out toward him from every corner of the car, Cadel began to cry like someone whose heart was breaking.